**Amarna
The Complete Series**

By

Grea Alexander

Shoved out into the cold, cruel world shivering and naked by SeaMonkey Ink
A division of the sick mind of Grea Alexander

Copyright © 2016 by Grea Alexander.

All rights are reserved. No part of this work may be reproduced or transmitted in any form or by any means possible in both the human and alien spectrum of existence including any and all oral, mental, physical, emotional, spiritual, sexual, electronic or mechanical means including but not limited to photocopying, scanning and/or recording by any information storage or retrieval system and/or by any means yet to be invented without the express written permission of Grea Alexander or SeaMonkey Ink.

Genre: Historical Novel
Rating: Mature

Printed in the USA AKA the United States of America or as I like to call it Uuusah

Are YOU the bastard spawn of a Seamonkey?
Well, would you like to be?

www.SeaMonkeyInk.com

SERIES INTRODUCTION

In an paradoxical twist, I am a novelist who reads/studies far more nonfiction (particularly history) than fiction.

Hearing the tale of the Curse of Tutankhamun when I was young, I wanted to know more.

So, I researched King Tutankhamun which lead to me learning about his sister-wife, Ankhesenamun which lead to me learning about their father which lead to me learning about their parents, Ay, Horemheb, etc, etc. As I worked my way through this particular portion of history, I found it interesting how after "King Tut's" death (when he was around 18/19) the throne jumped around eventually (basically) ending up in the hands of the military and commoners. That made me say, hmmmm. Thus, the original concept for the series was born.

While digging deeper into the aftermath of Tutankhamun's death, I discovered the whole Prince Zannanza fiasco which lead to researching about his father King Suppilu then learning about Mursili II who I found deliciously fascinating. That this whole colorful Hittite History not only was going on at the same time as the King Tut drama but was actually historically linked at several points throughout history was the icing on the cake. I decided to write Mursili into the series and to deepen the link between the two civilizations.

The Amarna Series explores this period and its figures and was created in three parts. Casting the Egyptian slave Ida and the Hittite boy Prince Mursili II as the protagonists, the series spans from the period after Akhenaten's death all the way through the reign of Ramesses the Great. It speculates about the how and the why both the fates of the Egyptian kingdom & the Hittite kingdom seem so intimately intertwined during this period.

You have Tutankhamun's father, Akhenaten, who decides to transform Egypt into a monotheistic state and who is married to Nefertiti (arguably one of the most beautiful women in history) who then produces among his spawn Pharaoh Tutankhamun - hands down probably the most famous pharaoh of all time.

During the same period, you have the Hittite King Suppiluliuma who commits these great sacrileges against his kingdom's charters and the gods (including murdering his brother for the throne). Among this king's spawn is Mursili II who is deeply religious, claims to be receiving messages from one of their goddesses and who vows to atone for the wrongs of his father no matter the cost.

The series begins immediately following Akhenaten's death, when you have this mad clamor for control first of Tut and then of the throne.

Following Tutankhamun's death, the throne quickly changes hands - falling into the hands of men of various stations and capabilities. In addition, there is this tremendous effort to try to erase Akhenaten and his descendents from all of history and to revert Egypt back to polytheism.

Queen Ankhesenamen really does send for one of King Suppiluliuma's sons to secure power. The Prince he sends, however, is murdered en route and so begins war with Egypt (after some letters back and forth trying to get to the bottom of it). Through a series of unfortunate but favorable events, Mursili II (who no one expects and is still a boy) ends up King. Under Mursili II, not only does the Hittite kingdom recover from a series of epic disasters but peace is finally made with Egypt under both Horemheb and Ramesses the Great.

While I've dramaticized and put my own spin on some things in this series, it's about 95% historically accurate in regard to events in the story as well as some of the controversies that existed in ancient Egyptian times - necrophilia by the priests, usurping of other's monuments, grave robbing sanctioned by high officials, power struggles between Upper & Lower Egyptian Royals etc. Many characters in this book DID exist in real life. In fact, the only fictional characters in these books are the minions (with Lord Bietek being the only royal exception): Ida, Galeno, Nacamakun, Esnai, Clizi, Hazrene, Azra, Faium, Galeno, Lord Bietek, Saphik and their offspring.

Unbelievable as it may seem, I'd say about 90% of what I wrote regarding the actual historical figures' actions in this series comes from actual historical fact (AKA what the people clever enough to have recorded it and lucky enough for their recordings to be found's version of the facts). For instance, the section of prayer included in Book II credited to Mursili II is a real excerpt of a prayer actually written by Mursili II. Even some of the seemingly more outlandish parts of the book such as the mention in Book I of the rebel leader who sent out his mother to plead with Mursili for his life REALLY happened. The conflicting stories of the Battle of Kadesh in Book III - with both sides claiming victory when it was likely a tie. True. Mursili's struggle with Mal-Nikal and the resulting death of Gassula. True.

While most of my historical novels are set in the past and do contain nods to actual historical events, customs, etc., the Amarna series goes far beyond that. It is by far the most historically accurate series I've written to date. The true story was just too good and had just too many possibilities for me to want to do anything more but fill it out and have a conjecture field day. It was a challenge to be sure – working within so many pre-set parameters but I really enjoyed writing this series.

I hope you enjoy it.

Cheers!

Grea.

**Amarna Book I:
Book of Ida**

By

Grea Alexander

Shoved out into the cold, cruel world shivering and naked by SeaMonkey Ink
A division of the sick mind of Grea Alexander

Copyright © 1997 by Grea Alexander.

All rights are reserved. No part of this work may be reproduced or transmitted in any form or by any means possible in both the human and alien spectrum of existence including any and all oral, mental, physical, emotional, spiritual, sexual, electronic or mechanical means including but not limited to photocopying, scanning and/or recording by any information storage or retrieval system and/or by any means yet to be invented without the express written permission of Grea Alexander or SeaMonkey Ink.

Genre: Historical Novel
Rating: Mature

Printed in the USA AKA the United States of America or as I like to call it Uuusah

Are YOU the bastard spawn of a Seamonkey?
Well, would you like to be?

www.SeaMonkeyInk.com

Dedication

I would like to dedicate this book to myself, without whom none of this would have been possible. Without my tireless talent, faith, energy, effort, ability to exist in a fog of complete denial, questionable sanity and financial backing none of this would have been possible. I truly am the wind beneath my crown.

I would also like to dedicate this book to the trees who so tirelessly and unwittingly and well.... involuntarily gave their lives to print this book because I prefer good old-fashioned paper books that I can actually hold in my hand and read.... or use as paper weights or tear out the pages of and clean my windows with (for that streak free shine) or hurl discus like at bad Seamonkeys.

And last but not least, I would like to dedicate this work to GOD who had the incredible sense of humor, mind-boggling ingenuity and questionable taste to create me and grant me what appears to the untrained eye to be a talent for stringing together such bizarre, twistedly amusing and vaguely disturbing thoughts in such a way as to actually create something semi-logical or at least decidedly nonsensical enough that it almost makes some sort of coherent sense but entertains and absorbs nonetheless.

Please note that this work is a Novella.

A novella is a written work running between 20,000 and 49,000 words. It is generally considered too long for most publishers to insert comfortably into a magazine (hhhmmmm), yet too short for a novel.

Why should you BUY a novella?

Well, because I am your queen and I say so. But also, if you're like me, you may actually have a life outside of this book (scary to imagine but true). You may not have the time or inclination to read a 1,000 page monster novel or you simply may not care about how 3 paragraphs of comfortable the chair in the center of the room is (unless of course its comfort is caused by the corpses stuffed inside of it or something of the like). You may have a low threshold for magazines with all of their endless pages of ads, tireless celeb gossip dribble or writers telling you (and quite authoritatively at that) what's best for you and how you should live your life (not to mention that that's my job). You may also be wanting something to read a little more substantial than how to wear stripes or position your package in your underthings for maximum effect. Then again, you may just have a really, really short attention span.

That's were a novella comes in handy. It's just long enough to keep you occupied for a nice chunk of time but not so long that you end up neglecting your family (thus resulting in divorce and CPS involvement), spending your whole vacation in a book (thus being mugged by local thugs) or going to work the next day a stressed out, sleep-deprived wreck because you just HAD to finish it (thus causing you to get fired for sexual harassment). Not only that, several completely fabricated studies show that people who do not add novellas to their library diet run a 300% higher risk of stroke, heart disease, impotence, diarrhea, brain damage, Tourette's, drug, alcohol & gambling addiction, schizophrenia, depression and Alzheimer's than those who don't. If you can't do it for yourself, do it for your family.

Amarna Book I:
Book of Ida

Thebes, Upper Egypt. 1324 BC

The last living male descendant of the Amarna line, Pharaoh Tutankhamun, has died suddenly under mysterious circumstances. His wife, Queen Ankhesenamen, is left without a male heir. The ambitious vipers Ay and Horemheb are nipping at her heels in their bid to seize power.

Queen Ankhe has but one hope to maintain her hold on the throne - an alliance with the Hittites. With Ay and Horemheb watching her every move, there is only one person she can trust to save her and her line - a girl, a slave - Ida.

Introduction

Book I follows the time period following Pharaoh Akhenaten's death through to the final year of Pharaoh Ay's reign. While the main focus of this book is on Ida and Tutankh's relationship, the fallout from that relationship and the struggle to hide Ida's continued existence from their enemies - particularly Horemheb and Suppilu, we see an emergence of a new relationship - that of Ida and the then Prince Mursili - 6th in line for the throne at the time.

Prologue

Thebes, Upper Egypt. 1274 B.C.

Queen Tuya did as she was bade by her father. She waited until she was completely alone, until not even her beloved son, Pharaoh Ramesses II, was present before she broke the seal of the first scroll.

For years she had wondered about what the scrolls, so carefully cared for and preserved by her father, contained, about what great secret he had safe-guarded so doggedly.

Still, now that she had been entrusted with their care, she was not so sure she should read them.

She stared down unseeingly at the neat rows of hieroglyphics, her mind drifting to the day her father had given the small chest of scrolls over to her. It was shortly before his death, not long after Ramesses had taken over the throne.

As he had lay on his sick bed, her father's handsome face had been so intense.

"Protect these," he had told her. "This is my greatest gift to you: the knowledge of your past. Read them. Learn from them. Know that what Aten would have be will be regardless of implausibility, time or distance."

Even then, his grip on the chest had not loosened. It was only after he had drawn his last breath, a few hours later, that she was able to take the chest into her possession.

Snapping back to the present, Tuya re-rolled the scroll and tied the binding back into place. She set the first scroll down, went to the window and stared out of it.

At last she had the secrets of her family's shrouded past in her hands.

But did she really want to know?

She was, after all, no longer just Tuya, daughter of a soldier, but Tuya, once Queen of all of Egypt, mother of Ramesses II. What if the information contained in these parchments could cause her harm somehow? What if it illegitimatized Ramesses' succession to the throne?

Perhaps she should destroy them, she pondered, have them burned.

Her mind nearly set, Tuya hurried back to the chest, frantically returning the scrolls to its keeping. Gathering the chest in her arms she moved hurriedly towards the door.

She stopped just short of it. Her eyes drifted down to the chest.

If the scrolls *did* contain horrible secrets, perhaps others existed who knew what these secrets were. Would she not be better served by knowing what was contained within?

And what of her father? He had worked painstakingly for so many years to piece together their past - gathering accounts from diaries, witnesses, the words of her predecessors themselves. Who was she to dishonor her ancestors by burning their precious histories -

potentially dangerous or not?

Her mind finally made up, Tuya returned the chest to the table.

She reopened the chest, stared at the set of scrolls for a time. Then sitting down at the table, she slowly re-released the binding of the first scroll.

I

Thebes, Upper Egypt. 1332 B.C.

One of Queen Ankhesenpaaten's hands lay on her stomach, the other gripping the arm of her seat so tightly that it had grown pale. Her face was drawn, wan. Dark circles ran under her eyes.

Idaten, Ankhesenpaaten's childhood playmate and favorite slave girl, worriedly applied kohl to Ankhe's eyes. She had already been at the task of beautifying the queen for quite some time now and found herself less than impressed by her results.

Standing back to judge her work, she sighed heavily, shaking her head.

"Why do you do this to me, Ankhe?" Ida said half to herself.

Ankhesenpaaten gave no sign of having heard her, of even having *seen* her though Ida stood directly in front of her.

Ida tried once again to improve Ankhe's pallid appearance - with little success. She put down the palate of powders and the brush, studied the queen intently for a long moment.

Ida was no fool. She did not doubt that should Ankhe appear in such a state, that it would be she who would pay the price. Still, what more was there for Ida to do?

Frustrated, Ida continued to study Ankhe's face as she pondered her predicament.

Perhaps food might help to bring some color back to the queen's cheeks.

"Esnai," Ida snapped at the new slave who was perfecting Ankhesenpaaten's wig, "go and get Queen Ankhesenpaaten her morning meal."

When the girl continued her work, unmoved by Ida's dictate, Ida's already brewing agitation turned quickly to anger. "Esnai, now!"

Suddenly having heard her name, Esnai paused in her work. She looked to Ida, awaited further instruction.

"Well go!" Ida ordered, making a shooing motion with her hands.

Esnai's expression mirrored her confusion. "Go where?" she asked.

Ida glared angrily at the girl for a long moment before walking swiftly around Ankhesenpaaten and slapping her.

The girl covered her injured cheek and scurried behind Batau, the well-seasoned slave at Ankhesenpaaten's feet.

Batau glared at Ida. "Ida," she reprimanded, "none of this is Esnai's fault." She turned now to Esnai, speaking loudly, slowly and clearly. "The Queen's morning meal."

Esnai nodded. She rose slowly, careful to stay out of Ida's reach as she backed out of the room.

Batau turned a hard glare upon Ida.

Ida, however, remained unapologetic.

"What?" Ida asked. "So much has happened just now. Pharaoh Akhenaten is dead, our Ankhe pregnant with his child and Smenkhkare's ridiculous mandate forcing us to abandon El-Amana.

"Now Ay and Horemheb are trying to groom Tutankh to become Pharaoh, are trying to force a marriage between he and Ankhe. How am I supposed to remember that that girl is a half-wit?"

"Ida, you know full well that Esnai is deaf in one ear."

"Excuse me, a cripple."

"Well, your memory for gossip certainly seems to be faring well enough. Apologize when she returns."

Batau turned her attention to massaging oil into Ankhe's other foot.

"Why?" Ida pressed, defiant. "I didn't make her a cripple. She should learn to listen."

Ida, smiling at her own cleverness, picked up the palate again. She turned back to the queen, dusted at the dark rings.

"Mark my words, girl," Batau warned, "One day your insolence will cost you dearly."

Batau shook her head. "As if the entire world is to blame for Horemheb forbidding Tutankhaten from seeing you anymore."

Ida spared Batau only a dismissive glance.

"It is for the best, Ida," Batau continued. "You are becoming a woman, with a woman's heart. You are already too attached to him as it stands.

"You wear the anklet he gave you as proudly as any peacock. You even disappeared with him during the last Nile Flood Feast. No one could find either of you for hours.

"That is not fitting behavior for the future Pharaoh nor for one of the Queen's slaves."

Ida's hand paused, her grip on the brush tightened to the point that her knuckles turned white. "From where did you hear that I was with Tutankh Nile Flood Feast?" she asked. "Esnai?"

Though Batau did not confirm her suspicions, Ida knew that it was she.

"Esnai has far too much ambition to ever be truly trustworthy," Ida said, wishing now that she had slapped the girl even harder.

"Tutankh may well mean everything he has said to you. I have seen with my own eyes that his affections for you are indeed genuine and that the two of you have been almost inseparable from the very beginning.

"But Ida, you must understand that his duty will not allow this no matter how much he may want it to be so.

"He is still a child, Ida. His will is not his own."

Ida did not reply as she continued to makeup Ankhe's face, her own face set like stone.

Batau stood and grabbing Ida's forearm, turned her towards her. "When he becomes Pharaoh do you honestly believe they will allow you to be anything more to him than a servant, than just another plaything at the most?"

Ida trembled with fury, tears stinging her eyes.

Batau had no right.

"I know that right now you think I am just being spiteful, but Ida, you are *just* a slave girl, however favored you may be, a slave girl."

Ida pulled her arm away. "My father is of noble blood," she retorted, "blood every bit as noble as theirs. My grandfather's defeat in battle and enslavement does not alter that fact."

"You think you're the only slave here who can trace their lines back to royalty?" Batau asked, incredulous. "You think your grandfather was the first and only vassal ever to be put down by Pharaoh, stripped of his power and privilege and enslaved?"

Ida gave no reply though Batau could tell by the girl's wounded expression that her words had hit their mark.

Batau sighed. "I'm sorry for your family and for you, Ida. Truly I am. But as things stand now, of noble line or not, you are no higher than I or even Esnai.

"You are just a slave, and we are all the same."

"I will never be like you," Ida retorted fiercely. "I will never bend and break my back until the day I die."

"Only time will tell," Batau replied wearily, her patience with the girl wearing thin. "Time will tell all.

"Still, for now, you are just another slave, and therefore, should consider yourself blessed if only to kiss the ground upon which Pharaoh has walked."

Ida shook her head defiantly though tears stung at her eyes.

"If you do not learn to bend," Batau counseled, "to play the game, you will break."

"I will *never* break," Ida swore vehemently.

"Won't you?

"How many times have I watched you locked in the confines, watched you released sobbing and wretched only to wind up in there again and again and again? How much more of that do you think you can take?"

A fleeting look of terror cracked through Ida's bravado.

The confines.

There was no punishment that terrified her more than being locked in that small, dank, windowless box of a cell.

Batau's expression and tone gentled as her hearted softened towards the child.

"I will not lie to you," Batau said. "First affections are always the hardest to let go of, and you will probably never forget him, but Ida you must stop this self-deception."

Ida turned towards the window as she fought to control the tide of her emotions, to keep the bitter tears back. "Your warnings come too late, Batau."

Ankhesenpaaten bent forward suddenly. She groaned in pain.

Ida whirled to face her.

"Ida," Batau called stooping over Ankhesenpaaten, "the midwife!"

Ida ran from the room.

"Breathe, Ankhe," Batau told the queen.

Ankhe grabbed Batau's hand.

"May Taveret protect you and your baby," Batau said softly as she stroked Ankhe's back. "May Taveret protect you."

II

8 ½ years later.

"Mother, what's going on outside?" Heketya asked as she ran to Ankhesenpaaten's side.

Ida dashed to the window and peered out of it. There was a small procession of soldiers coming up the wide lane that led to the palace. Towards the front of the procession there was an elaborate golden palanquin, Tutankhaten's empty chariot just behind it.

Ankhesenpaaten was suddenly there next to Ida, Heketya holding tightly to her arm.

"They've killed him," Ankhesenpaaten cried angrily. "They've killed Pharaoh and there is no heir."

Ida placed a hand over Ankhe's mouth. She had, after all, vowed to protect the queen.

She looked around at the other servants in the room, then to Batau. Batau nodded and left the room.

Ida took Ankhe's arm and led her outside to the garden courtyard, close to the fountain where Horemheb and Ay's spies could not hear them.

Ankhesenpaaten was on the verge of tears now.

Ida watched her, unmoved by her display of emotion - knowing well that Ankhe's tears were of anger, for what would happen to her and her daughter now, not for Tutankhaten.

She wanted to scream at Ankhesenpaaten, shake her.

She took a step away from her instead.

"Tutankhaten came to me," Ankhe said. "He came to me and he told me that Ay and Horemheb had grown too powerful, that he planned to de-elevate their position and revert back to Aten."

Ankhe sighed heavily. "He was ready to take full charge of his reign. I could see the determination, the wisdom, the power of Aten strong within him."

"He would have made a brilliant Pharaoh," Ida said, "the likes of which Egypt had never seen before and will probably never see again."

"But now..." Ankhesenpaaten broke off. She shook her head as the tears spilled from her eyes. "Now we are at the mercy of our enemies."

Batau came out to them. "They're saying it was a fall from his chariot, that he hit his head," she told them.

"That's a lie," Ida said. "Tutankh was an expert chariots man, an exemplary hunter. He would not have just fallen off."

"Ay has ordered Esnai be taken down to the harem," Batau whispered. "Horemheb has ordered for Ida. I think they're planning to seize power."

Ankhesenpaaten turned to stare at the water as it spewed from the fountain, as she searched her mind for an answer.

"Ida," she said at length, "take word to Suppiluliuma."

"To the Hittites?" Batau asked.

"Tutankhaten has no heirs," Ida supplied, "and Suppiluliuma has many sons."

Ankhe nodded.

"Ask that he send one of his sons to me - to become my husband and continue the royal line," Ankhesenpaaten ordered.

"Don't you mean Prince Zannanza?" Ida asked, not bothering to hide her distaste.

Ankhesenpaaten slapped her.

Her chest heaving, Ankhe continued. "You do whatever it takes to get to King Suppiluliuma, and I do mean *whatever*."

Anger flashed in Ida's eyes though she held herself fast.

"I am, as always, your slave," Ida replied stiffly, "I shall do as you have commanded. However, with Tutankhaten dead, there will be no one left to protect you."

"Nor you," Ankhesenpaaten retorted pointedly. "*My* position at least will be enough to keep me and my daughter safe for the time being."

Their eyes locked in open hostility.

Ida had had enough. She couldn't wait to be rid of Ankhesenpaaten - even if only for a couple of weeks.

"They won't just let Ida go," Batau interjected.

"They will if they think I'm dead," Ida replied. "Galeno has told me of a potion that makes one appear to be so."

"Galeno will tell you anything to get between your thighs," Batau said.

"At least men still *want* to get between my thighs, Batau," Ida retorted.

"Stop your bickering," Ankhesenpaaten snapped, "and do as I have bidden." She reached into the small purse woven into her gown and handed Ida all of its contents.

Bowing rigidly to Ankhesenpaaten, Ida left to begin preparation for her death and for her journey to the land of the Hittites.

III

Ankhesenpaaten, Heketya, and Batau made a good showing of Ida's passing.

Esnai, emboldened by her arrogant rival's passing, had the gall to wear the traditional garb of a royal consort and stand just behind Ay.

As Ida's small procession came to the embalming chamber, Batau could have sworn she saw a small smile flicker across Esnai's face.

Horemheb's features, in contrast, were stony, wrathful - as though he would avenge himself upon death itself for stealing his desired consort away from him.

Powerful and powerless alike watched now as priests of Amun came to stand at the temple doors, as Ida's body disappeared inside.

Indifferent to the plight of a dead slave, the priests' faces remained completely expressionless as they waited for the bearers to come back out again.

Then, without a single word, the priests retreated inside and the door closed.

It took but a couple of hours for the potent serum Galeno had given Ida to wear off.

Still, a couple of hours was all it took. A priest was already on top of her, taking his pleasure.

Though Ida screamed on the inside, she forced herself to be still, not to stiffen. Though she closed her eyes, she could not keep her tears from sliding down the side of her face.

Everyone thought they knew Ida.

They assumed she had lain with many men because many men wanted to lay with her.

They couldn't have been more wrong.

As at last the priest climbed off of her, she opened her eyes and stared up at the ceiling. Against all instinct, she fought to lie motionless as the priest righted himself.

Her mind drifted.

She thought of the Harvest Festival two summers past.

It was when everything had changed.

There had been a banquet at the palace. Most of the guests were drunk before the 2nd hour had passed. Ida, as usual, had managed to slip away before the greedy eyes and hands of the intoxicated aristocracy found her.

She liked at these times to walk through the royal rooms, to touch the beautiful, priceless things she would never own.

Ida had felt bolder that night than usual. Finding the passageway to the throne room completely empty, she had crept into the main state room.

In her naivety, she had been quite certain that no one was there, that no one would find her there.

She had sunk down onto Pharaoh's gilded chair, ran her hands along the gold, the embedded jewels. She had sighed in her contentment, the coolness of the metal feeling heavenly through her short semi-diaphanous dress.

She had pulled the formal wig that the servants were required to wear from her head.

Contrary to popular trend, Ida's hair fell all the way to her waist. Though she may not have had anything of any real value besides the anklet that Tutankh had given her, she made sure that her hair was the most beautiful in all of Egypt.

She spent many hours every day tending to it as she daydreamed, as she imagined that she was someone else, somewhere else - as she thought of the boy king whom she had been reduced to stealing rare, distant glimpses of for many years now.

Pulling her hair from behind her, she laid it over her shoulder. For a wig made of hair like hers, Egyptian aristocracy would pay gold enough to buy her freedom three times over – if only Ankhe would allow it.

Ida leaned back and closed her eyes.

Somehow, she managed to doze off. When she opened her eyes again, the moon was higher, illuminating the sky more intensely.

She listened. She could faintly hear the musicians playing and the loud, drunken laughter of the guests.

Her senses slowly returned as she continued to lay there.

Then, like a sudden splash of cold water, the realization came. She had been there much too long.

Hurriedly grabbing her wig, Ida rose from the chair.

She had barely managed two steps before she tripped over something and fell. Her heart pounding in her chest, she had stared towards the throne, into the darkness.

Someone else was there.

She could see a shadow now - slowly separating itself from the side of Pharaoh's chair.

She blinked rapidly as her eyes adjusted to the darkness.

A man.

The figure moved towards her.

"You should be more careful of where you tred," his voice said.

He took her arm and helped her to rise.

"Are you alright?" he asked.

"Yes," she answered breathlessly, taking a few steps back.

What she had just done was treason and this man, whomever he was, knew it.

"I must be getting back to the banquet," she choked.

She turned.

"Wait," the shadowy man called.

Ida turned back to face him.

"You seem somehow familiar to me," he said. "What is your name?"

"Idaten," she answered.

"Ida," he whispered softly.

Strange though it was, the way he breathed her name sent a delicious quiver down her spine.

"I am head slave of Queen Ankhesenpaaten," she said.

"Why are you here, Idamun, head slave of Queen Ankhesenamun?" he asked softly.

Ida cursed herself silently. She had never gotten used to the name of Amun that Horemheb had forced upon Ankhesenpaaten and Tutankhaten, upon them all, in place of Aten.

"Yes," she said, "Queen Ankhesenamun."

The man waited.

"I...I ..." she stumbled.

Try as she might, Ida could not seem to think of a satisfactory lie, of even the slightest explanation for why she, a slave, was asleep in Pharaoh's chair.

Flustered, she lifted her chin in defiance.

Why was she even *trying* to explain?

She did not owe this strange man any explanation. He had as little right to be there as she.

Ida nodded. She would tell him as much if he dared press her.

"My lady will be wondering where I have gone off to," she said.

All at once, the moon seemed to be directly behind him. It illuminated her to him but only painted a bright halo around his body.

Ida squinted, searching for some clue as to his identity.

The man, for his part, silently bore her bold attempt at perusal.

He was wearing a long, pleated linen kilt, as the nobles wore, and expensive jewelry. His torso was lean and muscular. He was without a headdress and his hair, fashioned in the manner of a wig, hung just past his shoulders.

"You have grown even more beautiful with the years, Ida," he said softly.

He reached out and touched her hair. "And still just as proud and strange."

"You have me at a disadvantage," she replied. "Who, may I ask, are you?"

"I suppose that without my headdress and in the dark I would be quite difficult to recognize after so many years." He reached out both hands to her. "Come," he said.

She hesitated.

"You will be safe with me, Ida," he said.

Impulsively she had taken them - the action sending a frightening yet exciting tingle through her palms, a tingle which spread through the rest of her body.

Though she could not see his eyes, she could feel him staring at her in the darkness. She colored, her eyes fleeing to the floor.

She felt him moving her towards the balcony. When she looked up at him again, she had gasped. She was speechless.

It was *him*!

A strange delighted happiness spread through her chest.

She smiled. His eyes glowed in response, an answering grin upon his lips.

No, her mind screamed, breaking the spell. *Your Tutankh died 7 years ago. This man is a stranger. This man is Pharaoh.*

Her smile faded. Pulling her hands from his, she prostrated herself at his feet.

"Forgive me, great Pharaoh," she said, her voice trembling.

"Don't," he replied.

He stooped and, gently grasping her arms, made her rise. "You have no need to prostrate yourself at my feet, Ida."

She looked into his eyes. They were so wise, so intense, so wistful as he gazed down at her.

She could still see her Tutankh in them - as if the last 7 years had never been. She was 11 again, a girl with the boy she would do anything for on the roof of the palace, watching the Nile waters swirl about the fields just before he had given her the anklet.

She pulled away from him and stepped out of his reach - the intensity, the vividness of her emotions terrifying her.

Tutankh's eyes became sad and weary. He looked down at his hands, then back up at her.

His brow furrowing, he turned and looked down into the garden courtyard.

The loneliness, the sadness in him was like a physical force. It reached out to her, encircled her, buried itself within her. She wanted nothing more at that moment than to take the terrible unhappiness away from him.

Against her better judgement, Ida slowly approached him, tentatively reached out and touched one of his shoulders.

He had tensed at first, relaxed but moments later as one of his hands covered hers. He had turned back to face her, his hand softly touching her face.

He drew closer to her, brushed her nose with his.

She closed her eyes, letting the sweet sensation of his nearness to her fill her.

His hands were on her waist now. She looked up at him. She saw her own turbulent emotions reflected back at her in his eyes.

He pulled her to him gently - his head lowering and his lips lightly brushing against hers.

She shivered, a tear trickling from her eye and him gently kissing the cheek down which the tear had fallen.

"Pharaoh!" they heard one of his personal guards call.

Ida was snapped back to reality.

She stepped back from him once more.

Going to the side of the gilded chair, he retrieved his headdress.

He glanced back at her once more. Then, putting on his headdress, he left.

The loud sound of the embalming chamber door snapped Ida back to the present. She slid from the slab and stretched her stiff muscles. She looked down thoughtfully at her wrist and ran her fingers along the gold of her bracelet, an anklet she had years ago outgrown, that she never was without.

It had always had a strange effect upon her. It made her feel loved, protected, strong.

She began to pace.

She started when some time later the coded knock she and Galeno had agreed upon sounded at the door.

She went to it and opened it.

Galeno walked in and laid the girl down upon the slab. It was strange for Ida to look at her. The resemblance to her was quite uncanny.

Galeno gave Ida the dress and wig of a trader's wife.

Ida hurriedly stripped save for her tight sheer tunic and donned the trader woman's costume. Galeno, in turn, dressing the dead girl in Ida's clothing and wig.

"The caravan leaves from Cartunk at dawn," he told her.

She nodded.

Impulsively, she had hugged him. "You have been such a good friend to me, Galeno."

He smiled. "Just returning the favor, Ida. When they tried me for being with men, it was your testimony that spared me. I could have lost everything."

"I guess then that we have been good friends to each other."

He smiled sadly. "I suppose we have. I just don't want to lose you now, Ida."

"You won't. Not ever."

Galeno smiled again, more convincingly this time. If only he possessed the conviction of the young.

"My horse is at the east wall," he said. "Please be careful, Ida."

She kissed his cheek. "You sound as if you'll never see me again. I will return very soon."

"I will pray that you do."

IV

Only when Ida had joined the caravan and she was moving across the desert towards the Hittite land did the full force of what she knew descend upon her.

Tutankh was dead.

The grief hit her hard, consumed her - mercilessly, fiercely. Her thoughts became plagued with his quiet voice; his sweet, sad smile; his fragile, fleeting laughter; his gentle, comforting strength. She felt like she was dying inside, wanted very much for it to be so.

By the time she was before King Suppuluiuma her grief was embedded in her every glance, her every word, her every gesture. It made her beauty all the more remarkable.

Though King Suppuluiuma did not doubt her sincerity, he knew well that Ay and Horemheb were not to be trusted.

"I will send one of my scouts into Egypt to see if Pharaoh Tutankhamun has truly died," he said at length, "and if Queen Ankhesenamun or one of his harem is not with a suitable heir. If I find it so, I will send one of my sons to your Queen. But you Idamun must stay here."

"But Queen Ankhesenamun...." Ida began.

"It is the only way I will consent to send a son of mine into Egypt.

"I remember you from the Nubian banquet. You were very much favored by your Pharaoh.

"I have also heard tale that you are the favorite of Queen Ankhesenamun - very highly prized, well trusted. If this proves to be some sort of snare, Ankhesenamun will be more motivated to intercede if I have her much treasured pet."

Ida almost wanted to laugh. Ankhe would never let her go not because she loved her, but because she hated her and she wanted her to suffer.

He turned to the guards.

"Nacamakun, see that she is taken to the harem," he ordered.

A sturdy, dark brown man graced with unruly, raven black hair with gray streaks running from his temples and fierce black eyes nodded. He bowed to his king.

Without warning, the world began to tilt and swirl before Ida.

One of the King's sons, Prince Mursili II, caught her as she collapsed.

Shortly after the banquet that had seen Ida and Tutankh reunited, Queen Ankhesenpaaten had suggested that Pharaoh take Ida with him to the banquet in Nubia. It was a matter of impressing upon the Nubian King and the other great leaders who would be attending the vast wealth and superiority of Egypt to their own kingdoms.

Each year, the Pharaoh took with him his best finery; his bravest, most handsome soldiers; his most beautiful, efficient slaves. It was considered a great honor to be chosen to represent the best of Egyptia.

Ankhesenpaaten had brought Ida before Pharaoh. "Is she not beautiful enough?" Ankhe had asked him.

Tutankh had only glanced briefly at Ida.

He nodded. "She is more than beautiful enough."

"She is also an extraordinary dancer," Ankhesenpaaten had boasted, "not to mention a very well-trained and efficient servant."

"Mistress..." Ida had began.

"Now Ida, you are more than qualified and you deserve this great honor.

"Some of the foreign nobles have even been known to take slave girls to wife," Ankhesenpaaten pressed. "Particularly with your pedigree..."

"I have no designs to be taken to wife by anyone, my Queen," Ida answered.

"Oh husband," Ankhesenpaaten went on ignoring Ida's lack of enthusiasm, "do not refuse me this chance to show off my beautiful little Ibis."

Tutankh looked at Ida again.

He turned to Ankhesenpaaten. "We leave at dawn. Have her prepared."

He left the room.

"My Queen, I don't think this is such a good idea. With the Pharaoh away, who will look after you and Heketya?"

Ankhesenpaaten kissed Ida's cheek and embraced her. "Ida, you are my truest, dearest, most loyal servant and I want the best for you," she said loudly. Then in a whisper, "Esnai has grown Ay's fangs. Horemheb's puppet himself will be accompanying Tutankh. Our Pharaoh will be hemmed in on all sides by vipers."

"Ay and Horemheb are up to an intrigue?" Ida asked.

"I can't be sure. They may try to ally the other kings against our Pharaoh. As a dancing girl, a servant, circulate through them, play the innocent fool, strain your ears so that you may hear any words meant to stir them against my brother-husband.

"You are the only one I can trust with his life, Ida. If you were of my own blood, I could not trust you more than I do now."

"Yes, mistress," Ida answered.

Ankhesenpaaten released her. She spoke clearly again. "As a token of my esteem please accept this ring."

Ankhesenpaaten pulled her most cherished ring, one given to her by her father Akhenaten, from her finger.

"I can not," Ida said.

"You must," Ankhesenpaaten said softly as she took one of Ida's hands and slid the ring upon her finger. "Should anything happen to me or Tutankh," she whispered, "I want you to ensure that the memory of the Amarna bloodline does not die as well."

Ankhesenpaaten kissed both of her cheeks. "Now prepare yourself for your journey," she said.

Ida bowed, dutifully obeyed.

Ida had had no contact with Tutankh the first night they had spent in camp.

He seemed to be slighting her, choosing instead to have Esnai serve him.

Ida had felt stung by this. Just a few nights prior he had been Tutankhaten again, the boy who had given her an anklet of which a slave girl was hardly worthy, who had looked at her as if the sun rose and set with her before the role of Pharaoh was placed upon him and he no longer was allowed to associate with slave girls.

Ida was still surprised that remembering affected her so deeply. She had long ago buried her feelings for him, the memories. She had assumed that they were dead, but ever since that night in the throne room, they had descended upon her mercilessly - like vultures upon a carcass.

She had been absently picking at her figs when Esnai appeared at the entrance to the women's tent. Ida ignored her presence.

Esnai came to stand directly over her. "Pharaoh wishes you to dance for him," Esnai said in that sneering way she had taken to addressing the other slaves since she had found favor with Ay, as if she were their mistress instead of Ankhesenpaaten.

Ida gave no acknowledgment that she had heard anything Esnai had said.

Esnai repeated herself.

Ida continued to ignore her.

"Pharaoh will hear of your insolence," Esnai said storming away.

Ida offered the remainder of the figs to a group of young slave girls and rose. She pulled back her hair into a thick braid and weighted down the end with a beautifully adorned silver hair ornament - another gift from Ankhesenpaaten. She changed from her dress into a short tunic. She put kohl on her eyes, slipped on tiny dancing bells.

Ida had padded barefoot to the king's tent.

She found him staring absorbedly at a painting of the Nile. He did not even seem to hear the jingle of the bells as she moved.

She stood there uncertainly, not wanting to disturb his reverie.

"I've been thinking about you a great deal, Ida," he said at length. "About when we were children, before Ay forbid me to consort with slave girls."

He paused.

Ida had remained silent.

"Do you remember that last Nile flood feast when we snuck away to sit on the roof of the palace and watch the water rise in the fields?"

"Yes," she answered quietly.

"Do you remember what it was I said to you just before we heard Batau calling for you and you had to return?"

Ida swallowed past the lump in her throat. "Yes."

When he continued to remain silent she realized he meant for her to tell him.

She cleared her throat. "You said...you said that I was the most beautiful girl you had ever seen."

"And?"

"And that once you became Pharaoh you would pledge your love for me before all of Egypt and take me to wife."

"You remember."

"It is not often slave girls receive such ardent declarations from their masters."

He turned around to face her. "I meant every word."

His expression was serious, his eyes probing. "I have never made such a proclamation to anyone but you."

She had to look away.

"We were just children then," she said.

He turned back to the paining for a time.

Ida looked back up at him.

After a long moment, he turned back to face her. "My Queen has told me you are an impressive dancer."

Ida could not stop the proud grin from lighting up her entire face. His eyes glowed in response.

"Dance for me, Ida," he said.

"Now? Without any music?" she asked.

He smiled, and he nodded.

Ida failed miserably to contain her laughter. "What would you like me to dance for you, Great Pharaoh?"

"Tutankh," he corrected, his eyes glowing in a way that made her heart thump loudly in her ears.

"What would you like for me to dance for you...Tutankh?" she repeated.

His gaze warmed her from head to toe.

Without warning, he took her hand and began to dance with her, whirling her around wildly as they used to do with they were children, before the world had become such a complicated place in which something as simple as their dancing together was clandestine.

They had fallen, laughing onto his makeshift bed.

They now lay on their backs.

"Aten, but I've missed you, Ida," he said smiling. "I'm glad to have you on my side."

Ida rolled onto her side to face him. "Pharaoh?"

Tutankh sat up and repositioned himself facing her. A sly smile spread across his face. "It has been ages since I have so enjoyed myself. Actually, I have not laughed like that since last I was with you.

"There's just something about you, Ida, that makes me feel free, as if I can tell you anything, can share anything with you."

Ida sat up. "That is not what you meant."

Tutankh laughed. "You are still very perceptive," he replied. "I have known Ankhesenpaaten for as long as I have been alive. I am also quite aware of Ay's and Horemheb's spies amongst us and I place my life in your hands - as I had my heart all those years ago."

"I shall do my best."

He reached out and gently cupped her cheek. "I know you will," he answered softly.

There it was again, this unnamable thing drawing them together.

"I never forgot you, Ida," he said huskily.

His lips tasted hers, gently, entreatingly.

Ida broke the kiss and stood abruptly. She turned her back to him.

He stood and came to stand behind her. Her breath caught. She did not dare turn around.

His hands were on her arms.

"Ida," he whispered, his lips brushing her ear lobe, his voice raw with emotion.

She trembled involuntarily.

"I've been so lonely for you, Ida," he whispered. "I want to bury myself in you, my precious jewel."

He softly kissed her earlobe. Her eyes fluttered closed.

"I want you so much, Ida," he sighed. "For all of these years I have dreamed of you, have longed for you. Your hold over me has not lessened with the passage of time."

His hands were sliding down her arms as his mouth moved along the tender flesh of her neck. "Let me love you."

Ida was weakening. She turned around to face him.

"We must not," she whispered breathlessly. "Ankhesenpaaten is like my sister, and if we are caught ..."

He put two fingers over her lips. "Tell me you don't want me," he said pulling her against him. "Tell me you don't feel this between us stronger than it's ever been, as if no time has passed. Tell me your heart belongs to another and I will bother you no more."

Ida could not.

He gazed into her eyes. "You are the only love I have ever known, Ida," he said huskily. "Love me."

His mouth was centimeters from hers.

"I can't," she whispered.

His head slowly drew back from her.

She had hurt him. She could see the pain in his eyes.

Her heart dropped to the floor.

He let her go and walked away from her, turned back to the paining.

Ida looked down, then to the entrance flap of the tent.

She stood there for a moment, uncertain.

She wanted to tell him that she had meant that she couldn't do *this*, not that she couldn't love him, that she *did* love him. She wanted to make him understand that there would be no going back for her if she made love with him, that her heart was greedy and it would never be able to go on as it had been if she gave in to it.

Instead, when he continued to ignore her presence, she left.

V

The noise level in the dancing girls' quarters was staggering. Ida had been silent, withdrawn since that night in Tutankh's tent. Even now she did not speak to anyone as she prepared herself.

One of the Nubian girls looked over Ida's modest dancing garb with disapproval. "That will not do," the girl said.

"Egyptian dance is more about movement than costume, about weaving a spell with the body than dazzling the eye with jewels," Ida replied defensively.

The Nubian shook her head. "I still say a little finery never hurts."

She went to one of the closets and pulled from it a long white dress. "Put this on," she said.

Ida stood glaring at the girl with her hands on her hips.

"Oh come on," the girl said laying the dress across her arms so that Ida could better see it. "None of the other girls have the flare to carry it off properly. Not to mention that the last girl who wore this dress won the heart of a sheik."

"I'm not looking to win the heart of anyone."

"Not even the heart of your handsome Pharaoh?"

Ida refused to give the girl the satisfaction of the effect her observation had upon her - though her cheeks burned.

The girl laughed knowingly. "You're probably right though. I can tell you don't need the dress to win his attentions."

Ida flushed.

"Yes," the girl pressed. "I see the way his eyes follow you when he thinks no one gives notice. The rich and the powerful never pay much attention to or even care what the slave sees."

The girl laughed again as she proffered the dress to Ida once more.

Impulsively, Ida had taken it from her and put it on.

When she looked in the mirror she hardly recognized herself. The dress was of linen. The bodice was sleeveless, tight, and cut low in front to show off the rich curves of her breasts. It had no back.

There were two sections to the skirt. One section ran in the back to the middle of her thighs, lengthwise. The other ran across the front of her, its edges just barely covering the edges of the back section. Whenever she moved, the sections separated, revealing the length of her firm thighs.

The front section was embroidered with gold thread in an intricate design, a fine sheer gold-colored material covering the wide waistband.

She looked like a queen.

Ida felt the girl loosening the braid that ran down her back. She let her.

The girl ruffled Ida's hair, letting the thick mane tumble wildly about her back and shoulders.

A gold armband slid up Ida's right arm. The anklet that Tutankh had given her when they were children served as a bracelet on the left. The ring Ankhe had given her adorned her finger.

The girl sat on the floor and put glass-jeweled rings onto Ida's toes.

The girl looked in the mirror at Ida who seemed to be mesmerized by her own image. She laughed.

"What did I tell you?" she asked Ida. "You must keep it all."

"But I can not," Ida protested.

"You must," the girl insisted as she began gathering Ida's clothes. "It fits as though it were made for you."

"But..."

"It was my sister's. Now it is yours."

Ida didn't know what to say. When she turned around, the girl was gone.

Ida stalled for as long as she could before heading for the great hall.

When she arrived at the banquet, all eyes were upon her. She ignored them and began serving Tutankh. His eyes were the only ones that had any effect on her - a mixture of longing and pain when they fell upon her. They made her chest ache. They made her want to run back to the Dancing Girls' quarters and strip the dress from her body.

She was playing a dangerous game she knew, but she was unable to stop, addicted somehow to it. She could not deny the electricity that passed through her when their eyes met.

Though she forced herself to look at him as little as possible, her eyes could not seem to get enough of the sight of him.

One of the princes beside him inquired as to who she was, told Pharaoh that she belonged in the harem, not the slave quarters. Pharaoh barely even acknowledged the compliment, instead sinking even further into the dark mood that had been descending upon him since his last meeting with Ida.

Ida's dancing had been spellbinding. Her remarkable beauty coupled with her natural grace and sensuality brought every man in the room to her feet. They had offered

Tutankh insane amounts of money and jewels and perfumes for her - enough to purchase 20 slave girls, support 10 wives.

Tutankh refused them with: "She is not my slave to sell." "She is property of my Queen. Only Ankhesenamun can sell her."

Ida pretended not to hear them as she resumed serving her Pharaoh.

As the liquor flowed, Faium, Horemheb's puppet, became freer. He began whispering in the ears of those around him of how weak the Pharaoh was, of how it was *his* master who truly ruled the kingdom.

As Ida walked past, he tried to grab her. Though she dodged him successfully, she knew it would soon be time for her to slip away. The rest of men were beginning to show signs of drunkenness as well.

Tutankh, however, was still on his first serving of beer. He was one of the few people there, besides herself and his personal guard, that chose not to indulge in the spirits.

The party was becoming rowdy, the other women loose. Ida discretely slipped away, back to the dancing girls' quarters.

There, she had removed the costume, carefully placing it and all of the jewelry, save the bracelet from Tutankh and the ring from Ankhesenpaaten, in the small trunk that held her belongings. She put back on her opaque undergarment. She sat down facing the mirror and began brushing her hair.

Ida heard the crash first.

She looked around the room. She was the only girl there.

Perhaps another of the girls had drunkenly stumbled back to another of the rooms to sleep off the liquor. At least that's what she told herself - though apprehension still gnawed at her.

She stood, hurriedly slipped on the short, semi-transparent dress she usually wore.

She refused to just sit there, an easy target. Brush in hand, she went to investigate. Slowly, she made her way down the corridor, peering into the other rooms as she went.

Suddenly, Ida was grabbed from behind, a male hand clasped tightly over her mouth.

He began dragging her back towards one of the beds.

Ida pressed the faux jewel on the brush's head and a blade shot out from the end of the handle. She jabbed it full force into her assailant's thigh.

The man cried out, let her go.

Ida dashed towards the door to the main hallway. She could hear the man stumbling behind her, cursing at her.

She flung open the door and dashed down the hall. Rounding the corner, she ran right smack into Pharaoh. His captain and lieutenant were with him.

"What is the meaning of this?" the lieutenant asked, catching her roughly by the arm.

Faium came limping down the corridor towards them. "Don't let her go," he slurred. "That bitch stabbed me."

Pharaoh looked from Faium to Ida. "Is this true?"

"Great Pharaoh, he attacked me," Ida answered.

"Did you attack her, Faium?" Pharaoh asked him.

"She told me to meet her in her quarters, then the little whore stabbed me."

"He lies," Ida said angrily. "I never asked him to my bed nor am I a whore"

"You lying harlot!" Faium exclaimed.

He raised his hand to strike her, Tutankh catching his hand before it could make contact with Ida's flesh.

"You're not going to let a slave get away with attacking a nobleman. Are you?" Faium demanded, incredulous.

"Ida is the property of our queen. When and if she is punished, it shall only be by my or the queen's edict," Tutankh answered.

"Oh. I see," Faium said looking from Pharaoh to Ida. "You're bedding the little tart yourself." He laughed sinisterly.

"I warn you to hold your tongue, Faium," Pharaoh said.

"You of all people, *Pharaoh* should know the penalty for adultery.

"Unless of course her cunt is so good you don't mind having your nose or ears cut off, public flogging, banishment, burning at the stake or being fed to wild animals for it."

"It is well that you know the punishment for adultery, but tell me Faium, do you know the punishment for heresy?" Tutankh asked.

"My master will not allow it," Faium said smugly.

"Perhaps you are right. Harsher. Gizom. Cut out Faium's tongue instead."

The two men grabbed Faium before he could back away.

"I'll take the girl to her quarters," Pharaoh said. "After you finish with Faium, send for Esnai. Instruct her that Ida is to receive twice the workload and no food for so long as we are here. She is to stay confined to her quarters unless specifically summoned."

"Yes, Great Pharaoh," Harsher and Gizom intoned. "As you have commanded, so it shall be."

They led Faium away, Faium yelling and fighting against them quite futilely.

Pharaoh took Ida's arm and escorted her back to her quarters. There she wretched her arm from his grasp.

"Why am I being punished for defending myself from rape?" she demanded.

He put two fingers over her mouth.

"You should have killed him," he said.

He gently pushed her hair back from her shoulder. "Still, no matter the provocation, it cannot be known that I chose the side of a slave over a noble."

"But I did nothing wrong," she answered in a sharp whisper.

"Which is why your punishment is for appearances only. I will summon you frequently.

"Then you shall eat. Then you shall rest."

"But Esnai -" Ida began

"I am well aware, as is everyone, that there is bad blood between you and she. Who would be judged more believable than your own enemy in regards to your penance.

"Trust me, Ida. She *will* gloat."

He touched her cheek briefly, then, without another word, he left.

VI

Ida was only vaguely aware of her surroundings.

"How long has she been unconscious?" Nacamakun asked the old slave woman who tended Ida.

"She has been ill since first she fainted, two days ago. She drifts in and out of fever, of consciousness." The woman was dabbing a cool, wet rag upon Ida's forehead as she spoke.

Nacamakun stood.

"I will check on her again when I return from my journey," he told the old woman. "While I am away, contact Prince Mursili. He will see to it that you have everything you need."

The woman nodded.

Ida drifted off again.

True to his word, Tutankh had summoned Ida often - though things remained tense between them. More often than not, he was not there when she arrived. When he was there, he kept busy, kept his distance from her.

After their return to Egypt, he did not speak to her at all.

Ida was sitting on her bed, staring thoughtfully at the bracelet, gently running her forefinger over the gold when Batau entered the room.

"Ida," Batau called.

Ida looked up at her.

"Ankhe has called for you," Batau said.

"I'm sorry," Ida said. "I did not hear."

She rose and followed Batau to the queen's chambers.

"You have been very distracted these last weeks," Batau said. "You've hardly been eating."

"I'll try to do better," the girl answered absently.

"What's the matter, girl?"

"Nothing."

"Ida -"

Ida slipped hurriedly into Ankhe's chamber, before Batau could press her further.

Ankhe looked up at her.

"What's the matter with you lately, Ida?" Ankhe asked impatiently. "I have been calling for you."

"I'm sorry, my mistress," Ida answered. "I've been feeling ill."

"Come closer."

Ida did as she was bade.

"I want you to deliver this message to Tutankhaten for me," she whispered.

She softly touched Ida's face, let her hand trail in such a way that she was able to discretely slip a small note into Ida's bosom.

When Ida tried to leave, Ankhe discretely detained her.

"Not now," she whispered in Ida's ear. "Take it to his room at midnight, along with the sweets."

Ankhe moved away, the volume of her voice returning to normal.

"Take this to Pharaoh," she instructed, handing Ida a dish of sweets. "Sinic gave these to me in tribute."

Ida took them.

"And make sure you have some as well," the queen added. "I'm sure you'll find them quite enjoyable."

"Thank you, Great Queen," Ida replied, bowing low.

"Oh and one more thing before you go. See what you can do to dress up this gown," Ankhe said, gesturing to a gown strewn across her bed. "Sometimes I don't know why I even bother sending away to have them made, not when I never quite find them satisfactory until you've worked your magic upon them."

A small smile of bemusement spread across Ankhe's lips. "You should have been an exemplary seamstress.... were you not born a slave."

Ida went to the bed and examined the gown.

She picked it up. "I shall see what it is I can do," she replied.

"When I return from my outing, do come and sit with me a while," Ankhe said rising from her chair.

"Yes, mistress," Ida said bowing to her.

Ida had stood outside of the door to Pharaoh Tutankhaten's chamber for a time before she actually knocked.

"Enter," he said.

Ida hesitated before she pushed open the door.

"Shut it behind you," he ordered.

Ida pushed the door closed.

"Come," he said.

Ida went to him. She assumed the subservient position at his feet.

"All of the servants have gone. You may speak freely," he said.

She stood and reached into her bosom. She handed him the note.

He took it. He looked down at the tempting looking cakes.

"Are those for me?" he asked.

"Yes, Great Pharaoh," she said bowing her head and offering up the dish to him.

He picked one up and examined it.

"My taster has already retired," he said. "Do have one first."

"But it is from your queen."

"Do not argue with me, Idaten."

Ida stood and took one of the sweets. She put it into her mouth, Tutankh watching her chew and swallow it.

"How is it?" he asked after a time.

"It's delicious," she replied, "and I feel no ill effects."

"Have another," he said.

She looked uncertain.

"Go on," he prompted.

She took another one, ate it.

They waited a time more - to make sure it was safe.

"How do you feel now?" he asked.

"The same. Will you not have any?" she asked.

He put the one in his hand into his mouth. He opened the note as he chewed it and read. He swallowed it, then took up another of the delectable sweets.

He seemed lost in thought as he re-folded the note.

He looked at her. "You do still read do you not, Ida?" he asked.

"Yes, sire."

"And did you read this note?"

"No, Great Pharaoh, I did not."

"Why not?"

"It was not meant for my eyes."

"The last section concerns you," he said.

Ida gave no reaction.

"Come now," he pressed. "Aren't you the least bit interested in its contents?"

"I believe I already know what it says," she replied.

"Do you now?"

"I have been lapsing in my duty these last weeks."

"And why is that?"

Her eyes fled his.

"Do you not feel strangely now?" he asked her.

"My Pharaoh?" she asked returning her gaze to his.

"Do you notice any difference in yourself since you have entered this room?"

"I feel warm. My skin is tingling."

"Is it unpleasant?"

"No. It's quite the opposite."

He smiled. "According to this note, these sweets contain mandrake."

Ida dropped the dish, the remaining cakes sliding across the floor.

"I don't understand," she said.

"Mandrake is an aphrodisiac."

"I know what mandrake does," she snapped. "I just don't understand why Ankhe would -"

"Send them to me?"

"After yet another stillbirth, the second of our two daughters, it was determined that Ankhe's womb had to be removed in order to save her life. Did you know this?"

Ida nodded.

"It is Ankhe's hope that I might become nymphotic by the mandrake's properties and thus impregnate some woman, *any* woman, so that we may adopt the resulting child and thus continue the Amarna line."

"But I ate two cakes of it," she said.

"Mandrake will make you do nothing you would not have desired to do otherwise. It simply frees you of the fear that would stop you from doing so."

"It robs you of the ability to see the consequences," she answered sharply.

"What's the matter, Ida? Would it not please you to carry my child?" he asked.

When she did not answer, his expression soured. "How about to carry *Pharaoh's* child?"

Ida shook her head. She didn't know what to say, felt that whatever came forth would be wrong.

Pharaoh stood. He stepped down from his chair, Ida taking a couple of steps away from him.

"I'm curious as to what will happen next," he said. "I want to know if the legends are true."

Tutankh reached out and softly ran his fingers down her arm.

Ida trembled, her eyes fluttering shut but a moment as she took another unsteady step backwards.

Melancholy crept into Tutankh's features.

He chuckled humorlessly. "Even drugged with mandrake you do not want me."

He stared down at her a moment more before he turned his back to her.

"Take the leave you so much desire," he ordered her.

Ida stood rooted.

He whirled back around and grabbing her arms, pulled her against him.

"Leave while you still can," he commanded between clinched teeth.

Though he let her go, she still could not move. Even as his lips came down solidly upon hers, forcing her back flat against the wall.

His hands grasped her face now, his body covering hers.

When at last he broke the kiss, his eyes were wild with desire. Ida was breathless.

His mouth covered hers again, his tongue sliding between her lips. When it met hers, all of her bones melted. The mandrake induced heat turned to flame.

Ida found herself unable to think of anything but the man who was kissing her, whose warmth she could feel through her dress.

Her hands were on the sinewy muscles of his back, her mouth just as greedy as his. His need was pressed against her. One of his hands had found its way to her breast.

One of her legs lifted, her foot sliding down the back of his leg. He tasted the hollow of her throat as he repositioned himself - his throbbing organ pressed directly against hers.

Ida gasped, her hands tangling themselves in his hair. He whispered her name as his mouth explored the tender flesh of the side of her neck.

His hand slid down to the edge of her dress, sliding it up her thighs. Her hands began loosening his kilt.

When he thrust into her, she stifled her cry of pain. Tears slid from under her closed eyes, dampened her long lashes, but she could not stop this, did not want him to stop this.

When at last it was over, she clung to him and wept.

"Ida?" he asked stroking her hair.

She abruptly pushed him away and ran from the room.

Tutankh watched her retreating back in confusion.

He looked down, saw the crimson drops on the white of his kilt. He looked at the door again in shame.

Ida had been a virgin.

VII

The day was hot in King Suppiluliuma's palace. Though Ida's illness had not passed, it had lessened considerably.

She rose slowly and went to the window. She watched the children playing in the pool of water in the gardens below the citadel.

She sighed heavily.

The days here seemed long. It had been 4 days since she had awoken and still there had been no report from Egypt. She worried about Heketya. She wondered if she was safe, if she was even still alive.

"Miss," a voice said.

Ida turned.

It was Clizi, the old slave woman Prince Mursili had assigned to her.

"Yes, Clizi," Ida answered.

"I see that you are better."

Ida nodded. "Much. Thank you."

Clizi smiled. Noticing that some of Clizi's teeth were rotten, Ida redirected her gaze.

"Do you think it will be a boy or a girl?" the woman asked.

"Do I think who will be a boy or a girl?" Ida asked.

"The baby. Do you think it will be a boy or a girl?"

Ida still did not appear to comprehend what the woman was saying.

"Your baby," the woman stated - louder, slower. "Do you think your baby will be a boy or a girl?"

The color drained from Ida's face. "My baby?"

"You are with child."

"But that cannot be," Ida replied shaking her head.

"Oh, but it is," Clizi reassured her.

"You don't understand. I *can't* be pregnant."

"And why not?" the old woman asked. "Is something the matter with your womb?"

Ida shook her head.

"When was your last woman's time?" Clizi pressed.

Ida thought for a moment. "About three months ago," she answered quietly.

"Do you think the father will marry you or at the very least claim the child?" she asked.

"He can not."

"He's already married and cannot afford another wife or child," Clizi surmised, self-satisfied.

"He's dead," Ida whispered.

"That's too bad. Still you shouldn't fret, young one. You're a handsome enough woman. I'm sure you can find a man that will overlook your condition."

Clizi collected the dishes from the floor next to the bed and left the room.

Ida suddenly felt weak again. She went to the bed and sank down onto it.

She clasped the pillow to her chest. Then, she began to weep.

Ida could have let it all end there - the night she had run from Pharaoh's rooms.

It had become afterwards as though she and Tutankh were strangers.

For the next weeks, they neither saw each other alone nor spoke to each other. Sometimes Ida wanted to scream with the madness of it.

The night she had made up her mind to put an end to the silent, awkward tension between them, it had been raining. It was late and the lights had long since gone out all over the palace.

She had seen the light in his rooms still burning from across the courtyard.

Ida had raised her hand to knock, decided against it. She did not want to give him the chance to turn her away.

Instead, she had slowly pushed opened the door and stepped inside. He was sitting on his bed, reading a scroll.

His hair was damp. He must have gotten caught in the rain.

She closed the door behind her.

"I'm fine, Ekon," Tutankh called, not even looking up, a soft smile played on his lips. "You worry too much. See my wet clothes are drying." He gestured to a nearby chair.

When he did not hear the sound of the door opening again, he looked up.

Ida swallowed passed the lump in her throat and approached him.

She sat on the floor in front of him, took the subservient posture of those wishing an audience with him.

"You may speak," he commanded.

"I apologize for the other night," she said. "I had no right."

Remorse filled his eyes. "*You* had no right? It is I alone who should bear the brunt of shame, Ida."

"It was not your fault alone," Ida answered. "Know that I will keep this between us."

He came to his knees next to her. He took her head in his hands, holding her face so that her eyes looked into his.

"I hurt you," he said.

Ida looked away.

"I wasn't thinking," he whispered.

Ida pulled away and stood.

His words stung her. Worse still, she could see it in his eyes. He regretted making love to her.

Tears threatened. Tears she did not want him to see. She turned her back to him.

He grabbed her hand and bowed his head against it.

"I'm so sorry," he said in an emotion raw voice. "I was like an animal. I defiled you and I hurt you. I tore your innocence from you in a wave of mad lust. Please forgive me, Ida."

She turned back to him, knelt in front of him.

She reached out and cupped his face. His cheek was damp, as was her own.

"There is nothing to forgive," she answered. "I wanted that night. I've wanted it for a very long time now."

"But your first time shouldn't have..."

Her mouth upon his silenced him.

His eyes searched hers as she gently broke the kiss.

He stood wearily and went to the window. He sighed heavily. "I cannot be your friend Ida and I want more from you than just your flesh."

Ida stood.

He turned to face her. "Is this only lust, loneliness, pity or do you truly love me, Idaten?"

Ida was torn between the desire to flee and the longing to stay.

"All of Egypt loves you, Pharaoh," she answered at length.

"I asked if *you* love me."

"Of course I love you. You are my master."

"Enough with the games, Ida. You know well that I ask not if you love me as a slave loves a master but as a woman loves a man."

Ida fought her heart. "It is forbidden. That night was forbidden. Even this is forbidden.

"We should not speak of such things. I should not even be here."

"Yet you are," Tutankh replied.

"I can no longer bear this, Ida. It's tearing me apart. Please. Just tell me the truth.

"Are you in love with Tutankhaten, the man you see before you stripped of all marks of Pharaoh, who is not your master but your servant, who has worshipped you since first his eyes and his heart could make distinction between man and woman, who gave you the anklet that now faithfully adorns your wrist, who would tempt death just for the chance to make love to you once more."

She stared at him silently for a long moment. She looked down at the ring Ankhe had given her, lightly ran the tip of her finger over it.

At length, feeling his impatient gaze burn through her, she looked back up at him. She nodded shortly, her eyes fleeing back down to the ring.

He was before her now, his hands on her shoulders. She looked up into his eyes.

"I have wanted for an answer to that question for an eternity," he said softly. He gently stoked her hair. "It seems that I have loved you forever."

He delicately kissed her, before stepping back.

"I want all of you, Ida," he whispered huskily. "Your heart, your body, your soul."

"They are yours," she answered breathlessly.

Her eyes gazed into his as she slowly undressed herself. His did the same as he removed his kilt.

Their lips touched gently, probingly. Her body burned where the length of him melded against her.

He lifted her and carried her to the bed.

He was sweet, tender, lingering as he learned all of the secrets of her body. Ida had no shame with him. She touched him freely, answered his ancient signals with her own instinctive urges.

This time, as he entered her, he was slow, gentle. The ecstasy of it brought Ida to tears. She moved with him.

For many hours their lovemaking lasted, Ida even allowing herself to fall asleep in his arms.

In the morning, just as the first stirrings of life began in the palace, she finally slid into her own bed. When Batau would come to wake her, she would seem to have been there all night.

VIII

Ida felt it again, the strange gentle stirring in her stomach. Could it be their child?

She put her hand on her belly.

A child. A child conceived of purest love, forbidden love between a god-king and the lowliest of all servants, a slave. The only living child of Tutankhaten, the last true heir of the Amarna line.

Ida knew in her heart of hearts that it was Horemheb who had had her Pharaoh murdered. His wrath was terrible, his influence far reaching. If he ever found out that she was alive and carrying Tutankhaten's child....

There was a light knock on the door. Ida turned towards it.

Clizi.

Clizi ran to Ida excitedly. "Nacamakun has returned and held council with the king. He has agreed to send Prince Zannanza to your queen."

Ida half laughed, half cried in relief.

She had done it. She had saved Heketya. She might even be able to return to Egypt in time to say one last goodbye to Tutankh, to tell him that she carried his child before she fled forever from Horemheb's reach.

She hugged the old woman.

"There is to be a feast tonight in honor of Nacamakun's return and Prince Zannanza's departure. The king would be most pleased if you would come."

"Of course," Ida answered. "I can thank him before I return home."

"You will have time yet to thank him," Prince Mursili II interrupted from the door way.

Ida's smile faded. How long had he been standing there watching them?

"What do you mean I will have time yet?" she asked.

"My father has no plan to release you until my brother is safely installed as Pharaoh," Mursili replied.

"But that could be months," Ida protested.

"Indeed," Mursili agreed.

The joy fled from Ida. She sat down heavily upon a chair, her hand absently seeking out her stomach.

Mursili studied her for a long moment.

AMARNA BOOK I: BOOK OF IDA

"My father shall be glad to know you have accepted his invitation," he said.

Ida looked up at him, her gaze stony. Mursili smirked before excusing himself from the room.

"Ladies," he said with a short nod.

Ida stared at the spot Mursili had abandoned long after he had gone, her thoughts and emotions in turmoil. It was only when Clizi spoke again that she remembered she was not alone.

"How long has the father been dead?" the old woman asked quietly.

Tears came to Ida's eyes as she turned her attention to the old woman. "He has yet even to be sealed in his tomb," she replied softly.

"The child is of the Pharaoh Tutankhamun, is it not?" Clizi half asked, half stated.

Ida was taken aback. "My baby is none of your business."

"I just..."

"Get out," Ida ordered. "Now!"

Clizi rose hurriedly and scurried from the room.

A powerful wave of grief washed over Ida, threatening to drown her.

She took up a knife from the table and held the point over her heart. Her hands shook. Though she tried to will herself to do it, her hands refused to obey her.

She dropped the knife instead, sent it skittering across the floor.

"Why Aten?" she demanded angrily. "Why have you taken him from me and left me behind with child?

"I can not do this. I can not do this."

She buried her head in her arms in despair. Heavy sobs shook her body until she had cried herself into a fitful sleep.

That evening, with Clizi's help, Ida made herself presentable and went down to the banquet. The great hall was noisy, bustling. King Suppiluliuma had even hired a band of gypsies to entertain the throng.

She found she could not force herself to stay amidst the merriment for long. It felt false to her - base, like a mockery of her grief.

She excused herself and came to sit at the end of the corridor, upon a window sill. She stared unseeingly down into the garden.

"Why are you weeping child?" a rough, scratchy voice asked.

Ida turned. It was an ancient gypsy woman.

"Leave me," Ida said.

The old woman did not heed her. "Your husband is with your god," she said. "The child you carry within you shall keep the Amarna line alive. His seed shall return Egypt to greatness."

"You know not of what you speak," Ida answered sharply. "There are still three left in the Amarna line, women who can still bare children."

"That may well be, but it is the child within *you* that holds the key to the future of all of Egypt.

"Protect him at all costs. Amongst his descendants shall spring the greatest Pharaoh Egypt has ever known and ever shall know. His name shall spread across the centuries, across the boundaries of time, and through him the Amarna line shall live eternal."

Ida laughed humorlessly. "The pharaoh is dead. A dead pharaoh cannot adopt a child into his line of descent or bond him from slavery.

"And do you really think that Ay or Horemheb will allow a threat to their play for power to become Pharaoh?

"They tried that once, with Tutankhaten, and they failed. He began to rebel against them. Do you honestly believe they would risk it again?

"And what of me? I am nothing more than a pregnant slave girl who can not even go back to Egypt, yet from me shall come the greatest god-king of Egyptian history?"

Ida laughed again. "Woman you are mad."

"Heed my words girl," the woman warned. "Though times are dark, they will get darker still. Guard the child well and tell no one of who his father is."

Ida was angry now. "Go old woman and take your prophecies to those who will pay you handsomely for them. I have nothing I can bear to part with."

"I do not seek payment. It is only an honor for me to have been in the presence of the mother of the greatest line of Amarnas that will ever exist," she bowed to Ida.

"You *can* do this, Idaten," she said when she rose. "Your one god is with you. Tutankhaten is with you."

A tear trickled from the corner of Ida's eye.

The old woman smiled softly, reaching out to gently touch the tear.

She turned and returned to the party.

Ida watched the woman's retreating back. She could hear the jingle of dancing girls' bells and beads and bangles. The sound transported her back to Heketya's 8th birthday celebration.

Most of Heketya's guests had been so drunk that they could barely see by that time Ida and the other girls performed their last dance of the night. Ankhe and Heketya had long since retired.

How Tutankh's steady gaze had warmed her.

AMARNA BOOK I: BOOK OF IDA

They had been lovers for months now. He was becoming a Pharaoh in his own right, gradually seizing more and more power from the clutches of Ay and Horemheb.

He had refused to tear down the shrine of Aten and restore the priesthood of Amun. He had all but completely stopped the rebuilding of Amun's temples. He had even aspirations of returning the state back to monotheism as his father before him had, of changing his name back to Tutankhaten as it had originally been.

They were losing control of him.

Ida feared for him more and more each day. Yet, she could not help but be moved by his ever-growing wisdom and vigor, filled with love and pride.

Their lovemaking that night had been feverish. He was behind her, one of his hands stroking knowingly between her thighs as he thrust into her.

She could not contain a cry.

He had quickly cupped her cheek, turned her head so that his tongue could silence hers.

As they lay in his bed afterwards, Ida on top of him. Tutankh began to chuckle.

"What's so funny?" she asked.

"You," he answered.

She laughed softly. "Consider yourself complimented," she replied.

"Oh?" he asked gently flipping her under him. He slid himself against her.

She gasped loudly. He laughed.

"Promise yourself to me," he said rubbing himself against her.

"Tutankh," she gasped grasping his shoulders.

"Promise yourself to me," he repeated tasting her mouth.

She looked into his eyes. "I promise myself to you a thousand times and a thousand times again."

"And I to you," he answered as he stilled. "You know now that we are joined forever, don't you?"

Ida laughed. "That easily?"

"I am Pharaoh and I decree it so," Tutankh replied matter-of-factly.

"You know as well as I that neither the law nor society would recognize the marriage between a free man and a slave - especially not the Pharaoh and a slave. Not really anyway. At most it would be regarded as a concubinage."

"Alright, then I free you," he replied.

She laughed. "I am Ankhe's property, not yours. She was Queen before you were Pharaoh."

"Oh," he sighed exaggeratedly. "What am I to do when even my own love does not recognize my power as Pharaoh?"

She smiled mischievously, one of her hands roaming to the length of him.

She began to stroke him. "Oh but Great Pharaoh, you are mistaken. If anyone knows and recognizes your great "powers", it is I."

He laughed deep within his throat. "Then *we* shall recognize our marriage then. *Aten* will."

Ida gazed at him for a long moment, her smile fading. "I love you, Tutankh," she said. "With all that I am, I love you."

"I know," he replied, "and I love you, my hidden queen, my Ida."

They kissed.

"And as a symbol of our union," he said reaching for a small box on the table beside the bed.

He opened the box and reached inside. Extracting an elaborate gold pin, he handed it over to her.

"Wear it always inside of your tunic," he said watching her expectantly.

Ida read the hieroglyphs. His name and hers were inscribed upon it. All of Tutankhamun's royal wives had similar ones - though theirs were less remarkable than hers.

Inscribed upon on the back were the words: "My only true wife. My only true love."

She looked up at him. Tears of love had filled her eyes.

She had embraced him, then they had made love once more.

Ida glowed as she made her way back to her room, holding the pin tightly in her palm.

She went inside and began to undress.

She had stared at her naked body in the mirror, embraced herself as a warm smile spread across her face.

Tutankh. Her *husband*.

One of her hands slowly slid across her skin, her body tingling with just the memory of his body pressed against hers.

She set the pin on the shelf by the mirror and began to brush her tousled hair.

"My," a voice said from behind her, "don't you look smug."

Ida turned.

Batau.

"What are you doing in my room at this hour?" Ida asked.

"It's almost dawn, Ida."

"Why are you here?" Ida repeated.

"I heard you, Ida. I was walking through the corridor to check on Ankhe and as I passed Tutankhaten's chamber I heard your voice cry out."

Ida opened her mouth to speak.

"Don't bother denying it," Batau snapped snatching the pin from the shelf. Though she could not read, she had seen the like before. She knew well what it was and what it meant.

She slapped Ida.

"You whore!" Batau accused. "How dare you lie with Ankhe's husband?! Do you not have enough with Galeno and Persuti?"

Ida cupped her injured cheek. "How dare *you* judge *me*!"

Batau threw the pin at her. "I always thought of you as my daughter. I always had a soft place in my heart for you, but no more!

"And Ankhe. Ankhe raised you above all others, treated you like a sister and this is how you repay her, by stealing her husband from her bed?!"

"Batau, I love him. I have always loved him.

"And he loves me the same.

"If he were not Pharaoh *I* would be his one and only wife."

"Love does not excuse betrayal," Batau replied.

"Ankhe does not love him more than a friend. You know as well as I that since she lost her womb she hasn't been sharing his bed. She's been sleeping with Prince Zannanza."

Batau slapped Ida again.

Ida spun and fell to the floor with the force of it. She had to force herself to stay there lest she would rise and strike the old woman.

"I no longer see you, Idaten," Batau said. "Do you hear me? You are just another piece of rubbish, one of many."

Batau turned to leave

"Batau!" Ida called hurrying to her feet. "Please!"

Batau kept walking.

IX

"Idamun. ... Idamun....."

Ida looked up at the tall man-child who was calling her name.

Though she had seen him several times since she had arrived in Hattusa, she had never really *seen* him. He was handsome of face though lanky of frame. His coal black hair was even longer than hers, reaching almost to his knees. He couldn't be more than 3 years younger than she.

"Idaten," she corrected. "My name is Idaten. Ida."

"My mistake," he replied. "I was under the impression that all of your names were amended to Amun," he said.

"Not anymore," Ida replied.

"You were lost to us," the boy said, "in another world."

Ida stared at him expressionlessly.

"We have yet to be formerly introduced," he continued. "I am Prince Mursili II. Mursili they call me....amongst other things."

"I know who you are," she replied.

"My father has officially put you in my charge now. It would not do for you to starve to death in my care."

"I am not hungry," Ida answered.

"In your condition you *must* eat," he replied. "In fact, I insist."

"My condition?" Ida repeated.

"Clizi..."

"Is there anyone she hasn't told yet?" Ida asked, incredulous.

"Clizi only told me because it is her duty to. She told Nac because he might be suited to..."

Ida rose and tried to leave. He grabbed her arm.

"Boy or not, I am still Prince and you *will* show me all due respect."

"Forgive me, your highness," Ida replied. Though she struggled to contain her emotions, she still knew well her place. "I meant no disrespect. Truly, I did not. And I sincerely appreciate everything you, Nac and Clizi have done for me thus far -"

"But?"

"But it's just too soon." She smiled sadly. "You don't think I know it would be wise for me to accept Nac, that his support is a more than generous offer - far more than I deserve?"

She shook her head. "I haven't even *begun* to mourn."

"Mourn?" he replied. "You can mourn for the rest of your life if you like. This offer, however, is temporary - your pregnancy soon to be obvious to all.

"Nac may be far from young or rich but he does have rank, stability. He has a very healthy estate and an heir - not to mention the ear of the King.

"Nac wishes to marry soon. I would not dally long if I were in your shoes."

"I can not accept Nac or any other man of Hattusa - under any circumstances," Ida insisted. "Once Prince Zannanza becomes Pharaoh, I plan to return home."

"Then what?" he asked. "You think you or that child will *ever* be safe in Egypt?"

"I have friends, people who will help me start a new life away from the palace."

Mursili smirked cynically.

"As you will," he said. "You're making a serious mistake. But then it's yours to make isn't it?"

"It is," she replied evenly, though Mursili could all but feel the fire in her boiling towards the surface.

He nodded. "No one aside from Nac, Clizi and I know the paternity of your child and I plan on keeping it that way.

"So long as you remain in our land, and I draw breath, I promise that no harm will come to either you or your child.

"Neither of you will have anything to fear – not from my father, not from Zannanza and certainly not from Ay or Horemheb."

"I am honored to have your protection, Mighty Prince."

Mursili smirked. "I will leave you now, but I expect you to rejoin the banquet and eat well."

"As you have commanded," Ida replied with a bow.

She watched as the boy continued down the hall, away from the gathering, then returned to the banquet to do as she was bade.

Mursili found the old woman easily enough. She was waiting for him in one of the lower alcoves.

Angrily Mursili grabbed the woman's arm and pulled her into one of the empty rooms. He shut the door behind them.

Alone, he pulled the wrap and wig from the woman's head and threw it to the ground.

"What are you doing here, witch?" he demanded.

The old woman laughed.

"Is that any way to greet your mother?" she asked. "Your father and his Babylonian whore may well have banished me from Hattusa but never forget that *I* am still Suppiluluima's chief wife. *I* am still the one, true queen."

"Answer, woman."

"Can't a mother just want to visit her handsome son?" she asked reaching out a hand to stoke his face.

Mursili pushed her hand away. "Not when it may cost her her life or get her son banished."

"And who would dare turn me in?"

"That is not the point, mother. You know well how to reach me outside of the King's influence."

"I came to see the girl," the woman admitted.

"The one who calls herself Ida?" Mursili asked.

The woman smiled. "You've seen it too, haven't you?" she taunted.

"Seen what?" he replied.

The woman laughed. "I knew it! Suppilu did not drive *all* of the "witches" from the citadel did he?"

"I am nothing like you."

"No? Do the gods Arinna & Telipinu not speak to you?"

"Only in my sleep," he relented, relieved to share the truth of who and what he was - if only for a moment.

"And does *he* know?"

"Of course not. Only Nacamakun knows... and you."

"How long has it been happening?" she asked.

"Since my 13th year."

The old woman nodded, considering. "You must never tell him - no matter what.

"Your future depends upon it.

"Suppilu will banish you like he did me....or perhaps even worse should you fail to see what it is he wishes you to see."

"I remember well what he did to you. I will not make the same mistake."

"Suppilu has already started down a road to ruin, one from which there is no return. He saw to that when he murdered his brother Tudhaliya and usurped the throne.

"Your visions in his hands will only bring you ruin. But in *your* hands, in your hands Mursili our kingdom might yet be saved from your father's fate."

AMARNA BOOK I: BOOK OF IDA

"But how?" he asked.

"The girl, Mursili. You must protect the girl and her offspring at all costs. Her fate is tied to yours and to that of the Hittites. If her line falls, then so shall we."

Mursili stared at her for a long moment. "Just how far ahead have you seen?"

"I have seen shimmers, glimpses across the sands of times.

"Not all can be prevented, but if you protect her line, our kingdom will not only survive but thrive. And one day, when you are at your most vulnerable, she will protect *you*."

"You lay too much at the feet of a 4th level Prince and an Egyptian slave girl, mother."

"It is not I, my son. It's the gods.

"They are with you, Mursili. Heed them."

She picked up the wig and wrap, replacing them on her head.

"I have lingered longer than I had intended," she said. "I believe in you, son. Never forget that."

She turned to leave.

"Mother, I-" he called.

She turned back to face him, smiled knowingly.

"I know, Mursili," she said. "I know."

X

The past. Ida lived more in the past now than she did in the present. Once again, as she lay in the tub, Clizi's kind and careful hands bathing her, her thoughts returned to Egypt.

Batau's heart had hardened towards Ida - from the night she had caught Ida with Tutankh onward.

They hardly spoke, even now as they prepared Ankhe for a luncheon with the other royal wives.

"I have noticed a rift between the two of you these past few days," Ankhe said pointedly. "What has happened?"

Neither of them spoke.

"Pharaoh has changed as well," Ankhe remarked in that strange sharp tone.

Ida forced herself to remain passive. "Has he?" she asked.

"Indeed. He has been going against Ay and Horemheb's wishes. He is also happier than I have seen him since he has become Pharaoh. He is as he was when he was a boy."

Neither of the other two women spoke.

"He's in love," Ankhe said. "He radiates with it. It gives him strength. The sadness, the loneliness is gone from him."

Ida glanced pointedly at Batau. Batau looked back down to her task.

"I know it is not one of his other wives. He doesn't even look at them. It is someone else."

Ankhe looked directly at Ida. Ida's face burned.

Ankhe's eyes fell next upon the bracelet then drifted back up to Ida's face.

"Batau," Ankhe said, "could you go with Esnai to pick up my new wig?"

"Yes, mistress," Batau said rising and leaving the room.

Ida watched Batau leave.

"This woman, whoever she is, makes him very happy. No one deserves to be happy more than Tutankh, do they Ida?"

"No," Ida answered softly.

"I must admit though that I am quite jealous," Ankhe continued steadily. "In all our years of marriage he has never touched me out of more than conjugal necessity, never in love or desire. After my womb was corrupted, he stopped touching me altogether."

She stood. "Have you heard anything, seen anything that might give you suspicion as to who she may be or even if it is a woman at all?"

The way Ankhe kept pressing the matter with her, the way she kept glaring at her, there was only one conclusion Ida could draw.

She knows.

Ida sank to her knees before Ankhe. Tears spilled from her eyes.

"You know something, Ida?" Ankhe asked, feigning ignorance.

"Please forgive me," Ida begged.

"Forgive you?"

"I know Batau has told you. You know well that I am the woman in question."

"You, Ida?" Ankhe asked though she did not sound surprised.

"Please don't send me away," Ida begged. "I can't let him go again. It would destroy us both."

"How romantic or should I say.....melodramatic!"

Ankhe laughed humorlessly. "Of course I should have guessed long ago that things would turn out this way. Even when you were children you had this....unnatural attachment."

"I did not mean to betray you, Ankhe. You must believe me when I say I resisted as long as I could."

Ankhe walked away from her. She laughed that strange dry laugh again. "It was only an accident of birth that made him my husband. It's you he's always loved.

"Still, I can hardly fault him, Ida.

"I'm in love with you as well."

Ida stood slowly, her shock written all over her face.

Ankhe turned to face her. "Are you surprised to hear that I love you in that way?"

Ida didn't answer.

"I was never quite sure of how to approach you, could never quite figure out how to tell you."

She laughed dryly.

"Do you know we used to argue over you, Ida? Though he knew how I felt, he too refused to give you up.

"Almost anything else I have ever asked of him, he has given me. But when it came to you..." she shook her head.

"I was so glad when he became Pharaoh. All I had to do was put the idea into Horemheb's head that he was becoming too attached to you, that you could be a threat to his control over Tutankh.

"Day after day, I drummed it in. Until finally Horemheb came around to my way of thinking.

"I had hoped time and absence would erase this thing from the both of your minds. But I guess I was wrong wasn't I, Ida?"

"How could you do such a thing?" Ida asked, her hurt badly constrained. "You of all people knew how we felt about each other."

"Felt or feel?"

"I *never* stopped loving him. Even when all I had was this bracelet and a few distant glimpses of him, my feelings for him didn't die. They could never."

Ankhe laughed dryly. "How sweet.

"And to think I was murderously jealous when Batau first told me of your little run in the other night - angry at the both of you. My fury, however, can not change the way you look at each other can it? My wrath can not expunge him from your heart?"

"No," Ida admitted quietly.

"And you're sure about that, Ida?" Ankhe pressed.

Ida did not reply, her apprehension beginning to rise. She knew well that look in Ankhe's eyes.

Ankhe laughed again. "How can this be?" she asked.

"I am Queen. I am chosen by the gods to rule. I am above all others, yet, this love, this great immovable unyielding passion should be denied me, should be instead bestowed upon a mere slave, a slave I myself love nonetheless - and with my own brother, my own husband."

She laughed even harder. "What a cruel hoax this is!"

Ankhe's mad laughter gradually subsided. She was silent for a time now as she studied Ida.

Finally, the queen spoke. "I will not sell you or send you away. What fun would that be for me?

"And I *will* keep what I know a secret, for now, for the love I once bore the two of you. But if anyone else should find out about your affair or any of mine for that matter, I will have you thrown to the crocodiles. Is that clear?"

"Yes, my queen," Ida replied, her terror continuing to rise as Ankhe slowly approached her.

Ankhe pressed her lips against Ida's, wrapped her arms around her and pressed the girl to her. When Ida pushed away, tears were in Ankhe's eyes.

Ankhe sneered at her. "We'll see just how much this "love" between you and my brother really means to you."

She signaled to her private guard.

Just as Ida turned, she felt a blow to the back of her head.

Then, nothing.

When at last Ida came to, it was very dark. She could hardly move, hardly breathe. The temperature was stifling.

Panic quickly set in. She began screaming, banging desperately against her prison.

"Help!" she cried though she struggled to breathe, tears pouring from her eyes, blurring her sight. "Let me out!"

She cried out over and over again - until her voice was barely above a hoarse whisper, until her hair and clothing were pasted to her body with sweat.

Now, exhausted, all she could do was sob.

"Giving up so soon?" a familiar voice asked.

Ankhe.

"Please let me out!" Ida sobbed pitifully. "Please have mercy!"

"I will free you....in time," Ankhe promised as she sank down next to the coffin, "when you've learned your lesson."

Ida groaned in despair. "Why are you doing this?!"

"You need to learn your place. Years of favor have made you disrespectful. You have taken my kindness for weakness."

"That's not true."

"Isn't it? Even now you are insolent."

"No," Ida sobbed loudly. "Please don't do this!"

"You won't stop seeing my husband. Fine. Just know that each and every time you do, you will end up here.

"You will never know when or where or for how long but know this. It *will* happen."

"My queen..." Ida begged.

"*Every.* Time," Ankhe repeated.

"I trust it goes without saying that you are to tell no one about this, about our special time together, especially not Pharaoh. If you do or even if I *suspect* you have, I'll have you buried alive in the desert, right here in your cozy little home away from home."

"I won't say anything," Ida promised. "Please just stop this. I've had enough."

"I'll decide when you've had enough." Ankhe rose, a smile of satisfaction on her face.

"Ankhe? Ankhe!"

"I'm still here," Ankhe replied.

"By all the gods, let me out!" Ida cried out. "I'm sorry!"

"Not as sorry as you're going to be," Ankhe promised.

Ida sobbed loudly.

"How dark and tight it must be in there," Ankhe taunted. "How little air."

Ida began screaming uncontrollably, her fierce struggles against her confinement beginning once more with renewed vigor.

Ankhe laughed. She went to her men. "Release her before she suffocates," she instructed.

As one of the men moved towards the coffin, Ankhe held up a hand. "Not just yet. She still has fight in her to spare."

"Yes, my queen," he replied.

With that, the queen left the room, the sounds of Ida's hysterics following her down the corridors of the dark dungeon, bringing laughter to her heart.

XI

Things between Ida and the queen were never the same afterwards. How could they be? Every time Ida saw Tutankh, Ankhe sent her men.

Ida never knew what form her punishment would take.

Sometimes she was locked in a modified confine or a coffin or a box of some sort. Sometimes it was empty. Sometimes it contained water or mud or insects of various varieties.

Always they waited until Pharaoh was away. Always she was released in just enough time to recover sufficiently enough as not to arouse his suspicion.

No matter how careful Ida tried to be, somehow Ankhe always knew.

Ida didn't know if it was Batau, Esnai, someone else or a combination of spies who watched her. It became so she could trust no one.

The only time Ida felt secure and loved from then onward had been when she was in Tutankh's arms or with Heketya. Even then she could never quite relax between the lies she was forced to tell and the constant fear of being taken.

Still, Tutankh was one of the only two good things in her life, the one person she had that truly belonged to her, one of only two people who truly loved her.

She would never give him up. Even if it killed her.

A couple of months after the split with Queen Ankhesenpaaten, Ankhe had taken Heketya on a trip to Gebtu. Pharaoh Tutankhamun, at that same time, was away on a journey of diplomacy to of all places, Hattusa. Ida had never felt so isolated, so alone.

One day, out of the blue, Gizo had come to her, Galeno just behind him. They carried an order from the queen citing her hosts' slaves as incompetent and ordering Ida to Gebtu.

Ida had never been so afraid in all her life. Though she racked her brain, she could come up with no good reason why she was not able to comply with the queen's command.

Her mind finally numb, she had mechanically gathered her things.

The journey to Ankhe's side had been arduous, wearying. She had fallen asleep.

When she awoke, she found herself near the mouth of a network of caverns.

"Why are we stopping here?" she asked Galeno.

"These are our orders," he said. "You are to go on alone from here. Go though the entrance to that cave and wait." He gestured to it as he spoke.

Ida's eyes followed his hand. As she stared into the forbidding darkness, fear gripped her chest and squeezed.

She grabbed Galeno's arm.

"Is this a trap?" she whispered. "Does she mean to bury me alive?"

"I don't know why she has sent you here," he replied, "or why you would think she means you harm. However, I do know these caves. I used to come here before...to...."

He did not need to finish his sentence. Ida knew well what he meant. It was where he and his male lover met.

In silence, Galeno had dismounted before helping her down, before giving her rations and water.

"I don't know what you have done to incur the queen's ire," Gizo said, "but no matter what happens, we will come back for you as soon as we can."

Ida nodded.

"Now pay attention," Galeno said.

Ida nodded.

She watched as he drew a rough map in the sand with his finger.

"If you get in trouble, don't stop until you find the cavern of the skulls. It is one of the first 6 on the right side. Cross over the skulls and slip into the crevice. Follow the crevice until it gives to two tunnels. Take the left one. Turn right at the 3rd opening. Go down until you find a 2nd crevice. Squeeze into it. It goes on for quite some time but there is a lake at the end of it. There's edible vegetation, some fish."

Ida nodded.

He stood and kissed her temple.

"It grows late," he said. "We must go."

Again, Ida nodded.

Though tears stung at her eyes, Ida steeled herself and took a few steps through the entrance. Then, having no other choice, she sat down and awaited her fate.

Ida was not sure how long she had sat there in that cavern, but during that time, she had emptied both water bags and eaten what little rations the two men were able to spare. She had waited until the little sunlight visible through the gaps and crevices in the rock began to fade.

Ida stood now, began moving groggily towards the entrance.

Voices. Two of Horemheb's spies.

She could not let them find her.

Ida ran.

Searching desperately, she at last spied the skull cavern. She took a deep inhale and squeezed through the crevice.

As Galeno had bade, she followed his instructions until at last the path gave way to the tiny expanse of lake.

Ida collapsed, gasping for air.

Her breath finally returning to normal, she took in her surroundings.

It was truly a little oasis. In addition to the lake and vegetation, there was a wide gap that ran across the massive cavern ceiling. Light streamed in.

Ida heavily made her way to the water's edge. She drank from her cupped hands. She lay on her back and stared up at the sky until she fell asleep.

At first Ida though it a dream.

She had become aware of his scent, then the soft brush of fingers pulling her hair back from her throat. His teeth were gentle on the end of her ear lobe.

A soft smile spread across her lips.

She turned her head and felt the soft press of another mouth against hers, the gently coaxing of a tongue seeking entrance. She welcomed it, rose to press her body against the lean male one that was now on top of her. Her hands tangled in his hair as his hands slid along the length of her body.

The kiss broke and she opened her eyes. She was smiling.

"Do you often allow strange men to molest you?" Tutankhaten asked her.

She laughed. "How could it be anyone else but you?"

"You peeked?"

She shook her head. "I'd know you anywhere...the smell of you, the feel of your touch, the way you kiss me, the way your body feels against mine."

The slow, half smile that spread across his lips, the gleam in his eyes made her heart pound.

"I'm sorry it took me so long to arrive," he said. "I had meant to be here before you, to surprise you and come with you through the chasm.

"I had it all planned out. I feigned sickness this morning and begged not to be disturbed until tomorrow. I slipped into this peasant dress and made my way out of the citadel easily enough.

"Just as I came over that last rise, I spotted the strangest thing - Horemheb's men just ahead of me."

Ida's mood darkened, her thoughts floating unbidden to the hell she would have to endure when she returned.

He smiled.

"Don't worry," he said. "I was never in any real danger. Even *I* can outsmart those two."

Ida laughed.

He stroked her face. "But if they had found you, had hurt you in any way...."

Ida put two fingers over his lips. "I'm fine," she reassured him.

"But the crevices-" he began.

"I got through the crevice the same way I get through the passageways to your rooms. I closed my eyes and pictured you on the other side."

He grasped the hand at his mouth and kissed her fingers.

"But the passageways are wide," he said. "It must have been hell for you to come here alone."

She softly touched his face. "But it was worth every second to end up here with you."

He sighed. "How I ache when we're apart. I see glimpses of you and I almost go mad with longing."

"Well, we can't let the Pharaoh go mad now can we?" she said as she shifted.

He was hard against her. It heightened her own excitement.

She slid her hands slowly down his back, then at his waist, around to the front to him.

He whispered her name hoarsely. "Ida."

She grinned sensually, relished the ragged sound of his breath as she touched him. His eyes flashed devilishly then his hand was upon her throbbing womanhood. She gasped and he chuckled deep in his throat.

It was instantaneous. Both of their hands disengaged as if by some instinctive agreement. Hands freed flesh from clothing.

As he thrust into her, her legs wrapped around him. Their mouths battled in frenzied desire.

When they at last exploded in shuddering ecstasy, he had lay his head against her chest. She played with his hair with one hand, the other on his shoulder. His arms were wrapped around her waist.

She could have stayed there with him like that for the rest of her life.

As he drifted into a light slumber, her thoughts turned to Ankhe, to the price she would have to pay for this little snatch of happiness.

Her mind raced, searched desperately for some way to keep this latest rendezvous a secret.

She was so absorbed in her thoughts in fact, that she hadn't even realized he had come awake, that he was studying her intensely.

"What's wrong?" he finally asked.

"Nothing," Ida lied, forcing a smile.

"Ida..."

Ida's gaze fled his. "It's just... I don't want this to end."

Tutankh cupped her cheek. "It won't," he promised. "Ever."

She forced another smile, kissed him deeply.

He broke the kiss, his eyes searching hers. "You *would* tell me if something was wrong, wouldn't you, Ida?"

"Of course I would," she lied. *And have Ankhe turn against you and ally with your enemies?*

"Ankhe hasn't found out has she?" he asked.

"Of course not. No one has. We've been too careful." Yet another lie.

"I know you, Ida. Something is wrong. It's been wrong for a while now."

"*Nothing* is wrong. I just get a little sad sometimes. I miss you."

He shook his head. "You're hiding something."

Ida laughed. "What could I *possibly* be hiding?"

"Ida.."

"Tutankh, please," she begged. "We have so little time together as it is. Let's not do this again. Let's not ruin it by bringing the outside world into it."

He looked away from her.

Ida turned his face back to hers. "I swear it. I'm fine."

"If anyone tries to hurt you, in any way," he said, "even Ankhe, you come to me."

"No one would dare hurt me. I belong to you."

"Promise me, Ida."

"I promise," she lied.

Though he had still seemed suspicious, he had let it drop.

As fate would have it, it would be the last time she would see him alive.

Ida lay now in her bed in the Hittite citadel. She let out a lonely, pitiful sob, holding herself tightly.

With all of these memories assaulting her like waking dreams, she had to ask herself if it'd all been worth it.

Without a moment's hesitation, the answer came to Ida.

Yes.

Her only true regret was that she hadn't given in to their love sooner, that they hadn't had more time together.

She touched her hand to her softly swollen belly.
Gods, yes. It had definitely been worth it.
She reached inside of her tunic and felt the pin.

XII

The sudden great commotion outside of Ida's rooms in the citadel awoke her. She rose and slid on her dress.

The door to her rooms burst opened. There was a blur of dark silhouettes. Someone grabbed her arms roughly and half dragged her out onto the terrace.

There was an enormous throng below carrying torches and weapons.

"Kill her!" someone yelled.

"Throw her over!" another shouted.

The mob was hungry for her blood.

"But I've done nothing wrong!" Ida exclaimed.

Someone lifted Ida and placed her on the railing as if to throw her to the mob. The mad frenzy below grew.

They were shouting, pushing each other, fighting amongst themselves to get a position closer to the balcony. People were disappearing within the sea of angry Hittites, trampled underfoot.

"Stop this madness, this instant!" a familiar voice boomed from just inside the open terrace doors.

Her assailants turned to face its source.

Mursili.

He and Nacamakun appeared now on the balcony, Mursili's guard surrounding the crowd on the ground below.

"Release the girl," Mursili commanded.

Her assailants looked to one another, confused. They were not accustomed to taking orders from this royal whelp.

"By Telipinu's will, I am your Prince and I order you to release her!"

Ida's assailants relented – with great reluctance.

A path made, Nac made his way to her side. He took her from the oaf that had put her on the railing, setting her feet back down on the ground. He blocked her from the other men's reach with his form.

"But she set the trap for Prince Zannanza," one of the conspirators protested to Mursili.

"She knew not of the plot to kill my brother," Mursili replied. "She has been under my careful surveillance since her arrival and she has conspired with no one.

"Surely you have no doubts as to the competence of a Prince of the Hittites?"

"Of course not, my Prince," the man replied. "Perhaps she came here knowing from the start what they had planned."

Ida pushed passed Nac to face her accusers. "I only came here to save my queen from the evil men who threaten to seize control of Egypt - Ay and Horemheb," she replied impassioned. "It is *they* who have plotted to undo not only Prince Zannanza but my Queen. It is *they* who killed Pharaoh and tried to make it seem an accident. It is *they* who have done all of this and more.

"Prince Mursili is right. I am innocent."

"See, Great Prince?" one of the men replied. "How well the little viper spins her lies, even now."

"It matters not your decision," Mursili said. "Only the King has the power to pass a judgment of death."

He took Ida's arm and hurriedly led her from the room, Nac right behind them.

The men on the terrace protested angrily. Though they followed the three they dared not challenge Nacamakun.

In the corridor, a small command of soldiers came to block their path.

"I am taking her to the king," Mursili said releasing her, one hand on the hilt of his weapon. "Stand aside or die."

The soldiers looked uncertain. While Mursili was 4th Prince, the deceptively thin and fairly introverted teenager was not one from whom they had ever been instructed to take order.

"Now!" Mursili growled as Ida leaned weakly against him.

The soldiers obeyed.

"Carry her," Mursili ordered Nac.

Nacamakun lifted her easily into his arms, hurried behind Mursili towards the throne room. They were well on their way when someone grabbed Ida's arm and pulled her from Nac's grasp. Ida screamed.

Nacamakun turned, pulled her free again before he began to scuffle with the man. More men came to the aide of Ida's assailant.

Mursili grabbed hold of her arm once more, pushed her behind him as he fought beside Nac.

"Ida, run!" Mursili gasped after one man got the better of him, slashing his arm.

Ida did as she was bade. She flew to the throne room and threw open the door.

She ran down its great length towards the hurriedly clad men who clustered around the man on the throne. She fell on her knees before them.

One of the men drew a dagger and raised it to plunge it through the base of her skull. A 2nd dagger flew at him, piercing his arm. The man dropped the knife.

Mursili went to the man and pulled his knife from the man's wrist. He wiped the man's blood on the man's clothes.

Mursili turned now to King Suppiluliuma. "Sire, I bring Idamun here for your judgment and your judgment alone."

"Then have it," Suppiluliuma answered. "For what has happened to my son, she and her kind shall be put to death,"

"But she is with child," Mursili said. "Nacamakun's child."

"Nacamakun's child?" Suppilu repeated. "How can you be sure this girl tells the truth?"

"I learned of it not from her mouth but from Clizi's."

The King studied Mursili skeptically for a long moment before he turned to Nac.

"Is this true?" he asked.

Nacamakun nodded. "Yes, sire," he lied. "The child is mine."

The king stood and walked to the window. He stared out of it as he weighed Mursili's words.

Just what was the witch's son up to? His behavior, when it came to this girl, had been far out of his usual character - to put it mildly. Could the child somehow be Mursili's and Nac, loyal to the boy to a fault, be covering for him?

The King frowned.

Nac would do most anything for Mursili, even something like this.

King Suppilu turned back to them at length. He looked at Ida who was still prostrate, then to Mursili and the old soldier.

At last he spoke. "Because you have so faithfully served me Nacamakun, I make this edict. No harm is to come to Idamun whilst she is with child.

"She is to serve the court as any other slave might so long as she is able to do so. I will not pass judgment on her until after the baby is let from her body."

"And then?" Mursili asked.

"The child shall stay with Nacamakun."

"And Ida? She is still the child's mother," Mursili pressed. "Surely, it would only be true justice to spare her."

"Justice? You dare speak to me of justice for this creature?!" the King demanded moving menacingly towards Ida.

Mursili quickly moved forward and pulled Ida to her feet, out of the King's reach. He stood now in front of her, Nac just behind her.

"Was it justice that Zannanza, your own brother, was murdered?!" the King demanded.

Mursili knew better than to answer. Any further point he tried to make now would be wrong in his father's eyes.

"A postponement of her sentence is all I am willing to offer you, boy," the King said. "Take it."

Mursili bowed his head. "As you have bidden, My King."

He and Nac waited, heads bowed respectfully as the King and his entourage left the chamber.

"What now, My Prince?" Nac asked.

"He said she is to serve the court did he not?" Mursili asked.

"Indeed."

"Well I'm a member of court am I not?"

"You are," Nac replied.

"And the child is to remain in your care?"

"Yes."

"Then we'll both take her to the house in Syria. She will be safe under my brother Sarri's protection."

"And your father?"

"Let Sarri and I worry about father. You just have our quarters packed and ready to go by first light."

"Yes, sire," the grizzled soldier replied. "But what is to be done with the girl until then?"

"Ida will stay with me in my rooms until the household is ready to move."

"Yes, sire."

Mursili waited until Nac left the throne room before he grabbed Ida's wrist and triggering a hidden door, led her through the passageways to his quarters.

Ida was lost in speculation. She stood there, unseeingly, as Mursili gave his guard instruction and barricaded his chamber door.

He turned now to look at the girl. "You can share the bed," he said.

Ida looked over at him. "Why are you doing this?" she asked.

"If you think I mean to take advantage - "

"I mean why are you helping me?"

"Why not?" he replied flippantly. "I'm a Prince. You're a pregnant woman. What kind of a man would stand by and watch a pregnant woman be murdered?"

"Man? You're still a boy."

"Perhaps, but a boy who is man enough to protect you."

"And to go against your father?"

"It's about time someone did," he replied. "And who better than the witch's son?"

He rolled up his sleeve, examined the wound on his arm.

"The witch's son?"

"The old gypsy woman at the banquet who cornered you."

"The fortune teller?" Ida asked.

"She's my mother, my exiled mother."

Suddenly it all made sense to Ida. "So you believe it too. You believe that this child I carry is somehow destined to save the Amarna line."

"I believe what the gods have shown me," Mursili replied.

"And just what is that?"

"That your fate and my fate, that the fate of the Hittites and the fate of the Amarnas are intertwined. If one falls, they both fall. If one rises, they both will rise."

Ida laughed humorlessly.

"What's so funny?" he asked as he applied salve to his cut.

"That you people think I or any child issuing from me is special. That you think I have the strength to guide and protect this child, that I have it in me to fight against your father, Ay and Horemheb."

"It doesn't matter to me if you believe. It only matters that you and your line survives. Nac and I are going to make sure that that happens."

"And just how are you going to do that?" Ida demanded. "Do you even realize how many times tonight alone my child and I were almost killed?"

"I know exactly how many times you were almost killed tonight. Nacamakun and I were there, remember? And we kept the both of you safe, didn't we?"

"Maybe you got lucky. Maybe we all did. But how much longer do you think you can possibly delay the inevitable?"

Mursili shrugged. "I think you'd be surprised."

"Don't kid yourself," Ida replied. "I knew my life would be a short one the moment I gave in to my feelings for Pharaoh, especially after my queen found out. I knew it would be shorter still when he was murdered. Shorter still when I crossed the desert into Hattusa, when I found out I carry Pharaoh's child.

"Now Prince Zannanza's murder has cut my time down to what? Maybe another few months at best?

"You may by some miracle be able to save my child, but don't fool yourself. Be it by Egyptian or Hittite hands, I will not live to see 20."

"Maybe you will," Mursili countered. "Maybe you won't. That still doesn't mean I will ever give up fighting for you."

Ida laughed harshly.

"What's the point, Mursili?!" she asked. "To fulfill some outlandish prophecy? I can't even leave this *room* by myself."

Her laughter turned to hysterical sobs. "Even if I do make it out of Hattusa alive, I will have to spend the rest of my life in hiding from one faction or the other."

"A life in hiding is better than no life at all," he replied.

He stared at her for a long moment.

"Don't you think you've wasted enough time and energy on self-pity?" he asked.

Ida was taken aback, momentarily forgetting her despair.

"What?!" she choked.

"I have no plans to spend the next months listening to you cry every time the wind blows. It certainly can't be good for your baby either."

He nodded. "I know now why your queen sent you here. She was sick of your whining, wasn't she?"

Ida's tears were all but forgotten in her temper.

"How dare you?" she demanded. "You think my life has been easy? You think these tears have been easy?

"I have just lost everything I ever cared about. *Everything*. And you dare mock my pain?"

She shook her head. "I would rather take my chances in my own rooms in the citadel than be trapped in Syria for a *hundred years* with a spoiled jackass like you."

She stormed towards the door.

Mursili smiled, applauding.

Ida whirled around to face him.

"Good for you," he said. "You do still have a backbone after all."

"You don't know a damned thing about me," Ida spat.

"I know that you're a lot tougher than you let on. I know that there is a great deal of fire and resiliency behind that puffy, weepy face of yours."

He moved towards her. "I know that you carry the child of Pharaoh Tutankhamun - whom you obviously loved a great deal and who loved you enough to claim you to wife. I know you faked your own death and snuck here right under the nose of the very same men that just a few minutes ago you claimed you could not outmaneuver. I know when you thought that mob on the terrace might turn on me, you risked yourself to try to make them understand the truth.

"I also know you're right about me. Many would call me an ass.

"While my advice is sound, it is often delivered with far too much pragmaticism to be palatable to even the slightly sentimental. However, I am good at keeping confidences and most all would agree that there is no one better to have on your side or more loyal than I.

"I'm also not tactful like my older brothers or as war-worn as my father, but I'm learning."

He gave a small smile. "You should also keep in mind that asses are stubborn. Asses don't give up - no matter what."

Ida stood uncertainly at the door.

"Give it a try," he said. "What's the worst that could happen if you cast your lot with me?"

"I could end up dead," Ida replied.

Mursili laughed. "You'll probably end up dead either way, just that much sooner if you try to go it on your own."

A soft chuckle escaped Ida's lips inspite of herself.

"Now what say you help me bandage this arm?" he asked.

When she continued to stand there uncertainly, he added. "Don't worry. You'll have plenty of time to run away later."

Ida hesitated for another long moment. Then, with little other choice, she went to him and began to dress his wound.

XIII

Time is man's greatest enemy. No one knew this better than Idaten. The last year and a half had simply flown by.

Though Ida had a determined and resourceful ally in Prince Mursili, she knew well that each day she spent in the Syrian palace was borrowed. It was only a matter of time before the chaos that had broken out in the wake of Prince Zannanza's death seeped through the cracks of even these high stone walls.

Every morning she woke with a mixture of relief and dread. Every night she went to sleep with a mixture of hope and fear.

In spite of the happiness of her days there, there was always this anxiety gnawing at her. It was worse than waiting for Ankhe's guards to find her and lock her in the confines.

Some days she almost wished it would all collapse already, that this half nightmare, half dream would end.

Adding to Ida's unease, Mursili had been summoned to the capital, his father having fallen victim to the plague. He had been gone for almost a month now, each day of his absence adding to Ida's dread.

As Ida watched her son stumble clumsily about the yard, laughing merrily as he chased Nacamakun's 3-year-old son, Kadar, she wished it would never end.

Her son, Abidos, was so beautiful. He looked more like her than Tutankh - which she was certain might well save his life one day. He possessed Tutankh's gentle nature, though sparks of Ida's fire showed through when he was angry.

Abidos fell on top of Kadar, laughing so hard tears filled his eyes. He didn't even seem to mind Kadar's flailing, as the other boy struggled to slip from his grasp.

Kadar's mother had given birth to him 2 months too early and had died shortly thereafter. It was a miracle that the little boy himself had survived. He was very small for his age and prone to fits of illness. Her son dwarfed him.

Abidos clumsily climbed to his feet and began to run after the little boy who had finally managed to escape him. Again, Abidos fell.

Ida chuckled softly.

She was so absorbed in the little boys' play, in fact, that she did not even hear Clizi come out.

"Ida," Clizi called softly from behind her.

AMARNA BOOK I: BOOK OF IDA

Ida turned to look at her.

"Prince Mursili has returned," the old woman said.

"Is he in his rooms?" Ida asked rising.

Clizi nodded. Ida did not fail to notice that the old woman would not look her in the eye.

Stiffly, Ida made her way to Mursili's rooms. She hesitated outside of the door for a time, gathering her composure.

When finally she entered, she found Mursili pacing frantically. He stopped suddenly, picked up a statuette and flung it violently against the wall.

Ida gasped.

He turned to face her.

"Ida," he breathed.

"Are you alright?" she asked quietly.

Mursili shook his head. "I warned him, Ida," he said, his anguish etched upon his handsome features. "I warned him of the folly of attacking Egypt without first consulting the oracle and receiving the gods' blessings. I warned him about gloating over his ill-won victory and bringing the Egyptian captives to Hattusa.

"Even the *gods* tried to warn him, Ida. They brought forth first a plague upon our people. When he heeded them not, the drought came.

"Even with all of this, arrogant, foolish King Suppiluliuma, breaker of the covenant of the Telepenus's Proclamation, refused to heed.

"Now he lies dead - a victim of the very plague he carried here from Egypt."

Tears pooled in his eyes.

"Oh, Mursili," Ida breathed. "I'm so sorry."

"The old fool brought it upon himself," he said sitting down heavily upon the stair, his head hanging down.

Ida went to him. She sat down beside him, intertwining her hands with his. They sat there in silence for a long while.

"Prince Arnuwanda's coronation is imminent," he said quietly.

He needn't say more.

Ida knew well what it meant. Prince Arnuwanda and his wife Mal-Nikal had made no secret of their desire to execute all Egyptians within their borders, a sacrifice to the gods in hopes of regaining their favor. They had been Mursili's greatest enemies when it came to Ida. Now, with Suppilu out of the way, they would come for her.

"I'm sorry," he continued, "but there's nothing more I can do. I can no longer keep you safe here."

Ida nodded, silent tears falling from her eyes.

"I got to see 20 at least," she said.

They both chuckled softly.

She sobered.

"How long do I have?" she asked.

Mursili's smile faded.

He rose, went to stare out of one of his windows. "You leave tomorrow."

"I see," she replied, she too rising.

Mursili turned back to face her.

"I'd better go spend time with my son," she said wiping away her tears and struggling to regain her composure.

She turned to leave.

"Ida," Mursili began, walking towards her.

She turned back to face him.

"In time," he said, "when things blow over..."

"I know," she replied.

She then did something she had wanted to do for many months now. She placed a lingering kiss upon his lips.

Mursili was taken aback but for a moment before he pulled her to him and kissed her back.

A noise in the antechamber broke them apart.

As Ida turned to go, Mursili grabbed her hand. He held it for a long moment before letting it go.

Ida lay awake in her bed late that night, Abidos asleep on her chest as she stroked his back.

She could not bear to think of leaving her son, would not allow herself to until she was well away from him - knowing now that losing him would be the blow that killed her.

Still, there was no scenario she could image in which Abidos would be safer with her than with Mursili and Nac. Once she crossed that border into Egypt, it was only a matter of time before her enemies found her. She would not let them destroy Abidos too.

The child began to fuss in his sleep, interrupting the train of her thoughts.

Ida rose, began to pace the room as she gently bounced the boy in her arms, as she soothingly stroked his face.

Her thoughts turned to Mursili.

Mursili was no longer the quiet, lanky boy he had been when first they had met.

Their time in Syria and the challenge of protecting her had strengthened his body as well as his mind.

The two of them had grown close these months. Very close. So close, in fact, that she felt guilty - as if she were betraying Tutankh somehow by having feelings for this man. Still, Ida could not see how she could not care for Mursili.

Mursili had taken good care of them, had been with her every step of the way. He had never let her feel sorry for herself, always coming up with some distraction or goading her into an argument or project until the dark thoughts were driven away.

He had shown her her first snow, held her hand when she went into labor. He had been the first man to hold Abidos and remained to this day Abidos' favorite person outside of Ida. He had held her when she cried, listened tirelessly as she rambled on and on about her dead Pharaoh and all she had suffered under Ankhe.

He was the first person in her life, the only person she had never lied to, that she had never pretended with. She felt free with him, like it was safe for her to be Ida in spite of all of the baggage that came with it.

Could she now just give that up and go back to the way she was? Back to all the lies and the paranoia and isolation?

After all they had been through, could she really just leave him now, now when his world was on the verge of falling apart?

Though she did not, could not love him in quite the same way she had loved Tutankh, she had to admit to herself now, before it was too late, that her feelings for him were no less real. Mursili was under her skin.

Ida's mind drifted to their earlier encounter in his chamber.

After tomorrow, she may well never see him again.

If Arnuwanda's forces had their way, she was dead. If Ay, Horemheb or Ankhe caught her, she was also dead. And that was only *if* the perils of the journey, her broken heart or slavers didn't remove her from the equation first.

Setting Abidos in his bed, Ida kissed his forehead. She stared down at him for another long moment before leaving the room.

Ida found Mursili awake. He was staring, unseeingly, out of the window. He turned to glance briefly in her direction as she entered, before returning his gaze to the sky.

Ida's heart pounded loudly in her ears as she shut the door and moved towards him.

Though he did not turn, Mursili was acutely aware of her approach. His chest heaved, his blood rushing loudly in his ears. The task of not turning towards her was becoming more and more unbearable with each passing second.

She was right behind him now. He could feel her there though she had yet to speak or touch him.

Behind him, Ida reached out a hand to touch his arm, pulled it back before it made contact. She stood there uncertainly for what felt like an eternity, her resolve fast abandoning her.

And there he was, his back to her, pretending she wasn't even there.

Maybe this was a mistake, Ida thought. Maybe he didn't feel the same way about her. Maybe Mursili was being the gentleman he was, trying to make an already ridiculous situation less so.

She turned to go instead, was surprised when Mursili grabbed her by her wrist, holding her fast. She looked up into his eyes. They glittered like jewels in the torchlight.

His mouth came down hard upon hers, the long-denied desire consuming them both without thought, without care for what was to come.

He gently guided her backward towards the bed, hands leisurely divesting bodies of clothing and mouths rarely losing connection.

He carefully laid her naked form down upon the bed, covered her body with his.

He stared now into her eyes, said a million things in that silence that neither of them dared give voice to before he reclaimed her mouth.

The rest of the night slipped away unnoticed as they explored each other's bodies, as he forever removed any doubts from her mind that Mursili was no longer a boy but a man.

Dawn broke far too soon.

The household would be awake any time now. She could linger no longer.

Silently, they kissed their goodbyes. Then Ida quietly padded back to her rooms.

XIV

The next day went all too quickly for Ida. By late afternoon, her escort was preparing to start out.

Ida was playing with Abidos in their rooms when Nacamakun came to her.

"Ida," he began.

"I know," she replied, though she hesitated.

Tears pooled in her eyes, a thousand conflicting thoughts and emotions flowing through her all at once.

She took a deep, shaky breath before at last picking up Abidos. She held him to her, stroking his hair.

As she turned to face Nac, she spoke. "I know I have already asked too much of you, of all of you, but I'm *begging* you. Please take my son as your own."

"I promise you," he replied. "So long as I have breath in me, no harm shall come to him. Everything Kadar will have so will Abidos.

"And I won't be alone either. No grandmother could love him more than Clizi and no father could fight harder for him than Prince Mursili."

Ida nodded, the tears falling.

She reached into her shift and took off the pin Tutankh had given her. "Give this to him when he begins to become a man. Never let him doubt that I loved him more than my own breath, that he was conceived in purest love between a man and a woman."

Nacamakun took it from her, looked down at it.

He looked back up at her. In that moment, Ida knew he knew well what it was.

"You have my word," he promised.

Ida nodded again.

When she continued to stand fast he spoke again. "It's time."

Though Ida nodded, her grip on Abidos tightened.

"Ida..."

She at last forced her legs to carry her out of the room and into the courtyard.

The caravan was ready. Clizi and others were gathered to say their goodbyes.

Mursili was not among them.

Ida barely heard anything any of them said to her, bore their kisses and hugs stiffly as she slowly made her way towards the caravan.

She stood just short of her horse, frozen, Abidos still in her arms.

"Ida," Nac urged. "He will never be safe in Egypt, never as your son."

"I know," she replied.

When she continued to stand frozen, Clizi approached. "I'll take him," she said softly, reaching out her arms for the boy.

Ida looked to the old woman, the pity in Clizi's eyes almost unbearable. She began to tremble. She turned her back to her.

"Mommy loves you so much," Ida said to Abidos. "Always. Always. Always. More than all the treasures in the world. More than the sun, the moon and the stars. Never forget that." She planted a lingering kiss on his head.

She turned now to Clizi, gave the boy over to her.

"I'm sorry, Ida," the old woman said before hurriedly carrying the boy away.

As if sensing something was wrong, very wrong, Abidos began to cry and squirm in Clizi's arms. He cried out for his mother. Over and over again he cried out, his cries ripping into Ida's very soul.

It would be the first time in his life that his mother would not come.

Ida no longer had the strength to stand. She sank to the ground, stared through tear blurred eyes in the direction in which Clizi had carried her son.

Nac watched her uneasily. He was no good at this sort of thing. Where the hell was Mursili?!

Almost as if hearing Nac's thoughts, Mursili appeared. He stared at her for a long moment before he sank down to his knees before her.

"Ida," he said softly.

Slowly, she turned her gaze to his.

The sorrow in his eyes was too much. A great, heaving sob shook Ida. He pulled her into his arms, held her tightly. More heart wrenching sobs came, the flood of her grief finally spilling forth. In all his life, Mursili would never forget how she had cried.

He let her feel sorry for herself but for a few moments before he pulled away. He held her now, firmly by her shoulders.

"I need you to listen to me," he said, his eyes boring into hers. "I know this is hard, the hardest thing you have had to endure yet, but you need to be strong right now. We *all* need you to be strong, but most especially Abidos needs you to. The longer you linger, the more danger you put us all in."

Ida stared at him for a long moment. Then, with more strength than even she knew she had, Ida began to fight her grief, to bring her sorrow back under control.

"Good girl," he said. "I won't let them win. Things *will* get better. I promise you. And, when they do, you can return.

"But if Arnu or his queen or many others like them get their hands on you, it's all over. *Everything* is over.

"You need to leave *now*, before it's too late. You have to be gone before Arnu's coronation, before his proclamations become public knowledge."

Ida took a deep breath, shaky breath. She pulled away from him and stood. Mursili rose as well.

Silently, he helped her mount her horse, watched as she struggled valiantly not to fall apart. He took her hand in his, pressed it to his lips. Ida turned to look at him, their gazes holding for a long moment before he released her hand and backed away.

The caravan lurched forward.

"If any harm comes to her," Mursili proclaimed, "there will be nowhere for the man who lets her be hurt to hide."

"Sire," his men intoned.

He stood back helplessly, watching them go.

XV

Egypt. Ida had never loathed any place as much as she did her beloved Egypt at this moment.

As they neared the border, she could see it was still just as beautiful as it had always been.

Still, in her heart, it no longer felt like home - not without Abidos, not without Tutankh. She was certainly no longer the same girl who had slipped across the border almost 2 years ago.

She gazed out now at the riverbank, saw she, Tutankh and Ankhe playing there when they were children.

It seemed so long ago.

A couple of miles across the Egyptian border, the caravan came to a halt. The head of the caravan and Nac spoke briefly, after which the caravan veered southeast, leaving Ida and her escort behind.

Ida's escort led her through Lower Egypt.

It was only when they continued on around Thebes that Ida became confused.

She rode up alongside Nac.

"Where are you taking me?" she asked him.

"Upper Egypt."

"Upper Egypt?" she asked, her confusion growing.

"Napata."

"Napata?! I know no one in Napata."

"Good," Nac replied. "We were not certain."

"But why?"

"Prince Mursili asked that I make sure you arrive safely and that's what I intend to do."

"In Thebes. But Napata?"

"The Prince has a great many allies, even in Upper Egypt. We have only a fraction of an idea of what Arnuwanda's next move will be, of his agenda as a whole. Mursili does not want you anywhere near the northern border."

"And I am to survive how in Napata?"

"The Prince has secured you a position with a noble family there.....as a wet nurse."

"A what?!" she asked. She felt as if the wind had been knocked out of her.

"You can trust in Mursili, Ida. His plans have plans have plans."

"A wet nurse?!" she breathed shaking her head. "How could he?"

"He cares a great deal for you, Ida. Even so, he knew well the day would come when you would have to return home."

"So he forces me away to strangers, to a land I've never been to, into a trade that he of all people should know I could not do?" she asked.

"Sometimes, we all have to do things we wish we did not."

Ida fell silent for a long moment. "And how can you even be sure we can trust these people?"

"As Mursili is sure, so am I," he replied. "But then Mursili's plans have plans have plans. Should you need it, you will find more than enough in your packs for any eventuality.

"Still, money can only get you so far. People you can truly trust are hard to come by in these turbulent times."

Ida fell into silence as she contemplated Napata and her alternatives. There was little of appeal to choose from in any scenario.

"Will they know who I am?" she asked at length.

Nac remained impassive. "The household only know what they need to know. Your husband was killed in the Hittite Sac. Your daughter died in a cart accident shortly thereafter. You have served in two prominent households in wet nurse capacity and come highly recommended."

"And if I refuse this post?"

"Then I shall have no choice but to remain by your side."

Ida scoffed.

"The Prince has determined that you will live to a ripe old age," Nac added, "that you will return to him."

"And the children?" Ida asked. "Mursili? Who will protect them while you're here babysitting me?"

"I trust my men."

"Your men?"

"Prince Mursili and his household were ordered back to the citadel. He in turn ordered the boys be taken to my private estate in Hattusa - out of Arnuwanda's sight but close enough should he need to act."

"So I have even less choice than even I knew?" Ida asked.

"In Napata you will have comfort, protection, an open conduit to the Prince should you need it and a legitimate reason to keep your milk flowing – a thing that might be useful should you be able to return before Abidos reaches his 3rd year."

Ida studied Nac's face for a long moment. "Alright," she conceded. "I will do as Mursili wishes."

XVI

Will I ever get used to it? Ida wondered as she sat at the mirror and brushed her long, blonde locks.

It had been nearly 2 years since she had come to Napata and still she saw a golden-haired stranger whenever she looked in the mirror.

It had been Lord Bietek's mandate that she dye her hair, as it had been that she take on the name Hawara.

She set down the brush, absently stroked her wrist where her bracelet had been. Upon Nac's instance she had given it over to him for safekeeping – it so obviously being a token of imperial favor.

She began to braid her hair.

Yes, it had been yet another lifetime since she had arrived - the Bietek edifice almost as impressively defensible as Mursili's estate in Syria. Lord Bietek, a staunch supporter of the Amarna line and of peace between the Hittites & Egypt, had proven stern but trustworthy.

It had been difficult at first for her to mask her broken heart, to touch, let alone to hold and suckle someone else's child.

Still, even that had grown easier.

Ida rose and went to the nursery, knowing well the little Lord would be awake soon. She greeted the other staff as she went.

Inside the nursery, she closed the door, sat down on the window seat as she waited.

Things were not well in the land of the Hittites. Though the drought had finally ended, the plague pressed onward.

King Arnuwanda had been furious to learn that he had been outsmarted by Prince Mursili. Though Prince Sarri made sure no harm came to Mursili, much of Mursili's household was executed. The gods be thanked, Nacamakun and Clizi were not among them.

Mursili had also taken a wife. One who, by all accounts, he had grown to love a great deal. A woman by the name of Gassulawiya.

Still, he had never forgotten Ida. Even to this day, he worked tirelessly on her behalf.

Almost a year ago, Arnuwanda succumbed to the plague leaving his conniving viper of a queen, Mal-Nikal, to rule as Tawannanna – Queen Dowager and conduit to the gods.

To their vassals' surprise, Mursili had managed somehow to maneuver himself into the position of King. It had outraged many that they should be forced to accept what they considered the inexperienced rule of a man-child - especially when there were two older, seemingly more capable Princes who should have by all right superseded him.

His right to rule was under constant challenge from all sides – from within by Mal-Nikal and her allies, and without by numerous tribes including the Kaskas, the Arzawa and the Kaskans.

In Egypt, Ay and Horemheb still reigned supreme, watched with interest the disorder in the Empire to the North.

They worked steadily to erase all memory of Tutankhamun and his father, Akhenaten, from official record, to undo all that both men had accomplished. Both names were stricken from all public and palatial inscriptions, Ay and Horemheb even going so far as to usurp their monuments.

As of late, rumor had begun to spread that Ay even intended to steal Tutankhamun's tomb.

It had been almost a month since Lord Bietek had last held private audience with Ida, and now her nerves were on edge. She simply had to know what was going on back in Hattusa, that Abidos, Kadar, Nac & Mursili were still safe.

As it was now, all she could do was pray to the gods and make sacrifices each holy day.

The little Lord cried out, breaking Ida's train of thought. She rose and went to him, soothingly stroking his hair as he began to suckle her.

Lord Bietek's audience chamber was overflowing. Though Ida could find no legitimate reason to be near its doors, she could not stop herself from drawing near.

"How can we be sure it is so?" Lord Bietek demanded.

"How can it not be?" one of the men replied. "Manapa-Tarhunta has betrayed King Mursili. The king and his comrades were ambushed near the Seha River."

"But there were survivors."

"Mostly foot soldiers. Of the commanders only Chief Urhib was found and even he is in and out of lucidity.

"There has been no sign of the King nor the captain of his personal guard, Nacamakun."

Ida could hear no more though the debate continued inside. She stood rooted in shock as tears began to fall from her eyes.

If Mursili had fallen and Nacamakun had fallen ...

Ida could not even bear to think on it.

She suddenly found it difficult to breathe. She had to get out of here, away from this place.

Hurrying to her rooms, Ida began to pack, her vision blurred by her tears.

Home. She needed to go home. She needed to tell Tutankh goodbye, then she needed to go back to the land of the Hittites, to find her son before it was too late.

XVII

When at last Ida came to the Imperial City, she was unrecognizable. Between her Bedouin dress, her blonde locks and her carriage, no one would ever take her for the girl she had once been.

As she moved through the city towards the palace, she was keenly aware of her surroundings.

Once at the palace, she took the hidden corridor to Tutankh's quarters, a corridor she had used a thousand nights before. She wanted something of his she could carry with her, needed to know where he was buried.

At the trap door she listened. Hearing nothing, she slowly pushed it open.

She peered into the chamber. Empty.

She climbed into the room, leaving the door ajar should she need to exit the rooms in a hurry.

She went to his bedroom and began to dig through his things.

She was rummaging now through a trunk in Tutankhamun's chamber when she came across it - the document which confirmed the rumors about Ay's plans for Tutankh's tomb.

According to the document, everything had already been set into motion to move Tutankh from his rightful place in the Valley of the Kings and to dispose of him. The precious goods in Tutankh's tomb would then be re-inscribed for Ay and when the time came, Ay would be placed in the tomb along side them.

The move would take place in three months time, while the capital was distracted by the Nile Flood Feast.

Ida's mind reeled.

How could even Ay stoop so low?

She shook her head. She would never let that happen. She would never let Ay damn the man she loved for all eternity. She would see Galeno before she left for Hattusa, would make sure that her people beat Ay to Tutankh's tomb.

Folding the document, she slid it into a hidden pocket of her dress. She resumed her dig.

She froze, listened. Yes, someone was coming.

She hurried back to the trap door. She could hear the voices more clearly now.

Someone was definitely in the hidden passageway. Horemheb.

Carefully Ida re-closed the trap door. The last thing she needed was for one of them to find it open and decide to investigate.

Her mind raced. *What now?*

Hoping against hope, she went through the rooms, towards the second hidden passageway in his personal audience chamber. Just as she was about to enter the audience chamber, the main door of the chamber swung open.

Ida hurriedly slid out of sight. She listened.

Ankhe & Ay.

Out of time, Ida managed to scurry back into the connecting room before she was seen.

What was she going to do? She was trapped!

Quietly, Ida padded back into the bed chamber. She pressed her ear to the initial trap door. Silence.

She slowly pulled the door open, carefully maneuvered her torso inside to look around.

Horemheb and his men were still about, no doubt spying on Ankhe & Ay. Stealthily pulling herself back into the bed chamber, she re-closed the door once more.

There was movement to her left. Ay and Ankhe were moving through the rooms.

Ida desperately scanned the bed chamber. Though her eyes landed upon the bed, she stood rooted, the sweat already breaking out all over her body.

They were just outside now.

Without further hesitation, Ida triggered the panel hidden in the bed's base, slid into the cramped compartment before triggering the door closed again.

It was not long before she felt them settle on the bed above her, before she could hear the old man's raspy moans, Ankhe's soft sighs.

Seconds seemed like minutes, minutes like hours as Ida's own psyche turned against her.

Though it had been years, her experiences in the confines had not lost their potency.

Still, she had to endure. She had to do it for Abidos and in some ways she owned it to Mursili & Nac who had sacrificed so much for her survival. She couldn't let it all end - not here and not now.

She clasped a hand over her mouth to stop herself from screaming like a mad woman.

It was only when Ida heard the snores that she dared open the compartment.

She lay there for a long moment, silently gasping for air as the warm air generated in the compartment began to dissipate.

As quietly as she could, Ida crawled towards the door. She had made it all the way to the threshold when she heard the cry.

Scrambling to her feet, she ran desperately through the rooms towards the audience chamber's trap door. She glanced behind her at the scream's source.

Seeing her face, Ankhesenamun screamed again.

Ankhe had just seen a ghost. She hurriedly covered herself as Ay sprang from the bed, still relatively spry for a man of his advanced years.

"Guards!" he bellowed as he gave chase.

Ida pulled open the trap door, was just about to fly through it when the guard burst into the room and seized her. They held her fast as Ay then Ankhe entered the room.

Ay's jaw dropped as the realization of the spy's identity hit him.

"Take her to a cell," he ordered, "and send for Horemheb."

Ankhesenpaaten hurried back to the bed chamber. She hastily began to dress – even as the guards led Ida from their rooms.

"I have not given you leave," Ay said, entering the bed chamber.

"I am still queen…if only to further your ambition," Ankhesenpaaten said. "Idamun is *my* property. I mean to find out where she's been all this time."

"As do I," Ay replied, the threat clear in both his tone and expression. "As do I."

Ankhe steadily met Ay's glare for a long moment - before she hurried from the room to the dungeons.

"Guards, open the door," Queen Ankhesenamun snapped.

"Pharaoh has instructed us to await Horemheb," one of the guards replied. "Until then, no one may question the prisoner."

"You dare disobey your Queen?! Idamun is *my* property not my husband's. I have full rights to her."

The guard captain eyed her thoughtfully for a long moment.

"I'll handle this," he stated, dismissing his men. He waited until they were out of view before he extended his hand, expectant.

"What is this?" Ankhe demanded, indignant.

"You know well what it is, Your Highness," the man replied.

Ankhesenamun offered him the only thing of value she had on her at that time – a necklace given to her by Ay. She would see to it that this rapscallion and his hand were parted soon enough.

The man took the proffered bribe with a slimy smirk. He studied it for a long moment. Then, seemingly satisfied, he unlocked the cell.

Ankhesenamun entered.

"I see you haven't lost the common touch," Ida said, not even bothering to look up at her.

Ankhe's blood boiled. "How dare you come back here," she growled.

"It had to be a surprise to say the least - my return," Ida replied. "With what happened with Zannanza, surely you expected they'd kill me.

"Yet, here I am, alive and blonde."

Ankhe grabbed her up by her hair. "Perhaps your stay in Hattusa has made you forget yourself, but Ida, you are still my property."

Ida pushed her away, her eyes glittering with hatred. "Not anymore, Ankhe. I belong to me now.

"I will; however, honor the vow I made to you all those years ago, to serve you and protect you. Though you have gravely wronged me and dishonored Tutankh, though I despise you and everything you stand for with everything in me, I will not tell anyone of your involvement in this."

"By all the gods you won't," Ankhe threatened.

The door behind them opened. Ankhe turned to face the intruder.

Horemheb.

Horemheb's eyes glittered intensely. He smiled harshly, his graze drifting from Ankhe to Ida.

"Well, isn't this interesting?" he mused.

He reached out his hand and took a tendril of Ida's hair between his fingers.

"You look very vibrant for a dead woman, Ida." He said to her. "And very wheat-haired."

Ida did not respond.

His gaze returned to Ankhesenpaaten. "And to find you here too, Queen Ankhesenamun.

"This night is just full of surprises, isn't it?"

"She is my property," Ankhe replied. "I have every right to be here."

"To learn as I learn?" Horemheb asked. "Or perhaps to make sure her tongue stays silent against you?"

"She is just a slave. What could she possibly have to say that would be truth in regards to the Queen of all Egypt."

"You'd be surprised what the lowly know, what they are capable of discovering.

"I myself am not from nobility, but have I not .... advised, been that little voice in the heads of three separate god-kings?

"Idamun is a slave, yes. But I'm willing to wager she knows quite a lot."

Ankhesenpaaten fell silent.

"So, Idamun," he said, "Tell me. Where have you been all these years?"

Ida stared at him defiantly.

He sighed exaggeratedly.

"Oh, Ida," he said. "It would be such a shame to ruin such a pretty face."

He reached out and touched her cheek.

Ida pulled away as though he had seared her.

Horemheb chuckled. "I am quite certain I already know the answer to my little question. I mean, how *else* could the Hittites have known so quickly of Tutankhamun's little...accident?"

Ida slapped him.

Horemheb laughed. "I do so admire your fire, girl, your courage. I only wonder how it is that a lamb like Tutankh was able to tame a lioness such as you. I mean aside from the wealth and the power."

Ida did not answer.

"How did you do it, Idamun? Fake your own death?

"Who helped you, *tried* to help you commit treason against Pharaoh?"

Ida laughed harshly now.

"Ah, so now you are amused," Horemheb said.

"I am. I conspired to commit treason against *Pharaoh*? And by Pharaoh, I believe you mean Ay?"

Horemheb smirked, his anger thinly veiled.

Ida continued. "I must admit, I am surprised to have returned to find Ay and not you upon the throne. See as you do so prize yourself of your cunning, deviousness, treachery. How is it that the old turtle beat you to the finish line? How is it that that old man made a fool out of you?"

Horemheb forced a hard smile. "I suppose that even the most unlikely of candidates can worm their way to power - just as a slave girl can worm her way into a god-king's bed.

"But don't fret, Ida. Ay is old and without blood heirs. Accidents happen all the time.

"Surely you know that by now?

"And me... I am a patient man."

"I'm sure Nakhtmin will beg to differ," Ankhe taunted. "Ay means for him to rule in his stead."

Horemheb turned, eyed the queen pointedly. "Surely even you are clever enough to see that your little love toy is hardly a match for me.

"Even if he were, by some miracle, to get within a 100 yards of the throne, how long do you think you'll hold onto him – especially once he finds out about your shriveled, little womb?"

The look of outrage and shock upon Ankhesenamun's face brought a chuckle to Horemheb's throat.

"Yes, I am aware of your plight," Horemheb said with feigned consideration, "but poor ancient Ay, he has no idea that when he dies, his line dies.

"Still, it is a kindness you do the man. Riding a woman as ancient as his wife, Tiy, must be like plowing through the desert with a 50 sna pack."

"No," he mused, a lecherous smile upon his face, "not nearly as desirable as a nice, warm, firm little piece of ass like you, Great Queen.

"Of course, from your end it must be like getting rutted by a dried out piece of driftwood. Still, we all make sacrifices in the end. Don't we?

"You just keep right on spreading your favor and believing in Ay & Nakhtmin, keep hoping that they can save you from me.

"As for me, I control the military and I dear Ankhesenamun have no room in my court nor in my bed for vipers."

The color drained from the Queen's face.

"You may take your leave now, my Queen," Horemheb suggested.

Ankhesenpaaten stood rooted.

"Now!" he barked.

Ankhe scurried from the room.

Horemheb returned to Ida. He closed the space between them, cornering her.

"There is no need for games," he said. "We both know where you were, why you were there and who sent you there. That quite frankly is a waste of my time," he said waving it away.

"I know you are bound by your oath not to expose your queen, and that you will not - though you murder her with every glance. You have honor, know the meaning of loyalty though your mistress does not.

"Your little deception is of no real consequence to me. You were only doing as you were commanded, as all good subservients should.

"Besides, I don't need your testimony to condemn Ankhesenamun. The walls are closing in on her, even as we speak."

He grabbed Ida's wrists forcing her hands behind her back. He pressed himself against her.

Ida's eyes glittered angrily.

"I don't want to have to hurt you," he said, "but make no mistake, I will."

He greedily tasted her throat.

Ida's chest heaved with angry outrage.

He abandoned her throat and returned his eyes to her face. "All you have to do is become one of my concubines, swear an oath of allegiance to me."

"Never," she spat.

Fury burned in Horemheb's eyes. "Women all across Egypt would pluck out their own mother's eyes to be a consort of the Pharaoh, yet you reject me for the love of a dead boy?!"

"Did you forget, Horemheb?" Ida spat. "You are not Pharaoh."

"I am not Pharaoh in title only, and very soon, that too will be remedied."

"Let go of me," Ida demanded.

Horemheb's eyes glittered. "You want me to let go of you?

"As you wish.

"Perhaps you prefer instead to lie with the rats, the rot, the cold, the darkness, the stale bread and water, the disease?"

She did not answer though defiance burned steadily in her eyes.

He released her. "Hykis!" The man appeared at the door. "Lock her in one of the confines."

Horror flashed briefly in Ida's eyes. The confines were only 6 feet by 3 feet, no windows, no air.

Horemheb smiled slowly, then he left Hykis to his charge.

XVIII

Ida was on the verge of insanity three days later. She had clawed at the metal until her nails broke and bled. She had screamed until her voice had failed her. She had balled up as best as she could and wished for dead.

At last her mind fled, a jumble of memories assaulting her all at once - in bits and pieces.

At last exhausted, sleep claimed her.

Ida's peace, however, was short-lived. She was awakened, not an hour later, by the sudden damp chill at her chest.

She opened her red-rimmed eyes slowly, as one hand rose to touch her breasts.

They were leaking milk again.

Ida forced herself to sit up. She opened her dress and began to pump them by hand.

The sudden squeal of the door being thrown opened, the sudden powerful burst of sunlight made Ida fall back in agony.

She balled herself up as tightly as she could, tried to hide the moisture.

Rough hands were upon her forearms, forcing her to stand. The light was so bright to her dark accustomed eyes that she had to wince for a time before the outside world came into focus.

Ankhesenpaaten was there, staring at her in disbelief.

Ida could see it in her eyes.

She knew.

Ida silently pled with the other woman to hold her peace, her head shaking slowly.

Ankhesenamun's disbelief gave way to jealousy. A slow smile began to form on her lips.

Ida knew then, beyond a shadow of a doubt. Ankhe would tell Horemheb.

As if sensing his name in the women's thoughts, Horemheb appeared at the main gate of the dungeon.

"She has borne a child," the queen proudly announced.

Horemheb entered the cell, shouldered past Ankhe.

He went to Ida and tore aside her dress. He stared in comprehension at the faint stretch marks that marred the perfect flesh of her stomach, at her engorged breasts which even now leaked milk. He let the material go.

He looked at Ankhe, a look of distaste upon his face. "Are you really so hateful that you would lead your very enemy to what could possibly be the only living child of your dead brother?"

He shook his head. "In sealing the fate of Idamun and her child, you have sealed your own. I will not have such a monster loose in my kingdom."

Ankhe stepped back from him.

"Guards!" he called.

Two men stepped forward.

"Take her out into the desert," he ordered. "Make sure no one ever finds her."

A grin of satisfaction played on Ankhesenamun's lips.

The men nodded and moved towards Ida.

"No," Horemheb said gesturing to Ankhe, "Her."

They took Ankhesenpaaten into their custody.

"Wait!" she called as they dragged her away. "You can not do this! I am Queen!"

Ankhe's voice gradually faded until her words were no longer comprehensible.

Once again in silence, Horemheb's attention returned to Ida. "So. Did the boy's seed finally flower or is some other buck to blame?"

"The child is not Pharaoh's," she lied.

Horemheb studied her for a long moment. "Somehow, Ida, I just can't quite bring myself to believe you."

"Grand Vizer, please-"

Horemheb smirked. "Ah, so *now* I have your respect?"

"My child has *nothing* to do with any of you or any of this."

"Perhaps not, but it's always better to be safe than sorry, is it not? Make no mistake, girl. I *will* find you and Tutankhamun's or whoever the hell's bastard and when I do, I will pluck its little heart from its chest and serve it to you for supper."

"Please, no!" Ida sobbed.

"Perhaps we should start in the Land of the Hittites?" he said. "Hattusa, perchance?"

He nodded. "Yes, we'll start there."

He turned to his men. "Take her back to the holding cell," he ordered.

"No!" Ida cried, struggling every step of the way.

The guards did as they were bade, Horemheb following behind them.

Once she was locked in her cell, he spoke loudly enough for her to hear his every word, his sly eyes watching for any reaction.

"Handpick some men and join Ay's next caravan to Hattusa," Horemheb said. "Your presence should be unmarked as such.

"Once you are there, discretely check out every member of Mursili's court - from the slaves to the members of his personal guard, everyone. Do not return until the child is found."

"Hattusa?" one of the men asked. "Why would Pharaoh be going to Hattusa?"

"Because Mursili is trying to broker a peace treaty with him."

"Mursili?" Ida breathed.

Horemheb turned his full attention to Ida. He studied her intensely.

"Know him personally do you?" Horemheb asked.

"No," Ida lied.

"Wasn't he killed?" one of Horemheb's men asked another. "By Man...Man-"

"Manapa," Horemheb supplied, turning back to face the men.

"Yeah, that's him," another of the soldiers said.

"It would seem this Mursili is more clever than even I had originally imagined," Horemheb replied. "It was he himself who spread the rumor of his untimely defeat.

"Then, soon as Manapa let his guard down, wham! He crushes Manapa and his forces."

Horemheb and his men chuckled.

Horemheb continued. "Word is, when the time came to pay the piper, Manapa sent his own mother out to Mursili to beg forgiveness and to ask that Mursili accept him once more as a vassal of his state.

"Imagine that!"

The men broke into hardy laughter.

"The old bag was even said to grovel right there at Mursili's feet - prostrated and everything!" Horemheb added.

"Mursili, feeling sorry for the old biddy, shows them mercy," Horemheb concluded. "I, on the other hand, would have laughed myself to death and then, beheaded them both!"

Ida sank to the ground and sobbed in her relief. If Mursili was still alive, there might still be hope for her son.

XIX

The days seemed endless as Idaten rotted away in her cell. She could barely eat or sleep. Hope was the only thing keeping her alive. Hope that Horemheb would never find her son.

In the weeks that passed, she had grown gaunt, horrifyingly thin. Her once glorious mane was now wiry.

Every time the door to the dungeons opened, her heart stopped.

Every time she held her breath.

Every time nothing.

She tried to convince herself that Horemheb would never find her son. And though, with each passing day, it seemed more likely he would not, she could not let herself believe it.

Horemheb was relentless, an unstoppable, omnipotent force.

Then the day had come.

Ida had grown so weak that she could hardly rise from her bed anymore. Not that she had any reason to.

It had been the middle of the night when they had roused her, supported her as they led her to one of the side torture chambers.

Horemheb was there. He looked down at her, smiled.

Rather than torture, he had a journey in mind. They set out into the deep desert.

It was cold and inspite of the wraps she wore, she could not keep herself from shivering violently.

They came now to a small cave.

One of the men dismounted her and half-carried her inside. He let her go, leaving her to fall to the ground like a broken puppet.

It was so dark inside that Ida could see nothing. She could only hear the sound of the soldier's footsteps as he walked away.

She began to feel her way along the floor, stopping only when she felt something soft and damp just in front of her.

Her heart stopped in her chest.

Suddenly, a flood of lantern light illuminated the darkness. Ida shielded her eyes against the sudden brightness.

To her horror, the soldiers were walling her up in the cave.

She looked back before her, began screaming hysterically.

There, in the center of the floor, was a tiny body. The face had been bashed in - to the point of being unrecognizable. The tiny heart lay crushed in the dirt next to the corpse. On a gold chain around the child's neck was the pin that Tutankh had given her.

"No!" she screamed over and over again.

"No!" she cried as she let her head fall to rest upon the tiny, empty chest.

She screamed like a mad woman with all of the grief that overwhelmed her heart. Not only had they murdered the child, but they had ensured it would not be able to pass on to the next world.

"I curse you, Horemheb!" she yelled. "Your line shall die with you!"

Horemheb laughed. "I have a healthy wife. Soon, when I am Pharaoh, I shall have dozens more."

"Your line shall die with you!" she repeated.

She turned her attention back to the child. "Oh, Aten," she sighed taking the lifeless body into her arms and pressing it to her chest. "Oh, god."

XX

Ida thought she was dead at first.

By the time she realized she was neither dead nor hallucinating, a single, thin ray of sunlight had broken through the wall Horemheb's men had built at the mouth of the cave.

The pin was still clutched in her fist, her head still lying on the child's chest as she watched the gap become larger and larger, as she watched brown hands pulling the stones from the entry.

When the hole was large enough, Galeno climbed through and hurried to her side.

"Ida?" he whispered.

She did not answer. She simply stared at him.

He said something loudly in Bedouin. Two of the desert dwellers climbed through the hole and came to Galeno's side.

The men tried to lift her. She would not, however, let go of the dead child.

Galeno finally had to pry her fingers loose, all the while promising to see the child properly buried.

It was all like a dream to Ida. Nothing made any sense. Everything seemed surreal, to be moving in slow motion.

The world tilted, then Ida was still.

Epilogue

"My Queen?" Tuya's personal attendant asked, concerned. She had been awaiting audience with the queen for quite some time now, had at last entered the Queen's chamber without her acknowledgement.

Queen Tuya looked up at the girl, her cheeks streaked with tears.

"Is everything alright?" the girl asked.

Tuya nodded absently. Remembering herself, she wiped away her tears with the back of her hand.

She placed the scrolls on the table back into the chest and locked it. She placed the key around her neck.

Still, even now, she stared at the chest as though she contemplated re-opening it.

"Forgive me, My Queen," the girl gently pressed, "but Pharaoh awaits."

The Queen nodded. "As you will," she said.

The girl bowed to her, then she went to the antechamber and commanded the rest of the Queen's attendants to enter.

Even as they prepared her, Tuya's thoughts remained upon the scrolls.

If it had been anyone else's audience, she would have postponed them. But this was Ramesses, her son, and he needed her.

Even as she left the room, she made herself and her father a vow.

As soon as she was able, she would return to the scrolls.

How True is Amarna Book I: Book of Ida?

Okay, this is all being done by memory of research done decades ago. It's as accurate as I can make it without trying to dig up said research.

- The only people who did not specifically exist in reality (though they can be said to be composites of real people) are all of the non-royals and one royal.
- The actual personalities of the Egyptian royals are unknown (except for Akhenaten who left behind lots of clues). I used creative license in a way that I believe supports their known actions (with the except of Ankhe who I just had a bit of fun with).
- A LOT is known about Mursili II, however, as the Hittites were fastidious chroniclers – especially Mursili II himself.
- There really were scandals involving the accusation that priests were engaging in necrophilia -hence Ida waking up with the priest on top of her.
- It was not uncommon for successors to "erase" previous rulers/lines by erasing their names from written history and destroying or reclaiming their deeds/monuments. Ay and Horemheb were particularly determined to erase the Amarna.
- Ironically, it is believed that Tutankh's tomb was found so intact because one of his successors usurped his intended royal tomb. This means that Aye and Horemheb helped PRESERVE and renew interest in the Amarna (particularly "The Heretic King" and his line) instead of erasing it. Just think about it. How many people have heard of Ay and Horemheb vs. the people who have heard of "King Tut", Nefertiti (his mother) and his father, "The Heretic King" (Akhenaten)?
- Mandrake really was believed to be an ancient aphrodisiac. It was also believed by some to grow as a result of the release of semen, urine and/or blood into the ground by executed criminals at the time of death.
- The penalty for adultery really ranged from having your ears or nose cut off, public flogging, banishment, burning at the stake or being fed to wild animals.
- Beer and other alcohol was often drank more than water (by those who could afford it) as water quality was often not the greatest.
- Egyptians really did wear wigs - some even shaving EVERY HAIR off of their entire body.
- Royal wives really were given a pendant engraved with their and Pharaoh's name.
- It was not uncommon practice in the ancient world for victors to take members of the vanquished ruler's family/household and "adopt" them or put them into service in their household in order to prevent retaliation/rebellion or in order to further subjugate and/or humiliate the defeated – hence Batau and Ida both being of royal blood though slaves.
- The only royal in the book who did not exist in real life? Lord Bietek.
- Akhenaten (Tutankh's and Ankhe's father) was a monotheist. He moved the capital to El-Amarna and took away much of the money and power from polytheists and their

- priesthood. This did not make him or his many friends.
- Ankhe, Tutankh and others from Akhenaten's household all originally had names that ended in -aten which basically dedicates them to Akhenaten's mono-theistic god, Aten.
- After Akhenaten's death, (various "advisors" and interim rulers) moved the capital back to Thebes, reinstated polytheism and changed the endings of all names to -amun (which rededicates them to the god Amun.
- Tutankh was a child when he became Pharaoh. It is likely that most of that which was implemented by him as Pharaoh was actually implemented through Any's machinations.
- Ankhe was indeed impregnated by her father Akhenaten. Their resulting daughter was her only surviving child.
- Ankhe also married her brother, Tutankh, who was a young child at the time (and who may have been the son of their father's sister AKA their aunt).
- Tutankh, however, was believed to be in his late teens – somewhere between 17-19 when he died.
- Ankhe is believed to have given birth to two children fathered by Tutankh – both girls and both who died shortly after birth/in the womb.
- Ay was largely credited with "helping" Tutankh to rule once Tutankh was coronated Pharaoh.
- That is until Tutankh was claimed to have mysteriously died after a fall from a chariot in his late teens.
- Originally it was believed that Tutankh was murdered due to the extent and placement of damage to his skull.
- Later forensics has disputed the assassination theory.
- I, however, don't place much faith in forensics conducted thousands of years after the fact (and some days after in some cases thanks to all of the contamination/falsification scandals).
- If you think about it, Ay is doing what he wants, having a grand old time. Then Tutankh hits puberty. What happens when kids hit puberty? As my father would say, they start smelling the musk under their arms. A Tutankh on the verge of adulthood might have been a lot more difficult to control than Tutankh the child. Especially considering his controversial upbringing in monotheism, it is not inconceivable that perhaps he was starting to allude to Akhenaten-like beliefs or otherwise trying to assert his authority and that Ay, Horemheb or others might have wanted him gone.
- After Tutankh's death, Ankhe really did send a messenger to the Hittites seeking a marriage to one of King Suppiluliuma's sons in order to keep hold of the throne. I chose to make that messenger my fictional character Ida (who was secretly carrying Tutankh's child).
- Suppilu was a real King and a character in and of himself. He murdered his own brother to get the throne (against the law).
- Suppilu also exiled Mursili's mother to marry what some scholars describe as a Babylonian princess in order to solidify/increase his power.
- Some believe the Babylonian princess Suppilu married was Mal-Nikal. (Yes, she was

real). Some believe Mal-Nikal was the wife of one of Suppilu's sons. As remarriages between fathers, sons, brothers, siblings, etc. was NOT uncommon amongst royalty and throughout the ancient world, I decided to make Mal-Nikal both.
- After verifying Tutankh was really dead, Suppilu sent one of his sons, Zannanza to marry Ankhe and take over the Egyptian throne.
- Zannanza, however would never make it to Egypt. He was murdered in route.
- While it could be argued it was because the Egyptians did not want to see a Hittite on the Egyptian throne, it could also be argued that Ay and company were wrapping up Operation Usurper.
- Lord Bietek is a composite of all of the royals who objected to Ay and Horemheb's succession. Such a person would likely help hide someone he believed could dethrone them.
- There was frequently tension between Upper and Lower Egypt - particularly after Tutankh's death. At times Upper and Lower Egypt were even ruled by separate kings. The famous Egyptian double crown represents Upper Egypt and Lower Egypt combined under the same rule.
- After the so called Zannanza Affair, Ankhe married Ay. This gave Ay's claim to the throne some legitimacy (though many were not happy about his succession).
- Ankhe disappears from history sometime after this marriage and before Horemheb ascends the throne.
- Ankhe's daughter with Akhenaten disappears from history sometime after Tutankh's death.
- What actually happened to both females is a mystery.
- Ay's connection to the Amarnas is controversial. Some believe him to be of some blood connection to the Amarnas or at least to royalty. Some think not.
- Horemheb's accession, on the other hand, was the most controversial as he was NOT noble.
- However, Horemheb controlled the military.
- Suppilu was very angry and upset by his son's murder. He sent missives to Egypt demanding explanation for this betrayal.
- Egypt didn't even bother to respond.
- Suppilu decided to teach Egypt a lesson. He consulted the oracles who told him NOT to invade Egypt.
- Suppilu ignored the oracle and invaded Egypt anyway.
- Though Suppilu succeeded on a military level, he ended up bring back plague to Hattusa (via Egyptian prisoners) - a plague that ended up killing both him and his successor.
- A famine also devastated Hattusa at the same time as the plague.
- Mursili II wrote what can be considered one of the 1st known personal diaries/autobiographies in history. Much about the events after Tutankh's death and in Hattusa at the time comes from his first-hand accounts.
- Deeply religious, Mursili II believed that all of these actions on the part of his father Suppilu (from the murder of his brother to ignoring the oracle and invading Egypt) was

the cause of all of the misfortunes that plagued the Hittite Empire.
- As a result, Mursili became obsessed with appeasing the gods – specifically his patron gods: Telipinu and Arinna.
- Mursili also believed he could actually commune with these gods. This led me to make him a psychic who had inherited it from his banished mother.
- Mursili was known for being fairly tolerant of other's beliefs and reasonably fair.
- Mursili II really was NEVER expected to ascend to the throne, yet a series of unexpected events catapulted him to power as a teen.
- Many of the Hittite vassals DID rebel as they figured the teen could not stop them.
- Brothers Arnuwanda and Mursili's conflict over Ida, however, was added for dramatic effect as Ida isn't real.
- Mursili proved his doubters wrong. He WAS a great warrior, strategist and king.
- However, Mursili's loved ones really DID drop like flies around him – and for the causes as described in the books.
- Mursili DID fake his own death to lull rebelling states into a sense of complacency.
- The account of a vanquished rebel vassal sending out his mother to plead with Mursili is TRUE.
- And Mursili actually DID take pity on him.

Amarna Book II:
Book of Hawara

by

Grea Alexander

Shoved out into the cold, cruel world shivering and naked by SeaMonkey Ink
A division of the sick mind of Grea Alexander

Copyright © 2014 by Grea Alexander

All rights are reserved. No part of this work may be reproduced or transmitted in any form or by any means possible in both the human and alien spectrum of existence including any and all oral, mental, physical, emotional, spiritual, sexual, electronic or mechanical means including but not limited to posting online (in excerpt or in whole), file sharing, photocopying, scanning and/or recording by any information storage or retrieval system and/or by any means yet to be invented without the express written permission of Grea Alexander or SeaMonkey Ink.

Genre: Historical Novel
Rating: Mature

Printed in the USA AKA the United States of America or as I like to call it Uuusah

A product of Seamonkey Ink, LLC

www.SeaMonkeyInk.com

Dedication

This book is hereby dedicated to GOD, the trees that provided paper for it, the screens that illuminate to allow it to be read electronically, myself, the real-life characters that inspired this work and this series' fans who waited so patiently for Book II to be released and who will wait even more patiently for Book III to be borne into the world....but not *necessarily* in that order.

Please note: This work is also a Novella

What's a novella? A novella is a written work running between 20,000 and 49,000 words. It is generally considered too long for most publishers to insert comfortably into a magazine without charges being filed against them yet too short for a novel.

I personally LIKE novellas. They let me get my work out faster which benefits both you who are dying to know what happens next and I who have a short attention span and limited time/energy to work on my books (as I suck so much at and don't have the time, money, know-how or energy for mass marketing nor do I have the sales to be able to live by writing books alone). Even if that were not the case, I don't like filler. I write what I feel needs to be written to get what I want to get across across. Sometimes more but rarely less.

So there you have it. It is what it is and I am unrepentantly unapologetic about it. I even wrote a song about it. Wanna hear it? Ok, read it?

Who writes short books? I write short books. If you dare read short books, read this short book.

Awesome right? (laugh)

In conclusion, yes, this book is short. It is a novella. I enjoy writing novellas and apparently series as well. While I do, however, have a few looonnng novels. (For some reason the Rebellion books in particular each just grew into big, fat, literary monsters.) This, however, is not one of them.

While I won't promise that I will stop with the novellas or the serializations, I will however promise you one thing. Ok, so I will loosely make an effort to guarantee one thing. Okay, so I will kinda, sorta try to uphold one thing. No, a few things:

1. Each series will last no longer than 3 books (which may or may not have spin offs or continuation series that will each last no longer than 3 books).
2. All of the answers to all of the big questions and the loose ends I deem important will be wrapped up by the 3rd book in the series.
3. I will remain one of the world's worse synopsizers. It is what it is. All of my creativity is poured into the story and the characterizations. I'm afraid by the time it's all over, there's very little left for synopsis..es or titles. Besides, my stories are kind of hard to sum up without giving anything pertinent away.
4. My book titles won't improve much over the course of the years either I'm afraid.
5. I will finish all of the books I start in serial form...eventually.

Now that we've gotten that swill out of the way, on with the show!

Amarna Book II:
Book of Hawara

How far are you willing to go? How much are you willing to sacrifice?

These are the questions King Mursili II has had to ask himself every day since his thirteen year – the year the gift of prophecy had awakened within him, the year Queen Ankhesenamun's slave Ida had come to his father's court begging for one of Mursili's brothers to marry the queen and save the throne of Egypt.

Despite the unfortunate turn of events – his brother's murder and the fall of Queen Ankhesenamun, the gods had been quite clear. The fate of the Hittite Kingdom was linked to that of Egypt. His fate was linked to that of Ida. If one fell, so would the other. His only hope to restore his own Hittite Kingdom to greatness was to restore the Amarna line to power in Egypt, to atone for the sins of his father.

Yet, with those closest to him being sacrificed in the process and the tide continuing to rise against them, how far is King Mursili prepared to go to see the prophecy fulfilled?

Introduction

In book II, we pick up where book Book I left off - at the end of Pharaoh Ay's reign. This book covers the period all the way through Year 11 or so of Mursili's rule in Hatti.

In this book, the fight continues to hide the continued existence of Ida as well as to protect King Tutankhaten's legacy from not only their enemies but from those who would martyr them in order to challenge Horemheb's rule or for their own personal gain.

King Mursili continues to try to help Ida in this regard in addition to trying to deal with the weight of his own destiny. Although once the most unlikely to ascend the throne, Mursili is charged with not only restoring his famine and disease-ridden kingdom to glory but with making amends to the gods for his father's transgressions against them and with fulfilling a prophecy which ties the success of restoring the Amarna line to power with the future of his own kingdom.

Prologue

Ancient Egypt. 1274 B.C. Reign of Pharaoh Ramesses II.

Queen Tuya sat in a place of prominence, amongst the lines of royals and nobles who lined the main avenue that ran from the palace entry gates to the main doors of the palace. Her son's queens, concubines and offspring flanked her on either side.

Tuya was anxious, one hand tightly gripping the seat of her sedan chair as they waited for her son, Pharaoh Ramesses II's, return.

What did it all mean? she wondered.

Before she could return to read more of the scrolls her father had entrusted to her care, war had erupted between her son's empire and the Hittite empire ruled over by King Mursili II and Queen Gassulawiya's son, Muwatalli II. If the fates of the Egyptian and Hittite empires were as tightly intertwined as the first scrolls she had read indicated, why this? Why now?

Could her son be destroying not only Hatti but Egypt - even as she sat there in her golden finery, in her golden chair, awaiting his return?

Tuya's grip on the chair tightened. She fought the urge to rise, to run back to her quarters, throw open the trunk and read more. She had to know the answer. If there was even the slightest chance...

Just as she could fight the urge to flee no more, the sound of cheering reached her ears.

Ramesses. He was near.

She sank back down in her chair and she waited.

It seemed to take an eternity before his procession wound through the streets and through the main gate.

Just a little longer, Tuya, the queen counseled herself as the first glimpse of the double crown of Pharaoh came into view.

Hurriedly dismounting the moment he was before his mother, Ramesses ignored royal protocol and stalked determinedly into the palace, his top aides and advisors right behind him.

The royal family and honored guests were in shock.

Tuya sat there for a long moment before she too could wait no longer. Abandoning decorum as well, she rose from her sedan. As soon as she was sure none of the stunned spectators could see her, she ran.

Tuya quickly caught up to the men. Slowing her pace, she called to one of Pharaoh's lesser advisors. The man turned to greet her.

The Queen Dowager waived away the formalities as soon as they began to flow from his lips.

"What's happening?" she demanded.

"Negotiations with Hatti failed," the man admitted. "We go to war."

"War?" Tuya breathed, her skin turning pale.

The advisor nodded. "We meet the enemy at Kadesh," he confirmed.

Tuya took a stumbling step backward.

"My Queen," the man said hurrying forward to steady her. "Are you ill?"

Tuya nodded absently.

"Guard!" the man called. "Take the Queen to her chambers."

The men did as they were bade, a dazed Tuya barely aware of what was going on around her. It was not until her eyes took in the main door to her suites that she snapped back to reality.

Regaining her composure, Tuya dismissed the guard. As soon as the guard was out of sight, she entered her chambers.

Impatiently, she dismissed her staff. They puzzled as she closed and locked the main suite door behind them.

Alone at last, Tuya moved hurriedly to the far wall. There she triggered the panel that hid her secret room from view. Retrieving her father's chest, she pulled the key from around her neck and unlocked it. She hurriedly rifled through the scrolls until she found the one she had been reading when she had been called away by Ramesses' command.

Unrolling it, she sat down and she began to read.

I

The scrolls.

Ancient Egypt. Between 1319 and 1323 BC. Final year of the reign of Pharaoh Ay.

Idaten thought she was dead at first. By the time she realized that she was neither dead nor hallucinating, a single, thin ray of sunlight had broken through the wall Horemheb's men had built at the mouth of the cave.

The pin was still clutched in her fist, her head still lying on the child's chest as she watched the gap become larger and larger, as she watched the brown hands pulling the stones from the entry.

When the hole was large enough, Galeno climbed through and hurried to her side.

"Ida?" he whispered.

She did not answer. She simply stared at him – her eyes vacant as tears slowly slid down her cheeks.

He said something loudly in Bedouin. Two of the desert dwellers climbed through the hole and came to Galeno's side.

The men tried to lift her. She fought them, refusing to move, clinging obstinately to the dead child.

Time was running out.

With no other option left to him, Galeno had to pry Ida's fingers loose, all the while promising to see that the child was properly buried.

It was like a dream to Ida. Nothing made any sense. Everything seemed surreal, to be moving in slow motion.

The world tilted, then Ida was still.

For days Ida drifted in and out of consciousness, unaware of all that was going on around her. Names came to her lips, tossed forth from her muddled memory like crickets jumping through the reeds: Kadar, Nacamakun, Mursili....Tutankhaten.

The final name to leave her lips and awaken her from her fevered dreams was that of her and Tutankhaten's son.

"Abidos!" Ida cried as her eyes shot open in the darkness. She sat up abruptly, the world around her tilting at odd angles with the action. Her skin was covered in sweat, her breathing labored as at last she was able to maintain her hold on the present.

"Thank the gods!" Galeno, her long-time friend and fellow conspirator cried as he hurried to her side.

"My son!" Ida cried desperately clutching his arm, tears streaming down her face. "Where is my son?!"

"The boy?" Galeno questioned, confused. When had she...

"The boy," Ida repeated as her memory slowly returned.

She covered her mouth in her horror. "Oh, Aten," she choked.

She tried to rise from the bed, found her weakened body unable to sustain her.

Galeno caught her and held her upright. "Ida, it's too soon."

"The boy," she said, anguish and desperation burning in her eyes. "I have to see him. I have to see him now."

"That's not possible," Galeno replied.

"Not possible," she repeated, not fully comprehending.

"Nacamakun took the body to Hattusa."

Galeno felt Ida go limp in his arms at the mention of the man's name.

"Oh, Nacamakun," she sobbed. "I'm sorry. I'm so very, very sorry."

Galeno eased her back down upon the bed. He watched helplessly as great sobs shook her far too frail body.

Galeno rose. Leaving Ida in Clizi's capable hands, Galeno slipped from the room.

After a few dead ends, Galeno found Lord Bietek in the main audience chamber, in whispered conference with his supporters.

Lord Bietek was the most powerful man in Lower Egypt and an ally of Mursili II, the current Hittite king. In addition to great wealth and influence, Lord Bietek had royal blood that was traceable to before the time that Upper and Lower Egypt were united under Pharaoh Menes.

With the last of the true Amarna royal line gone, Lord Bietek was considered by many to be best suited to take over the Egyptian throne once Ay, now stricken with ill health, passed.

It was no secret. Although Nakhtmin was Ay's official heir, no one doubted that so soon as Ay closed his eyes forever, Horemheb would seek to displace him. To those of royal lineage, it would be an outrage – a commoner upon the Egyptian throne.

In addition to being Vizier, Ay had at least come from royal stock – his daughter being none other than Nefertiti, Akhenaten's Great Chief Wife – thus his reign was tolerated. But this Horemheb – a mere advisor and soldier? Never.

"My Lord," Galeno interrupted. "I realize I am hardly worthy but may I have a word with you...in private?"

"Surely, whatever you have to say to Lord Bietek you can say in front of us," one of the men replied, floored by Galeno's audacity in asking that men of his stature be dismissed.

"It's about Ida," Galeno pressed.

At the mention of Ida's name, Lord Bietek took notice.

"Do as he asks," Lord Bietek ordered.

"My Lord, this is highly irregular!" another of the aristocrats protested.

"Now!" Lord Bietek commanded.

The men bowed, did as they were bade. They were further surprised when Lord Bietek followed them to the door and shut it firmly behind them.

Lord Bietek turned to face Galeno, his face stony. "Hawara," he corrected. "Her name is Hawara."

"But - " Galeno began.

"Ida was Queen Ankhesenamun's slave. Ida died not long after Pharaoh Tutankhamun and is interred in a grand tomb worthy of a state official in Thebes. Ida no longer exists. There is only my wet nurse, Hawara. Hawara who was kidnapped by slavers and only by the grace of the gods has been returned to my household."

"With all due respect, my Lord, there is good reason Nacamakun sought the aide of my men and I in finding and rescuing Ida. Ida and I are friends, true, but beyond that, it was I who helped her fake her death, who arranged her passage to Hattusa in a vain attempt to save the Amarna line. I may be no more than a peon in your eyes, but I believe I have more than earned the truth."

"As I said, Hawara was kidnapped by slavers."

"Cut the shit," Galeno said, losing patience with the man. "You can dye her hair every color of the rainbow and you can call her whatever the hell you like, but that girl lying in the west wing of your compound is still Idaten."

Lord Bietek was both shocked and impressed by Galeno's boldness. He was nothing as Lord Bietek had pictured him, especially in light of Galeno's scandalous, sexual liaisons and the resulting trial.

Perhaps Lord Bietek had dismissed him too readily.

Galeno struggled to regain his composure. "Look," he said. "I apologize. I just care about Ida – very much. I need to know what's going on so that I can help her. I need to know, for her sake, what happened between the time she reached Hattusa and now."

Lord Bietek studied him for a long moment. Finally, he replied. "If anything I'm about to tell you gets out, I will have you skinned alive."

"If anything you're about to tell me gets out, I will skin *myself* alive."

Lord Bietek smirked. "As well you know, in response to Queen Ankhesenamun's plea for King Suppiluliuma to send a son for her to marry, in order to save her throne from Ay and Horemheb, Prince Zannanza was chosen. The messenger, Hawara, was held in Hattusa as collateral.

"It was during this time that Hawara became acquainted with then Prince Mursili II. When his brother Zannanza had his little accident on his way to marry Ankhesenamun, the then King Suppilu accused her of plotting with Ay and Horemheb. In retaliation, he ordered her put to death. Only...."

"Only what?" Galeno pressed.

"Only Hawara was found to be with child. Her life was spared as Nacamakun, the head of the king's guard, claimed to be the child's father. This led the king to suspect that the child's true father might well be his son, Mursili."

"But neither was, were they?" Galeno surmised.

Lord Bietek smirked. Yes, this Galeno was a sharp one.

Without answering the question directly, Lord Bietek went to a hidden cabinet built into the wall and opened it. Reaching inside, he pulled out a golden pendant. Re-closing the cabinet and re-crossing the room, he handed it to Galeno.

Galeno took it and examined it.

He had seen the likes of it before.

Turning it over, he read the inscription. His face betrayed his surprise.

"Is this what I think it is?" he asked Lord Bietek.

Lord Bietek nodded. "I thought it might be a fake so I had it examined by the foremost experts on royal seals and emblems. I can assure you, with great certainty, that it is indeed genuine."

Galeno examined the pendant once more.

All of the royal wives had them. It was a symbol of their status and affirmation of the legitimacy of their marriage to Pharaoh. Only this one bore a personal inscription and tied Ida to Tutankhamun.

If Ida was bound to Tutankhamun and already with child when she arrived in Hattusa, that could only mean...

Galeno shook his head.

No, that couldn't be.

Surely, Ida would have told him if it were true – if she were carrying the last living descendent of Pharaoh Tutankh. They had been friends since childhood and had always shared everything. Surely, Ida wouldn't have kept such a big secret from him.

Unbidden, Galeno's mind fled to the child they had found in the crypt with Ida, everything suddenly falling into place.

Ida had probably given birth and somehow been sent back into Egypt under Lord Bietek's care. But how did Ida and the child end up in Horemheb's hands, sentenced to be walled in and left to die - the brutalization of the child an obvious attempt by Horemheb to destroy the last of Tutankhamun's line not only on earth but in the afterworld?

He looked to Bietek, suspicion burning in his eyes.

Bietek smirked again.

"It was not I," he assured Galeno. "Hawara returned to Thebes of her own accord, without either my permission or knowledge. She was captured in Pharaoh's rooms and imprisoned.

"From what I gathered from Nacamakun, a source loyal to Mursili informed the king of her plight. Mursili in turn sent Nacamakun back into Egypt to oversee her rescue.

"Nacamakun, however, seemed just as stunned as you are right now to find out about the murdered child."

Galeno once again fell victim to his thoughts, momentarily forgot the other man in the room.

Suddenly snapping to the present, Galeno spoke. "Pharaoh Tutankhamun had a male heir – a legitimate male heir but now that heir is dead?"

"From what we can tell. If you wish to learn anything more, you will have to ask Hawara herself."

Galeno nodded. "I'll do that," he said.

"Now, if you'll excuse me," Lord Bietek said clasping his hands behind his back. "I was in the middle of a conference."

"Of course, My Lord," Galeno said. He proffered the pin to the other man.

Lord Bietek kept his hands clasped. "It was given to Hawara and to her care it should be returned."

Galeno nodded his understanding. He bowed and paid his respects before he left the room.

II

Hattusa, capital of the Hittite Empire. Royal citadel.

King Mursili II scrawled hurriedly in his journal - anxiously awaiting word from Egypt. The king was a fastidious chronicler - the Hittites long having realized the importance of history and record keeping.

Still, it was unusual for someone of his eminence to keep their own history. That work was usually left to the royal scribes.

Mursili, however, was not like the kings before him. He had been entrusted by the gods with a mission, a mission he knew most would not understand, with a destiny he could not even bring himself to trust to the scribes - honorable and learned as they were.

Still, Mursili recognized the importance of these events, felt he would be dishonoring not only the gods but all who had sacrificed and would have to sacrifice in the future to appease the wrathful deities and return the Hittite Kingdom to their favor.

To keep their peace and to honor those who would fall in the course of his destiny, Mursili had taken to chronicling his life himself. He had done so for the past handful of years, since his 13th year – the year the visions first began.

The completed journals he kept in a secret room under lock and key. He showed them to no one - not even his beloved wife, Queen Gassulawiya. Nor did he have plans to reveal them to anyone until he was on his deathbed, until he had done all that he had been charged to do.

Finished with his current entry, King Mursili set down his writing instrument. He stared down, unseeingly, at the neat rows of cuneiform, his thoughts drifting to what was yet to come.

As eagerly as he had received the news of Ida's rescue, he was not eager for the confrontation with Nacamakun that would inevitably follow.

Nacamakun had been a father figure to Mursili his entire life. He had always done whatever Mursili had asked of him, without question or complaint. Even when Mursili had revealed to Nac that he had been cursed with the same connection to the gods, the same visions that his father had used as an excuse to exile his mother and marry his Babylonian whore, Nac had stood by Mursili's side and kept his secret.

The calamity with Ida had been no different. When Mursili had revealed his connection to the girl, that the fates of Ida and Mursili as well as the fates of the Hittite Kingdom and the Egyptian Kingdom were intertwined, Nac had accepted it without question. He had not even hesitated to back Mursili when Mursili had come up with the scheme to claim that Nac was the child's father.

What's more, Nac had also not batted an eyelash in supporting Mursili as he outmaneuvered first his father, then his brother and his enemies to not only keep Ida safe but to keep the child safe. When Mursili asked that Nac adopt Ida's child, Nac had not hesitated - just as he had not hesitated to watch over Ida and deliver her into Lord Bietek's care. Even when Mursili began to maneuver to claim the throne and as he fought to keep it, Nac had been right there by his side.

Mursili did not doubt that he would not be where he was today if not for that man. Yet, how had Mursili repaid him?

Mursili exhaled sharply.

He felt sick at the thought of what he had done. He had lied to Nac. He had sent him into Egypt to rescue Ida knowing full well what would befall the child in his absence. He had done as the gods had commanded and he had sacrificed the boy in the name of attrition for his father's many sins against the heavens.

To save his plague and famine weakened people, he had struck a deal with the devil himself – the soon to be Pharaoh, Horemheb.

In exchange for a peace treaty with Egypt, he had called away Nac's personal guard and left his household open to Horemheb's men. Then, in the dead of night, with Mursili's full knowledge and complicity, Horemheb's men had attacked Nac's home.

Nac's people had stood no chance. Unprotected and taken by surprise, they were easily overtaken. The boy was found and as the vision had prophesied, he was carried away, back into Egypt.

Mursili sighed heavily.

The child's life in exchange for peace with Egypt and Ida's life - just as the oracles had promised him. The child's life to atone for the sins of his father and raise the Hittites from the depths to which the once great empire had been plunged by his father's arrogance - just as the visions had foretold.

But what consolation would all of that be to Nacamakun? Nac who had been more loyal to Mursili than anyone else ever had. Nac who had risked all to support Mursili, who had taken Mursili under his care as he had his own child, as he also had taken care of Abidos?

Nac would never forgive him. How could he? How could Mursili ever forgive himself?

Mursili fought to contain the tears that even now threatened to spill from his eyes.

His bond with his 2nd father would be severed forever by what the gods had commanded. Yet, after all his father Suppilu had done to dishonor his line, to dishonor the Hittite Kingdom, to dishonor the gods, what choice did Mursili have?

Balance had to be restored. Reparation to the gods had to be made.

Though Nac remained alive, Mursili would forever count him as his 5th sacrifice to the will of the gods. First there had been his brother, Prince Zannanza. Second, his father – a victim of the plague his father had brought to Egypt with his Egyptian captives. Third had been his oldest brother – also taken by the plague. Fourth, there was the child. Now there was Nac.

Mursili fell to his knees and began to pay to his patron gods – the Sun Goddess Arinna and the Storm God Telipinu.

Almost as if in answer to his prayers, Mursili heard his name.

He listened. There it was again, echoing through the citadel.

"Mursili!"

Mursili took a deep breath and rose.

It was time to face his destiny.

III

Lower Egypt.

Ida had cried herself to sleep.

When next she awoke, she found Galeno sitting in the darkness, in a chair next to her bed. Hearing her shift, his fingers closed around something he had been studying in his palm.

Ida forced her weakened body into a sitting position.

He looked up at her, forced a thin smile that didn't quite reach his eyes, that did nothing to hide the worry that was etched on his features.

"Galeno?" Ida asked, worried for the state of her friend.

Galeno sighed. He rose, began to pace the room as he kneaded the pendant in his hand.

He suddenly stopped. He stared at Ida for a long moment.

Ida looked every inch like someone who had barely cheated death. Her once glorious mane was brittle, thin and straw like. Her once beautiful face was gaunt, her once golden skin now pale. Her once athletic and voluptuous body was now rail thin, her bones grotesquely visible through her now dry, thin and battered skin.

How could she possibly survive what was to come – a life in hiding, a life on the run?

"Galeno, please," Ida begged.

"I had a long talk with Lord Bietek," he began. "He told me everything, Ida. Everything he knew anyway."

"I don't understand," she replied.

"Maybe this will refresh your memory," Galeno said returning to the bed. He handed her the pin.

Ida hesitated for a long moment before she took it from his hand, the cool golden metal feeling both cold and warm in her hand at the same time. She stared down at it, her memory drifting to a time that seemed now so long ago.

"Why didn't you tell me?" Galeno asked, breaking through her revere.

"I couldn't tell anyone," she replied simply, her eyes still glued to the pendant.

She looked up at him. She shook her head. "I'm sorry."

"So the boy we found with you....He was your son?" Galeno gently prodded.

Ida thought it over a long moment before she answered, tears falling from her eyes as memories of the times she spent with the child flashed before her eyes.

"Yes," she replied, "and no. I was the only mother he had ever known, but it was not I who bore him."

"And the child you bore?" he asked, though he was quite sure he already knew the answer. "Who was that child's father?"

"It was Tutankh," she whispered quietly, her grief evident in her eyes.

Galeno was taken aback, the wind knocked out of him. He could barely bring himself to utter his next words. "So your son, the true heir to the throne of Egypt, lives?"

Ida nodded shortly.

"Yes," she breathed. "At least I hope so."

Galeno gasped. He stood, began to pace the room once more as the implications of what she was telling him began to sink in.

Did Lord Bietek know the whereabouts of Ida's child, of his only legitimate competition for the Egyptian throne?

He thought back to his earlier conversation with Lord Bietek. Although haughty, Lord Bietek certainly seemed earnest enough. Perhaps he did genuinely believe that the dead child was Ida's.

Galeno turned to Ida. "Who else knows of this?"

"No one outside of the original players," Ida replied. "Me, Nac, Mursili I'm certain and now you."

"What of Lord Bietek? He believes your child is dead."

"Good," Ida replied.

"Good?" he questioned. "Is Lord Bietek a danger to you? Is that why you snuck back to Thebes?"

Ida shook her head. "You misunderstand," she said. "Lord Bietek is quite a noble and honorable man. He's as good as they come. However, the fewer people who know Abidos is still alive, the better. Letting everyone believe my son is dead is the best chance he has at life."

Galeno resumed his pacing as he considered Ida's words, as he added these new pieces to the puzzle of events in his mind.

He stopped again. "Do you have any idea of where the child is now?"

Ida shrugged. "He's probably still in Hattusa - probably with Mursili or someone he trusts," she replied.

The man frowned. If her son was still in the land of the Hittites, why then had she gone to Thebes?

He decided to ask. "Why did you go to Thebes then, if not to save your son?"

Ida thought on it for a long moment, pushing through the fog that even now threatened to overcome her.

"Tutankh," she breathed as the realization hit. "I went to say goodbye to him. Only...."

She began to pat her body for the hidden pocket. Empty.

Her mind drifted to her capture. She had had the document that would lead her to Tutankhamun's grave and evidence that Ay planned to rob it and claim both the tomb and its riches for himself hidden on her body when she was thrown into the dungeons.

Then what? Think.

She had it. Fearing that Horemheb or one of his men might discover the evidence, she had torn it into small pieces and little by little swallowed it.

"Only what?" Galeno pressed.

Ida's eyes rose to focus on him as she pulled herself from her thoughts. "Only I discovered Ay's plot."

"What plot?"

"Ay plans to usurp Tutankh's tomb."

"What?" he asked, incredulous. "Even the likes of Ay would not dare to..."

"He would and he will," she said. "I found evidence – a document written in Ay's own hand. He plans to strip Tutankh of his treasures and stature in the afterlife, just as he and Horemheb have stripped him from history in the present world."

Galeno was in shock. Just when he thought the current reigning Pharaoh could sink no lower, he did.

Was it not enough that he and Horemheb had stripped the Amarna children of first their religion, then their name, then their power, then their lives in this world? Was it not enough that they had destroyed the Amarna temples to their one god, their Aten, and had the names of Akhenaten and Tutankhamun literally chiseled away from all monuments, statutes, tombs and records? Was it not enough that they had found what they had believed to be the only remaining true royal Amarna heir, Ida's son, and mutilated him so that he would not be accepted by the gods in the afterlife? Did they also need to do this to?

"We have to stop them," Ida entreated. "We have to get to Tutankh's tomb first and we have to hide him and his belongings were no one would ever think to look for him."

"But how?" he asked.

"I memorized it," she said. "I know exactly where the tomb is. But we need people we can trust - preferably people from far away lands who wish to return there and have no stake in Egypt. We need men for the labor but we also need warriors to take on the tomb guard and to secure the haul.

"We'll need a place for him – a tomb that is well appointed, well protected but not intended to be used. Perhaps one for someone of note who was killed abroad and whose body was never recovered.

"Lastly, we need a diversion. We need the eye of Pharaoh and his men to be turned elsewhere while we make our move."

Galeno nodded. "How about during the Nile Flood Feast?" he suggested.

Ida shook her head. "That would be too late. That's when Ay's people plan to move."

"Then that doesn't leave us very much time. Nile Flood Feast is less than a month away."

"Then we'll need all the help we can get. I'll send word to Mursili. In the meantime, arrange an audience for me with Lord Bietek."

IV

Hattusa.

King Mursili II sat in his audience chamber and waited on the throne.

It was not long before he spied Nacamakun stalking determinedly up the stairs towards the open door.

"Mursili!" Nacamakun cried out in rage and anguish. Tears were pouring down Nac's cheeks as he clutched the small, wrapped form of a child in his arms.

There was a mad, murderous gleam in Nac's eyes that made the blood of even the king's bravest, most battle-hardened guard run cold.

Still, it was the guard's duty to protect the king. They barred Nacamakun's entry.

"Let him pass and leave us," Mursili ordered.

His men could not hide their surprise - even as they obeyed the order. Nac too seemed momentarily taken aback as the men moved from around him and closed the door in their wake.

Yet, when Nac's gaze returned to Mursili, the malicious gleam returned to his eyes.

He began to move deliberately towards the King, Mursili rising and meeting him halfway.

Nacamakun smirked as he offered the bundle to Mursili.

Gingerly, the king accepted the boy's body.

"So this was the reason you sent me to find your precious Ida?" Nacamakun demanded. "Not because you trusted me but because you planned to stab me in the back?"

"I had no choice," Mursili replied, gently setting the child down upon the alter.

Nac was not surprised to find the alter already prepared for the performance of the boy's death rites. Not only did Mursili have the power to see through the veils of fate and time, as king, he was also the chief priest and conduit between the people and the gods.

"We owe the gods," the king continued. "You know well the prophecy. I had no choice but to save Ida and her line - in order to ensure the survival of our empire. Her life is tied to my life. The Egyptian empire is tied to our empire. If one should fall, so shall the other."

"So you sacrifice my only son?!" Nac yelled.

Mursili replied evenly, as he slowly began to unwrap the boy. "Horemheb found out about Abidos. He sent a group of his soldiers into Hattusa to search for the boy. It was only a matter of time before they put the pieces together and figured out that the dead Pharaoh's son was in your household. They never would have stopped searching otherwise.

"We also needed peace with the Egyptians. We needed time to grow strong again, to rebuild, to secure our borders. None of this would have been possible without this sacrifice."

Mursili forced his face to remain passive as he took in the state of the child – the smashed in face, the crushed chest and pulverized heart. The Egyptians meant for this child not to even be accepted into the afterlife. The Hittites, however, did not share these beliefs. As heinous as the Egyptian's treatment of the body, as long as the soul had been pure at the time of death, the child would be welcomed into the heavens.

This, however, was of little consolation for either the boy's father or the king who had loved the child as a little brother.

"But why *my* son?" Nac demanded, his pain and anguish shaking Mursili to his core though Mursili's expression remained impassive.

Only Mursili's eyes betrayed the true turmoil in which his soul was mired.

"You could have sacrificed anyone else's child," Nac continued, "and no one would have been the wiser. The gods showed you what would happen yet you did nothing to protect Kadar. Why?!"

"It had to be Kadar," Mursili replied as he began to clean the boy. "Telipinu demanded a sacrifice worthy of him. No lesser child would have appeased him."

"You're a father yourself, yet you speak of sacrificing the life of my son with as much compassion as you would a bull."

"I feel compassion for all living things, Nac," Mursili replied. "You know that. But you wrong me greatly to speak to me as if the loss of Kadar has as little effect on me as the loss of a fine piece of chattel. Kadar was like my little brother. I grieve his loss no less than I did those of my own flesh – my father and my brothers.

"Nacamakun, I am more sorry than I can ever express that you and yours got caught up in all of this, that you were hurt, that you had to suffer for your loyalty to me and my line.

"I know it is of little consequence to you right now, but some day all of this will prove to have been worth it. With our pain, humility, contrition and sacrifice, we will bring peace and prosperity to two empires. We will save the lives of thousands upon thousands. You have to believe that. You can't ever lose sight of that fact or you won't survive this."

"I won't survive this or you won't?" Nac demanded.

Mursili didn't answer. There was no need for him to.

Both he and Nac knew that it was of himself that he was speaking, that it was himself he was trying to reassure, that it was himself he was trying to convince.

"What good are these visions if you can do nothing to change what is to come?!" Nac demanded, his frustration and anguish beginning to turn into despair.

"That I am shown the way and must comply - no matter how painful or difficult, is part of our penance," Mursili said. "As great of a man and a king as my father was, his transgressions against the gods were great. From the moment he killed my uncle to take the throne, he set this path in motion.

"If we do not stay strong, if we dare not repay every ounce to the gods that they demand in recompense, the consequences will be disastrous.

"As long as we keep to our end of the bargain, so long as we keep Ida safe and return Tutankh's line to power, we will be redeemed."

"So you keep saying," Nac replied. "But I'm beginning to wonder. If it was for anyone other than Ida, would you have made such a sacrifice?

"I too was young once. A beauty such as Ida has great power over men, especially once she gets under their skin, once they have tasted her flesh."

Mursili paused in his ceremony. For the first time since the conversation had began, he looked Nac in the eye. The king's eyes were hard.

"I realize you have every reason in the world to hate me right now," Mursili conceded, "but you go too far."

"Do I?" Nac pressed.

"I love my wife."

"I know you do. But you still feel for Ida as well, do you not?"

"That's beside the point," Mursili replied.

"Is it? Tell me you didn't share a bed with Ida. Tell me you didn't love her, that you don't love her still and I will believe."

Mursili thought on it a long moment before he replied. "The boy I was will always hold a place in his heart for Ida but the man I am now loves his wife. Surely, even in your pain, you know I would never put either of us through such torment unless there was no other way and surely not just for the sake of my loins."

"I don't know what to believe anymore," Nac replied. "Just a few days ago, I never in a million years would have believed you capable of what you have just done."

"I –"

"Had no choice," Nac interrupted. "Yes, I know. The prophecy. The gods."

"We still all have sacrifices to make before it is all said and done," Mursili said. "Even I."

"Is that true, Great King? When the gods turn on you too and demand of you a sacrifice such as this - one so terrible that you feel a great hole has been torn through your very soul, will you be able to make it?"

"I shall do what must be done," Mursili said with more confidence than he felt, "no matter what it costs me. I have to put things right again."

Mursili began to anoint the child's skin with the blessed oils and recite the prayers of passing.

Nac watched him for a long moment before he forced aside his torment long enough to consecrate his son's passage into the afterlife.

Closing his eyes, Nacamakun began to recite the prayers in unison with the king.

V

Hattusa.

Nacamakun and those select trusted few who were allowed to gather, to pay their respects. watched as King Mursili II himself set fire to Kadar's funeral pyre.

Kadar's rites had been as grand as those put on for any Hittite King.

As the last of the flames began to die down and the guests said their final words of consolation, Mursili watched Nacamakun.

Over the course of the 2 days of rites, the two men had not spoken again save as was required to pass Kadar into the netherworld.

Now, as Nac strode purposefully towards him, Mursili braced himself.

"We need to talk," Nac said.

Mursili nodded. "Meet me in my chambers in 20 minutes," he agreed.

Making his excuses, Mursili departed for his chambers. Once inside, he changed from his priestly trappings into his normal attire. Though his heart pounded in his chest, he appeared outwardly calm.

He had just finished his latest entry into his journal when Nac entered.

"Leave us," Mursili instructed his personal servants and guard.

Nacamakun watched as the door closed behind him. Then, without warning, he was upon Mursili.

Mursili stood now with Nac just behind him. Mursili's long hair was entangled in Nac's grasp, Nac's blade pressed against his throat.

"I should kill you for this," Nac growled.

"But you won't," Mursili replied calmly.

Nac released him, shoving him away from his person. Mursili turned back to face the man.

"Instead," Nac continued, "I demand to be released from your service."

"Denied," Mursili replied.

"Denied?" Nac repeated indignantly.

"You have a role yet to play in our salvation."

"Haven't I given up enough? Is not the life of my only son more than I owe you, more than I will ever owe your regime?"

"Your only son?" Mursili repeated. "Is there not another – a child hiding in the storage closets of your compound, a child who is frightened and alone, a child who has for the better part of his life looked to you as a father?"

"Abidos," Nac breathed. He had been so overwhelmed by his grief that he had not even given the other boy a thought. He had simply assumed that Abidos was under Mursili's care.

Mursili nodded. "The Egyptians still have eyes in the citadel. I dare not bring the boy here.

"I know it is asking a great deal of you, but I need you to keep your word to Ida. You promised her that you would take care of Abidos as though he were your own. Now, I need him to become just that."

"What are you saying?" Nac asked through narrowed eyes, though he knew well what Mursili was asking.

"I need the boy that was laid to rest here today to be not Kadar but Abidos and I need the boy that remains in your household to be not Abidos but Kadar."

Nac inhaled sharply.

"I know it's still too soon," Mursili assured him. "But in time, perhaps..." He swallowed passed the lump in his throat, tears stinging at his eyes.

Nac considered the proposal. As angry as he was with the gods, with Mursili, with everyone and everything at that moment, the child was not to blame.

Abidos was just a boy. Perhaps he might even one day be able to use the boy to pay Mursili back for his treachery.

"I will do as you ask," Nac conceded at last, "but only under one condition."

"Name your condition," Mursili replied.

"From this day forth, you and I are finished," Nac said. "Except for as it applies to protecting Abidos or to Ida, I want nothing further to do with you."

Mursili nodded shortly.

"Then so shall it be," Nacamakun said. "Now, if you'll excuse me, Your Highness. I have my son's ashes to attend to."

Mursili stood frozen, watched as with rigid shoulders and on stiff legs, the man who had been a second father to him walked out of his life – knowing in his heart of hearts that from that day forward, Nac would be little more than a stranger to him.

With a shaky breath, Mursili came back to life. He trembled in his grief, tears falling unchecked down his face.

Unable to contain his anguish a moment longer, he began picking up things and flinging them around the room - a vase, a chair, some books, anything in his path.

His wife, Queen Gassula, burst into the room at the commotion – just as yet another vase sailed across the room to smash against the wall.

"Mursili!" she cried out, alarmed.

It was rare that her husband gave way to such violent displays of emotion. Something had to be very wrong.

Mursili put the stool he had in his grasp down, turned his wild, grief-stricken gaze upon his beloved.

Gassula went to him, threw her arms around him.

Mursili clutched her tightly. Then, burying his face in her shoulder, he finally let go of the grief he had been holding inside for the last two weeks.

Finally, he mourned for Kadar, for Nacamakun, for Ida and for himself.

VI

Thebes. Upper Egypt.

The gods were on Ida's side - their favor coming in the form of a lunar eclipse.

Pharaoh and his priests were preoccupied with the oracles and rituals that accompanied such celestial events, as were the majority of citizens from the highest of nobles to the lowliest of slaves.

Galeno threw a lavish lunar affair in Thebes. Among the nobles and notables in attendance were the Tomb Governor, the Mayor of Thebes, the Vizier, the High Priest and other high-ranking officials who presided over the Valley of the Kings.

Mursili, for his part, had sent a small group of his most trusted personal guard. The guard was able to, through the use of actual violence and the threat of violence, quarantine the Tomb Guard.

With the tomb officials and tomb guard effectively neutralized, Lord Bietek's laborers came into play.

The laborers came in the form of slaves from distant lands. The promise of their freedom, the freedom of their families, passage back to their homelands and a sizable financial payoff was more than enough to buy their silence.

Still, as an extra measure of precaution, the laborers were blindfolded until they reached Tutankhamun's tomb.

They worked quickly, half of Mursili's guard keeping watch as they did.

Once they finished loading Tutankhamun's coffin and funerary treasures into the wagons, the laborers were once more blindfolded - until they reached the new tomb.

The new tomb had been created a few years before as a gift for none other than Galeno's female lover – the daughter of a Theban aristocrat. Once Galeno's dalliances with a male lover were exposed, the girl had deserted Galeno, thus never receiving the grand gift.

As the sun's shadow began to cover the moon, the laborers unloaded the wagons, were left in relative peace as they lowered Tutankhamun's coffin into the awaiting sarcophagus and arranged his goods.

Done, the men filed out, leaving Ida alone with her dead lover's coffin.

Ida unrolled the scroll Galeno had procured from one of the former High Priests of Aten. In a clear, strong voice, she read the required prayers from the Book of the Dead – prayers meant to consecrate the tomb and allow Tutankh to pass peacefully into the Land of the Dead.

Done, she re-rolled the scroll.

Reaching inside of the sarcophagus, Ida gingerly stroked the golden face of his outer coffin. Tears slipped from her eyes.

"Be at peace, my love," she whispered.

She stared at his coffin for a long moment, etching every detail into her memory. She rose and walked among his things, touched those things he had touched during his lifetime for the last time.

"Hawara!" one of Mursili's men called. "It's time!"

Hurriedly wiping at her eyes with her bare hands, she went outside. The laborers re-entered and slid the heavy stone lid on top of the crypt.

Ida watched helplessly as they began to set the booby traps and wall up her love for all eternity - a part of her wanting to stay down there with him. Almost.

But Ida would not. She could not.

Though she did not believe in such things as prophecy, she believed in Mursili. And if Mursili said it was possible for her to ensure the everlasting glory of the Amarna line and to return Tutankhamun's descendents to power, she would dedicate her life to making it so.

She took one last shuttering breath before she stepped outside into the night air.

The first signs of sunrise inched on the horizon as the laborers finally sealed the outside of the tomb.

It was done.

Ida sighed heavily. She was suddenly exhausted as she watched the laborers being re-blindfolded and set into the wagon. They would remain so until they reached Lord Bietek's estate.

One of Mursili's men, Saphik, noticed her leaning heavily against one of the horses. He had heard tell of this woman from his Great Aunt Clizi. He was surprised that this emaciated waif with coarse, breaking, bleached blonde hair and dark roots was the great beauty who had not only stolen the dead Pharaoh's heart but also the heart of the Hittite king when he was just a boy.

He moved towards her, caught her just as her legs gave way.

VII

It was several days after Nacamakun laid his son to rest before he could bring himself to return to his estate. There were just too many memories there.

He was grateful at least that his estate had already been restored, that all traces of the horror that had been committed there had been removed. Still, none of the survivors could quite meet his eyes. It was as though they all felt somehow guilty, somehow complicit in Kadar's kidnapping and murder.

Still, Nacamakun remembered his vow to Mursili and to Ida. Holding in his grief as much as he could, he had packed Abidos up that very night and moved to a new city where no one knew the child.

Nac would also, over the course of the next few months, piece together exactly what had occurred.

On that most fateful of nights, the captain of Nac's guard had just been returning to the estate, from a meeting with King Mursili, when he saw the invaders.

One of the Egyptian men was passing Nac's son into the arms of another on horseback. The captain had managed to spear one, knocked another from his horse, but there were simply too many. Before he could stop him, the one with Nac's son had broken away from the skirmish and galloped off into the night. There was a sudden sharp pain at the back of the captain's head. Then darkness.

When the captain had awakened many hours later, he had run back inside to find most of the household murdered. In the boys' room he had found the wet nurse raped, lying on the ground with her clothes still disheveled, her skull split opened. He had called to Abidos but had received no reply. He had searched and searched until at last he had found the traumatized little boy hiding in one of the storage bins.

Nacamakun would later learn from Abidos that Kadar had ignored Abidos' persistent tugs, had instead frozen at the sound of the wet nurse's screams. When the screams finally stopped, Abidos had run away to hide while Kadar still stood rooted. The men at last came into the room, found the boy who appeared to be Abidos' age, found the pin on the nightstand next to the bed and assumed that he was Abidos. And just like that, Nac's son was gone.

VIII

Seven years later. Lower Egypt. Lord Bietek's Estate.

A lot had changed over the course of the last seven years.

The Nile Flood Feast, during which Ay had planned to usurp Tutankhamun's tomb, had come and gone.

Pharaoh Ay had been astonished and incensed to find his intended plunder already stolen.

A grand investigation had ensued. Those members of the tomb guard who had foolishly remained after Mursili's men had released them were executed. The Grand Vizier was stripped of power as were the Tomb Governor and the Mayor of Thebes.

Still, no one could be found who knew or admitted to knowing anything about what had happened to the boy king and his treasures.

A few short months later, old Pharaoh Ay had died. Still refusing to admit defeat at the hands of the boy king's supporters, he was buried in Tutankhamun's abandoned tomb nonetheless.

After a brief power struggle, Horemheb easily defeated Nakhtmin and emerged as the new Pharaoh. In an attempt to lend legitimacy to his reign, Pharaoh Horemheb married Ay's daughter and Nefertiti's sister, Mutnodjme. He also set about on a campaign to erase his 4 predecessors from history by dating the start of his reign from Amenhotep III, from the time of Tutankh's grandfather. Just as Ay had before him, Horemheb replaced all of these predecessors' names with his own - on every public monument, statue and royal record.

Taking Ay's intention to restore the polytheistic religions of tradition even further, Horemheb destroyed every record of the monotheistic religion of Aten, the religion instituted by Pharaoh Akhenaten, Tutankh's father. He had even used the blocks from the destroyed Aten temple to fill the interior of the temple of Amun.

In what would prove to be an incredible irony, Horemheb performed the very desecration upon Ay's tomb as Ay had planned for Tutankhamun. Though Ida despised Horemheb, this act gave her a great deal of personal satisfaction.

In Hattusa, things for King Mursili II had finally began to settle down. Horemheb held true to the treaty he and Mursili had made in exchange for what Horemheb had believed to be Tutankhamun's son. Mursili's vassal states also finally seemed, for the most part, to accept his rule - though occasionally one would test him.

Casualties from the plague that had ravaged the Hittite Empire for nearly two decades were becoming few and far between. The fields once again were fertile, yielding more than enough food to feed Mursili's people and even allowing for the building of copious stores at the citadel, a guarantee to ensure against future famine.

Still, all was not peaceful in Hattusa.

Yes, these days most of Mursili's battles were directed inward, took place within the walls of the citadel itself. Mursili's queen, Gassulawiya, had set her sights on the role of Head Priestess – a role still held by his father and brother's widow, the current Queen Dowager or Tawannanna, Mal-Nikal. Although his brother Arnu II's death had opened the path for Mursili to become King, his stepmother Mal-Nikal's grip on the queendom and the accompanying role of High Priestess had not lessened. In fact, with the years, she only seemed to become more powerful.

Taking the side of his beloved queen, Mursili found himself caught between the two factions.

Ida had changed as well. She had regained her health and her former stunning beauty. Her hair had been shorn and regrown into a thick, healthy, though now auburn, mane. The contrast between the unexpected hue of her hair and her brown skin was arresting.

Gone was the reckless, impulsive girl she had been. Now she was deliberate and shrewd.

Though crushed by the news that Nacamakun had taken her son the gods knew where, with Galeno's support, she had thrived and risen to a position of great prominence within Lord Bietek's household. She used her now considerable resources to discretely seek the man and her son out, never giving up hope that one day she and Abidos would be reunited.

Saphik now occupied the role Nacamakun once held as the captain of King Mursili's personal guard. He was also now the primary catalyst for Ida's search for Nac and the main conduit between Mursili and Ida.

Galeno, Saphik and Ida were gathered now in Ida's rooms.

Ida reread the missive King Mursili had sent with Saphik for the third time, still not quite believing what was written there. She sank into a chair, lost in her thoughts as the letter slipped from her grasp.

Galeno went to her side, retrieved the fallen letter. As he read, he too seemed too stunned for words.

Saphik went to Ida, crouched down on his haunches before her.

"Hawara, what is it?" Saphik asked.

"It's Nacamakun," Ida replied. "He and....Kadar have returned to Hattusa."

IX

Saphik stood now looking out over the courtyard, his naked form outlined by the moonlight, lost in thought.

Ida turned over in her bed, realized that she was alone. She opened her eyes, spied Saphik standing there - as beautiful as any Minoan god.

A soft smile played on her lips as she silently admired him. His form was finer than that of any of the statues she had seen on display in Knossos. His golden skin bore the scars of a warrior, each one with its own story to tell. His jet-black hair fell around his face in thick, loose curls. His clear, alarmingly blue eyes - so different from her chocolate brown ones - were piercing when he turned them upon her.

Ida slipped from the bed and padded quietly over to him. She wrapped her arms around him, pressing her naked body to the back of his as she rested her chin on his shoulder.

Saphik smiled, one of the dimples hidden in his cheeks making an appearance, complimenting the dimple that pierced his chin.

"What are thinking about so intently?" Ida asked.

"Nothing," Saphik lied.

Ida slid around to face him. When he pulled her against him, she smiled.

"It certainly didn't look like nothing from where I was standing," she teased.

He smiled and planted a slow, lingering kiss on her lips. "You'll think I'm a fool," he said when he broke the kiss.

"Then you've nothing to fear in telling me," Ida teased. "Because I already do."

She laughed as he tickled her in just the right way, in a very ticklish spot. Grabbing her waist, he turned her around, pulled her firmly against his muscular frame. His hands slowly slid across her skin as his mouth moved to leisurely taste her neck.

She turned her head towards his and their mouths met in a more than demure kiss.

At this rate, she would never find out what was bothering him. She broke the kiss, one hand rising to stroke his face as she gazed into his eyes.

"Tell me," she pressed.

Saphik sighed heavily. "It's Hattusa," he admitted at last.

"What about Hattusa?" Ida pressed.

He released her and moved to the other side of the room.

He turned back to face her. "It's just that I don't want things between us to change." he said.

Ida went to him and cupped his face. She smiled reassuringly. "They won't," she said. "I promise."

"And King Mursili?" Saphik pressed.

"What *about* Mursili?" she asked throwing up her hands.

Saphik placed his hands on his hips. "It's obvious he still has feelings for you."

"What was between Mursili and I was a very long time ago."

"So you deny still having feelings for him?" he asked, unconvinced.

"I will *always* have feelings for Mursili, just as I will always have feelings for Tutankh. But they are the past and you are the here and now."

Placing her hands on his shoulders, she tiptoed and reclaimed his mouth with sweet, coaxing kisses.

"You say that now," he said against her lips.

Ida shoved him forcefully to the bed. She jumped on top of him, straddling him. They both laughed as she bent lower, the curtain of her long hair hanging around them as her mouth sought out his.

"Of course," Ida teased between kisses, "if you're really that concerned, you should probably just marry me already."

Saphik cupped her face, held her still so that he could look into her eyes.

"Are you serious?" he asked, his eyes piercing into hers.

"I assume by the dozen or so times you have asked for my hand that that is what you want," she teased.

"You know it is," he said.

"Then let's do it," she said. "Before we leave here, make me your wife."

Saphik pulled her mouth to his, his kisses no longer playful but full of desire as he rolled her under him and possessed her.

X

The citadel. Hattusa.

There was tension in the air between the four. Ida and Saphik sat in the small private audience chamber with King Mursili and his wife, Gassulawiya.

Though Mursili had introduced Ida to Gassulawiya as Hawara, an emissary from Lord Bietek, Gassula knew well who she was, who she had been to Mursili.

Mursili, for his part, had seemed genuinely happy to see Hawara. His smile, however, had faltered when he dismissed Saphik, only for Ida to ask if Saphik could stay. When Ida went on to explain that Saphik was now her husband, all pretense of merriment had faded from the young king.

Now the four sat in the audience chamber eating their meal, Saphik and Gassula occasionally making attempt at small talk while Mursili's moody glare drifted between Saphik and Ida.

Ida, for her part, tried her hardest to avoid meeting Mursili's gaze. She instead concentrated much too hard on her meal, the hand Saphik had slipped into hers under the table the only thing keeping her from fleeing the chamber all together.

Mursili, still not one to mince words, rose abruptly. He turned, addressed his wife and Saphik. "If the two of you don't mind, I would like to speak with Hawara in private. The two of us have much we need to discuss."

Gassula paled. "Of course, My Liege," she said, rising.

Saphik forced a smile. "Of course, Your Highness," he intoned as he too rose. Ida, however, had still not let go of his hand. He looked down at her. Her eyes were begging him to understand. Giving her a reassuring squeeze, he escorted the Queen from the chamber.

When the door closed between the two, Ida rose. "Why did you do that?" she demanded.

"I did it because I need to talk to my friend," Mursili replied. "Do you have any idea how hard it's been for me since Nacamakun left and my mother died, always hiding what I am from everyone, even my wife?"

"Your mother died?" Ida repeated. "When?"

"Last Spring," he said.

"Why didn't you tell me?" Ida asked, sorrow for him in her eyes. Although he would never admit it, in his own strange way, Mursili was very close to the woman.

"You had enough on your plate with your son missing. I didn't want to add to your burden."

"Mursili," Ida said going to him and wrapping her arms around him.

He took comfort in the familiar feel of her embrace, wrapped his arms around her in return.

They stood there like that for a long moment before Mursili pulled away. He put distance between them.

Ida could see he was deeply troubled.

"Ida," he began. "The visions are getting worse. They had stopped for a time after...after..." He couldn't even bring himself to say the words. "Now, they've started again with a vengeance. Death is in the air again, Ida, only this time, I think it comes for my youngest boy, Hattusili."

"Oh, Mursili," Ida breathed.

"It's Mal-Nikal's doing," Mursili continued. "I can feel it. She has found favor with the dark gods, is using their influence to strike down Hattusili as a warning to us both. Gassula, however, will not heed her and Hattusili grows sicker by the day. If only Gassula would stop, maybe the gods would have mercy and spare our boy."

Mursili frowned, momentarily lost in his thoughts. He returned his attention to Ida. "I love my wife more than I have ever loved any woman and the gods know I speak the truth. It's just that she just keeps at it, just keeps pressing me to remove Mal-Nikal as High Priestess. I have warned Gassula time and time again that the oracles remain on the side of Mal-Nikal, that she must be patient until the gods are ready to accept her but my wife grows more and more impatient with each and every moon.

"Just last night, I found her praying to other gods for their favor - though I have expressly forbidden it."

He shook his head. "Gassula is taking us down a road from which we may not be able to recover, and I don't know what to do about it."

Ida thought on his dilemma. "Perhaps I can help," she offered. "I can get to know Gassula, perhaps try to counsel her in the lack of wisdom of this path."

Mursili laughed dryly. "You, Ida, are absolutely the last person on earth from whom my wife would accept council. Mal-Nikal, perhaps, is another story entirely."

"Mal-Nikal? The woman despises me," Ida replied. "She's hated me ever since Prince Zannanza was murdered."

"Perhaps," Mursili conceded. "But she hates Gassula more. If she buys into the rumors about the two of us perhaps..."

"The friend of my enemy is my friend," Ida finished.

Mursili smiled.

"Alright," Ida conceded. "I'll give it a try though I promise nothing."

"That's more than I could ever ask," he replied.

One of Ida's hands clutched her skirt. "Speaking of sons," she began, "have you seen him?"

"Abidos," Mursili stated.

Ida nodded.

"Only from a distance," Mursili admitted. "Nacamakun won't let me anywhere near him. Of course after what happened to Kadar, who could I blame him?" There was a great deal of pain in Mursili's eyes.

Ida placed a reassuring hand on his shoulder.

Just as she did, the door flew open.

"Oh," Gassula breathed.

Ida's hand dropped to her side.

Gassula was clearly shaken by what she had seen, though it was completely innocent.

"Pardon me," the young queen managed, averting her eyes. "I didn't realize the two of you were still in here."

"It's perfectly fine," Ida reassured her. "Mursili and I are finished here."

Ida looked to Mursili. When he nodded his confirmation, she headed for the door.

"We'll talk later," Mursili called behind her.

Ida nodded.

Leaving the king and queen alone, Ida walked the familiar open-air corridors of the citadel, until she stumbled across Saphik. He was standing with one shoulder leaning against a column, staring unseeingly into the fountain.

"There you are," Ida said, genuinely happy to see him. "I was looking all over for you."

"Where you?" he asked, doubt burning in his eyes.

"Of course I was," she replied with an uncertain smile.

"You sure about that?"

Though Ida's smile faltered, she refused to bite. She was in no mood to argue with him.

Instead she turned her attention to the fountains and the beautifully landscaped gardens that surrounded them.

She sighed contently. "This was always one of my favorite places," she mused.

"I'm sure it was," he replied, tossing one of the pebbles in his hand into the water.

Ida turned to face him, forced a smile. "It's getting late," she said, "and it's been a long day. What say we go on up to our rooms and get out of these clothes?"

Saphik didn't reply. He just stood staring at the fountains.

"Saphik, please don't do this," she said.

"Do what, Ida?" he asked. "I'm not the one already having secret meetings with my former love."

"For the sake of the gods, Saphik. It wasn't like that."

"Then what was it like, Ida?" he pressed.

"He just needed a friend," his wife replied. "That's all."

"Okay. So what did your *friend* need to talk to you about so urgently that he kicked his own wife and your husband out of the room?"

Ida looked away.

Saphik chuckled humorlessly. "And so it begins," he said.

"So what begins?"

"The lying, the keeping secrets, the sneaking around." He laughed that same hollow laugh. "And we haven't even been here a full day yet."

"Saphik, please," Ida begged.

"Please what, Ida?"

"I chose you, Saphik. You. Please don't push me away."

"So I should just wait until he steals you from me instead?" He smirked, his hurt in his eyes. "I should have known that it was too good to be true when the former consort of a Pharaoh and a King decided to slum it with a solider."

Ida slapped him.

"I'll not hear anymore of this," she said, her chest heaving and anguished tears pooling in her eyes. "I married you because I love you, because I want to be your wife, because I want to have a life, a family with you."

She blinked back her tears, turned to leave. She stopped in her tracks. "And for the record, Saphik, the only man who can take me from you is you."

XI

The next morning, Ida found Mursili in the stables. Like clockwork, he still rode first thing in the morning. Ida smiled.

Hearing her approach, Mursili looked up at her. "You look like hell," he greeted.

Ida laughed inspite of herself. "You don't look like you had such a good night yourself."

Mursili nodded agreement. "It seems it is still too new for either of our spouses – us being in the same place, at the same time."

Ida nodded.

"You should go see Nac," Mursili suggested. "He'd be happy to see you and you, in turn, would be happy to see your son."

Ida nodded again. "I was thinking the same thing," she admitted. "I just didn't want to hurt you by bringing it up first."

"It's fine," he replied. He eyed her thoughtfully for a long moment.

"What?" she asked.

He sighed heavily. Now was as good a time as any. "I think we need to give Gassula and Saphik some time to get used to the idea of us being in each other's orbits again, to try to avoid being alone together as much as possible until they do."

Ida thought it over for a long moment. "You're probably right," she admitted. "Still...."

"I know," he replied giving her a small smile.

Ida turned to go.

She turned back to face him. "Just promise me one thing," she said.

"Anything," he replied.

"Promise me that they won't come between us, that we'll always be as close as we are now."

"Always," Mursili replied without hesitation. "No matter what."

Their eyes held for a long moment before Ida pulled her gaze away. She stared down at the ground for a moment before her gaze returned to his. "And about that matter we discussed."

"Second thoughts?" he asked.

"No," she reassured him. "I just want you to know I will be working on it no matter what. Even if I can't take care of the matter myself, I will see to it that it is handled discretely."

Mursili smiled. "Thanks."

Ida returned his smile. "You're welcome... Great King," she added with a mischievous glint in her eye.

The two laughed.

Ida looked back to the citadel. "I should be going," she said. "Saphik will be up soon."

Mursili nodded his understanding. He stood watching her go, until he could see her no longer. Then mounting his stead, he spurred the animal into a run.

Saphik couldn't help but panic when he awoke to find Ida gone. He had made the mistake of allowing himself a few drinks with his regiment after Mursili had thrown him and Gassula out of the audience chamber. Ok, if he was honest with himself, more than a few.

Rather than lift his spirits, the drink had only managed to dampen them further. All of his old insecurities came rushing to the surface, his mind unable to focus on anything but the way Mursili had brooded as his gaze drifted between he and Ida, on not only the way Mursili had had the audacity to remove him from his wife but on the way that Ida had let him.

By the time Ida had found him by the fountain, he was more than a little drunk, more than a little jealous and feeling more than a little spiteful.

When she had left him there at the fountain at the end of their argument, he had felt like a gigantic ass. Instead of going to her and begging for her forgiveness, he had instead taken the coward's way out. He had waited until the light had gone out in their bedroom before he had stuck into the main chamber, made himself a makeshift bed on the floor and slept there instead.

As the first glints of dawn broke, he opened his eyes. He had slowly pushed open the door to their bed chamber and watched her sleep. She was so beautiful. Who could blame Mursili or any man for that matter for still desiring her?

He had crept further into the room, closing the door behind him. Slowly, silently, he slipped into the bed next to her. He lay staring at her for a long moment, drinking in the sight of her before at last he gave in to his fatigue.

Now here he was in their bed alone. Had she wised up and left him? he wondered.

Just as he was about to rise and go in search of her, she came back into the room. She was dressed impeccably, had obviously been up for quite some time judging from the elaborate hairstyle into which she had arranged her mane. She carried a large tray in her arms.

"I brought breakfast," she announced.

Saphik gingerly sat up in the bed, feeling more like an ass than ever now. He couldn't even meet her gaze.

Ida set the tray on the table next to the bed.

"Well?" she said. "Go on. Eat up."

He finally forced his eyes to meet hers, his sorrow filling them. "Ida, I - " he began.

"Ssshh," she said bending to cover his mouth with hers. They kissed for a long moment before Ida pulled away. "Hurry before it gets too cold," she said.

"I don't care if it gets cold," he said pulling her mouth back down upon his.

"But I do," she said pulling away again. "We have a long ride ahead of us today."

"Ride?" he asked. "Where?"

"To see my son."

XII

As their party pulled up outside of Nacamakun's new estate, Ida was pensive.

"Nervous?" Saphik asked.

"A little," Ida admitted. "It's been such a long time. What if he doesn't want to see me?"

"Who? Nacamakun or Kadar?"

Ida shrugged. "Either," she replied. "Both."

"Well," Saphik reasoned, "we certainly won't find out just sitting here staring at the gate."

Ida sighed heavily. "I hate it when you're right," she said.

Saphik dismounted before going to her mount and helping her down. She stood there uncertainly, staring at the gate, one of her hands clutching her dress.

Her heart dropped in her chest as she looked at her husband.

"What?" he asked.

"I don't want to hurt you again," she began. "But...."

"You want to see them alone first," Saphik supplied.

Ida nodded, sorrow in her eyes. "It's not you. I swear. It's just that maybe they would be more comfortable if it was just me...at first."

Saphik smiled reassuringly. "It's fine," he said. "It makes sense."

Still, she stood rooted. After a few long moments, she sighed heavily. "Who am I kidding?" she said. "I might not even be welcome myself."

He cupped her face and looked into her eyes. "Of course you're welcome. You did nothing wrong and you have every right to see the boy. You're the only mother he has ever known."

Though Ida felt a pang of guilt at never having told him that Kadar was really her son Abidos, she took strength from his confidence. She smiled softly and nodded.

"You're right," she said. "Besides, what do I have to lose right?"

"Right."

"Ok," she said taking a deep breath. "Let's go."

As soon as they walked to the threshold, the gate opened. Ida and Saphik exchanged a surprised glance.

"We've been expecting you," the men at the gate offered. "The commander is in the audience chamber."

The couple entered the compound.

"Right this way," one of the men directed.

Ida kissed Saphik quickly before she left to follow the man.

Ida took in the new estate as she went. It was nothing like his previous estate. She suspected that that was much of the compound's appeal for Nacamakun.

It seemed to take an eternity for Ida to reach the audience room. Once inside, she found the man staring out of the window at the courtyard below.

"He's a handsome one," Nac said without even bothering to turn around. "He seems familiar. Who is he?"

"His name is Saphik. He came with you to Egypt to find me."

Nac nodded. "Ah, yes. Saphik. Clizi's great nephew. He's Captain of the King's Personal Guard now is he not?"

"Yes," Ida replied. She anxiously wrung her hands.

He turned to face her. "You look beautiful as always," he said.

"Thank you," she replied. The once handsome middle-aged man now looked many years beyond his age. There was a sadness, a weariness about him.

"Does the king know about you and Saphik?" he asked.

The king. It was the 2nd time he had avoided saying Mursili's name.

"Yes," she replied. "Mursili knows Saphik is my husband now."

Ida didn't fail to notice how Nac winced at the mention of Mursili's name.

Nacamakun chuckled, pleased. "The king can't be happy about it."

"Mursili has a wife, a family. Why can't I have the same?"

"Why not indeed?" he replied, his mirth fading. "Just make sure that that beautiful boy you call a husband watches his back."

"What are you saying?" Ida demanded, though she knew exactly what Nac was implying. "Mursili would never hurt my husband - someone who makes me happy, someone I love."

"Wouldn't he?" Nac replied. "I used to think I knew the king. I used to think I knew what he was and wasn't capable of. I was wrong.

"Face it, Ida. The boy you used to know is gone. The man that remains cares for nothing but his prophecy and he's willing to sacrifice anyone and anything in the mad pursuit of his hallucinations."

"How can you say that?" Ida defended. "You used to believe just as much as he."

"That was before he decided to betray me."

"Mursili had nothing - "

"To do with what happened to Kadar?" Nac smirked. "That's where you're wrong, Ida."

His eyes narrowed. "Just how much has he told you about that time?"

AMARNA BOOK II: BOOK OF HAWARA

"He told me he was sent a vision that I was in danger so he sent you to Lord Bietek's estate to find me. While you were investigating my disappearance....." Ida couldn't even bring herself to say it.

"While I was investigating your disappearance?" Nac repeated with a laugh.

"I can understand why you would blame Mursili for what happened but -"

"You understand nothing!" Nac yelled at her, his pain and anguish etched in his features and burning in his eyes. He crossed the room to her, his eyes burning into hers. "I guess Mursili neglected to tell you the entire truth.

"You see, Ida. Mursili had a much broader vision. Yes, that you were in danger was part of it but he also saw what was to happen to the boys. But, rather than warn me or try to protect them or substitute some other poor children for ours, he decided that it should not only run its course but that he should help it along. That's right, Ida. Mursili sent me away on a wild goose chase while he told Galeno your true location.

"While I was in Egypt chasing shadows, he made a deal with Horemheb - exchanging the life of your son for a peace treaty with Egypt. Of course Mursili knew well that it would be my son, Kadar, and not Abidos that would ultimately been sacrificed. Still, he did nothing to stop it. He just let it happen."

"Oh, Nac," Ida gasped, tears flooding her eyes. She shook her head, could not accept that Mursili would do such a thing to someone he loved as dearly as he loved Nac. "There must be some kind of misunderstanding."

Nac shook his head, grabbing her arms. "There is none. He admitted to it out of his own mouth. He just kept going on about the prophecy and about how the Storm God required that it specifically be Kadar and about how it would all mean something in the end."

Tears glistened in Nac's eyes. "It was as if he had stepped on my toe or stolen a trinket from me. As if the greater good would be consolation to a man whose only son was just brutally murdered. And do you know what he asked of me next, even as my son's ashes were still hot?"

Ida shook her head, tears streaming down her face.

"He asked me to deny my son, to pretend that it was Abidos that had died instead of Kadar. It made me sick to my stomach. I couldn't even stand to look at him anymore. I couldn't stand to be anywhere near him or Hattusa anymore. I had to go."

Ida sank to the ground. She couldn't accept a word of what she had just heard. Yet, she knew Nac was not one to lie.

At long last, she looked up at Nac. "This is all my fault," she said. "Isn't it?"

A great sob shook her frame. "Oh, Nac. I'm so sorry."

She buried her head in her hands as her sobs grew more violent.

Nac sank to his haunches next to her, pulled her into his embrace.

"Ida, you are not to blame," he said. "You had no way of knowing that Mursili could be capable of such a thing. I had known him his whole life and even I never suspected."

He tilted her head to look him in the eye. "Look, Ida. I came back to Hattusa for you, because you didn't deserve to suffer the loss of a child like I had, because of what Mursili had done. If I blamed you at all, I would have never come back."

Ida nodded her understanding.

"You need to pull yourself together for your son's sake," Nac said. "He'll be here any moment now."

Ida took a few deep breaths as she struggled to bring her emotions back under control.

"That a girl," he said helping her to stand. "You were always a strong one."

"Is there somewhere I can wash up?" Ida asked.

Nac nodded. He called in one of his men and directed him to lead her to one of the spare rooms.

XIII

Hattusa. Nacamakun's estate.

Once in the spare room, Ida was left alone. She sank down onto the bed, Nacamakun's words replaying in her head over and over again.

She shook her head. Nac had to be wrong. He *had* to be. The Mursili she knew would never have....

Ida shook her head again.

It was a misunderstanding. It just had to be.

Whatever the case, Ida would get to the bottom of it when she returned to the citadel. For now, she just needed to pull herself together, to see her son.

Ida rose and went to the basin. She splashed water on her face. Drying it, she looked in the mirror. Her eyes were moist and bloodshot. Her golden skin was red and blotchy from her eyebrows clear down to her nose. She couldn't face Saphik in the state she was in, let alone her son.

"Get it together, Ida," she said to her reflection. "Think of Abidos. Think of your son."

She instantly started to calm, felt the heat begin to fade from her face and with it the signs of her emotional distress. She took a few deep, calming breaths.

The sound of laughter caught her off guard. She rushed to the terrace, looked over the railing.

Ida's heart skipped a beat. It was him. It was Abidos.

He was playing some sort of sword play game with Saphik and some of Nacamakun's men. Others of the staff were laughing and cheering them on.

Ida flew from the room and down the corridor. Only at the threshold to the courtyard did she stop and catch her breath. The last thing she wanted was to scare the boy during their first meeting since he was a year and a half old.

She stared at him from the shadows in amazement. He was almost 11 now and tall for his age. His hair was long in the Hittite way and he was dressed every inch the high ranking Hittite son. He was amazingly skilled with the wooden sword and shield for a boy his age, his lean muscular form a testament to the intense training regiment Nacamakun had obviously instituted for the boy.

The resemblance to Ida was striking though she could still see some of his father in him – especially when he laughed.

Ida smiled as he parried Saphik's lunge with a merry cackle.

Nacamakun was the first to spy Ida as she stared at boy from the shadows. He waved her into the courtyard.

Ida discretely made her way to Nac's side.

Catching a glimpse of her from the corner of his eye, Saphik surrendered to Abidos in a grand, comic flourish that set not only the boy but all of the observers into a hysteria of cheers and laughter.

Nac took Ida by the elbow and led her through the spectators to the boy and man in the center.

Saphik smiled brightly at her. However, as she drew nearer, his smile faltered. Although she might be able to fool others who did not know her, he could tell she had been crying – hard.

What the hell had Nacamakun said to her?

His smile gone, Saphik turned to glare at Nacamakun.

Nac ignored him. Instead, he turned his attention to the boy.

"Father," the child said, flying into Nacamakun's arms.

Nac pulled away from the embrace, his hands on the child's arms. "Well fought young solider," Nac said.

"Thank you, commander," the boy said standing up straight and tall.

Nac smiled. "Remember how I told you we would have lots of visitors when we returned to Hattusa?"

The child nodded.

"You've already met Saphik," Nac continued. "He's the Chief of King Mursili's personal guard. He used to be under my command."

The child nodded again.

"Now I want you to meet his wife, Hawara. She's an emissary from Lower Egypt, sent by Lord Bietek."

The boy looked up at Ida, was instantly struck by her beauty. He had never seen such a beautiful woman in all his short life.

Or had he?

Abidos's eyes narrowed and his head tilted as he tried to place her.

Yes, there was definitely something familiar about this Hawara.

"I'm your aunt," Ida supplied. "Your mother was my sister."

Satisfied with her explanation, the boy smiled - his short-lived suspicions already dissipating.

Ida held out a hand, a smile lighting up her face as she blinked back happy tears.

"Hi," she said. "I'm Hawara."

The boy took it. "I'm honored to make your acquaintance," the boy said. "My name is Kadar."

Ida's heart lurched at the mention of the name Kadar.

"You're very beautiful," the boy said eliciting smiles from those gathered.

"So are you," Ida said with a happy laugh.

The boy frowned. "I'm a boy. Boys can't be beautiful."

They all laughed once more.

"Of course not," Ida said. "I meant handsome."

The rest of the afternoon was spent pleasantly enough as mother and son became reacquainted. As much as Saphik was dying to know what had happened between Nac and Ida, he knew better than to push it, especially not now. If he had learned anything over the course of the time he had known Ida, it was that he would never have all of her, that there would always be things she kept from him.

As much as he wanted to call her on her lie – that she was not Kadar's birth mother, pressing her only caused her to push him away. Especially now, after their recent row over Mursili, and with her just now becoming reacquainted with a boy who was obviously her son, he would have to swallow his own stung pride and hurt feelings and just be there for her should she need him.

After the boy retired for the night and after Ida had sat next to him stroking his hair and watching him sleep for a time, Nacamakun, Ida and Saphik went to his private chambers for a late supper.

Ida was quiet as she absently picked at her food.

"You alright?" Saphik asked.

Ida nodded.

"You don't have to go back there you know," Nac sad. "You can stay here as long as you want."

Ida looked up at him. "You know I can't do that. Not now."

"Why not?" Saphik asked.

"If I abandon him too, he'll have no one," she said, her eyes on Nac.

"What do you mean he'll have no one?" Saphik pressed.

Though he was in the room, he still felt like he wasn't. He sank back in his chair and gave up trying to compete with Ida's past.

"All he had was you, me and his mother," Ida replied, still speaking to Nacamakun. "You left and his mother passed. If I leave him too..."

Nac's brow furrowed as he considered her words. "His mother passed?" he asked. "When?"

"Last spring," Ida replied.

"I didn't know," Nac admitted. He had always been fond of Mursili's mother – banished witch or not.

"Nac, no one else knows," she said cryptically - knowing full well that Nac would catch her true meaning. The oracle was one thing. But having visions in the land of the Hittites - a direct unmonitored, uncontrolled link to the gods was a very dangerous thing, especially when those visions didn't align with what the powers that be wanted them to. Mursili's mother had been exiled, in part, because of it.

Nac didn't reply.

She studied him for a long moment before she spoke again. "On top if it all, Sarri is still in Assyria, his youngest boy Hattusili has fallen ill and Gassula is obsessed with becoming high priestess, pitting him against Mal-Nikal and her supporters. Though he holds it in, he's suffering.....and not just because of the present."

Though Ida saw a crack in Nac's angry exterior, he replied: "He brought it all upon himself."

"Perhaps. Still, no matter what he may or may not have done, I owe him. I owe him my life and the life of Kadar. If it wasn't for him, neither of us would be here."

"If it wasn't for him, the other boy *would*," Nac countered.

"You don't know that," Ida replied.

"No," he said. "I don't. And thanks to him we never even got the chance to find out."

"He's doing the best he can. I have to believe that."

"Of course you do. If he's right, your line stands to gain everything."

Ida looked as if he had slapped her.

Nac immediately felt guilty. "I'm sorry," he apologized. "I shouldn't have said that."

"It's fine," she said. "Maybe I deserved that. If I were you I might even have worse to say. Still, I have to talk to him, to hear his side of things."

"You have to know you can't trust him now," Nac said.

"Maybe not like I used to but I have to have faith in him. I made a promise to someone very dear to me – a promise that I mean to keep. If Mursili is the conduit that will help me to do so, I will have to stand by him. I have to believe that all we've lost – you, me...him – was for a reason. I have to believe that there is some kind of great, universal justice at work, that it isn't all for naught. Otherwise, what would be the point of us going on?"

"The point is in that room down the hall, asleep," Nac replied. "The promise of the future is in that boy's smile. I'm done with..." he glanced at Saphik. "Mursili."

Ida nodded. "I understand. Just know that he hasn't given up on you."

Nac smirked. He took a long drink. "You have chosen your path and I have chosen mine."

Ida nodded her understanding. She seemed uneasy. "I hope this won't - "

"Of course not," Nac said waiving her concern away. "I'm not going anywhere. This is my home. This is Kadar's home now too and you and Saphik are welcome.... anytime."

Ida smiled. "I'll hold you to that."

She rose.

"It's getting late," she said. "We should be heading back now."

Nac nodded as he too rose. "I'll see you out."

Saphik stood watching the two for a long moment before he too rose and followed.

XIV

Hattusa. Royal Citadel.

The ride back to the Citadel was tense. Neither spoke – Saphik brooding and Ida lost in her thoughts.

As soon as she entered their suite, Ida had the servants draw her a bath.

Saphik watched as Ida undressed.

"So this is it?" he asked. "Five years as lovers, barely one month of marriage and it's over?"

Ida turned at last to face him. "Is that what you want?" she asked, her impatience thinly veiled. "Is that why you're acting like this?"

"Of course not," he replied. "I just want you to start treating me like your husband… and not just in the bedroom either."

Ida chuckled humorlessly.

"I'm too tired for this right now," she said slipping on her robe and leaving the room.

Saphik followed. Ida had just sank into the welcoming warm water and closed her eyes when he spoke again.

"Ever since we got here I feel more like a pretty decoration, a body guard more than your husband," he said.

Ida opened her eyes. "What do you want me to say? You knew well there were parts of my life I can never share with you and you've known since the day we met."

"Things are different now. I was just a fling back then. Now -"

"Now *what*?" she demanded angrily. "Now, I'm supposed to magically transform into a completely different person because I became your wife?

"You *knew* how I was. You knew there were things I can never speak to you about. You were fine with it.

"At least you pretended to be. Now, you're acting like a spoiled child."

"A spoiled child?" he asked, wounded. "I'm a spoiled child because I want my wife to stop treating me like a stranger, because I want my wife to let me in, to trust me?"

"I *do* trust you!" she replied, frustrated. "You know that! I have told you things I've never told anyone. I have never kept anything that was solely my secret to share from you. However, when it comes to confidences I have been entrusted with, confidences that involve other people." She shook her head. "I can't share with you that which isn't mine alone."

"If you really trusted me -"

"I'd prove it, right?" Ida supplied. Her blood was boiling.

The warm water suddenly losing its appeal, she the left the bath, rewrapped and tied her robe around herself. She stalked back into the bedroom, Saphik on her heels.

She whirled to face him. "You'd have me prove I find you trustworthy by making myself untrustworthy?" She laughed again.

He grabbed one of her arms, pulled her to him. "Don't you dare mock me, Ida," he warned.

Ida snatched her arm away from him. "Or what?" she taunted.

Their gazes locked for a long heated moment before Saphik took a few steps away from her.

He shook his head. "Maybe this was a mistake," he said.

Ida was momentarily stunned into silence.

She blinked back the tears that threatened. "Is that how you feel?" she asked.

He ran a hand over his face. "I don't want to," he admitted, "but how do you expect me to feel? How would you feel if you were me?"

Ida went to him. She cupped his face with one hand. "Saphik, my life is complicated. It might well always be. I love you and the last thing I want is to lose you."

"Then let me in," he whispered, stroking her face.

Ida sighed. "I can't," she said. "Not into this. Not now. Not ever. You're the one thing, the one person that I have that's pure, that isn't complicated, that has nothing to do with the past."

Her eyes traveled his face then returned to his eyes. "I need you more than you will ever know, Saphik. I need you with me when it all becomes too much for me to bear. I need you to hold me when I feel like the whole world is closing in on me and I can't hold the pain inside. I need you to tell me I can do this, I can survive this - even when you don't know what's going on or that I can. I need you to believe in me, to have faith in us - even when I give you every reason to doubt. I need you to be my strength.

"You're my light. You make the dark thoughts disappear. Please don't take that away from me," she begged.

At that moment she looked so earnest, so lost, so beautiful that any thoughts Saphik had of saving himself while he still had the will dissolved. Instead, he found his lips crashing down upon hers.

It was not long before Ida's robe floated to the floor, before she lay naked underneath him. Heartache quickly gave way to passion as mouths and hands made the reassurances their words had not.

The last few hours of the night passed unnoticed as they spent them lost in one another, as they shared the most intense night of lovemaking they had ever shared.

But even then, even as Saphik's hands moved across her skin, it was not Saphik's hands that heated her flesh. Even as his mouth brought her to dizzying new heights, it was not Saphik's mouth that set her ablaze. Even as her nails bit into the flesh of his back, it was not Saphik who moved within her.

It was daybreak as at last Saphik drifted off into a satiated slumber, his body entwined with his wife's.

Ida waited until she was sure he was deep in sleep before she carefully detangled herself from him.

Sliding from the bed, Ida padded quietly to her travel trunk. Pulling out clothing, she began to dress herself.

She needed to see Mursili.

XV

It was a dream that was not a dream. King Mursili had had visions long and often enough to tell the difference.

Though the images changed and the intensity of the visions was increasing, the message was always the same. It was time for another sacrifice, and the gods wanted his youngest son, his most beloved child, his Hattusili.

Mursili awoke with a cry. His body was drenched in sweat and his breath leaving him in heavy gasps.

Queen Gassulawiya sat up next to him, one hand on his shoulder. Her face was drawn with concern. "What is it?" she asked.

Mursili sat up slowly, his mind still reeling from the images the gods had implanted there.

"Another nightmare?" Gassula pressed. He had been having them more and more often.

Mursili slowly met her gaze. As much as he wanted to tell his wife the truth, he knew he never could. A husband with visions might well be the ammunition his wife needed to usurp the role of High Priestess. However, it might also be just the ammunition needed to dethrone him or worse – the anti-"witch" hysteria cultivated by his father still not completely eradicated from Hatti.

So, instead of telling his wife the truth, he nodded.

Gassula stroked his face. "Maybe you should see someone," she said.

Mursili pulled away from her. "I'll not visit one of your witch doctors," he snapped.

Gassula fell silent, her face drawn.

Mursili studied her for a long moment before he climbed from their bed.

The young queen watched as he moved across the room to his writing stand. He opened his great book and began to write.

"Perhaps you suffer so because Mal-Nikal is using her power against you," Gassula suggested. "A woman like that has no place as a conduit to the gods."

Mursili glanced up at her, his eyes piercing. "Or perhaps I suffer so because my wife has become so greedy for Mal-Nikal's power, a power for which her very gluttony proves her unworthy."

He went back to his furious scribbling as though he hadn't spoken.

Gassula was hurt. She blinked back her tears as she rose from the bed and crossed the room towards him.

Mursili immediately closed the book and snapped the lock into place before she could see what he had written. Taking the book with him, he moved passed her and towards his dressing chamber.

"Where are you going at this hour?" Gassula asked.

"The temple," he replied simply.

King Mursili and his guard were just coming to the main gate of the citadel when he heard Ida call to him.

He drew his escort to a halt, watched as she ran to him.

"I need to see you," she cried before she could even catch her breath.

"I'm on my way to the temple," he replied. "We can talk when I return."

Ida could see it in his eyes. Something was wrong – very wrong.

Whether Mursili knew it or not, he needed her.

"It's urgent," Ida insisted.

Mursili studied her for a long moment. "If it's that urgent, you can come along," he said.

Ida's head turned to gaze at the window of her suite.

His eyes followed hers. "I can send Jonkina to advise him and you can take over Jonkina's stead."

Ida returned her gaze to Mursili's. She was in no mood for yet another argument with Saphik. Yes, she would rather ask for forgiveness later than permission now.

She nodded her assent.

Jonkina dismounted. Once Ida was settled on his stead, he started back on foot.

The escort restarted their journey.

Tawannanna Mal-Nikal watched with interest from her window.

So *that* was the infamous Ida, she pondered, a slow smirk creeping across her face.

Nikal had always been quite perceptive. Still, it would not have taken anyone of great discernment to catch the undercurrent of attraction between the King and his former charge – the intense, unspoken chemistry.

All it would take was the right match for it to turn to flame - a flame that would burn pretty little Gassulawiya and thus her bastard of a stepson in the process.

Nikal's smile widened.

She would use Ida to drive a wedge between Gassula and Mursili. Then, when Mursili had only Ida left, Nikal would expose "Hawara's" true identity.

Who among the nobles would dare support a king who still consorted with an Egyptian spy, with his brother's betrayer no less? It would be enough to plant the seeds of

AMARNA BOOK II: BOOK OF HAWARA

dissention among his supporters and to shift them to her side. As the walls closed in on the two, while Mursili was down, she would send word to Pharaoh Horemheb that his little phoenix Ida has risen from the dead.

Mal-Nikal had met Horemheb on multiple occasions. He was a narcissistic, insecure little man who methodically destroyed all that reminded him of his betters – his Amarna predecessors and all who remained loyal to them. His ego would not allow him to suffer that Ida still lived, that the most loyal of all to the last of the Amarnas still drew breath. He would come after her.

Whether Mursili chose to continue to protect her or to send her away, he would still lose in the end. He was too pious, humane, sensitive and conscientious when it came right down to it – especially when it came to those he loved. He would never simply hand her over to Horemheb no matter how much Horemheb threatened. That Mursili would not give in to Horemheb's overblown ego would infuriate the small man that ruled their neighboring kingdom. It would be enough to destroy the treaty that had kept the peace between the two nations these last seven years.

Even those supporters who had not abandoned Mursili at the revelation of his consortship with the enemy would not dare to stand by his side should he bring the threat of war down upon the heads of the still recovering kingdom. They would beg the Tawannanna to take over control of the throne.

That poor, beautiful Saphik would be hurt and left broken-hearted in the end was a shame, but Nikal would do her best to console him.

She sighed, her hands slowly sliding across her body at the thought of Saphik.

She shuddered as one hand slid between her thighs. It had been so long since she had ridden a stallion such as Saphik.

Too long.

XVI

Temple of the Sun Goddess Arinna.

Ida waited until she and Mursili were alone before she spoke.

"Have your visions gotten worse?" she asked.

Mursili nodded.

He sighed heavily, suddenly quite weary.

"There is no longer any doubt," he said. "The gods demand the life of Hattusili."

"Oh, Mursili," Ida whispered, tears glistening in her eyes.

Mursili finally let the tears he held in in front of Gassula fall.

"Hattusili grows weaker by the day," he continued. "I see his mother sitting next to his bed every day, helpless, trying everything she can think of to heal him, not knowing that nothing she does will save him. And I can't tell her a thing. I can't tell her that soon he will close his eyes forever."

A great sob shook Mursili.

Ida went to him and wrapped her arms around him. He clung to her, buried his head in her neck as he let out his grief.

His pain cut Ida to her core. She too began to sob.

They stood like that for a long time, until finally Mursili was able to pull himself together again.

When at last he pulled away from her, he put distance between them.

He turned his back to her, his tear blurred gaze fixed upon the idol at the front of the room.

"Look at me," he said. "I'm such a hypocrite. I'm getting exactly what I deserve for what I did to Nacamakun. I sacrificed his son's life to appease the gods – a man who was never anything but good and loyal to my family's son."

He turned back to face her, swallowed past the lump in his throat. "That's what you wanted to talk to me about isn't it? About if what Nacamakun had to say about me was true?"

Ida nodded, her own tears still flowing down her face though her sobs had quieted.

"Well, it is. Every word." He laughed humorlessly. "And you want to hear something funny? The day he returned, the day he confronted me, he asked if I would be so willing to make the same sacrifice if it was my son. And you know what I told him?"

Ida shook her head.

"I told him that when the time came for me to make such a terrible sacrifice, as the one I chose to make for him, that 'I shall do what must be done.'"

Mursili laughed that same hard, hollow laugh.

He laughed harder and harder until the tears were streaming down his face again.

Ida held herself as her heart broke for him.

He went to her, held her by her arms. "Get away from me, Ida," he said. "Far away from me."

Mursili cupped her face, a thousand emotions burning in his eyes. "Everyone who comes near me, everyone who loves me pays a price – a terrible price. If something were to happen to you because of me...." His brow furrowed. He couldn't even bring himself to say it.

His eyes drifted to her mouth and then back to her eyes before he took a few stumbling steps away from her.

He closed his eyes briefly, took a couple of calming breaths to regain his focus. Being so close to her had a dizzying effect on him. That he saw those same desires mirrored in her eyes in that moment did nothing to stem the pounding of his heart.

When he opened them again, Ida was staring at him, her confusion mirroring his own.

Finally, she spoke. "I won't leave you," she said. "Especially not now. Who will you have left if I do?"

Mursili bowed his head. He sighed shakily. It took great effort for him to regain his composure.

"Leave me now," he said as he moved past her to the alter. "I have much to do."

Ida nodded. She stood staring at him for a long moment as he opened the trunk of blessed oils and offerings he had brought with him, before she turned and left him to his prayers.

Saphik was in the training yard with his men.

He took his pain out on any man foolish enough to tangle with him. So far seven lay in the dirt at his feet, beaten and bloodied.

After the night he and Ida had had, he had fallen asleep, sure that their bond was stronger than ever. Yet, when he had awakened, he had found not his wife but one of his men in his room.

Worse still, the man had brought tidings that his new bride had ridden off with the king, and without so much as doing him the courtesy of telling him to his face.

Saphik snarled, the eighth man falling as Saphik's shield smashed into his face.

"You might want to take it easy on them," Jonkina said stepping between Saphik and the next man in line for a beating. "It isn't their fault."

Saphik grunted and threw down his sword and shield.

Jonkina formally ended the exercise and turned his attention to the fallen men.

Saphik stalked determinedly towards the soldier's bath house. He stood under the cool water as one of the servants pumped it in. Even the feel of the refreshing liquid against his skin did little to cool his hot blood.

The temple of the Sun Goddess his ass.

Saphik closed his eyes, fought to drive the jealous thoughts from his mind. His thoughts, however, would not obey. He found himself bombarded with images of Ida and the King doing all sorts of things to each other – things his wife had no business doing with any man but he.

Saphik hurriedly opened his eyes again. He would never let that happen. If he even imagined he smelled another man on her, king or otherwise....

The water stopped. Saphik swore softly as he wrapped a drying cloth about his waist and strode around to the pump room. Instead of the boy whose job it was to keep the water running, he found Mal-Nikal.

She appreciatively took in his half naked form.

"Tawannanna," he breathed, hurriedly prostrating himself before her. "Forgive me. I had no idea..."

"Neither did I," she replied with a lecherous smirk. "Please rise."

Saphik did as he was bade, stoically bore Mal-Nikal's bold perusal of his strong, hard, glistening body. She could just see the outline of his member through the drying cloth. Impressive indeed.

When her eyes returned to his, she spoke again. "Did my stepson not grant you leave to celebrate your nuptials?"

"He did, your highness," he replied.

"Yet, you're here," she replied. "Strange. And here I chastised and sent away the water boy for wasting water."

"Forgive him, my queen. It was all my doing."

Mal-Nikal looked past him. "And where is your blushing bride?" she asked. "Hawara isn't it?"

Saphik hesitated before he answered. "At the temple of the Sun Goddess."

"The Sun Goddess," she repeated with furrow brow. "The temple of Arinna, the King's patron goddess?"

Saphik nodded shortly. Though he did his best to remain impassive, a muscle spasmed in his jaw.

Nikal smirked. This was going to be easier than she thought. "And you let her go alone?"

"She's not alone."

"No?" she pressed.

"She is with the king and his men," Saphik managed though the very words made the bile rise in his throat.

"The king?" Nikal replied. "That's strange. Mursili was never one to take to strangers easily, yet here he is taking her to temple with him, and not just any temple at that, but the temple of his patron goddess. She must have made quite a strong impression on him indeed."

Saphik's blood was boiling, she could tell.

"This is not their first meeting," Saphik said. "She was a high-ranking member of Lord Bietek's household."

"Oh, so that's how you met!" Nikal exclaimed. "She was one of his castoffs."

Saphik could not contain the hard glare that pierced into Nikal. "My wife was never any man's castoff."

"Oh you mistake me," she said. "Hittite is not my native tongue. Sometimes I mix my words. What I meant was..." she pretended to think for a long moment. "Ah, yes, emissary."

Goosebumps came to Saphik's skin.

"Look at that," Nikal said, her eyes once again traveling down his body. "I have kept you far too long. Please forgive me."

"Your highness," he replied. He stood rooted for a long moment as she left the pump room.

XVII

Queen Gassulawiya had insisted on attending Tawannanna Mal-Nikal's invocation - much to Nikal's delight.

Nikal relished every opportunity to rub the fact that she was still the true Queen, the High Priestess, in the young upstart's face.

That the ceremony was outdoors and would afford all of the attendants, most especially Gassula, a prime view of the King and Ida's return pleased Nikal all the more. Now if only she could find a way to get Saphik to come down.

Nikal had caught glimpses of Saphik throughout the day, always with that same morose look on his face - as though someone had killed his favorite war horse.

After lunch, he had retreated to his quarters and not come down.

Of course as Queen Dowager she could certainly force him to come down. He was, after all, a servant of the crown. However, as she planned to seduce the man, a more subtle tactic might prove more wise.

Nikal looked at herself in the mirror as her slaves dressed and perfumed her. Though ten years Saphik's senior, she was still quite comely. Of course, what she had to offer a man by the way of money and power only added to her natural graces.

Still, Saphik did not strike her as the type to fall from grace for reasons as base as desire or power. No, the only way she would be able to seduce him was to hurt him, to play on his insecurity, to make him doubt Ida's heart and fidelity.

Nikal smiled.

Jealousy. That would be Nikal's weapon of choice.

Saphik sat stewing in his and Ida's suite as the sun began to dip in the horizon.

Ida and the King still had not returned – though the temple was less than an hour's ride from the citadel.

What in the hell is keeping them? he wondered.

As if in answer, images of his wife riding the king appeared in his mind's eye.

He took another long swig of alcohol.

Just as Saphik finally resolved to go after them, he heard the main door to his suite open.

Ida!

Setting the bottle down on the floor next to him, he rose and entered the reception area.

Instead of his wife, he found Mal-Nikal. He prostrated himself before her as he greeted her.

She waved his formality away. "Please stop doing that every time you see me," she replied. "My friends have no need to bow before me."

Saphik rose. "Are we friends?" he asked her, his eyes narrowing.

"I would like us to be," Mal-Nikal replied, her eyes glittering sensually.

"I'm newly married," he said.

"A fact irrelevant to your wife," Nikal retorted.

"I thought we were to be friends."

"We are," she reassured him.

"Then watch what you say about my wife," he warned.

"It's not your wife I don't trust," she reassured him. "It's the king. He's used to getting whatever he wants, is willing to sacrifice anyone or anything to get his way."

That muscle in Saphik's sculptured jaw spasmed again.

"But then Mursili's never gone against a man of your obvious....assets," Nikal said, her eyes slowly drifting down Saphik's body and up again.

"Still, tongues do wag," she added. "If you continue to skulk about the grounds and hide in your rooms, you'll only add fuel to the fire."

"So, what would you have me do?" Saphik asked, his anguish burning in his eyes.

Nikal smiled. "I would advise you to make yourself seen. Come down to the invocation and to the dinner that follows. Make merry like all is right in the world. And when your wife returns, be welcoming and warm to both she and Mursili as though you have all the faith in the world that nothing is going on between them. In this way, you can prove yourself not the cuckold but the gossips fools."

Saphik weighed her words.

After a few moments he spoke. "When and where is the invocation?" he asked.

"It will be in 2 hours time, in the front courtyard."

She turned to go, then turned back to face him. "Oh and formal dress is required. You might want to do something about your appearance before you come down. You look disheveled and smell of spirits."

Saphik nodded his understanding.

Nikal smiled.

XVIII

King Mursili and Ida's return couldn't have gone better for Mal-Nikal if she had sacrificed a bull to the gods. That the pair missed the invocation and did not arrive until the gathering had moved inside to the main hall, as the guests mingled prior to dinner, worked out even better than her most vivid machinations.

Every time the main door had creaked open, curious guests had turned to see who was arriving - the king and Ida's return being no exception.

Having no idea that half the nobility in Hattusa would be in the main hall, Ida and Mursili were still well at ease. As the main citadel door opened, they were standing close together. She was laughing at something he was saying close to her ear – as she gave him a sidelong glance and he gazed warmly at her, a wicked grin upon his face.

Of course, once they realized they had an audience, all merriment had faded.

The only thing better than the looks on Mursili and Ida's faces when they realized how inappropriate it must all appear, were the answering looks on Queen Gassulawiya and Saphik's faces.

Nikal smiled wickedly, mischief gleaming in her eyes.

"Welcome back, your highness," she greeted as she approached the king. "I do so hope you and your guest can join us for dinner."

"Thank you for both the greeting and the invitation, Tawannanna," Mursili replied. "However, we must decline. It's been a rather long day of prayer and purification."

"Of course," Nikal replied.

Mursili nodded and Ida bowed before they left the room. Mal-Nikal watched slyly as the two headed down opposite corridors to their private suites.

Although she continued to play the lady bountiful, she kept an eye on Gassula and Saphik. Neither was putting up a very convincing front.

Nikal only wondered how long it would take them to go chasing after their wayward spouses.

When the doors to the great dining room opened, Nikal got her answer. As the throng began to move, Gassula slipped down the side corridor.

Oh to be a fly on that wall, Nikal thought, her smile widening even further.

Nikal had expected Saphik to follow suit.

Much to her surprise and secret delight, he did the exact opposite. He followed the throng into the dining room.

XIX

Alone in his chambers, the walls began to close in on King Mursili II once more.

He paced furiously for a few long moments before he went to his journal. Unlocking it, he began to write.

Though he fought hard to contain his anguish, his normally precise cuneiform showed obvious signs of strain.

At the temple, the Sun Goddess had made it clear.

She would accept no substitute.

It must be his beloved son, Hattusili, sacrificed at her alter if Mursili desired her continued patronage, the continued prosperity of his kingdom and the continued protection of the last of the true Amarnas – Abidos....Ida.

Mursili turned now to his patron god, Telipinu, wrote a prayer in his honor.

Telipinu, you are a mighty noble deity. Mursili, the king, is your servant.

You, Telipinu, are a noble god. Your godhead and the gods' temples are firmly established in the land of Hatti. But in no other land anywhere are they so. In the land of Hatti they present festivals and sacrifices pure and holy to you. But in no other land anywhere do they present them so.

You are the father and mother of every land. You are the inspired lord of judgment. You are untiring in the place of judgment. Among the Primeval Gods you are the one who is celebrated. You, Telipinu, assign the rites for the gods, you assign the portions for the Primeval Gods. They open the door of heaven for you. You, the celebrated Telipinu, are allowed to pass through the gate of heaven. The gods of heaven are obedient to you, Oh Telipinu. The gods of earth are obedient to you, Oh Telipinu. Whatever you say, Oh Telipinu, the gods bow down to you. Of the oppressed, the orphan, and the widow you are father and mother. You, Telipinu, take the cause of the orphan and the oppressed to heart.

Turn with favor toward the king and the queen, and toward the princes and the land of Hatti. Take your stand, Oh Telipinu, strong god, beside the king, queen and the princes. Grant them enduring life, health, long years and strength. Into their souls place light and joy! Persuade mother Arinna to turn now from this path. This, your humble servant, begs of you.

Mursili stopped writing, read over his entreaty. He was just about to continue when one of his guard entered.

The queen was on her way.

Closing and locking the journal, Mursili placed it in the hidden panel. Just as he closed the panel, Gassula entered.

He turned to face her.

"What am I to you?!" she demanded. She trembled in her hurt and fury.

"You are my love," he replied. "My queen."

"Then why now do you dishonor me so? Why now do you flaunt your lover in front of everyone?"

Mursili went to her. "There is nothing between Hawara and I - save friendship. Nothing improper has passed between us."

"It didn't look like it," she replied. "First you abandon my side – to go to the temple you said. Then I find out, along with half of Hattusa's nobility, that you were instead with *her*!"

"I did not lie to you," Mursili replied. "We went to the temple. We performed prayers and purifications on behalf of Hattusili."

This made Gassula even angrier. "And who is she that you would take *her* to temple to pray for Hattusili. *I* am his mother. He is my son, and yet you choose she and not I to accompany you to the temple. You choose she and not I to perform the sacred rights.

"No wonder I am not High Priestess. Even my own husband does not have faith in me!"

Mursili was stung. "You know well that's not true."

"Isn't it?" she pressed.

"Of course not."

"Then show me," she said. "Show me what it is you keep secreted away in your journals."

Mursili looked away guilty.

Gassula laughed humorlessly. "I bet *she* knows though doesn't she?"

"Gassula -" he began reaching for her.

"No, don't," she said pushing his hands away.

She stared at him a long moment, tears pooling in her eyes, before she turned and stalked to the window.

She wrapped her arms around herself as finally her tears began to stream down her face.

Mursili stared at her for a long moment before he left the room. He needed to gather the oils and offerings to solidify his entreaty to the Storm God. As much as it pained him to leave things as they stood with Gassula, Hattusili was running out of time.

XX

The scribe Mittanna-muwa sat at Prince Hattusili's side as usual. When Muwa was a child, the then Prince Mursili had plucked him, more than half dead, from the streets of Assyria. The Prince had seen something of worth in the bedraggled child, had been impressed that the child understood him when he spoke in Hittite to his men.

When the child also demonstrated rudimentary knowledge of five other languages, the Prince had been amazed. He had thanked the gods and taken the boy under his care. When he came of age, the newly crowned King had had Muwa indoctrinated into the trade of scribe.

Muwa was determined to repay the King's kindness. He would save the King's favorite son. He had to.

During the day, Muwa spent hours poring over documents brought from every land inside and outside of Hatti, in search of a cure for the frail boy. Under his careful instruction, the boy's doctors had administered each and every promising curative.

Still, despite the occasional remission of his condition, Prince Hattusili inevitably fell ill again - the treatment that had temporarily restored his health suddenly ineffective.

Muwa wanted to scream. He was almost at the end of the latest pile of medical research papers and he could find nothing of promise.

He looked to the King. Mursili was in the next room, performing a dedication to Telipinu. Perhaps he would be more successful than Muwa.

Muwa rubbed his weary eyes, returned his attention to the papers in his lap.

Suddenly, there was a crash.

Muwa rose, the papers falling from his lap and remixing on the floor at his feet. He rushed to the ante-chamber in which Mursili was working.

He found the King on the floor. Mursili's entire body was trembling, his eyes rolled back in his head. Blood seeped from his eyes and nose.

Muwa was horrified.

Just as he opened his mouth to call for the guard, Mursili grabbed his ankle. Muwa watched as the tremors ceased, as the king's eyes rolled back into place.

He sank to the fallen man's side.

"My King," Muwa breathed. "Are you well?"

The king nodded heavily.

"I'll fetch the physicians," Muwa said beginning to rise.

"No," Mursili whispered. "Bring Hawara instead," he said. "Only Hawara."

Though Muwa was perplexed by such a request, he was loyal to the king.

He nodded his acquiescence, helped the king to sit upright. Leaning the weakened monarch against the wall, Muwa rose to do as he was bade.

Muwa found Ida in the courtyard.

"Lady Hawara?" Muwa asked. Though he had seen her from a distance, he was not well enough acquainted with her to know if it was indeed she.

Ida nodded.

"It's the king," Muwa said, a bit too rushedly. "He requires your immediate presence."

"What's wrong?" Ida asked, picking up on the man's agitation.

"There's no time to explain," Muwa said. "Please come."

Ida nodded, followed.

It seemed an eternity before they reached Mursili. Upon the sight of him, Ida gasped, one hand covering her mouth.

"Help me," Mursili ordered extending his arms.

Muwa took one arm and Ida the other. They helped Mursili to a chair.

After a few ragged breaths, Mursili again addressed Muwa. "Now leave us," he said, "and tell my men to allow no one else entry."

"Yes, My King," Muwa intoned though he stood rooted, his eyes drifting uncertainly between the woman and Mursili.

"I'm in good hands," Mursili reassured him.

Muwa nodded before he left the room.

As soon as the door closed, Ida sank to her haunches before Mursili, her hands cupping his face.

"By the gods, what has happened to you?" she whispered, her horror in her eyes.

"I had another vision," he said.

Ida frowned. Although she was often privy to what the visions revealed, she had never before been there when one had come.

She had had no idea they could be so violent.

"Are they always like this?" she asked, concerned.

"No," he replied. "They usually come quite peacefully, unbidden in the night. This vision I called to me.

"Adopted son of the gods or not, receiving their will in waking form..." He smiled sheepishly. "Well, you can see for yourself how that manifests."

"Do you want me to fetch your physician?" she asked.

"No," he replied. "I need to speak to you more urgently than I need medical care. Though I will be weak for some time yet, I have no grave or permanent injury."

Ida, however, did not appear reassured.

He smiled again. "It's not nearly as horrible as it appears," he assured her.

"The cleansing cloth is there." He gestured to his son's bedside.

Ida rose and took up one of Hattusili's cleansing cloths. She picked up a water basin and placed it at Mursili's feet.

As she knelt in front of him, they continued to speak - she gently cleansing the blood from his face.

"And what was it that the gods had to say with such violence?" Ida asked him.

"The Storm God has accepted my offering," Mursili said with a smile. "He will save my son."

Ida smiled, hugging him. "Mursili, that's great!"

Mursili smiled, returning her embrace for a long moment. When she tried to pull away, he held her fast to him. His smile faded.

"Mursili?" she asked, dread beginning to rise with her. "What's wrong?"

"To save my son, I must slight the Sun Goddess," he said. "I must dedicate my son to the goddess Sausga."

His grip loosened and Ida pulled back slightly to look into his eyes. She found sadness there.

"I don't know if I should do this, Ida," he admitted. "The Sun Goddess has been my patron goddess since I was a boy. I want to save my son but I can't harm the path of our fate, of our people."

"The Storm God is your patron god is he not?" Ida replied. "Surely, he would not have offered you this option if it would lead to your ruin."

"Perhaps," he conceded. Mursili studied her face for a long moment, his mood visibly deteriorating.

"There's more isn't there?" she asked, knots beginning to form in her stomach.

"Yes," he breathed.

"What is it?"

Mursili looked away from her.

"Mursili," she called to him.

He returned his gaze to her. He gently stroked her face with both hands.

"Ida," he whispered. "My poor, beautiful Ida."

Ida grasped his wrists, tears pooling in her eyes. "Mursili, you're scaring me," she said.

He swallowed passed the lump in his throat. "You have to leave this place," he said.

Ida shook her head. "I already told you. I'm not leaving you or my son."

"Listen to me," he said gripping her shoulders. "This is not just about you or I. It's Mal-Nikal. If you stay here, she will destroy us both and not just us, both of our lines and our kingdoms. If you don't go away and stay away - far from me, both Egypt and Hatti will be plunged into years of war and darkness. Gassula, my children, Nacamakun, Saphik, Kadar...you, me all of us will die and our lands will burn."

Ida shook her head, tears coming to her eyes. This wasn't happening. She had just found her son again, had just come back to Hattusa.

"No," she breathed, cupping his face. "Not yet."

Tears came to Mursili's eyes as they bore into hers. "She has already begun to put her plan into motion."

Ida's heart began to ache in her chest, her mind drifting to a day that felt like a lifetime ago, when she was forced to flee Syria and leave Abidos and Mursili behind. She opened her mouth to protest again, was silenced by his lips upon hers.

The fervor of the kisses between them set her afire like none other had before them.

If Mursili hadn't regained hold of his senses, hadn't remembered that his son, the son of he and his queen, lay in fitful slumber just a few yards away from them, there is no telling how far it would have gone between them.

Still, it took great effort for Mursili to stop himself.

He closed his eyes, one hand gripping her face as he rested his forehead against hers and fought to regain his breath. When he opened his eyes at last, when he dared see those things burning in Ida's eyes that were to be forbidden them, he knew well that the vision foretold the truth. If Ida remained in the citadel, in his life, he would eventually betray Gassula and bring all of the disaster he foresaw crashing down upon all of their heads.

He released her, sat back in the chair.

They sat in silence for a long moment before at last Ida spoke.

"When do I leave?" she asked.

"With the morning sun," he replied. "I will rescind Saphik's leave, reassign him to my brother Sarri's citadel in Syria."

"He'll be grateful for it," Ida admitted.

Mursili nodded. "As will my wife."

He stood, sighed heavily.

"So this is goodbye again?" Ida said rising.

"For now," he replied. "Just until I can find a way to neutralize Mal-Nikal."

Ida nodded.

"I'll make sure Nacamakun and Kadar know where you are," he offered. "I'm sure he'll be glad to bring the boy to see you when he can."

Ida gave a weak smile. "Thank you." she said.

Mursili nodded. Their eyes met and held for a long moment, longing burning within them.

Mursili cleared his throat, turned away from her. "You should probably -"

"Of course," Ida replied. "Saphik might return at any moment and we both have much to do."

Mursili nodded. It was only when he heard the chamber door close behind her that he released the breath he had not realized he had been holding. As he stood there a pain gripped his chest, a pain greater than even the vision had been.

He had lost her...again.

XXI

Ida's heart grew heavier with each mile that stretched between her caravan and the citadel. She tried to convince herself that it was because she would be far away from Kadar, but even then she knew it wasn't true. She knew well that Nacamakun would not keep her son from her, that he would find opportunity for her to remain a part of her son's life. It would hurt to be away from him but she knew it was only temporary.

No, the real reason her heart bled now was because of Mursili. A little while between she and him had been never a little while. If Mal-Nikal was as determined, powerful and conniving as Ida had been lead to believe, she might never see Mursili again. The thought twisted the dagger that was already buried in her chest.

As the miles continued to grow between them, Ida's pain grew. As the great citadel shrank behind them, she fought the growing urge to turn her horse around.

Although it hurt even more now then when she had lost Tutankhamun, she knew she could not afford to falter – for either of their sakes. If she turned back, she knew all would be lost.

Still, even knowing the stakes, knowing the greater purpose behind their sacrifice, it wasn't any easier. In some ways, it made it worse - the seeming unfairness of it all.

Why did *they* have to be so burdened? Why did *they* always have to suffer, to make these sacrifices?

For the first time she truly understood how horrible it must be for Mursili - the weight of it all, the terrible burden he forced himself to bear year after year after year, for all of their sakes. And now he was alone again. Now he had no one he could turn to to ease that burden.

Ida clamped her hands over her mouth to silence the sob that threatened.

Oh, Mursili.

Ida had never felt so terrible in her entire life - not even when she had left Abidos in Syria. At least when she had been forced to leave Abidos for his safety, she knew the child still had Mursili, Nacamakun, Clizi and countless others. But Mursili...

She shook her head, her heart aching more than she thought she could survive in that moment.

But why?

Tutankh was the love of her life....wasn't he? Yes, she loved Mursili well, was grateful to him but Tutankh had been her one true love, the mate of her soul....hadn't he?

Ida released a shaky breath, felt like the wind had been knocked out of her.

She startled when she felt Saphik's hand upon hers. She turned her head to meet his worried gaze.

He managed a weak smile of encouragement in reply.

Poor Saphik, Ida thought.

He didn't deserve any of this. He deserved a wife who would love him just as much as he loved her, who would be just as devoted. He was everything a woman could want. He just wasn't...

Mursili, her mind whispered.

A wave of guilt washed over Ida. Pulling her eyes away from Saphik, she tried to focus on the scenery around them - even as the tears began to slip from her eyes.

A few moments later, the caravan pulled to a halt. Saphik dismounted and came around to her side. Ida looked down at him.

"We must make camp for the night," he explained.

Ida nodded, allowed him to help her down.

It broke his heart to see Ida so miserable. "You'll see Kadar again soon," he said. "I promise."

Ida couldn't take his kindness. She did not deserve it. She finally broke, great sobs shaking her body as the flood gates of her grief finally burst open.

Saphik pulled her into his arms. "Hey," he said softly as he held her fast and stroked her hair with one hand. "It'll be okay. I promise."

Tawannanna Mal-Nikal presided over the morning invocation with great glee.

Everything was falling into place nicely. If they continued to progress at the rate they were going, she might well have Mursili off the throne before the end of next year.

Though Queen Gassulawiya had attended as usual - no doubt in a pathetic attempt to impress upon the nobles her great piety, the king had not. Neither was "Hawara" in attendance – a fact that would no doubt send the palace tongues wagging. Saphik was not yet accounted for either, but as the past few days had proven, it was not unusual for him.

As the ceremony drew to a close and the attendants gradually filtered out of the ceremonial chamber, Mal-Nikal sought out Gassula.

"Greetings, young queen," Nikal said.

"Greetings, Tawannanna," Gassula replied.

"I was hoping the king would be in attendance this morning," Nikal said. "All is still well with him I trust?"

Gassula nodded. "He had much to attend to on behalf of Prince Hattusili," she informed her.

"Ah, yes. No doubt Lady Hawara is proving to be of great assistance in that regard."

"Of course, Great Dowager Queen. Any prayers for Hattusili are of great help....from any distance."

Mal-Nikal's expression betrayed her surprise.

"Ah," Gassula replied, not bothering to hide her satisfaction at having won one over on the older woman. "Didn't your spies tell you?"

"Spies," Nikal repeated. "I have no spies – only friends."

Gassula smirked.

"And just what is it these friends of mine should have told me?" Nikal pressed.

Gassula gave no reply, appeared instead to be contemplating whether or not she should be the one to break the news to Nikal.

"Enough with the games," Nikal demanded, growing agitated. "It's obvious you can't wait to spill your little secret, so out with it."

Gassula smiled sweetly. "Captain Saphik has been transferred. He and his wife left with the sun."

Nikal's face fell. This couldn't be.

Gassula's smile widened. "Oh, Tawannanna. How insulting that you weren't told, that they didn't even bother to pay you your due respects before departure."

Nikal glared at the other woman.

"Now if you'll excuse me," Gassula said. "I must attend to the king."

Nikal watched the queen depart, her fury thinly veiled.

After a long moment, a slow, vicious smile spread across Nikal's face.

Mursili may have forestalled her plans...for now. There was, however, more than one way to skin a cat - some ways less pleasant than others.

The vicious mile widened.

It was time to implement Plan B.

XXII

Ida grew restless at the compound in Syria.

They had been there for nearly a month. Saphik was off soldiering for Prince Sarri. Nacamakun and Kadar had come and gone. Never had she felt so alone.

As she wandered the familiar corridors, she felt at once comforted and saddened. There were so many memories for her in that place. Memories of some of the happiest times of her life with Nac, Mursili, Kadar and Abidos and some of the saddest – when she had to leave them all to return to Egypt - had taken place here. Their shadows still permeated the hallways - the pale remnants of a time when they were all together, when they were all happy. It was at once comforting and devastating.

She worried endlessly about Mursili, about Hattusili.

She looked down at the scroll in her hand once more. It had come from Mursili, was written in his very own hand. She could almost feel his torment through his words.

Prince Hattusili was growing worse. Mursili could not bring himself to forsake the Sun Goddess – even with the Storm God's blessing, not after all she had done for him. So he watched helplessly, prayed endlessly for his son's recovery while Muwa continued to pour over medical doctrine after medical doctrine in hopes of finding a cure.

Ida frowned. If she could not be there for him in the flesh, she would be there for him in spirit. She went to her writing table and began to craft her reply.

King Mursili was weary, ill at ease. He had spent the past couple of weeks praying to Telipinu for an alternative way to save Hattusili, an alternative that would not so brazenly disregard Arinna. At the same time, he prayed to Arinna to release him from this demand, to release his son.

Telipinu, however, was as unrelenting as Arinna.

By the gods he wished Ida was there.

Mursili frowned. Just the thought of Ida brought pain to his chest.

He looked over at his sleeping wife. He could honestly say he was still just as much in love with her as he had been on the day he had taken her to wife. Still, that did nothing to diminish what he felt for Ida. Gassula was his great love but Ida was something different – something more.

Mursili shook his head. There was no use dwelling on it all now. Clearing his mind, he began to craft new entreaties to his patron gods.

Behind King Mursili, Queen Gassulawiya opened her eyes. He was at it again - drafting prayers in hopes of saving their son.

Gassula didn't understand it. According to the scroll her spies had intercepted from Hawara, Hawara seemed to be under the impression that the king had discovered something - some secret way to save the prince. Yet, the king did not act.

Even now, with their son in a slumber so deep he could not be awakened, Mursili hesitated.

But why? What could be so terrible that Mursili would risk losing his most cherished of children forever?

She studied him for a long moment, her mind made up. If Mursili wouldn't tell her the truth, she would find out on her own. In the morning, she would pay a visit to the oracle – even if that meant throwing herself at the mercy of Mal-Nikal.

XXIII

What a delicious development, thought Tawannanna Mal-Nikal.

She smiled at the sight of the young Queen Gassulawiya, prostrating and making offerings to her in the hope that Nikal would grant her access to the oracle.

To have Gassula gift-wrapped and placed right at her feet was nothing short of a miracle in Mal-Nikal's eyes. Perhaps it was true. Perhaps King Mursili *had* run afoul of his patron goddess after all.

Mal-Nikal relished in Gassula's forced display of humility for a moment longer before she retreated to the back to "consult with the oracle". Instead of a true consultation, she went through the herbs and drams she had collected over the years. There. That one.

She took up the small glass vial. Holding up the contents, she held it to the light. She swirled around the substance, a slow smile coming to her face. It was just potent enough to do the job but just subtle enough that it could not be traced.

Mal-Nikal's hand closed around the vial, hiding it from view. There was more than one way to drive a wedge between the King and his wife, more than one way to bring Ida back, more than one way to take over the throne.

Walking back out to the main chamber, the High Priestess was the picture of piety.

"The oracle will hear your petition," Nikal announced.

Gassula rose, for once grateful to the Tawannanna. Her earnest gratitude made Nikal feel guilty...almost.

"But first you must drink this draft," Nikal announced, "to purify your spirit and to open you up to the heavens."

She mixed the elixir in the usual way with all of the usual incantations and blessings. However, no one noticed as Nikal added the entire contents of the hidden vial as well.

Discretely hiding the now empty vial among the decorations on the alter, Nikal came around the alter and offered up the chalice to Gassula. Eagerly, Gassula took it, her hands over Nikal's as she drank the fill of the cup.

Taking the cup and resetting it on the alter, Nikal gestured for Gassula to follow. Gassula did as she was bade.

Gassula's head was spinning as she left the oracle and headed to the Temple of Sausga. Could it really be so simple? Was that all it would take to save her son?

A son alive and dedicated to Sausga was better than a dead son dedicated to Arinna. Even as she felt true hope for the first time in months, she found she also felt somehow....off - lightheaded, slightly nauseous. Something was wrong with her.

Gassula shook her head, reasoned away her symptoms.

Even as sweat began to break out on her body, as her limbs became unfathomably heavy, she pressed on. Nothing was going to stop her from saving her son.

XXIV

At last the Sun Goddess Arinna showed her mercy.

Late that very afternoon, Mursili's prayers were interrupted by an exclamation from Muwa. Startled, Mursili hurried into Hattusili's bed chamber.

Muwa looked up at the king, a broad, excited grin on his face as he held out one of the documents.

"I've found it!" Muwa exclaimed. "I think I've finally found the cure!"

Mursili took the proffered parchment from the man and read over it.

A smile broke across the king's face. "By the gods!" he exclaimed. "You might be right!"

He and Muwa laughed as Mursili clapped him on the shoulder.

"Get the doctors to work on this formula right away," Mursili ordered.

"Yes, Great King!" Muwa exclaimed excitedly, as he hurried from the room.

Mursili sat down next to his son. He stroked the boy's hair, held one of the child's hands.

"They've done it," he breathed. "Arinna and Telipinu have reconciled and given us a second chance."

Just as he spoke those words, Queen Gassulawiya came stumbling into the room. She was covered with sweat, her skin pale and pasty.

Mursili was shocked by her appearance. He rose, went to her just in time to catch her as she collapsed.

He shook her, calling out her name, "Gassula! Gassula!"

Slowly, the queen opened her eyes. She smiled weakly.

"It is done," she said happily. "Our son is saved."

"How did you - "

Gassula cut him off. "I knew you would never do it on your own so I did it for you. I dedicated the boy to Sausga."

"You did what?" Mursili asked, his devastation painted on his face.

"See for yourself," she said, her eyes drifting passed Mursili's face and to the boy on the bed behind him.

Mursili turned to look at Hattusili. First, the boy's fingers jumped. After a few long moments, his eyes began to flutter. But a breath later, they were slowly sliding open.

Hattusili's gaze slowly focused on his parents. "Mother?" he whispered hoarsely. "Father?"

Mursili's jaw dropped, he turned back to face Gassula.

"What have you done?" he asked softly, a solitary tear falling from his eyes.

"I've saved our son," she said, not understanding why her husband looked so unhappy at such a joyous moment.

"You think Arinna will take this lightly?" Mursili asked. "You've damned us. You've damned us both."

XXV

King Mursili could hardly concentrate as he drafted his latest prayers to the Sun Goddess. Even as Muwa administered the draught that Arinna had granted them to Hattusili, Mursili knew well that it would not be enough. Queen Gassulawiya had slighted the Sun Goddess, had degraded her place in the heavenly hierarchy even as the Sun Goddess had chosen to have mercy on her chosen conduit's offspring. There would be heaven to pay and the sacrifice of one child would no longer be enough. Mursili only prayed he was not too late to save his people.

Behind him, Gassula lay on their bed, racked by yet another fit of coughs - their physicians trying everything in their power to cure her. Despite their best efforts, she grew weaker by the day. Even as Mursili tried everything in his power to save her, he knew he would fail. She had crossed the Sun Goddess and it would cost her her life.

Mursili's writing instrument trembled in his hand though he forced himself to keep working.

At last, it snapped in two. Mursili threw it across the room, his red rim eyes and disheveled appearance making him look like a madman.

His slaves watched uncertainly.

Mursili turned to glare at them. "Send for Muwa," he commanded.

The minutes dragged on as Mursili awaited Muwa.

Finally, the man arrived.

"How may I be of service, Great King?" Muwa asked, prostrating himself before Mursili.

"I need you to write for me," the king replied. "I need to send warning to Assyria."

There was chaos at Prince Sarri's compound.

Ida watched helplessly as the prince's men, including Saphik, carried the stricken prince through the main gates and up to his suites. She followed behind them, waited anxiously for news as physicians and men streamed in and out of the chamber.

Sarri was Mursili's favorite brother. He had been the only one to openly support Mursili when he had been Prince and had dared to defy the crown in order to keep Ida and Abidos safe. He had also been Mursili's greatest supporter in his bid to become King, his help immeasurable in allowing Mursili to stabilize the empire after Mursili took the throne. The peace with Syria was also in large part thanks to Sarri's efforts.

Sarri was Mursili's right arm. Mursili could not afford to lose him.

It seemed like an eternity before at last Saphik came out to her.

"What's going on?" Ida asked him.

"I don't know," Saphik said. "One moment we were running drills and the next Prince Sarri had collapsed and fallen from his horse."

"Is his injury grave?" Ida asked.

"Not from the fall," her husband replied. He ran an anxious hand through his hair. "I don't know, Ida," he said. "I've never seen anything like it before. One moment he was strong and healthy then the next...." He shook his head. "He just wasn't."

A loud groan of pain issued from Sarri's room.

They both turned towards it. "I better get back inside," Saphik said.

Ida nodded absently.

Saphik hesitated for a long moment, his worry for his clearly shaken wife battling with his sense of duty. "You okay?" he asked.

Ida forced a weak smile. "Of course," she managed. "You'd better go."

He nodded, returned to the prince's side.

As soon as the door closed, Ida collapsed.

XXVI

Saphik sat at Ida's side, gently stroking her hair.

He looked to the sealed communiqué that sat on the table - a missive from the King, unsure if he should give it to her. He returned his gaze to his wife, a slow smile coming to his face as at last her eyes fluttered open.

"Welcome back," he said softly.

Suddenly remembering herself, Ida sat up abruptly. Her head throbbed with the motion.

She winced, one hand rising to gingerly touch the back of her head.

"Easy now," Saphik advised. "You hit your head when you fainted."

"I fainted?" Ida repeated.

Saphik nodded.

"How's Prince Sarri?" she asked.

Saphik sighed. He didn't know what to tell her.

"The truth," Ida pressed him.

He studied her face for a long moment before he replied. "It doesn't look good for him, Ida." he said.

Ida inhaled sharply, tears coming to her eyes.

"There's more," he admitted. Against his better judgment, he handed the message from King Mursili to her.

Ida looked at the note. Even before she began to read, tears fell from her eyes. It wasn't even Mursili's handwriting. Mursili *always* did his own writing. That he hadn't could only mean one thing. Something was wrong with him, very wrong.

Ida broke the seal and began to read. The content of the letter confirmed Ida's suspicions.

In it, Mursili told her everything – how his patron goddess Arinna had granted them the power to heal Hattusili only to have Gassula go behind his back to the oracle and dedicate Hattusili to Sausga instead; how Arinna was now out for blood; how Gassula had been struck down; how he prayed and made offerings day and night to try to stem the tide of the goddess' rage; how he feared that there would be more death and suffering ahead. Most of all, Mursili warned her that she must not, no matter if the heavens themselves should fall upon his head, not even if he should beg her in his weakness to come, return to the citadel. Until Arinna was appeased, until she forgave him, Ida was to stay put. If she disobeyed, things would only grow a thousand times worse. The Sun Goddess' wrath might well spread to those Ida loved and beyond.

Ida was in a daze as she clutched the letter tightly in her hand. Why was this happening to Mursili? He was a good, pious man. He did everything the gods asked of him - no matter what it cost him, yet they could still do this to him.

Ida was hurt and she was angry. She wanted to make someone pay, anyone.

"Ida?" Saphik asked.

He had never seen her look so before, and it scared him.

"Please leave me," she said not even meeting his gaze. "Leave me before I say or do something we will both live to regret."

Saphik remained rooted.

Ida turned to look at him, anger and hatred blazing in her eyes. "Please."

Saphik swallowed passed the lump in his throat. On stiff legs, he rose and did as he was bade. He stood outside of the door for a long moment before he headed down the hall.

If only King Mursili II would have known how accurate his words would turn out to be. His sky would indeed fall. In barely a fortnight, his most beloved brother, Prince Sarri-Kusuh, would succumb to his mysterious affliction.

XXVII

Saphik had never seen Ida as she was now before.

She was inconsolable. All she did was lay in their bed and cry or stare unseeingly out the window, day in and day out. When she wasn't crying, she was losing herself in his flesh or out cold from exhaustion. Getting her to eat was a task in and of itself. Getting her to talk to him - next to impossible. He was relieved when at last the royal convoy arrived.

Saphik hurried down to greet them, hoping against hope that his message to Nacamakun had reached the man in time, hoping against hope that Nac would agree to his request. His eyes searched the disembarking men and women for any sign of him. There.

Saphik rushed through the gathering crowd to the man, the look of relief on his weary face saying it all as he heartily greeted Nacamakun.

"I was worried you wouldn't get my message in time," Saphik admitted.

"Message?" Nac asked, seemingly confused.

"Is that not why you're here?" Saphik asked.

Nac shook his head. "I may have fallen out with the king, but I have served his family my entire life as has my father and my father's father and no doubt as will Kadar. What the king has done is no fault of Prince Sarri nor is it the fault of any other of the royal family. I would not dare dishonor Prince Sarri by not paying my respects, by not seeing with my own sword that the prince's body makes it safely back to the capital."

"So Kadar is not here then?" Saphik asked, his face falling.

Nac offered him a small smile. "Of course Kadar is here. As my son, my duties will one day become his."

Saphik looked around him but still saw no sign of the boy.

"Kadar is in the rear of the convoy along with the other military plebeians," Nac offered.

Kadar looked surprised. "But he is your son. Surely...."

"My family was not always so well appointed. In order to build a good soldier, you have to build him from the ground upwards. Come," Nac said guiding Saphik to the interior of the compound. "Kadar has duties to attend to before he will be allowed to join us inside and we have much to speak on."

Nacamakun watched Ida as she stood, stared unseeingly out the window. She took a deep shuddering breath then broke into tears.

Finally, Nac spoke. "Well, this certainly isn't the welcome I expected," he said.

Ida turned, her grief momentarily forgotten in her surprise. A smile broke across her face as she ran across the room and flew into Nac's arms. Nac held her tightly, felt the tension melt away from her.

Ida pulled away to look at him. "I can't believe you're here," she said. "It's as though my prayers have finally been answered."

"Prayers to see an old man?" he asked. "Surely, there are things closer to your heart for which you pray."

Ida looked away guilty. She pulled away from Nac completely and turned away from him.

"Let me guess," Nac surmised. "The king."

Ida turned back to face him. "You know me well enough to know I don't just weep for Mursili. Prince Sarri was always good to me."

"But still you shed the bulk of your tears and your prayers for the king," he replied knowingly.

"I can't help it," she admitted. "Know you of what happened with Hattusili, with Gassula?"

"Last I heard, the young Prince fell ill and as he recovered, his mother tragically succumbed to the same illness. She, however, seems to be having a rougher go of it than her son."

Ida shook her head. "You don't understand."

She proceeded to tell Nac of that last night with Mursili in Hattusili's room, of Mal-Nikal's machinations – of course leaving out the part about the kiss. She then went to her writing desk and withdrew the last two letters she had received from Mursili. She gave them to him.

Nac read, his expression deeply disturbed as he read through the 1st and even more disturbed as he read through the 2nd. He too had noticed that the 2nd was not even in Mursili's hand. When Nac looked back up at her, she spoke again.

"You know him. Mursili blames himself for *everything*. He takes the weight of the entire world on his own shoulders. With Prince Sarri gone, the queen ill at health and I forced to stay away......" Ida shook her head, fresh tears coming to her eyes. She couldn't even bare to imagine the state the king must be in at that moment.

Nac gave no response, knew well what she was about to ask of him.

"I know you have reason to be angry with him," Ida pled, "to hate him even, but please....you can't continue to disregard him. Not now. Even if only for the sake of your sense of duty, of your family pride, you must go to him. You must help him be strong and to face down his enemies."

Though tears welled in Nac's eyes, his jaw was set.

Ida went to him, her hands on his arms. "See," she pressed. "Even now I can see your pain. I can see you still feel for him, that you hurt for him just as I do. I know he has his faults, that he has made mistakes but he is a good king – the finest Hatti has had for many generations. If the Tawannanna has her way, he'll lose everything. Is a Hatti with Mal-Nikal at its helm one you want to live in, one that you want Kadar to grow up in?"

Tears fell from Nac's eyes, his anguish over the loss of his son battling with emotions long buried – his guilt over abandoning his duty to the crown, his feelings of betrayal and buried deepest of all, his fatherly love for Mursili.

"Loving him is hard," Ida said. "I of all people know that." She sighed. "I know you feel like letting him into your heart is betraying Kadar. I too used to feel guilty about it, like I was betraying Tutankh by allowing such feelings for him to exist. But now..."

She shook her head. "Now, I realize that every moment of my life - even my love affair with Tutankhaten, was leading me to this, was leading me to him.

"Even now, as my heart bleeds, as we are forced apart once more, I know he is my destiny. And I'm okay with it. No matter how much it hurts sometimes, loving someone is never wrong."

Nac's tears flowed faster, his body rigid though he still did not reply.

Though Ida was fast losing faith she could get through to him, she pressed on. "You read the words yourself. You know what would happen if I went to him. Yet, with each passing day, it grows harder and harder for me not to. If only there was someone by his side, someone we could both trust....."

A sob escaped Ida's throat. She sank to her knees, her hands clenching tightly around the fabric of his shirt. "Nac, please save him. Please."

She sank to the floor completely, a sobbing ball of grief at his feet.

Nac couldn't stand to be there one moment longer. Without a word, he left the room.

XXVIII

Seeing Kadar again did Ida a world of good.

Now, as the royal caravan began final preparations to return to Hattusa, she clung to the boy tightly, tears streaming down her face.

How much grief could one woman take in a lifetime? Nac wondered.

Ida looked up at Nac as he approached them, that same pleading, hopeful look in her eye that had been there every time she had looked at him since their conversation in her room.

"Do we have to go so soon?" Kadar asked. Even not knowing that this woman was really his mother and not his aunt, he had quickly grown attached to her. "The capital is in mourning so they'll be no training exercises for weeks."

"I have a duty to fulfill," Nac replied.

"He could stay with us," Ida replied, hope glistening in her eyes. "He'll be safe here with Saphik, Prince Sarri's guard and I."

Safer than at the capital, Ida thought.

Almost as if reading Ida's thoughts, Nac nodded. "You're right," he said. "The capital is no place for the boy right now and...." he stared pointedly at her for a long moment. "I have a duty to fulfill."

In that moment, Ida was so happy she didn't know whether to laugh or cry. In the end, she did both. Thank you, she mouthed to Nac.

Nac tore his attention from Ida to his son. Kadar was beaming.

"You really mean it?" Kadar asked excitedly. "I can really stay with Uncle Saphik and Aunt Hawara?"

Nac couldn't help but smile at the boy. "For the time being," he said mussing Kadar's hair. "But don't be so happy about it. You might hurt an old man's feelings."

Kadar's face quickly sobered.

Nacamakun laughed. Abandoning his normally formal public posturing, Nac held out his arms. "Now give your old man a hug."

Kadar gave Nac the strongest hug he could manage. Nac kissed him on the temple. "I'll miss you boy," he said pulling away from him. "Behave yourself and take good care of your aunt here."

"Yes, sir," Kadar said standing at attention and giving his father the formal salute.

"Hawara," Nac said.

Ida flew into his arms and hugged him tightly. Pulling away, she kissed his cheek. "I won't ever forget this," she said. "I'll take good care of him."

"I know you will," he replied.

AMARNA BOOK II: BOOK OF HAWARA

The horn sounded alerting those departing the compound that the caravan was about to leave.

"Tell Saphik I said goodbye," Nac said.

Ida nodded, she and Kadar watching as Nacamakun mounted his steed and joined the end of the caravan as it slowly ambled its way out of the main gate.

XXIX

The citadel. Hattusa.

"Well, aren't you just a sight for sore eyes," Tawannanna Mal-Nikal greeted Nacamakun from just behind him.

Nac glanced at her though he didn't respond.

"Even you couldn't resist a trip out to watch the spectacle, could you?" she continued with a low, throaty laugh.

Though Nac bristled, he did not respond. Instead, he kept his eyes glued resolutely ahead.

Nikal, not one to be deterred by something as trivial as being ignored, continued. "Just look at him."

Below them, King Mursili was performing Prince Sarri-Kusuh's rights.

Mursili's condition disturbed the older man. His face was gaunt, his eyes red rimmed. His robes were ill-fitted - an obvious sign of weight loss so abrupt and extreme that there was no time to refit them before the caravan had returned.

Even from the terrace, from where Nac watched, he could see Mursili's hands trembling, the tears Mursili fought to keep in his eyes as his shaky voice called out to the gods - entreated them to provide Prince Sarri a safe passage to the next life and a peaceful eternity.

At long last, the pyre was lit and Prince Sarri released from this world. Mursili stumbled backwards, the weight of his grief suddenly too much. He leaned heavily against one of the columns before he turned and disappeared into the citadel.

Nikal laughed, taking a sip from the chalice in her hand. "At this rate, he won't last the month let alone remain fit to rule for very much longer."

The hairs on the back of Nac's neck stood. He turned at last to face her, his eyes narrowed. "Did you have something to do with this?" Nac asked her.

Nikal smiled. "Of course not," she replied. "How could I, a mere figurehead, punish the "adopted son of the gods" with so much personal misfortune? And all the way to Assyria no less?"

"And the Queen?" Nac pressed.

"The queen...the queen. Oh, you mean Gassulawiya?" she teased setting down her cup.

"I know she went to the Oracle just before she was struck down."

"Don't look at me. It's obviously the Sun Goddess' doing. After all she did for the king and his little tart, Gassula dared to dedicate his favorite son to Sausga." Nikal laughed. "A thing like that can't be undone. She was just asking for trouble."

AMARNA BOOK II: BOOK OF HAWARA

Nac roughly grabbed her arm. "Arinna might well have allowed what came to pass to come to pass but if I find out that she had any *mortal* help in her vengeance..." Nac let the threat die unspoken though the murderous gleam in his eye left no doubt as to his meaning.

Rather than pulling away, Nikal pressed closer to the man. "Oh, Nac, you remember," she said with a lascivious grin. "It's been so long since I had it rough," she teased as one hand slid down to stroke his length.

"Maybe that's your problem," Nac said through clenched teeth as he grabbed a hand full of her hair and yanked back her head.

Nikal laughed.

Walking her backward, deeper into the room, he shoved her roughly against a table. Hurriedly ripping her dress upwards, he roughly entered her.

Nikal cried out in pain and pleasure. How she had missed their little trysts.

XXX

The citadel. Hattusa.

"Come to gloat?" King Mursili asked his unexpected visitor. "Come to see how well I 'do what must be done' have you?"

Nacamakun's face remained stoic as he took in Mursili's suites. The rooms were completely trashed – bits of pottery, furniture, everything scattered throughout. Thanks to the servants there was at least room to walk. He had not, however, allowed them to clean away his destruction. He was somehow comforted by the outward display of the chaos that raged within him. His rooms were the only place he could let go.

"Of course not, Your Highness," Nacamakun replied. "I come to pay my respects, to offer my condolences."

Mursili laughed humorlessly. "You sure about that?" he pressed. "After what I did to you aren't you even just a tad bit satisfied that I've come to this?"

"Surely you know me better than that," Nac replied. He eyed the other man for a long moment. "How's your son?"

"He grows stronger with each passing day."

"And Queen Gassulawiya?"

Mursili smirked. "She passed with the rising of the sun this morning. Does this please you?"

"Children losing their mother is never a cause for celebration."

"Except maybe in this case," Mursili replied. "She suffered terribly, especially in the last days." He eyed Nac for a long moment. "So is that why you came?" the king taunted. "To see after my children?"

"I came because Ida asked me to," Nac admitted, "and by the look of things, not a moment too soon."

At the mention of Ida's name, a spark of life came back into Mursili's eyes. "Ida," he said. "Is she well?"

Nac nodded. "As well as can be expected under the circumstances."

"She has not come has she?"

"No, sire."

Mursili nodded, his countenance visibly awash with relief. "Good. Make sure she does not," he said. "Even if you have no more sense of care or duty to me, for her sake, for Kadar's sake, you must make sure she stays far away from the citadel. It is not safe for her to be around me." The spark of life faded. "I have failed, Nacamakun. I have incurred Arinna's wrath and anyone close to me will suffer because of it."

Just then, a slave entered with a chalice of medicinal elixir. His physicians sent it to him each night in vain hope he would take it and at last get the rest his worn body so clearly needed. Although he usually ignored it, tonight he was in no mood to deal with the demons in his head. Without hesitation, he took up the chalice and brought the tonic to his lips.

"Wait!" Nac called crossing the room towards him.

Mursili hesitated, his chalice frozen mid air.

"Where is your taster?" Nac asked.

"Well to bed by now," Mursili replied.

"Then don't drink," Nac advised.

Mursili smirked again. "What does it matter either way?" he asked. He took a small swig of liquid. After the hint of elixir slid down his throat, he sighed. "I've done everything the gods have asked of me – twelve long years of total and utter obedience – since my thirteenth year of life. Yet here I am, only worse for wear – down two fathers, one mother, four brothers counting Kadar and one wife. And for what? To pay for sins that weren't even mine in the first place."

The king laughed hollowly. "I'm tired, Nac," he admitted. "I'm exhausted right down to my soul. I have nothing more to give or that I can bear to lose. If this draft is poisoned, so be it. I welcome it."

As Mursili raised the cup once more, Nac took the chalice from his hand and set it down on the alter.

"And what about your people?" Nac pressed. "They deserve to suffer? They deserve to be ruled by the likes of the Tawannanna Mal-Nikal or worse still, to be invaded or enslaved by Pharaoh Horemheb? What will become of them if you are gone?

"For all your faults, you are indeed a great and noble king – one willing to sacrifice whatever it takes for the greater good of Hatti. Could the same be said of the Tawannanna or Pharaoh?

"Even forgetting those you rule, what of your children? Do they too need to suffer as you suffer? Do they deserve to lose a father and their mother in almost the same breath? Do they not deserve at least a father's guidance and protection?"

"Then there's Ida and Abidos. If you're gone, who will protect them? Who will help them restore the Amarna dynasty? All of this suffering, all of this sacrifice – is this not what it is for? Does it not fall to you to restore Egypt's rightful rulers and thus ensure prosperity for Hatti?

"You've said it yourself a thousand times. Your destiny is linked to hers. Would you be so nonchalant if it was Ida drinking from that chalice?"

Mursili winced.

"Like it or not, Mursili," Nacamakun continued. "Your life is not your own. Your destiny is not your own. Killing yourself – purposefully or otherwise – does not change that which the gods have seen fit to place on your shoulders.

"You spoke to me once of prophecy and sacrifice and doing what must be done. Well now is the time, Mursili. Now is the time for you to stand behind your words. Now is the time for you to hold most steadfast to your faith."

Mursili fought to hold back his tears. Nac too found his eyes starting to water.

"You spoke once of all of this pain and sacrifice being for a reason, of it meaning something in the end. If you give up now, it will all have been for nothing. All those people dead, all of those lives cut short...for nothing.

"You say you're sorry to me for my son's fate? Then prove it. Make it up to me. If only so you can look those who were sacrificed in the eye in the next life, become once more the man you once were – the man I had complete faith in, the man I loved as my own kin, the man I could once again follow."

Mursili's nodded, his tears falling anew. "I will," he said. "I promise."

Nac's tears too fell as he squeezed Mursili reassuringly on the shoulder.

Not one for extended emotional displays, Nac turned his attention to the chalice. He picked up the abandoned vessel, turned his back to Mursili to regain his composure and to give the other man time to do the same as he examined it. He swirled around the liquid as he studied it.

He sniffed it, wrinkled his nose at the smell. "What's in here anyway?" he asked, turning back to face the king.

Mursili shrugged one shoulder. "My physicians send it," he replied. "It's supposed to help me sleep."

"Does it work?" Nac replied.

"I don't know. I've never taken it before."

Nac's thoughts drifted to Mal-Nikal's words on the terrace. "Mind if I try something?" he asked. "Just out of my own curiosity."

"Go right ahead," Mursili replied.

Nacamakun called for a prisoner. Once the prisoner arrived, he proffered him the chalice. "Drink," he commanded.

The prisoner hesitated.

"Drink it," Mursili added, "and you'll earn your freedom."

The man, one destined for execution, eagerly complied. He took a great sip and swallowed.

"All of it," Nac said.

The man did as he was bade. "Now what, my lords?" the man asked.

"Now, we wait," Nac replied.

"For?" Mursili asked.

"I'm not quite sure," Nac admitted.

Mursili laughed. "Well if you don't mind," he said. "I'm exhausted. Wake me if ever and whenever whatever you're waiting for occurs." He turned to start towards his bed chamber.

"Mursili!" Nac called.

Mursili turned.

The poor soul recruited to be the impromptu taster began to sway unsteadily on his feet. He began rubbing his head with one hand, the other across his midsection. A few minutes later he sank to his knees and began to retch uncontrollably. The color drained from his skin. Sweat broke out on his skin as he collapsed.

Mursili too paled as he stooped with Nac to help the man from the floor to a chair.

As the king watched the man convulse, his mind raced. He had seen the same symptoms before – though a milder version. They were the same as Gassula's.

Mursili's shock quickly gave way to anger. "Who would dare do this?" he asked Nacamakun.

"It's too early to be certain," Nac replied. "But I have a suspicion."

XXXI

Another two years flew by.

The investigation into King Mursili's attempted poisoning and Queen Gassulawiya's death tore Hattusa in two. As Nacamakun worked his way through the slaves and witnesses, as he tortured the king's physicians until one finally gave a name, the Tawannanna campaigned among the nobles.

Even after a thorough search of the oracle revealed Mal-Nikal's poison horde, the factions that supported each remained deeply divided and at each other's throats. Mursili's attempts to gain enough support to execute Mal-Nikal were futile. She still had too much influence – so much that he was not able to even strip her of the title of High Priestess, let alone arrest her.

By the time the oracle at Sarissa finally released an official ruling in support of Mursili's version of events and declared Nikal guilty, more than a year had passed. When at last the royal guard went to arrest her, she had already fled Hatti.

Feeling cheated and anguished, the King had no choice but to settle for an official banishment - with warning he would never stop searching for the Tawannanna and that if she dared set foot in Hatti again, she would pay with her life.

Those who had harbored her, who had helped her escape did not fare nearly so well. The fortunate ones' entire household was stripped of everything they owned, including title, and placed into bondage as an example to those who would dare stand beside an enemy of the king. The unfortunate paid with an excruciatingly painful death – the likes of which stilled even the few vassal states that had become increasingly emboldened by Prince Sarri's passing.

When at last the dust settled, the nobles of Hattusa turned their attention to more pragmatic pursuits – pressing Mursili to find a new queen. After much discussion, Mursili at last settled on Tanu-hepa. Tanu-hepa was everything that Gassula was not. She was plain, reserved, obedient, frigid and discrete. She was also the favored daughter of the most powerful house that had switched allegiance from Mal-Nikal to Mursili once the oracle made its prognostication of poison. She came ready made with sons, which the king adopted.

Tanu-hepa was everything Mursili wanted at the time. She was someone who could help reinforce his position as monarch but that did not require any attention or maintenance in return. In short, she was someone he would not get attached to, someone who would not take it too hard that Mursili bore her no affection.

As for Ida – he kept her locked away in Prince Sarri's compound. First, it was for fear of what the Tawannanna might have in store for her then it was for fear of what Arinna might have in store for him. Now it was out of protest of the new queen's family – the scandal involving the two at the main hall having grown to ridiculous proportions in the meantime, still fresh on their minds and gossips' tongues even after so much time had passed. Still, Ida and Mursili remained in constant contact – via letter.

Though Ida grew increasingly impatient to return to the citadel, she continued to play the part of dutiful wife to Saphik in Assyria. Her only reprieves were Mursili's letters, the occasional visitor, the occasional trip and that Nacamakun and Kadar spent part of their time at Prince Sarri's compound, when they weren't at the citadel. Sometimes, when Nac had a mission to one of the less tame frontier lands, he would leave Kadar solely in Ida's care. Now was such a time.

Prince Sarri's compound. Assyria.
"Galeno," Ida breath, surprised. She had been roused from her sleep in the wee hours of the morning by one of the servants. "What are you doing here?" she asked.

Galeno offered a small, crooked smile before the two embraced. They stood like that for a long moment before they broke apart. Galeno looked around nervously.

"What is it?" Ida asked, instantly picking up on his anxiety.

Galeno glanced pointedly at the servant. Ida dismissed her then returned her attention to Galeno.

"Where's your husband?" Galeno asked.

"He's at Mari outpost with his men."

"How long ago did he leave?"

"A few days."

"When is he due back?" Galeno asked.

"Any day now," Ida replied.

"And Nacamakun?"

"In Assur." She eyed Galeno suspiciously. "What is going on?" she demanded.

Galeno looked around nervously again. "Is there somewhere we can talk?" he asked. "Somewhere private."

"Of course," she said. "Come with me."

Ida led him to her suites. Inside, Galeno looked about the rooms, out the terrace, behind the curtains.

"What on earth are you doing?" Ida demanded.

"Making sure we're absolutely alone," he replied as he continued his perusal of the suite.

Ida folded her arms across her chest as she watched her best friend darting about her rooms. Finally satisfied, he returned to Ida.

"You plan on telling me what the hell is going on?" she demanded.

Galeno took a deep breath. "Ida, it's Saphik."

"What about, Saphik?" Ida demanded.

Galeno looked around nervously again. "Are you sure, he's really where he said he was going to be?"

"I guess."

Galeno reached into his pack and pulled out a parchment. He handed it to Ida. "This is Saphik's hand is it not?"

Ida nodded.

"Read it," he said.

Ida read it, the color draining from her face.

As I said, I have confirmed it with my own eyes. I stand by that it is more than just the vain hopes of a grieving mother. Pharaoh's son lives. Not only does she admit it with her own tongue, but I have listened and heard Nacamakun and others speak of him thus in private counsel. There is no mistaking it.

Even had I not heard with my own ears the truth, one look at the boy, especially beside Ida and one can not possibly doubt that he is her issue. I know that still you doubt. Once you look upon the boy yourself, however, you too will be so convinced.

The perfect opportunity has finally presented itself. If all goes to plan, you will have the boy before the next cycle of the moon.

She looked back up at Galeno. "Where did you get this?" she breathed.

"From one of Lord Bietek's men."

Ida was temporarily dazed by the revelation.

Lord Bietek, too?

She shook her head. It couldn't be.

Her mind sharpened. Abidos.

"We have to get out of here," Ida said, "Now."

Galeno nodded. "Is there anyone here you can trust?" he asked.

Ida thought on it.

"Jonkina." She looked back up at Galeno. "Have my servant fetch him while I go wake Kadar."

Galeno had been right to be suspicious. Just as they exited Prince Sarri's compound, Jonkina spotted torches in the distance. He halted the small group behind him – three of his most trusted men, Ida, Galeno and Kadar. All eyes turned towards the direction in which he had been staring.

"It's him," Ida said. "I know it is."

Jonkina looked back at her. "Shall we go on through the forest trail?" he asked.

Ida nodded. "You take Kadar and go. I'll go back to the compound and stall him."

"But my lady -" he objected.

"That's an order," she said. "Your priority is to get Kadar back to the citadel unharmed."

"Yes, my lady," Jonkina intoned. Turning his horse, he signaled for the rest of the group to follow him into the thicket.

Galeno hesitated.

"You too," Ida insisted.

"But Ida -"

"There's no time to argue. I need someone I can trust with my boy at all times." She dug out the incriminating letter and handed it back to Galeno. "See that Mursili gets this."

She smiled reassuringly, gave Galeno a kiss on his cheek. "I'll be fine," she said. "Hurry."

Against his better judgment, Galeno turned his mount and ran her to catch up with the rest of the group. Satisfied that her son was out of immediate danger, Ida turned her horse and rode back to the compound.

XXXII

Prince Sarri's compound. Assyria.

It was not two hours later that Ida felt Saphik slide into the bed next to her. She closed her eyes, forcing herself to lie still, to pretend to be asleep - even as her skin crawled. She felt him lean over her, plant a kiss on her bare shoulder as one his hands slowly slid up her leg, taking the hem of her night dress with it.

She shivered. However, instead of in anticipation, she shivered in revulsion. How could this man look her in the eye day after day, make love to her night after night knowing full well his end goal – to steal away her son? Especially when he knew well how much it killed her not to be in Kadar's life? How could he lie to her over and over again?

Ida could stand it no longer. She rolled over, forced a fake smile. "Welcome home," she said.

Saphik placed a lingering kiss on her lips.

When he pulled away, he smiled down at her. "That's a start," he said, the same hand once again trying to find its way beneath her gown.

"It's late," Ida explained, her hand upon his stopping his progress.

"That never stopped us before," he replied, a mischievous gleam in his eye.

"Besides, you don't have to do a thing," he promised. "You only have to lie there."

Ida stifled a yawn, smiled apologetically.

"By the gods, I'm sorry," she replied. "I would love nothing more than to have you inside of me, but I can't help it, I'm exhausted."

Saphik gave her a small frown. She lifted her head to gently kiss his lips before scooting across the bed and snuggling herself in his arms.

"First thing in the morning," she assured him. "I promise."

He grunted.

She looked up into his eyes. "Good night."

"Good night," he said though his disappointment was written all over his face.

Burying her face in his chest, Ida pretended to fall asleep. It was going to be a long night.

The sun was high in the sky by the time Ida was startled by her night dress being slid off her shoulders, by his hands on her naked breasts. She had not slept a wink the night before. Even as the sun had peeked into the room, she dared not move lest she cause him to stir.

Now, however, it seemed her prayers that he would sleep well into the evening were to go unanswered. It was barely now noon.

As his lips and hands moved across her skin, she tried to force herself to endure it, to respond as she always had. Something within her, however, would not comply.

"Good morning to you too," Ida said pulling away. She kissed him solidly on the mouth before rising from the bed.

"Yes," he said, a scowl on his handsome face. "It's *morning*." He emphasized the word morning - a signal to Ida that he remembered her promise of the night before.

"I know," Ida said apologetically, with a reassuring smile. "I just need a bath first." She made a face. "I feel really dirty this morning." It wasn't exactly a lie. "You've been on the road half the night to get home. The least I can do is get cleaned up – presentable for you."

Saphik rose to stand in front of her. He pulled her to him. "It wouldn't matter to me if you were covered in horse manure, I'd still want you. I'd still find you desirable."

He kissed her deeply.

Ida pulled away again. "I won't be long," she promised.

He watched as she hurried towards the bathing room. After a few moments of consideration, he followed.

"What time is it?" he asked as he noticed the light streaming into the room.

Ida startled. She hadn't realized he had followed her, had been lost in her thoughts as she stripped away her clothing. "I'm not sure," she lied.

Saphik went to the window and looked out of it. Below, his men were wrapping up their late morning exercises. "Shit!" he exclaimed. "Is it really so late?" He turned, made a beeline for the door.

He found his path blocked by a naked Ida. She pressed herself against him, one hand sliding down his chest. "Hey," she said with a pout. "What's your hurry?"

"It's almost time for afternoon drills," he explained, though his eyes begin to cloud with desire as her hand slid lower and lower and lower.

"Surely, they can go one afternoon without you?" she pressed, a mischievous glint her in her eyes as she slowly sank to her knees.

"Surely, you followed me in here for a reason," she asked, the wanton look in her eyes as her mouth and hands began doing delicious things to his member rendering him speechless and cutting off his mind's ability to think of anything else.

When he gasped and breathed her name, his hand tangling in her hair, she knew well she had him.

Day edged towards evening in much the same way.

As soon as Saphik would come to his senses and remember his duty, Ida would seduce him into staying.

Ida thanked the gods for crocodile dung paste. It was not only an effective contraceptive, but an excellent lubricant as well. Without it, it would have been a very uncomfortable day for Ida. She could go through the motions all she wished but there was no way she could muster up enough desire for him to welcome him into her without it.

Still, even with the dung and after the day's activities, she found herself so sore she could barely move. Now, as Saphik began once again to rise, she could hardly rise up on her elbows.

"Leaving so soon?" Ida asked with a small pout.

Saphik smiled. He bent over to kiss her pouty lips. "I don't think even you could handle another round," he replied.

"That doesn't mean we can't just lay around and enjoy each other's nearness," she said.

He laughed, standing upright once more. "Maybe another time. We've been too selfish today. Kadar isn't here nearly enough. I'm sure he misses his mother."

"He's 13 years old," Ida replied, "and hardly still suckling at my teat."

She sat up all the way. "Besides, there are other prettier and younger females with which his time is occupied these days."

"Younger, yes. Prettier? I doubt it."

Ida forced a smile, inwardly amazed how even now he could be so....normal, as if nothing had changed, as if everything were right in the world between them. She watched as he moved towards the bathing room.

Once she was sure he was in the water, she rose.

She gasped. It hurt to stand. Taking a deep breath, she followed him. She needed to give Jonkina as much time to get as far away as possible.

The warm water was soothing. Even though he had pulled her to him once more, he had thankfully only held her. She stalled him for as long as she could with talk of the time they were apart, with talk of his campaign, compound shenanigans and gossip.

At last the water begin to grow uncomfortable.

"We should go," Saphik said at last. "Dinner will be served soon."

Ida nodded, did as she was bade.

They had just finished dressing when there was an urgent pounding at their suite door.

"Who could that be?" he wondered aloud as he strode purposefully towards it, Ida at his heels.

Saphik opened the door, found one of Kadar's training buddies standing there. The color drained from her face.

"I know you said you were not to be disturbed this day, my lady," one of the guards at the door said. "But the boy was insistent he see the captain. He said it's a matter of utmost importance."

"Of course," Ida said turning away before anyone could read the expression on her face.

"What's the matter, boy?" Saphik asked.

"Captain," the boy greeted. "It's Kadar."

"What about Kadar?" Saphik pressed.

"He's disappeared," the boy replied.

"Disappeared?" Ida asked turning back to face them, her face the mask of parental concern. "What do you mean disappeared?"

The boy went on. "At first I assumed he skipped practice to spend more time with Hazrene, but it's check in now and he still hasn't returned."

"Maybe he simply lost track of time," Ida suggested.

"I thought so too," the boy said, "so when I went to Hazrene's house. No one has seen him all day."

"And Hazrene?" Saphik asked.

"She's in Nineven visiting relatives," the boy supplied.

"Give me a moment to ready myself," Saphik replied.

Ida followed him as he hurriedly made his way into their bed chamber and began to put on his captain uniform, to grab his weapons.

"You don't think something terrible might have happened to him, do you?" Ida asked.

He turned to her, reassuringly stroked her face. "I'm sure it's nothing," he said. "You know teenage boys. He might well have other girls he attends to in Hazrene's absence. Still, I'd rather be safe than sorry."

Ida nodded her understanding. She watched anxiously as Saphik turned to head back out the door. She followed.

Saphik turned to face her at the threshold to their suite. "Where are you going?" he asked.

"With you to find my son," Ida replied.

He shook his head. "I need you to stay here in case he comes back here or..." He let the thought die unspoken.

"Or he's really in danger," Ida finished, tears beginning to well in her eyes.

"He's going to be fine," he replied, gazing into her eyes. Then to his men: "Look after her."

With that he was gone, as were any hopes Ida had of keeping tabs on him.

XXXIII

Jonkina and his band made excellent time. They had already crossed the border back into Hatti by the time they had to stop for the night, to rest and water the horses.

Just as they approached Mari, Jonkina noticed a ragtag group of mercenaries camped near the brush along the main road into the city. He turned his horse, led the group off of the main trail.

Galeno rode up alongside Jonkina. "What's going on?" he asked.

"Trouble," Jonkina replied. "By the looks of it – big trouble."

Something wasn't adding up.

It was near dawn and Saphik was still no closer to finding Kadar than he had been the evening before. He was growing increasingly frustrated and suspicious.

It wasn't until well into the morning that he finally got a break. One of his men half walked, half dragged an ancient man into the impromptu search headquarters Saphik had set up in the courtyard.

"Repeat for the captain what you told me," the guard ordered, releasing him.

The man's attention turned to Saphik. "I saw Jonkina and a few men ride out with the boy late night before last," the old man repeated.

"Are you sure that's what you saw?" Saphik pressed. "My men switch watch every few hours."

The man nodded. "Quite sure, captain. I too thought it was a changing of the guard....at first. But then a woman joined them."

"A woman?" Saphik repeated, the hairs on the back of his neck standing. No, it couldn't be.

The man nodded again.

"Can you describe this woman?" he asked.

The man looked away from him.

"Talk!" Saphik demanded.

"It was your wife, sir," the old man said.

Saphik's jaw clenched as he stalked determinedly around the table and away from the command center. He made a beeline for the slave quarters, straight to the night porter.

The porter's eyes widened as he saw Saphik. It was all over now. May the gods forgive him.

Ida paced her bedroom. She had tried to leave the quarters a few times – once during each shift change – only to be refused. She was effectively trapped.

At the sound of the main door swinging open, she returned to the main chamber. Saphik was there, his face distorted in anger. Fear gripped Ida's heart. She waited, her heart pounding in her chest.

"Any news?" she asked when he did not speak.

He looked finally at her, a small smirk on his face. "You should know that better than I," he replied.

"Whatever do you mean?"

"What do I mean?" Saphik mocked.

Ida turned away from him. He went to her, grabbed her roughly by her arms and forced her to face him.

"You know well what I mean. How long did you think it would take me to figure it out?" he demanded.

"Figure out what?" she replied, her face the study of confusion.

Saphik laughed, releasing her and taking a few steps backward.

He nodded. "Play it however you like," he said. "But know that I *will* find them."

"Find who?" she asked.

"Your friend Galeno and Kadar," he replied.

He smiled darkly, "I should have known better. I should have distrusted Galeno's outward lack of ambition. Still, I guess your lover promising you the Mayorship of Thebes would be tough to resist."

All pretense faded from Ida. "What are you saying?"

"I'm saying that Galeno beat me to it." He smiled. "Surprised, Ida?"

She shook her head. "I don't believe you," she said.

"Of course not. Your good friend Galeno would never sell you down the river for his own ambition. But your husband.....he would right?" He shook his head. "So how did he do it? How did he convince you to go along with him, to hand the boy over to him on a silver platter?"

Ida paled.

Saphik smirked. "Let's just hope he decides to turn the boy over to Lord Bietek and not Pharaoh Horemheb," Saphik said. "Then again, Vizier is certainly a bigger boon than Mayor."

Ida shook her head again. "No," she breathed.

AMARNA BOOK II: BOOK OF HAWARA

"Yes, love. If you just would have stayed the hell out of it, you would have gotten your magical wish. Lord Bietek and his supporters meant only to use Abidos to rally support in removing Horemheb from power."

"Then Lord Bietek is a fool. Even if everything went as he had hoped, he would still never have enough power to remove Horemheb. Horemheb is not some green, overly pampered ruler without loyal boots on the ground. He was the commander of the military for many seasons and he has done much to ensure the military's continued support. All Lord Bietek would have done was made my son a martyr."

"Perhaps," Saphik agreed. "But if he had succeeded, he meant to place your son on the throne. Your son, Ida." He moved towards her again. "You see, you don't need your precious King Mursili to restore the Amarna line to power. You only need us."

"You?" Ida repeated incredulous. "Even if everything went to plan and by some miracle Lord Bietek dethroned Horemheb, my son would have been nothing more than Lord Bietek's puppet."

Saphik smirked. "Perhaps. Now we may never know."

"I don't believe you," Ida replied.

"You don't have to," he replied. "I don't need you anymore."

He turned to leave the room, Ida hurrying after him.

"What do you mean by that?" she demanded.

"I was hoping we could get you onboard, that you could help your son rule," Saphik replied, "but now, it's clear you're not to be trusted."

He turned to his guards. "Keep her here," he said.

Ida tried to follow, found the chamber door once more closed in her face.

She sank to the ground. Where the hell was Mursili when she needed him?

The hours dragged on for Ida as she remained prisoner in her suite. Soon, the hours became days.

She was beside herself, her mind coming up with and discarding plan after plan, scenario after scenario. She no longer knew who or what to believe, who or what to trust.

She would not, however, go down without a fight. She had even fashioned a weapon out of one of the fixtures, should she need to resort to violence.

Ida, however, would never get the chance to use it. Half-way through her evening meal, her surroundings began to blur. Realizing the food was most likely drugged, she tried to rise, instead collapsed to the floor.

As her eyelids began to drift closed, she saw soldiers' feet move into the room, their words incomprehensible as the drug lulled her into unconsciousness.

Then nothing.

XXXIV

Ida's eyes slowly drifted open. As the world gradually came into focus, she realized she was no longer in Prince Sarri's compound. She pushed her torso from the bed, her head screaming in protest.

Someone came to sit on the bed behind her. "Careful," he said, helping her to sit. "The drug is still wearing off."

Groggily, Ida turned her head to the speaker. Her face betrayed her disbelief. "Is this a dream?" she whispered.

Mursili smiled. "I hope not," he replied.

"Where are we?" she asked.

"Mittani," Nacamakun replied.

Ida turned her head towards his voice. He was standing just off to the side.

"Nacamakun?" she whispered. "But how?"

"The sun goddess," Mursili supplied.

"And Galeno," Nac added.

Ida struggled to push past the fog, the past days' events finally beginning to sharpen in her mind. Without thought, she tried to rise, sank weakly back to the bed as Mursili held her fast.

"My son," she murmured. "I have to find Kadar."

"He's here," another voice said. Galeno.

Ida turned to see Galeno and Kadar standing in the doorway. She started to weep in her relief. Mursili pulled her to him, gently stroked her hair.

"You're safe now," Mursili said. "You both are. Rest."

Though Ida tried to fight it, fatigue soon overtook her. Gently laying her down on the bed, Mursili rose. He turned towards Kadar.

The boy was staring at Ida in disbelief. Had she just said he was her son?

It was only when Nacamakun placed a comforting hand on Kadar's shoulder that the boy seemed to snap out of his daze.

"My mother?" Kadar asked Nac.

"There's a lot you don't understand," Mursili said.

The boy turned his attention to the king. "That woman is my mother?" he repeated.

Mursili looked to Nac. Nac nodded. Mursili returned his attention to Kadar. "Yes," he replied.

"Yes?" Kadar asked, tears coming to his eyes. How many nights had he wished for his mother - only for her to never come?

Kadar had been so happy when he had met his aunt - if only because it was like getting to touch a piece of his mother. These men, these people he trusted, knew well that she was still alive. This woman, his own mother, had continued to deceive him - even as she wormed her way back into his life and into his heart.

Kadar didn't know how to feel about any of it – about her, about Nac, about any of these people. He was at once happy, grateful, hurt and angry.

"We'll explain everything," Nac promised.

"But first," Mursili said, "we have to figure out what to do with her."

When next Ida awoke, she found Kadar sitting next to her.

He was staring at her, studying her as though he had never seen her before.

Ida smiled uncertainly.

"Kadar," she breathed as she sat up in the bed. This time, it was not nearly so difficult.

Tears came to the boy's eyes. "Don't you mean Abidos, mother?" he asked.

Tears came to Ida's eyes. When had he...

"They told me everything," Kadar supplied.

He opened his palm revealing the pin that bound Ida to Tutankhamun. Ida's eyes went to it, memories rushing to greet her. It had been another lifetime ago. She had been another person when Tutankh had given it to her.

She looked back up into his eyes, gently cupping his face and wiping away his tears.

"I'm sorry we lied to you," she said. "We were only trying to protect you."

Kadar nodded. "I know," he replied. He studied her face for a long time before he pulled away from her.

He stood. "I'll let them know you're awake."

Ida nodded.

He turned to go.

"Kadar," she called to him.

He turned towards her.

"I love you," she said, her love for him burning in his eyes, "and if there had been any choice, any way at all for you to stay with me, for me to be able to keep you safe, I never would have left you."

The boy studied her for a long moment before he replied. "I know."

XXXV

The city of Washshuganni. Mittani region. Hittite Kingdom.

King Mursili and Nacamakun filled Ida in on what had transpired with Saphik.

After receiving a vision from Arinna warning him that Ida and Kadar were in danger, Mursili and a small battalion began preparations to leave the citadel and start towards Assyria. As part of his preparations, the king dispatched his fastest riders to Assur to alert Nacamakun to his plans.

Galeno arrived just as the messengers were leaving the compound. He had been secretly working with Mursili for years - serving as the king's eyes and ears in Egypt - a double agent. Without knowing it, he confirmed Mursili's vision, filled in the missing pieces.

Knowing well that one man would be able to move faster than a small army and knowing how much Ida trusted Galeno, Mursili had sent Galeno on ahead to his brother's compound - to warn Ida and if able, to get them out of there.

Although Jonkina and his small band had initially gone undetected, Lord Bietek's mercenaries had eventually managed to pick up their trail 50 miles north of Mari. A game of cat and mouse – of hiding, backtracking and outright out running had ensued. As the pursuit continued, the mercenary force grew – joined by Saphik and his loyal followers from the compound as well as some of the other smaller bands scattered between Assyria and the citadel.

Still, the small group of Jonkina and his expert riders managed to keep out of the mercenaries' reach, always one step ahead. That is until just before they reached Washshuganni.

Thirty miles south of the city, an arrow had found its way into Jonkina's mount, disabling the animal. It forced the man to double with Kadar – the lightest rider and cost them their considerable lead.

Just as the mercenary force was bearing down upon Jonkina's men, Mursili's forces came bearing down upon them from the West. Nacamakun's forces soon joined the skirmish – arriving from the South.

In the end, Lord Bietek's forces were defeated. Those who weren't killed during the battle were executed on the spot.

As for Saphik, Mursili had personally relieved him of his head. Still warm and dripping blood, he had the head wrapped and sent to Lord Bietek – a warning that he was no longer welcome in Hatti.

Ida had been relieved - that was until Mursili told her she was not returning to Hattusa with them. Nacamakun had wisely cleared the room, leaving Ida alone with Mursili.

"What do you mean I'm not going with you?" Ida demanded, deeply wounded. "You came all this way for me yet you'd leave me behind?"

"Ida -," Mursili began.

She cut him off. "First you sent me away because of your father then your brother and his queen. Still, even after your brother's death, you left me there in Lord Bietek's care – forgotten."

"You know that's not fair," Mursili defended, quickly losing patience. "You know well you were never forgotten – not even for one second."

Ida continued, tears coming to her eyes. "And then finally, I come to the citadel only to be turned away from you again – first for Gassulawiya's sake then because of Mal-Nikal. Even when Gassula passes and Nikal is driven out, it is because of the Sun Goddess. Now, even after Arinna has given you leave to save me, you turn me away from you for the sake of your new queen's reputation. Do you really fear her family so much?"

"I do not fear any man and I do not turn you away for anyone's sake but your own....and mine."

Ida smirked. "And Tani-hoho's"

Mursili smiled inspite of himself. "It's Tanu-hepa."

"Whatever," Ida replied.

Mursili's smile widened. "You're jealous," he said.

"Of course not," she replied.

Mursili laughed. "You are. If you ever met Tanu-hepa you'd realize that she is no competition for anyone, let alone you."

"How dare you mock me?!" Ida replied, trembling in her fury.

"I'm not trying to mock you," he said reaching out to stroke her face.

Ida pulled away from him. "Don't," she said.

Mursili sighed heavily. "I know you're in no mood to believe me right now," he said, "but there is nothing that would please me more on this earth than to have you near me. Even so, I will not risk your safety for my own selfish desires. It's not safe for you at the citadel."

"Not safe? And the compound in Syria was safe?" Ida replied.

Mursili gave no answer.

"Why are you doing this?" she asked. "Why are you doing everything in your power to keep me away from you?"

Mursili shook his head, sadness creeping into his eyes. "Because I can't lose you too, Ida," he said. "I wouldn't survive."

"So you push me away? How well has keeping me at a distance worked out so far?" she pressed. "Did sending me to Egypt keep me safe? Did sending me here keep me safe? No matter where I go, my enemies will eventually find me. You know that."

"So you would come to Hattusa, to the citadel – the one place where everyone will think to look for you?" he asked anguished.

"I'm tired of hiding. I'm tired of running."

"So you would end up like Gassula instead?" he yelled.

"Yes!" she replied. "If it meant I could spend the rest of my life at your side, as a mother to my son, then yes. A thousand times yes."

Mursili was stunned into silence.

She cupped his face. "You say that your destiny and mine are linked," she said gazing into his eyes. "You say that what happens to you happens to me. Can you not understand how true that is? Can you not see that when you hurt, I hurt, that when you cry, I cry, that when you triumph, I soar? Can you not see that no matter how far away you are from me that you are still here?" She touched her chest.

A small smile came to her face. "I've been patient. I've endured it all. I've shared all of the pain," she said. "Do I not deserve to share the rest – your laughter, the sound of your voice, the sight of you, your scent...your touch?"

Her thumb moved to brush across his lips.

Mursili's heart was pounding in his chest. He pulled away from her, turned his back to her – his chest heaving.

Ida stood there uncertainly for a long moment. Finally, she reached out and touched him.

He turned back to face her. Their eyes held for a long moment before he pulled her to him and claimed her mouth. There was no shyness, no coaxing in his kiss as there had once been. Now his kisses were sure and passionate, his tongue against hers stirring a desire in her the strength of which no man before him had managed.

She was breathless as his hands seamlessly stripped her of her clothing, as his hands and mouth heated the newly exposed skin as it had never been heated before.

Her hands and mouth followed his lead, pressed against every part of his skin she could reach and pushed away his clothing to free that which she could not until they were both completely unclothed.

Picking her up, he set her on the writing table. He smirked before he slid to his knees, his tongue and hands doing things to her she had never dreamed them capable of. If she had not loved him before, she certainly would have fallen in love with him now.

His mouth upon hers again, she was just as impatient to be taken as he was to take her. With her legs, she pulled his hips to her. He rolled his hips, elicited a loud gasp from her as he moved in to claim what was his. He lightly nibbled at her neck as her nails dug into his back, as he slowly brought the crescendo of her gasps higher.

Now, as they moved as one, the sensation was unparalleled.

Yes, her Mursili had certainly learned a lot since last they were together. Even the first time they had made love, even all of Ida's imaginings since paled in comparison to this.

He was now behind her, his raspy, hot breaths in her ear as the friction grew between them, as one of his hands slid between her thighs.

The heat of it threatened to burn Ida from the inside out.

She cried out, her body no longer able to resist the inevitable.

She shook with the force of him a few more times as he too lost the battle to prolong their pleasure.

Ida turned now to face him, stared into his eyes before she kissed him – a long, intense, soulful kiss. When she pulled away to look into his eyes, she knew.

She had won.

XXXVI

Thebes. Egypt.

"This is an unexpected surprise," Pharaoh Horemheb said to his visitor.

They were in his private audience chamber now, Horemheb's eyes slowly drinking in the sight of the beautiful woman. She was dressed to seduce – the expensive clothing that covered her shapely form, the perfume coming off of her smooth skin, intoxicating.

The woman smiled sensually. "A pleasant one I hope," she responded.

Horem smiled in reply. "King Mursili has a bounty on your head," he replied. "What's to stop me from imprisoning you and collecting?"

Mal-Nikal was unafraid. "I am still Tawannanna," she answered. "Even if you were foolish enough to hand me over to Mursili, my supporters would never allow him to take my life.

"Besides, why look a gift horse in the mouth?"

"A gift horse, you say?" Horem replied, his eyes drifting down to her ample cleavage.

Nikal smiled. "Not that type of gift, Great Pharaoh. Information."

"What kind of information?" he asked.

"Information that might be worth permanent asylum and a comfortable living allowance," she said.

Horem chuckled. He did so enjoy this woman's spirit.

"So, you've said," he replied at length. "Still, I'd just as soon be the judge of that." He rang for his attendant.

"Bring Faium to me," Horemheb said to the other man, "and don't forget his pet."

"Yes, sire," the man said with a great bow.

Horem returned his attention to Nikal as the man left to do as he was bade. "Can I offer you a drink while we wait?" he asked.

"That would be most kind of you," she replied.

Pharaoh called for a second servant to bring in the refreshments.

It was not long after they finished their first cups that Faium and his boy arrived. He found the two royals sitting at a small table across from one another on the terrace.

Upon Faium's signal, the boy held out his hand. Faium made strokes and pressed points on the boy's hand.

"I am here, Great Pharaoh," the boy translated.

Nikal looked questioningly to Horem.

Pharaoh smirked. "Faium here had a little run in with Tutankhamun that cost him his tongue," he explained.

She nodded her understanding.

Turning his attention to Faium, Horemheb spoke. "Did you finish the contract?" he asked the man.

Faium nodded. He handed the scroll to the boy who in turn handed it to the pharaoh. Unrolling it, Horemheb read it. Seemingly satisfied, he handed it to Nikal for her perusal.

Reading it, Nikal smiled. Her smile, however, faded when Horem took it away again. She looked up at him.

"This is yours if, and I mean only if, what you have in trade is worth it," he said.

Nikal nodded. "I can assure you it is," she replied.

"Then out with it," he commanded.

"I was there when your men came to the citadel looking for the child – the child of the dead Pharaoh Tutankhamun," she said, "and I know well who the child's mother was."

"So?"

"So the woman has returned to Mursili. She lives now in Assyria."

For the first time Horemheb's smile faltered. "Come again," he said.

"Idamun, former slave of Queen Ankhesenamun, lives. Her hair is red now and she calls herself by another name – Hawara, but I know it is she. She caused far too much commotion in the courts of my husbands for me not to have marked her countenance well."

Horemheb stood, his eyebrows knitting. What kind of game was the Tawannanna trying to play? There was no way Ida could still be alive.

Horem's smirk returned. "I'm afraid you're mistaken in that regard," he said. "I saw to her death personally, more than a decade ago." He moved to tear up the contract.

"No," Nikal said, her cool composure finally cracking as she rose from her chair. "Wait!"

Horem ceased his efforts. "Why?" he asked. "You come into my court and you make up ridiculous lies in a foolish effort to force me into breaking my treaty with your stepson."

"I speak the truth!" Nikal insisted. "How dare you even suggest that a woman of my status would have cause to lie?"

"I dare suggest that all women have cause to lie based solely on the virtues of your sex. That you face me now - exiled from your land, marked for death by the king - is more than additional cause enough for you to create this deception."

"You say you personally attended to her death?" Nikal replied. "Where then is her body?"

"Walled up in a cave in the middle of the desert," he replied.

"Then take me there. If it is as you say, I will voluntarily go with your men to turn myself in to Mursili."

AMARNA BOOK II: BOOK OF HAWARA

Horemheb laughed. "What incentive is that for me?" he asked. "I could quite easily "persuade" you to go to Mursili anytime I wish it – no consent from you required."

"Then I will give you whatever of mine you ask," she replied.

"Anything?" Horemheb smirked, his eyes lasciviously traveling down her body. While he had managed to secure himself a royal after taking over the throne – Ankhesenamun's aunt no less - and to take his pleasure with her at his leisure, he had never had himself a queen.

Nikal swallowed passed the lump in her throat. She had little left to lose, Mursili having effectively "persuaded" those who would have helped her not to interfere. She was running out of resources. Like it or not, she needed this contract.

"Yes," she reluctantly agreed. "Anything."

Pharaoh Horemheb didn't know what to believe. He stood now staring out the window at the city below, the Tawannanna in the chamber behind him, waiting anxiously for his decision.

When they had arrived at the cave in which they had buried Ida, alive with the dead boy, they found the wall destroyed. Inside, there was neither the body of Ida nor that of her bastard.

Any number of factors could account for the destroyed wall – weather, tomb robbers – but what of the bodies? Had animals perhaps dragged off the remains? Perhaps those of the two-legged variety?

Horemheb frowned. Few knew of where they had taken Ida - none of which would bother to brag of so common or unimportant an event. Still, had Mal-Nikal somehow found out about the cave, had the remains removed herself to give credence to her ridiculous claims?

Or maybe, just maybe, had Ida managed to escape death yet a second time?

He had personally seen her body the first time she had "died", had himself been a witness to her lifeless state. Yet, but a couple of years later, he had been confronted with her – live and in the flesh.

"Give it to her," Pharaoh said at last.

Nikal smiled as Faium did as he was bade.

Horem turned to face her. "Don't get too excited," he warned. "The contract is valid only pending verification. If we do not find Ida alive within the year, I will personally make you work off your debt, on your back, in the barracks. Then, once you're good and used up, kick you out on your pretty, little ass."

"Yes, Great Pharaoh," Nikal replied, only the rigidity of her posture betraying her fear.

Horem smirked, turned to Faium. "Interview her carefully. Mark every detail down."

"Yes, Great Pharaoh," the boy replied on his master's behalf.

"And make preparations," Horem continued. "It has been quite some time since we last paid a visit to our brother nation. What better time than now?"

Epilogue

There was a knock on Queen Tuya's chamber door. She glanced out at the sky. It was near nightfall – no doubt time for her to dress for the elaborate war offering to the gods that would precede her son's departure.

Reluctantly, she returned the scrolls to their trunk. Locking the trunk, she returned the trunk to its hiding place and the key to its place around her neck.

She had learned much – true, but still nothing that would help her convince Ramesses not to go to war with the Hittites. She was certain that the prognostications of a now dead Hittite King would not be nearly enough. She needed something more.

Tuya sighed heavily as she went to the door and unbarred it.

There was a rush of activity around her as her dressers, dressmakers, hair stylists, makeup artists and the like moved in and out of her chambers. She stood and sat as she was bade – their very own living doll – while they poked, prodded and beautified her, determined that she would do her duty to Ramesses then she would return to finish what she had started.

How True is Amarna Book II: Book of Hawara?

Okay, this is all being done by memory of research done decades ago. It's as accurate as I can make it without trying to dig up said research.

- The only people who did not specifically exist in reality (though they can be said to be composites of real people) are all of the non-royals and one royal.
- The only royal in the book who did not exist in real life? Lord Bietek.
- Lord Bietek is a composite of all of the royals who objected to Ay and Horemheb's succession. Such a person would likely help hide someone he believed could dethrone them.
- Egyptians believed that desecrating a body (such as destroying the heart) prevented a person from moving on in the afterlife.
- Mursili II wrote what can be considered one of the 1st known personal diaries/autobiographies in history. Much about the events after Tutankh's death and in Hattusa at the time comes from his first-hand accounts.
- Ay/Horemheb and Mursili II really did enter into a peace treaty. Mursili wanted to give his plague and famine inundated people a break from war.
- It took about 2 decades for Hattusa to recover from these natural disasters. During this time, Mursili built up large stores of grain – a guarantee against future famine.
- There really were scandals regarding officials robbing royal tombs – the results of the biggest of these scandals is described in Amarna II though it did not happen during this period. The Grand Vizier, Tomb Governor and Mayor of Thebes were all stripped of their power. Lesser accomplices were executed.
- No record of the tomb Carter discovered and which contained Tutankh's body and things was ever found. In my version of events, I decided to make this because Ida had stolen the plans and moved Tutankh's body and belongings without permission.
- Ironically, it is believed that Tutankh's tomb was found so intact because one of his successors usurped his intended royal tomb. This means that Aye and Horemheb helped PRESERVE and renew interest in the Amarna (particularly "The Heretic King" and his line) instead of erasing it. Just think about it. How people have heard of Ay and Horemheb vs. the people who have heard of "King Tut", Nefertiti (his mother) and his father, "The Heretic King" (Akhenaten)?
- Ay really appointed someone other than Horemheb as his successor. However, Horemheb defeated Nakhtmin and seized the throne.
- Horemheb, as much in search of legitimizing his rule as Ay had been, married a woman who some historians characterize as Ay's daughter and Nefertiti's sister: Mutnodjme.
- There is a lot of controversy surrounding Ay's true lineage though one theory is that he was a grand level relation to Tut.

- Horemheb really did pick up where Ay had left off and set about erasing everyone from Amenhotep III to Ay from history and usurping whatever treasures, deeds and statuary that suited him.
- Horem really did continue in destroying the religion of Aten (Tutankh's father's monotheistic religion) and erasing all traces of it. He even went so far as to use blocks from the destroyed Aten temple to fill the interior of the temple of Amun. Ironically, this action helped PRESERVE the Aten stones.
- Muwa really was one of Mursili's scribes. He's the only non-royal in this book that was a real person.
- Mursili's loved ones really did continue to drop like flies around him – and for the causes as described in the books including his brother Sarri-Kusuh.
- Mursili II's marriage to Gassulawiya was a love match – at least on his end. (wink)
- Some believe the Babylonian princess Suppilu married was Mal-Nikal. (Yes, she was real). Some believe Mal-Nikal was the wife of one of Suppilu's sons. As remarriages between fathers, sons, brothers, siblings, etc. was NOT uncommon amongst royalty and throughout the ancient world, I decided to make Mal-Nikal both.
- Mursili II, as king, was Head Priest. However, it was Mal-Nikal (his stepmother/sister in law) and not his Queen Gassulawiya who welded the most power over the priesthood as Head Priestess.
- Mal-Nikal also remained Queen.
- Gassula wanted Mal-Nikal's positions and kept putting pressure on her husband Mursili to get it for her. Mal-Nikal, however, wasn't having it.
- Mursili's youngest son at the time, Hattusili, really did fall into a terrible illness. He really was dedicated to another goddess, Sausga – not one of Mursili's two patron gods, Arinna and Telipinu. It was believed that this would/did save the boy's life.
- Sausga was a real goddess in the Hittite pantheon of gods. She was also known as Ishtar.
- Hattusili would remain faithful to Sausga/Ishtar his entire life.
- When Gassula suddenly died of poisoning, all eyes really did turn to Mal-Nikal.
- Mal-Nikal, however was much too powerful. Even Mursili could not touch her. She REMAINED Queen and High Priestess despite Mursili's accusations.
- It wasn't until Mursili received backing from the oracle at Sarissa, until the oracle confirmed his suspicions, that he could even attempt to avenge his wife.
- Mal-Nikal, however, was a step ahead of him and still too powerful. She escaped.
- Despite the oracle's confirmation, Mal-Nikal's support was great. Mursili was forced to settle for an official banishment (though she had already gone) with her return only on pain of death.
- Mursili really did remarry – this time for political reasons.

- All of the places mentioned in Ida's flight from Saphik are real.

Amarna Book III:
Book of Raia

by

Grea Alexander

Shoved out into the cold, cruel world shivering and naked by SeaMonkey Ink
A division of the sick mind of Grea Alexander

Copyright © 2015 by Grea Alexander

All rights are reserved. No part of this work may be reproduced or transmitted in any form or by any means possible in both the human and alien spectrum of existence including any and all oral, mental, physical, emotional, spiritual, sexual, electronic or mechanical means including but not limited to posting online (in excerpt or in whole), file sharing, photocopying, scanning and/or recording by any information storage or retrieval system and/or by any means yet to be invented without the express written permission of Grea Alexander or SeaMonkey Ink.

Genre: Historical Novel
Rating: Mature

Printed in the USA AKA the United States of America or as I like to call it Uuusah

A product of Seamonkey Ink, LLC

www.SeaMonkeyInk.com
@SeaMonkeyInk

Dedication

Choose your own dedication:

- ☐ GOD
- ☐ Grea – Queen of all she surveys (which is right now 1 tiny room)
- ☐ Lions and tigers and bears - can't fly
- ☐ Myself (in this case, you the reader)
- ☐ Germanchökolätekäke ice cream
- ☐ Project Runway (with Heidi Klum)
- ☐ Ancient Egypt, Hatti and the keepers of history who laid the groundwork for this series

Please note: This work is also a Novella

What's a novella? A novella is a written work running between 20,000 and 49,000 words. It is generally considered too long for most publishers to insert comfortably into a magazine without charges being filed against them yet too short for a novel.

I personally LIKE novellas. They let me get my work out faster which benefits both you who are dying to know what happens next and I who have a short attention span and limited time/energy to work on my books (as I suck so much at and don't have the time, money, know-how or energy for mass marketing nor do I have the sales to be able to live by writing books alone). Even if that were not the case, I don't like filler. I write what I feel needs to be written to get what I want to get across across. Sometimes more but rarely less.

So there you have it. It is what it is and I am unrepentantly unapologetic about it. I even wrote a song about it. Wanna hear it? Ok, read it?

Who writes short books? I write short books. If you dare read short books, read this short book.

Awesome right? (laugh)

In conclusion, yes, this book is short. It is a novella. I enjoy writing novellas and apparently series as well. While I do, however, have a few looonnng novels. (For some reason the Rebellion books in particular each just grew into big, fat, literary monsters.) This, however, is not one of them.

While I won't promise that I will stop with the novellas or the serializations, I will however promise you one thing. Ok, so I will loosely make an effort to guarantee one thing. Okay, so I will kinda, sorta try to uphold one thing. No, a few things:

1. Each series will last no longer than 3 books (which may or may not have spin offs or continuation series that will each last no longer than 3 books).
2. All of the answers to all of the big questions and the loose ends I deem important will be wrapped up by the 3rd book in the series.
3. I will remain one of the world's worse synopsizers. It is what it is. All of my creativity is poured into the story and the characterizations. I'm afraid by the time it's all over, there's very little left for synopsis..es or titles. Besides, my stories are kind of hard to sum up without giving anything pertinent away.
4. My book titles won't improve much over the course of the years either I'm afraid.
5. I will finish all of the books I start in serial form...eventually.

Now that we've gotten that swill out of the way, on with the show!

Amarna Book III:
Book of Raia

Hell hath no fury like a spider caught in its own web.

The gods, even in their rage, had never been more clear.

Either King Mursili II succeed in placing the Amarna bloodline back upon the Egyptian throne or everything he has sacrificed, everything he has lost will be for naught. Everything he has put those closest to him through – Nacamakun, Idamun, his family – would be for naught. All of his prayers and faith would be for naught.

Yes. Even in their vengeance, the gods had never been more clear.

It's all or nothing. Either the prophecy is fulfilled and both Egypt & Hatti find salvation or Mursili and his allies fail - plunging both kingdoms into indescribable darkness.

Behold. Even in the terrible deafening silence of their abandonment, the gods had never been more clear.

The time has come for judgment.

Introduction

The overarching theme of this installment is Hell hath no fury like a spider caught in its own web. And boy there are a lot of webs & quite a few spiders! (wink)

In this, the final explosive installment of the Amarna trilogy, everyone's hand is revealed - the gods', Lord Bietek's, Ida's, Pharaoh Horemheb's, Mursili's, Nacamakun's.

Mal-Nikal makes an even more powerful ally and Mursili a new enemy with the power to destroy him and his from the inside out.

Lies, suspicions, insecurities are exposed. Long seething hatreds resurface.

It's all or nothing with each side clamoring for ultimate control of the Egyptian throne. Either the prophecy is fulfilled and both Egypt & Hatti are saved or it is not.

Prologue

Ancient Egypt. 1274 B.C. Reign of Pharaoh Ramesses II.

The palace at Pi-Ramesses was filled with frenetic energy – a blinding, colorful swirl of people coming and going at all hours of the day and night. It was a palpable energy - one that seemed to grow in intensity as the inevitability of war between the Hittites and Egyptians grew ever more certain. It was an energy that penetrated every cell, every nerve ending of Pharaoh Ramesses II's mother, Queen Tuya.

She sat now in the grand dining hall, at the head of its long, ornate table. Though she would rather be back in her rooms devouring the scrolls her father had left her, she had no choice but to be exactly where she was at that moment. It was the least she could do to support her son - charm and show the proper appreciation to her son Ramesses' allies.

Still, try as she might, the best the Queen could offer was an occasional forced smile, a nod of understanding every so often.

Even at that moment, as the tide of conversation turned to the war, as she sat poised and graceful upon her gilded chair, she wanted to weep. She wanted to tear out her hair and scream that it was not just their Pharaoh who was out there risking his life, but her son – the boy whom she had suckled, whom she had watched grow, whom had loved since first she had felt him moving inside of her.

Tuya forced her gaze downward, to her golden plate – afraid her eyes would give her true state away. Though it was filled with the rarest and finest of Egyptian delicacies, she could muster no appetite.

She suppressed a sigh as she began to force herself to eat.

A sudden commotion near the hall's entrance intruded upon Tuya's thoughts. All talk ceased as heads turned towards the disorder.

"But Her Highness instructed that I am to seek her immediately upon my arrival – regardless of the circumstances," the male intruder argued.

Grateful for the distraction, Queen Tuya excused herself from her guests and rose to see to it. As she turned, her pulse began to race.

It was him! He had finally come!

Though she wanted to sprint to the man and immediately pull him away somewhere private, Tuya was well aware of the eyes burning holes in her back. So, with great difficulty, she forced her feet to continue their slow, elegant gait towards the messenger.

Her voice commanding and even, she assured the guard that the intrusion was warranted and directed the man to follow her to her audience chamber.

Once inside, Tuya turned to face the man. As he opened his mouth to speak, Tuya raised a hand, silencing him.

Moving around him, the Queen went to the door and shut it soundly. Only then did she finally exhale, her shoulders sagging as she was finally able to let go of the burden of her charade.

The man waited patiently, his back to the Queen.

Taking a deep breath and standing erect once more, the Queen returned to the messenger.

"What news have you?" she asked.

"Two Shasu nomads were incepted by Pharaoh not a day's ride from Kadesh," the man replied. "They place the Hittite enemy far north in Aleppo - almost 200 km from Kadesh."

Queen Tuya nodded. "This is good news," she said almost to herself. "It means I still have time."

"Your highness?" the man asked.

She returned her attention to him. "Have my litter prepared. We leave at daybreak."

Without further delay, Tuya hurried to her rooms. Locking the door behind her, she removed the small trunk her father had given her from its hiding place. Taking the key from around her neck, she opened it and removed the final scrolls.

I

The Scrolls.

Thebes, Egypt. Circa 1307 B.C.

The former Hittite Tawannanna, Mal-Nikal, began to light the candles on her makeshift altar to the goddess Šaušga. It was the best she could do here - in this foreign land full of false gods.

Though she knew well it was not up to the goddess' usual standard, it was her last hope that Šaušga would hear her.

Mal-Nikal's pretty face distorted in the candlelight, her anger and bitterness boiling to the surface. This was all that bastard Mursili's fault!

It was his fault and his alone that she had been forced to kill his Queen Gaššulawiya. It was his fault that she had been exiled from her beloved Hattusa, that her allies had all turned against her. It was his fault that she had lost her position as Queen and Head Priestess.

It was also his fault that she was forced to flee for her life, to their enemy, Pharaoh Horemheb of Egypt - a king devoid of all noble blood and upbringing, a ruthless, lecherous man who was little more than a common solider.

Nikal's face twisted into a cruel smile as she lit the last candle, as she imagined what was to come.

Mursili had won – this round – but it was she who would win the war.

Already she had convinced the barbarian Horemheb to give her quarter and that Tutankhamun's former concubine and slave, Idamun, might still be alive. So long as Ida lived, there lived proof of Ida's marriage to Tutankh, proof of her having borne a child – a child who Pharaoh Horem had murdered and whose body had disappeared along with its mother's.

If it were ever proven that Horem murdered Tutankhamun's only living heir....

Nikal's smile widened at the thought.

This new outrage, coupled with the whispered rumors of Horem's hand in Pharaoh Tutankhamun's death and perhaps even Pharaoh Ay's & Queen Ankhesenamun's, might well be the last straw for this self-appointed Pharaoh.

As things stood now, Horem's grip on the throne was tenuous at best. He had many powerful enemies - enemies with royal lineage, enemies who would gladly embrace anyone bearing evidence that would turn the people and his soldiers against him, who would gladly take up any excuse to dethrone him.

Nikal unsheathed her sacrificial dagger, watched as the light glinted off of its razor-sharp blade.

If only Mursili hadn't been so foolish as to try to unseat Nikal for his precious Queen Gaššulawiya and to avenge his mother's exile, she might well have helped him to destroy this usurper once and for all. Still, as things stood now, she needed this rogue Pharaoh.

However, if things went as planned, she might not always. Her smile widened as she further considered the perfection of her plan.

It was only a matter of days now before Faium, Horem's Emissary to Hattusa, would leave Egypt to seek out Ida.

Faium finding Ida under Mursili's protection would put Mursili in an impossible position. The treaty with Egypt that Mursili had bought with the sacrifice of Ida & Tutankh's son would be broken. Mursili would either have to sacrifice the woman he loves or risk plunging the Hittite people, who had only just recovered from plague and drought, into war.

Either way, Mursili would suffer and maybe, just maybe, the kingdom would be thrown into enough chaos for Nikal to swoop back in and reclaim the throne.

All Nikal needed now was a little help from her patron goddess Šaušga.

Opening her palm, Nikal slid the sharp blade across the tender flesh. She held the sliced hand open for a long moment as blood pooled in the cut. Then, closing her fist, she squeezed – her eyes dancing as she watched her blood drip onto her offering.

While Šaušga might not be willing to challenge Mursili's powerful patron gods directly – Telipinu, the storm god and Arinna, the sun goddess, she may well be persuaded to tip the scale just a bit in Nikal's favor – if only to have one of her Priestesses in power over the whole of the mighty Hittite empire.

II

The goddess Šaušga was insulted. She was insulted that a mere moral would dare call upon her in such a way – with such a paltry offering. She was insulted that her High Priestess had been reduced to this sad little homemade altar while King Mursili's patron gods, Arinna & Telipinu, had beautiful, elaborate temples in Hattusa, temples overflowing with offerings of such perfection as to make the gods themselves weep.

Most of all, she was insulted by Mursili's arrogance, by his obvious indifference.

Though Šaušga had been the one to save the life of Mursili's favorite son, Hattusili III, Mursili still paid her little homage. Though Mursili did not interfere with Hattusili's training as one of her priests, he did little to acknowledge it either. It was as though he were ashamed of the fact.

To add insult on top of insult, King Mursili had yet to build Šaušga the temple she so well deserved - a temple in commemoration of her mercy, a temple his dead queen had promised Šaušga's high priests.

Mursili didn't even attend the high celebrations her priests held in her honor or keep her holy days.

It was as though Šaušga were insignificant - a necessary inconvenience that King Mursili all but ignored.

Though Šaušga did not have the power of Arinna or Telipinu, she was still a goddess. She still had the ability to affect the mortal world and everything in it – even Arinna & Telipinu's precious King Mursili.

III

Ida stared at herself in the mirror. She sighed.

It had been almost a month since the change and still she felt like she was looking at a stranger in the mirror.

She was dressed in Greek fashion – in fine white linen. A long diaphanous veil was fastened to her hair – one she had to pull down over her face whenever she went out. Strappy leather sandals adorned her feet.

Her elaborately braided and pinned hair had been dyed once again – this time a rich, mahogany brown.

With her new look came a new name: Raia.

She sighed again.

It seemed every time she got used to one look, to one identity, she had to change it. Slave, concubine, corpse, trader's wife, Hittite noble, Egyptian Nurse-maid, Desert-dweller, wife, Greek. Black hair, blonde hair, red hair, brown hair. Idaten, Idamun, Hawara, Raia. Sometimes even *she* had trouble keeping it all straight in her head.

At least this time she would get to stay by her son Abidos' side. At least this time she would get to stay by Mursili's side – sort of. At least this time she would have Nacamakun, Clizi and Galeno – people she trusted by her side.

That is if she considered spending most of her time hidden away, in the secret rooms connected to Mursili's, being by their side.

Yes, Ida had finally gotten her heart's desire: to be closer to those she loved, but it had come at a price – a heavy price. It had come at the price of her freedom.

Far too many people in Hattusa knew her face. Should the wrong one figure out she had returned, not only would her life be in danger but the lives of her son and the rest of those she loved.

So, for their sakes, she accepted her fate. For their sakes Ida dared not risk discovery though there were days she felt sure she would go mad - trapped as she was in these luxuriously appointed boxes. There were days she struggled to breathe despite the large well-appointed windows, days she threatened to topple from loneliness and despair despite the nearness of those she cared for.

Instead of the happy, carefree reunion she had expected this to become, it had instead become an exercise in isolation – the days between each of her reprieves seeming to stretch farther and father between with each day she remained there.

She sighed once more.

After more than fifteen years of hiding she was growing weary. She was beginning to lose faith in Mursili's gods and their prophecies.

Forcing her thoughts from their dark turn – something she found she had to do more and more often these days, she tried instead to focus on frivolity, on vanity. She turned to look at her reflection from different angles, as she positioned the veil different ways.

Still, no matter what she tried, it made little difference. It was all so plain, so prim – so different from the fitted, elaborate clothing she was used to. How was a woman to capture and keep a man's eye in such drapery?

Ida scowled. Between the new hair, the new clothing and the new name, she just didn't feel like herself.

She stilled, stood staring at herself in the mirror.

She sighed once more.

"You deserve better."

Ida's eyes widened. Though it had indeed been her own voice, it was not her voice as it was now. It was her voice as it had been many, many years ago – from when she had been little more than a wounded girl with a crush. More unsettling still, the voice had not come from within. It had come from just behind her. She had even felt warm breath upon her ear.

Yet, looking into the mirror now, Ida saw nothing and no one there.

Could this be the doing of Mursili's gods? Did they still mean them ill?

Though she began to tremble with fear, Ida forced herself to turn around – ever so slowly.

It was then that she saw herself, her younger self, on the day Queen Ankhesenamun had given birth to her father Akhenaten's youngest daughter, Heketya.

It all seemed so real, as though she had somehow been transported back in time to that very moment.

Her younger self was arguing with one of the older servants – Batau.

"I know that right now you think I am just being spiteful," Batau was saying, "but Ida, you are just a slave girl, however favored you may be, a slave girl."

Her younger self had pulled her arm away. "My father is of noble blood," she had retorted proudly, "blood every bit as noble as theirs. My grandfather's defeat in battle and subsequent enslavement does not alter that fact."

The present Ida shook her head in disbelief, squeezed her eyes shut. Though she covered her ears with her hands, she could still hear them.

Turning her back to the mirage, she began to pray to Aten, the sun god of Pharaoh Akhenaten, the first god's name she had ever known.

At last the voices fell silent. Slowly Ida uncovered her ears and opened her eyes. After a few long moments, she forced herself to turn around once more.

The vision was gone - the sun streaming into the room and birds once again singing as though it had never been.

Perhaps I imagined it, Ida thought.

The laughter that came from just behind her left shoulder, that burned in her ear proved otherwise.

Ida whirled around to face it... whatever it was.

It was her – the her from the vision.

"Who are you?" Ida demanded. "What do you want?"

"I am the Goddess Sausga," her younger self replied, "and I only want to help you – to save you and Abidos before it's too late."

"Save us from what?" Ida demanded.

"From Mursili and his gods," the thing responded.

"I trust Mursili," Ida replied. "He would never – "

"Never what?" it said. "Betray someone he loves? Sacrifice anyone – even a poor, defenseless child if it meant appeasing his gods?"

Ida fell silent.

"Mursili loves no one more than he loves his gods," Sausga taunted. "Not even you."

"You, whatever you are, are a liar."

"Am I?" it asked. "Why don't you ask him yourself? He sees what is to come. He knows what is to come and he's hiding it from you."

"Learn from Nacamakun's mistakes," Sausga warned. "Or your son will end up just like his."

Before Ida could find her voice, Sausga disappeared - leaving a shaken Ida in her wake.

IV

Nacamakun stood in the grand courtyard of the Military Training Barracks in Hattusa. He watched as Ida & Tutankhamun's son, Abidos, completed the drills that would determine his admittance into the Officer Training Academy - both pride and sadness in his heart.

He had been Abidos' guardian all of Abidos' life. He had watched Abidos grow, loved him, taught him everything he knew. When his own son Kadar had been murdered by Pharaoh Horem – mistaken for Abidos, Nac had taken Abidos away from Hattusa, raised him as Kadar instead. Pride and sadness.

Watching the boy, now known as Kadar, Nac wondered what his own sickly little boy – the real Kadar - might have accomplished had he not been taken. He sighed heavily.

Though at times it was quite difficult, Nac did his best not to dwell upon the past. *This was his Kadar.* This strong, striking, sharp-minded young man was his son now - as he had been since that dark, much too vivid night that had shattered Nac's world forever.

Pride and Sadness. Pride at all that Abidos had accomplished. Sadness not only that his son was gone, but that on some level Nac was glad that he had been spared Abidos' life instead. His own son, though much adored, was very weak, very sickly. He had not been expected to live a very long life, never would have been able to accomplish all that Abidos had.

Blood of his blood or not, Nac loved Abidos as much as any father could possibly love any son. And he would protect Abidos, from anyone or anything - even if that meant protecting him from King Mursili and his own mother, the King's current consort.

Nacamakun watched as the officers and fellow candidates congratulated Kadar on his performance, as Kadar made his way over to him.

Nac embraced him, held Kadar to him a moment longer than usual, a fraction tighter. It was all the sign that Kadar needed to know that something was amiss with his father.

Though they did not share the same blood, Nac had raised him since he was a baby. Nac was the only father he had ever known.

Kadar pulled back and searched Nacamakun's face. He was about to draw Nac away from the crowd when another of the newly accepted cadets interrupted.

Kadar turned to speak with the other boy. When he turned back around, his father was gone.

The abruptness of Nacamakun's disappearance only served to fuel Kadar's anxiety. He peered around the throng until he caught sight of Nac moving swiftly towards the entrance of the building.

Kadar followed. He ignored the other men that were approaching him. He cut passed them, determinedly following the path that he had seen his father take. When he reached the doorway, he found his father standing at the opposite wall, peering unseeingly out the window.

"What is it father?" Kadar asked.

Nacamakun shook his head. "This is neither the time nor the place," he said. "When the celebration has ended, I will find you." With that he turned and left, leaving a frowning Kadar in his wake.

Kadar paced restlessly some hours later, as he awaited his father's return. What had his father found out? Who had dared tell him?

Kadar worked very hard to be all that Nacamakun wanted - an exemplary soldier, a fair and honorable nobleman, a loving protector of his intended, Hazrene; however, he also played hard.

Still, Kadar was quite well-liked. He could think of no one who would lay his secrets bare intentionally. Unless....

Yes, that was it. Someone must have been speaking of his exploits. His father must have overheard.

Kadar began to mentally prepare himself, answering in his mind the questions his father most assuredly would ask him when he returned. He was so deep in his thoughts, in fact, that he startled when Nacamakun called his name.

"Father," Kadar breathed as he turned to face the man.

He exhaled loudly before he began. "I don't know what you've heard, but there is a perfectly reasonable explanation," Kadar began. "Before you jump to conclusions - "

Nac waived his explanations away. "This has nothing to do with your carousing," he replied. "It has to do with your past, the truth."

Before he could say more, Nac was racked by a fit of cough. He spit the blood into a spittoon.

"You're not getting any better, are you?" Kadar asked.

Nacamakun wiped his mouth with the sleeve of his cloak. He studied the young man for a long moment before he replied. "I fear I have less time than we expected."

"Father…"

"Kadar please. I need you to listen. It's time you knew the truth – the whole truth. I see far too much of your mother in your face to go on keeping it from you."

Kadar's brow furrowed. "The whole truth about what?"

"About everything," Nac replied. "But first, I must have your word. You must never let on to anyone that you know what it is I am about to tell you – especially not your uncle Mursili."

"You have my word father."

Nacamakun reached into his tunic and withdrew the bracelet that Suppiluliuma had taken from Ida. He handed it to Kadar.

Kadar took it. "It was my mother's?" he asked as he examined it gingerly.

Nacamakun nodded. "It was given to her by your father."

Kadar looked up at Nacamakun as the words sunk in. "My father?" he repeated.

Nacamakun had to turn away from Kadar's wounded eyes.

Kadar came closer to the man he had known as his father his entire life. "But I have no father but you," he said. "Though Pharaoh's blood runs in my veins, you have been my father in every way that counts for as long as I have been alive. I see no reason that that should be changed now."

The tension melted away from Nacamakun. He visibly relaxed as Kadar laid a reassuring hand on his shoulder.

Nacamakun turned to look at his adopted son, his love and pride increased a hundred-fold at that moment. "Nor do I."

Kadar smiled.

Another violent fit of cough seized Nacamakun. Kadar supported Nac, leading him to his bed.

"Rest now, father," Kadar said as he made Nacamakun comfortable. "What you aim to tell me has waited all of these years. It can wait one night more."

Before Nac could protest, a milder fit of cough racked his body.

Kadar hurriedly retrieved the powder the physician had left and mixed it with beer. He supported his father's head as he drank.

The drug worked swiftly. Before Nacamakun could object, before he could warn Kadar about Mursili and his fanatical pursuit of his gods and his prophecies, before he could warn Kadar about how dangerous it was for anyone to find out that Kadar was anything other than Kadar, Nac was consumed by a drug-induced slumber.

V

King Mursili II abruptly sat up in bed, awaking in a cold sweat. The goddess Arinna had sent him a message - a very clear and disturbing one.

The goddess Šaušga and his stepmother Mal-Nikal were working against him. More disturbing still, they were using Ida to do so.

He turned his head to look down at the naked woman who slept beside him. Was Ida now to become as his Queen Gaššula had been – always near but always at arm's length? Someone he loved but from whom he kept a large part of himself hidden?

Mursili's brow furrowed in anguish.

Did the gods wish to take everyone he held dear away from him? First had been his mother – exiled so that his father could marry the Babylonian whore, Mal-Nikal. Then had come his favorite brother Zanna – murdered on his way to wife Queen Ankhe in Egypt, a casualty in a desperate bid to keep Ay and Horemheb from seizing the throne. Next had come his father – a victim of his own sacrilege, whose sins caused the gods to curse the entire kingdom of Hatti and place the burden of the Amarna prophecy on Mursili's shoulders.

After father had come the deaths of brother after brother, Nac's son Kadar, his wife Gassula and nearly his favorite son Hattusili III. Though Nac was still alive, the king's second father still could not quite forgive Mursili for sacrificing Kadar to his gods.

The only other person he truly loved and who was still in his life – aside from their children – was Ida. Ida was his last confidante, the only person he had left in all of Hattusa with whom to share his visions, the only other person who had just as much to gain as he were the prophecy fulfilled, and the only other person who had much to lose if it wasn't. Did he now have to give her up too?

Mursili scowled.

The gods had always been very clear. His fate was linked to that of Ida just as the fate of his empire was linked to that of Egypt. Only by restoring the Amarna line to the Egyptian throne could Mursili save them all.

Ida, mother of Abidos, was the mother of that bloodline and she was no longer to be trusted. Could he really still succeed in fulfilling the prophecy without her? Did he want to?

And what now would become of the vision sent to him by his patron god Telipinu? Telipinu had decreed that the time to reveal Abidos to Pharaoh Horemheb was near. But how could he do so without trusting the boy's mother, while knowing that the goddess Šaušga might at any moment destroy everything they had fought so hard to build?

For not the first time, Mursili's personal desires and the will of his patron god and goddess came directly into conflict. For not the first time, Mursili wished he could be anyone but King Mursili.

Ida awoke to find Mursili kneeling on the floor beside her, just next to the bed - both of his hands clutching one of hers. Though his eyes were closed and he was deep in prayer, his brow furrowed. Though his lips moved, he made no intelligible sound.

Ida slowly sat up in bed - the sheet sliding off of her naked chest as Mursili's weary eyes slowly slid open, as he released her hand.

"Mursili?" she whispered, dread in her voice.

He didn't answer, the eyes that bore into hers full of sorrow.

She cupped his face with one hand, lovingly stroked his cheek with her thumb. "Did you have another vision?" she asked.

Mursili hesitated for a long moment before he shook his head no.

He's hiding something, the voice that was her own, but that lived outside of her head whispered. Sausga.

"Are you hiding something from me?" she asked, her hurt in her eyes.

Mursili rose and turned away from her. He sighed heavily.

"You are aren't you?" Ida pressed rising from the bed and moving towards him.

He turned back to face her. He cupped her face. "Ida, do you trust me?" he asked her. She nodded.

"Then trust that if I am keeping something from you, it is for the greater good."

Ida pulled away from him. "What's that supposed to mean?" she demanded.

That he doesn't trust you, the voice supplied.

"It means...." He shook his head. "It means that there are things I can't tell you, that I can't tell anyone."

"Since *when*?" she asked.

Since always, the voice echoed.

"I'm sorry, Ida," he said, "but the gods have demanded it."

See? He loves and trusts no one more than he trusts his gods, Sausga goaded, *not even you. How much longer before he sacrifices you or Kadar to them?*

"I must go," Mursili said moving away from her, as he began pulling on his clothes. "I have a meeting with my vassals."

VI

With each passing day, Sausga grew bolder.

She haunted Ida relentlessly – day and night. No matter how hard Ida tried to dispel her, to quiet her, she was always there – lurking, whispering, poisoning Ida against everyone around her with her insinuations and half-truths, playing upon Ida's insecurities.

Though at first Sausga only appeared when Ida was alone, she had begun of late to show herself even when others were in the room – always in one incarnation of Ida or another.

Ida felt like she was going mad – to see herself across the room as vividly as she saw any other person, to hear herself as clearly as she heard any living thing, yet have no one else around her aware of Sausga's presence.

It was only when Mursili was in the room with her that the goddess dared not appear. Ida wondered on this. Could it be because Mursili might be able to see Sausga? Surely, if anyone could, it would be he.

Still, as things stood between she and Mursili, she dared not ask him. She continued to carry her burden alone.

The nights were the worse. They seemed to be when Sausga was at her cruelest.

Ida's weary eyes would barely sink closed when she would be jarred awake again by the sound of the goddess whispering in her ear or rustling about the room. When at last Ida would finally become so exhausted that she sank into a restless slumber, she was trapped. Her dreams would be filled with nightmarish scenarios of death, of betrayal.

After weeks of this, Ida's nerves were on edge. Every sound or sudden movement seemed to startle her.

On top of it all, there was an uneasy tension between she and Mursili now – one that seemed to grow with each passing day.

Worst still, as much as Ida wanted to, she could not quite bring herself to tell Mursili the truth. Too much of what Sausga said to her rang true.

There was no question in Ida's mind that Mursili *was* keeping something from her – something big. Though he tried to hide it, she frequently caught him staring at her – wistfulness, anguish and sadness in his eyes for but a moment before he looked away from her.

Fewer and fewer words passed between them these days, as the secrets they both carried grew.

The love was still there, yes. It was always there and would always be, but their lovemaking had changed. There was an urgency, a desperation to it. It was as if they both somehow knew that everything was soon coming to a head and they were both afraid.

Even now, as he moved inside of her, as she felt her core contract forcefully around him, Ida had never felt so alone.

King Mursili's nerves were just as frayed as Ida's – the weight of his obligations to Egypt and Hatti, to fulfill the prophecy threatening to crumble him. He was being torn in two.

Though he could see the toll Sausga's antics were taking on the woman he loved, he was powerless to stop it. No, he had been *commanded* not to stop it.

As much as he hated keeping the truth from Ida, as much as he hated watching her deteriorate a little more each day, he knew that this was the only way. If they were to see the prophecy fulfilled and save them all, they needed Sausga distracted.

Still, it didn't make any of this any easier.

Every spare moment he made offerings to his gods. Every spare moment he fell to his knees and begged their mercy.

Always the answer was the same.

Just a little longer. It would all be over soon and the prophecy fulfilled. They just had to hold on a little while longer.

Mursili only hoped that Ida would last that long.

VII

Nacamakun stood before the mirror in his rooms as he dressed himself. He was to escort King Mursili to Ankuwa that very afternoon.

As he fastened his sword to his side, his body was racked with cough. Years of war and hard living had finally taken their toll.

He wiped his mouth with his sleeve, his eyes widening as they confirmed what his tongue had already told him. Blood.

He turned and took a great swig of the draught the doctor had prepared for him. Setting the cup back down, he turned to face his reflection. Though sweat had broken across his brow, he still seemed passably well.

"You don't have much longer," a voice said from just behind him. A voice that sounded far too much like his own.

Nac whirled around, drawn sword in hand, ready to engage the intruder.

He couldn't believe his eyes. It was *him*. Only it wasn't him. It was the Nac he had been long before.

He was kneeling – crying out in agony on the day he had ridden home and found his son Kadar gone and Abidos in hiding. It was the day when first Nac finally understood the lengths to which the man he had once considered a son would go to appease his gods. It was the day that not only Kadar had died but the day Nac had cut Mursili from his heart – or at least the day he had tried to.

"Remember that day?" the voice said from just behind Nac.

Nac whirled around to face the phantom that bore his face, shoved his sword into the specter - to the hilt.

He was unnerved when the thing merely smirked at him, when it slowly pulled the sword from its body and tossed it to the ground.

"What are you?" Nac whispered. "Why are you here?"

"I am the goddess Sausga," it replied. "And I am here to save you from reliving the same sad, bitter fate all over again. I'm here to save Abidos from Mursili and his gods."

"You lie," Nac replied with more faith than he felt, though Sausga could see right through him.

"I wish I did," Sausga replied.

"Not even Mursili would dare –"

"Sacrifice yet another of your sons if it meant appeasing Arinna and Telipinu?"

Nac could not speak, the blood in his veins turning into ice.

"Right now," Sausga taunted, "even as we speak, Faium and his entourage are on their way to the citadel. Though they travel under the guise of diplomacy, they have something very different in mind.

"You see, dearest Nacamakun, Mal-Nikal has told Pharaoh Horemheb of Ida's miraculous resurrection. Even without knowing that Tutankhamun's son lives, Horem knows that Ida and Ida alone can prove her marriage tie to the dead Pharaoh, that Ida and Ida alone can prove that Horem tried to kill Tutankh's only living heir.

"Horem can't afford to take that risk. He will stop at nothing to find Ida and in doing so, he *will* stumble across your handsome son – the beautiful boy with his mother's beautiful face."

"No," Nac breathed - even the thought of losing another son unbearable.

"Fear not," Sausga warned. "It's still not too late to stop it. It's not too late to hide Kadar and Ida from their enemies."

Nac turned away from his younger self, his mind whirling.

He didn't know what to believe. Sausga was the goddess of the harvest and fertility yes but she was also the goddess of war. Was Sausga truly trying to help save Ida and Kadar or had Mursili done something to make the goddess turn against him?

"Either way," Sausga said from behind him. "Can you really afford not to take me at my word? Would you really gamble with both Kadar and Ida's lives?"

Nac turned to face Sausga once more. The goddess, however, was no longer there. Instead, a new mirage unfolded itself before him.

He was bursting into a strange apartment, the sounds of women's wails filling his ears long before he came upon them. Inside the back room he found Ida and a woman-child he did not recognize huddled over a body.

Kadar!

Rushing to Kadar's side, Nac pulled the woman-child away. He sank to his knees, watched helplessly as Kadar tried to speak, as frothy blood bubbled forth from his lips instead.

But moments later, Kadar's spirit had passed from the world.

Nac was in a daze as the vision slowly dissolved around him. It took a long moment after it had fled for him to realize it hadn't been real.

Still, the intensity of the pain he had felt in that moment, that still haunted his chest, was.

That was all it took. Without further hesitation, Nac hurried out the door.

Sausga watched his hurried retreat, a slow smile coming to her lips. This was working out better than even she had imagined it would.

VIII

"What's going on?" Ida asked as she watched Clizi hurriedly packing her things.

"We have to leave," Clizi said. "We have to leave now."

Ida was taken aback. "Leave? But why?"

Before Clizi could answer, Nac entered the room.

Ida was even more confused. Wasn't Nac supposed to be escorting Mursili to Ankuwa?

"It's Horemheb," Nac supplied. "Nikal has convinced him that you live and he's sent Faium here to find you."

"What?" Ida breathed.

"It's true," Nac said. "I have men here still loyal to me. More than one witnessed Mursili himself sign Faium's diplomatic passage charter."

Ida shook her head. This couldn't be happening.

Ida's disembodied voice floated into her ear. "I told you you couldn't trust Mursili," Sausga whispered. "You can't trust any of them."

Ida stared wide-eyed at the phantasm of herself standing just behind Nac. It was her as Hawara – her tresses flaxen and breasts swollen with milk.

Nac turned to glace in the direction into which she stared – half expecting to see the apparition of his younger self there. When he saw nothing, he turned his attention back to Ida.

"We have to get you somewhere safe," he said.

Ida forced her gaze from Sausga and back to the imposing, dark skinned man who towered over her.

"And Kadar?" Ida asked.

"He's already there," Nac assured her, "where no one will find either of you."

Ida nodded her understanding. She turned to Clizi. "Leave the rest," she said.

Clizi nodded her understanding, rose to follow Nac and Ida out of the chamber door.

King Mursili's head ached. He sat now, holding a damp towel to the gash on the back of his head.

It had all happened so fast.

Nacamakun had entered his chambers as he was adding a quick entry into the great book of his reign. Before Mursili could even turn to face him, the older man had struck him in the back of his head with one of his idols – knocking him unconscious. When he had awakened, Nac, Clizi and Ida were gone.

How could this have happened?

Everything had been going to plan. Faium would be at the Citadel soon – bringing with him Kadar's destiny and the final element needed to restore the Amarna line to power.

Now...

Mursili shook his head.

No. He would not let it end like this. He had sacrificed far too much to see the prophecy fulfilled.

He had to find Kadar and Ida. He had to find them before it was too late.

IX

Ida had been horrified to see Mursili laying on his chamber floor – unconscious, blood pooling on the floor near his head. Though she had allowed Nac to pull her away from the prone man, she could not get the image out of her mind.

"I have to go back," she said.

"Absolutely not," Nacamakun replied.

"Nac, please," she begged. "What if he's..." She couldn't even say the words.

"Look," Nac said. "I know how you feel about Mursili, but Kadar's life is in danger. *Your* life is in danger. If you go back now, he will never let you leave and I will have to keep Kadar from you too. Is that what you want?"

Ida shook her head, tears pooling in her eyes.

"Good," Nac said. He turned to leave the room, was almost to the door when Ida spoke again.

"What if we're wrong?" she called from behind him.

Nac's shoulders stiffened.

He too had his doubts. Still, if there was even a grain of truth in the goddesses' words....

"What if we're not?" Nac asked over his shoulder.

Ida inhaled sharply. Even the thought of Mursili's betrayal hurt too much to bear.

She shook her head. There had to be more too it. There had to be something they were both missing.

Mursili would never sacrifice Abidos. He believed too strongly in the prophecy. He believed that saving the Amarna line was the only way he could save his own people. Surely, no force in the heavens or upon the earth could make him betray that cause....could it?

"It makes no sense," Ida said at length. "Why would Mursili go to such lengths to stop Saphik and Lord Bietek if he only meant to do what it is they were trying to do in the first place – to expose Abidos' existence to the world and dethrone Horemheb?"

"Because the will of the gods need not make sense to mortals," Nac replied turning back to face her, "and Mursili is a slave to those gods.

"Before he sacrificed my son, I never in a million years would have believed him capable of such a thing. Now..." he shook his head. "Now, I would put nothing past Mursili, Arinna or Telipinu."

"Still," Ida said. "After all he has done for me - for me and Abidos, should we not at least give him a chance to explain?"

"To explain what?" Nac replied, growing angry. "How he cares for nothing and no one the way he does for his gods, not even you?"

Ida stiffened, her blood turning cold. How many times had she heard those very words from Sausga?

Had Sausga gotten to Nac too?

Ida stared at him for a long moment. "You've seen her, haven't you?" she asked.

"Seen who?" Nac demanded.

"The goddess Sausga."

Nac laughed – a strange, hollow laugh. "You mistake me for your lover," he replied. "It is Mursili who claims to talk to the gods not I."

"He lies," Sausga whispered in Ida's ear. "They all lie. Don't trust any of them."

"I need to make final arrangements," Nac said. "You do as you will but know that if you leave, we will not be here when you return."

X

Ida found Mursili in Arinna's temple. His back was to her as he performed the sacrificial rites, his men standing guard at the temple's entrance.

He froze, suddenly aware of her arrival.

"Raia," he said setting the dagger in his hand down upon the altar and turning to face her. "Come."

As she crossed the threshold into the temple, he spoke again – this time to his men. "Close the door and allow no one else entry."

"Yes, Your Highness," the captain of his guard replied, doing as he was bade.

Mursili watched as Ida approached.

"I knew you would come," he said – both hope and despair burning in his eyes.

"How could I not?" she replied, her love for him tinged with pain.

She pulled her eyes from his, unable to stop her gaze from traveling about the temple, from searching for sign of Sausga.

Mursili watched her for a long moment. He knew well what she was about. Still, even Sausga would not dare enter Arinna's temple.

"Looking for someone?" he asked.

"No," she lied. "Just making sure we are truly alone."

He nodded.

She returned her gaze to his, stood staring at him for a long moment - longing, sadness and suspicion burning in eyes.

"Why'd you come back?" he asked.

She shook her head with a slight shrug of her shoulders. "I guess I just needed to know if it was true," she said quietly.

He looked down for a long moment, his brow furrowing before he looked back up at her.

"Did you give permission for Faium and his men to come to the citadel?" she asked.

He studied her face for a long moment before he answered. "Yes."

"Did you know they come seeking me?"

Another long pause before he answered. "Yes."

Ida was taken aback. "I don't understand," she said. "Why would you do this?"

"Because the gods have shown me what is to come. It's time, Ida. It's time to fulfill the prophecy."

"But at what cost?" Ida asked.

"That is for the gods to decide," he replied. "It is only my place to bear witness, to facilitate their will."

Sausga's words echoed in Ida's brain. *Mursili loves no one more than he loves his gods. Not even you.*

"And if the gods asked for Abidos' life?" Ida asked. "Would you give it to them?"

"The gods made no such request."

"And if they did?" she pressed.

He stared at her for a long moment before he replied.

"Abidos' fate is Abidos' fate," he answered cryptically. "With Faium comes Abidos' destiny. With Faium comes the final piece of the puzzle – the one piece vital to fulfilling the prophecy. If this meeting does not take place, all will be lost. All that we have lost, all that we have sacrificed, all that we have done will be for nothing if fate is not allowed to run its course."

"I don't care," Ida admitted, tears coming to her eyes. "I no longer care about the prophecy. I no longer care if the Amarna line returns to the Egyptian throne. I care about my son and I care about you.

"I have seen what this so-called prophecy has cost and I want no more of it. I just want to be with the people I love. I just want to live a normal life with you, Nac and my son."

She exhaled shakily, her tears breaking free.

She shook her head. "Mursili, I've had enough. I'm tired of running. I'm tired of hiding. I'm tired of fighting."

"Ida," he sighed cupping her face.

She pulled away, turned her back to him. "I'm with child," she said.

"What?" Mursili breathed. "Are you sure?"

Ida nodded, turned back to face him. "Clizi has confirmed it.

"Besides, you've seen the signs yourself. I've been weak, tired, barely able to keep anything down. Two moons have passed without my woman's blood."

She shook her head again. "I don't know what to do, Mursili. I won't sacrifice my son, yet I can't take this child from you either."

"Then stay," Mursili replied.

Ida shook her head. "Then I will lose Abidos," she replied. "Nac will never let him go nor will he ever trust me again."

"Then you have to convince Nac to bring Abidos back to the citadel," he said, his hands on her arms. "It's the only way."

"I can't," Ida replied pulling away from him. "I won't."

"Ida, please," Mursili tried to reason. "We have only just succeeded in winning back Arinna & Telipinu's favor. You know that. They have promised that all will be well in the end, that we will have everything we've ever dreamed of if only we see this through.

"However, if we don't act now, the gods will force action upon us. They'll turn against us once and for all and abandon us to fates far worse than any you could possibly imagine."

"Have they not already turned against us?" she asked. "Look at all they have done to us already, at all we have suffered. What if this is just another of their twisted, little games?"

"If I believed, even for one moment, that the gods meant Abidos harm," Mursili replied, "I would not ask this of you."

Ida studied him for a long moment. She shook her head. "I can't," she said. "I wish I could believe you but I can't.

"I know you. You would do anything the gods asked – anything at all if you believed it would save your people."

Her heart tore in her chest. "It's over, Mursili," she said. "You and your gods can only have one of us - either me and your child or Abidos - and I've decided to let Abidos go."

Mursili's anguish was written all over his face. "You think it's really that easy?" he demanded. "You think you can just tell the gods, sorry but no. You think they will just let you, me and our children live happily ever after simply because you've decided you don't want to play anymore?

"Don't you get it, Ida?! This is not just about you or I. It's about millions of people in both Egypt and Hatti, not just now but in generations to come. No one life – not yours, not mine, not even Abidos' - is worth their sacrifice."

He shook his head, tears pooling in his eyes. "I'm sorry Ida, but I can't let you or anyone else stand in my way."

Ida was stunned into silence.

"Guards!" Mursili called.

When the guard entered he spoke again.

"Take Raia to my quarters and see she stays there."

XI

Ida paced her rooms in the citadel like a caged tiger, Sausga - in the guise of a very young and heavily pregnant Idamun - watching her from across the room.

They had been there for more than a week without word from anyone.

"Why do you continue to pace so?" Sausga asked. "Will wearing through the floor change anything?"

Ida bristled, paused for a long moment before she resumed her pacing.

Sausga smirked.

"Just what did you expect from Mursili?" the goddess asked. "He is only a man. A man knows nothing of what it feels like to carry a child, to feel it growing inside of him."

Sausga rubbed her swollen womb. "How could Mursili possibly begin to understand the love of a mother for her son?"

Ida stopped, her gaze resolutely glued to the wall. She was trembling in her rage and despair.

"I warned you," Sausga taunted. "I told you you could not trust them. Now Nac has taken your son away from you for good and Mursili..."

The goddess smirked. "Now you finally see him for what he is.

"If he finds Abidos, he's going to place him upon Telipinu's altar with his own two hands. And once you birth his twin sons, he will place you upon Arinna's."

Sausga laughed.

Ida whirled around to face her, no longer able to withstand the cruel, hateful words that spewed from her very own mouth – words that burned into her very soul.

"Shut up!" Ida yelled.

"Why?" Sausga asked. "Is the truth not pleasing to your ears?"

"Shut. Up," Ida repeated.

Sausga laughed once more. "I tried to warn you but there's no getting through to you mortals is there? A handsome face and a well-skilled cock was all it took to get you to sell out your very own son."

Ida picked up a vase and flung it forcefully at the specter. Sausga laughed as it passed right through her and crashed against the wall.

"Tsk. Tsk. Tsk," Sausga said as her visage began to fade. "No getting through to you mortals at all."

XII

It was done.

Mursili watched now as a very curious and stubborn Kadar crept through the courtyard of the citadel, as he crept towards his destiny.

Though Mursili and his men had failed to find Kadar, though Nac and his men did all they could to keep Kadar hidden away from the Egyptian delegation, Kadar himself had found his way out, had found his way here, to this place, at exactly the right time.

Now, as Mursili watched the man-child – frozen in place, his chest heaving as first his eyes fell upon the beautiful Egyptian slave Azra, he knew it was done. Events had already been set into motion that would decide the fate of Egypt and Hatti once and for all.

Now, all Mursili had to do was keep Ida and Nac from ruining everything.

"Your highness," one of Mursili's men said from just behind him.

"Yes?" Mursili asked.

"Lord Faium seeks your counsel."

"Tell him I will be there shortly," Mursili replied.

"Yes, Sire," the man replied.

Mursili watched as Kadar slipped seamlessly among the banquet guests before he headed back inside to greet Faium.

It was not long after that Kadar, so enthralled and fascinated by Faium's slave Azra, found himself face to face with Faium. It was not long after that that Faium's eyes glowed with shock and recognition.

Mursili was not surprised. He should have known. They all should have known.

The gods always got their way in the end…one way or another. The only question that remained now was how high a price they would all have to pay for Ida and Nacamakun's interference.

XIII

"You can't keep me locked in here forever," Ida said, her eyes burning with anger.

"Of course I can," Mursili replied. "I'm king. However, I have no intention of doing so."

Ida's eyes glowed with suspicion, even as he stepped aside to reinforce his words. Her gaze drifted to the now open door, the door that had sealed her inside of her rooms, alone save for her servants, for nearly a month now.

She looked to him again. Just what was he up to?

"Why are you letting me go?" she asked.

"I'm not," he replied. "I'm merely giving you room to breathe."

"And Kadar?" she pressed. "Did you find him?"

Mursili shook his head.

Ida sighed relief.

"Fate did," he amended.

Ida's eyes widened in fear. "Where is he now?"

"With Faium's slave Azra," Mursili replied. "The two stole away in the night a few days hence."

"And you let them?" she asked in disbelief.

"Mmmm," he replied with a slight nod.

Ida was confused. "And Faium?" she asked.

"I'm quite sure he is doing everything in his power to find them."

"And you're not?" she asked.

"No."

Ida's brow furrowed. Surely there was something Mursili was not telling her. Surely Nac was also working to keep Kadar from harm.

Before Ida could ask, Mursili spoke again.

"I have said all I can say about Kadar's fate," Mursili added at length, "except for this. Stay out of it. If you interfere, things will end very badly for not only our people but for Kadar himself. Do you understand?"

Ida stared at him for a long moment before she finally nodded.

"Good," he said. "You are free to do as you will, to come and go as you please. Only take heed of my warning and mind the safety of the unborn children you carry inside of you."

"Children?" Ida asked.

"Twins," Mursili replied. "You carry my twin sons."

XIV

Kadar was happy. At least as happy as he could be after months on the run, as happy as he could be with the entire Egyptian and Hittite delegations hunting he and the woman he loved down like dogs.

Azra stared out of the window now, Kadar just behind her with his arms wrapped around her waist. She smiled softly as he placed kisses down the side of her neck.

He smiled as she turned around in his arms to face him.

Seeing the love and hope in his eyes, her smile faltered. It was not the first time he had noticed it do so.

"What is it?" he asked.

She turned away from him, unable to look him in the eye as she blinked back her tears.

"Kadar," she said a length. "There's something I have to tell you. Something bad."

She pulled away from him, crossed the room. He stood there watching her, unsure if he should go to her or stay where he was.

"I'm not who you think I am," she said.

"Are any of us really?" he joked.

She turned to face him. "No," she said. "I mean it. My name is Azra, yes and I work for Faium, yes but I was not sent with the delegation to serve him. I was sent with the delegation with one purpose and one purpose alone. I was sent to find the escaped slave Ida."

The color drained from Kadar's face.

Azra closed her eyes against the pain and fear she saw on his face.

"That was until Faium saw you and he began to suspect that...that it was not Pharaoh Tutankhamun's son who had been killed all those years ago but another, that Tutankh's heir might still live and that that heir might be you."

Kadar inhaled sharply. "What are you saying?" he asked though he already knew.

"I'm saying that the real reason I have been with you all these months, the real reason that I am here with you now is because I know who you really are."

She reached into her clothing and produced the pendant his father, Pharaoh Tutankhamun, had given his mother as a sign of their marriage. She held out her palm, showing it to him.

Kadar was stunned. He had kept the pendant well hidden in the floorboards of his home, that is until he and Azra had decided to run away together.

Still, he knew how precious and dangerous it was. He had never told Azra of its existence, had kept it well hidden among the things he had brought with him while they traveled and hidden in their rooms when they settled.

The only way she could have it now was if....

Kadar was devastated. "Why are you telling me this now?" he asked.

She crossed the room, came to stand before him. Taking one of his wrists in one hand, she unclenched his fist with the other. Placing the pendant in his palm, she closed it again.

She looked into his eyes, willing him to understand what it was she was trying to say. "Because I'm not the same person I was when this began," she said.

She blinked back her tears. "And because they're coming for you – soon. Though I have done all in my power to mislead Faium, my contact is a very shrewd man. I don't believe he trusts me any longer.

"Still, time is on your side. The trail I've left leads to Carcamish. It will take Faium's men days to search there and the cities between Carcamish and Washshuganni. By the time they reach Washshuganni, you could be as far away as the citadel in Assyria."

Kadar forced himself from his fog of pain and shock, his military training quickly taking over.

"That gives me a week, two at the most," he said half to himself as he hurried about the room gathering supplies.

Azra watched helplessly as Kadar hurried across the room to his armor and weapons, began hurriedly strapping them on.

He went to the door, Azra at his heels. After he unbarred it, he stood there for along moment.

"What of you?" he asked.

"I have to stay behind," she said. "It's the only way I can buy you more time."

He nodded. Still, he stood there.

"Kadar," she whispered, her voice trembling.

He turned around to face her.

"I...." she shook with the force of her sob.

Kadar pulled her into his arms and placed a long, lingering kiss upon her lips. When they pulled apart, there were tears in his eyes as well.

He rested his forehead against hers for a long moment, as he gathered the strength to leave her.

Finally, he released her, turned and left the apartment before he changed his mind.

Kadar was almost to the bottom of the stairs when he was confronted by a small group of hooded figures. He drew his sword, readied himself for what was to come.

He exhaled heavily, sagged against the wall in relief when one of the hooded figures pulled back its hood, revealing itself to be his mother.

For all of his bravado, Kadar was still little more than a teenaged boy.

Ida sobbed her relief, flew into his arms. He held her for a long moment before pulling away.

"We have to go," Kadar said. "Faium's men – "

"We know," Ida said, "but I'm afraid it's too late to run. They're just outside."

"Outside?" he asked puzzled. "But how?"

"I don't know," Ida replied.

"We should go back inside and barricade ourselves in," Galeno advised. "I have already sent word to Nacamakun. We only need hold out long enough for reinforcements to arrive."

Kadar nodded. He turned and led the way back upstairs, to his and Azra's quarters.

Azra was startled when Kadar burst back through the door - Ida, Galeno and a few of Galeno's men behind him.

"What's going on?" Azra asked.

"It's too late to run," Kadar said. "Faium's men are already here."

"But that's impossible," she said.

"Impossible or not," Ida replied. "They're here.

XV

King Mursili lay on the floor, his entire being shaking with convulsions, his eyes rolling towards the back of his head. Blood began to seep from his eyes, ears, nose and mouth as the gods filled him with their message.

Finally, the convulsions ceased.

Mursili lay there for a long moment – spent as his muddled mind struggled to make sense of the images with which the gods had filled it.

Something was wrong. Very wrong.

It was rare that the gods entered him in his waking state.

Mursili struggled to sit up, his breathing labored though he fought to return it to normal.

As the physical trauma began to subside, the images in his head became clearer.

He saw Azra warning Kadar of what was to come. He saw Kadar, Ida, Galeno and their band barricading themselves in Kadar's apartments. He saw Faium's men break through their defenses before Nac and his men could arrive. He saw....

Mursili stood clumsily, stumbled his way to his chamber door.

"Guard!" he called.

Even as the door swung open, even as his guard caught the weakened man and helped him keep his feet, he was calling for his horse.

XVI

Nacamakun felt like he was in a nightmare from which he could not awake.

He had just entered the rooms – rooms the goddess Sausga had shown him in her vision. There were Egyptian soldiers and hooded men strewn all across the floor – some dead, others in various states of injury.

Knowing well what he would find, Nac forced his wooden legs to carry him deeper into the apartment, towards the back room. There he found Kadar, Galeno, Ida and the woman-child.

Galeno was leaning heavily against the wall, clutching his wounded side. Kadar was lying on the ground between Ida and the woman-child, still alive but mortally wounded.

And the blood. There was so much of it.

As Nac had done in the vision, he rushed to Kadar's side, pulling the woman-child away. He looked down at Kadar now, feeling more helpless than he had in his entire life.

This wasn't happening again. It *couldn't* be happening again.

Nac was in a daze. Even the noisy, grief-filled wails coming from both Ida and the woman-child seemed to be coming from very far away.

As Nac looked down at his adopted son, it seemed to take an eternity for Kadar to breathe his last labored, raspy breaths. When at last Kadar's chest stilled, Nac felt his own heart stop in his chest.

Ida screamed – a cry so full of agony that it rattled him from his fog. He watched as his friend desperately shook her son, as she tried to yell and shake him back to life.

Nac gradually became aware that they were no longer alone. Someone was at the door.

Nac turned, watched in disbelief as Mursili entered the room. He stood, drawing his sword.

"This is your doing," Nac growled, madness and grief consuming him.

Before Mursili could respond, Nac charged him. Mursili's guard, however, were able to block the assault.

Though in Nac's crazed state he managed to kill four of the king's guard, they at last managed to subdue him. As one of the guard lifted his blade to cut Nac down, Mursili stopped him, ordering instead that Nac be taken to the dungeons – at least until he regained his senses.

"And take these two under my protection," Mursili ordered gesturing to Azra and Galeno.

He waited until his guard, Nac, Azra and Galeno were out of the room before he turned his attention to Ida.

He watched her for a long moment before he slowly approached she and her son. He sank down next to her, his sorrow filled gaze going first to Kadar then to Ida.

For the first time in his life, Mursili didn't know what to do.

So, instead, he did the only thing he could. He began to pray.

Ida was in complete shock as she silently stared down at her dead son, tears streaming down her face. She didn't seem to realize that Mursili and his men had arrived. She didn't seem to realize that Nac had tried to kill Mursili or to have been aware of the fierce fray that had taken place not 5 feet from where she sat.

Even now, she didn't seem to know that Mursili was there next to her or to hear Mursili's prayers for Abidos' safe passage to the next world.

So, when Mursili called to her, she startled.

"Ida," he breathed.

Ida's eyes slowly lifted to look at him. It took a long moment for her to come out of her fog, for recognition to register in her eyes.

"Mursili?" she whispered.

He nodded.

She shook with the force of her sob. "Abidos is not breathing," she whimpered.

"I know," he said quietly reaching out to take her hands in his.

She stared back down at her son. "And why is he so still?" she asked.

"Because he's gone," Mursili said softly.

Ida shook her head, her eyes fleeing back to his.

"No," she whimpered, her pained sobs beginning anew. "No."

"Ida, I'm sorry," he said pulling her into his arms. He held her tightly to him as she cried.

Ida's tears, however, seemed to be without end. When at last she pulled away from him, it was because she could no longer breathe. She was hyperventilating.

Mursili grabbed her arms. "Ida, breathe," he said.

Try as she did, she could not regain her breath. It wasn't long before she finally ran out of air.

At last she collapsed, Mursili catching her before her head made contact with the floor.

Then…. darkness.

XVII

Ida had never felt so keenly a stranger in Hattusa as she did right now - as she watched her son Abidos' body burn.

They were Egyptian. This was not their way. Abidos deserved to be embalmed. Abidos deserved to be mummified. Abidos deserved to have passages from the Book of the Dead read at his funeral and to be buried with the things he would need in the next life.

Instead, Mursili had read foreign prayers to foreign gods who meant nothing to her but misery. Instead, Abidos' body was set aflame and left to burn to cinder.

It wasn't right.

"No, it's not," Sausga whispered in Ida's ear.

More wrong still was the fact that Azra was still alive.

"While Kadar burns like some barbarian," Sausga breathed. "Even as you watch your son burn, the scribe Mittanna-muwa makes arrangements for Azra's escape."

Azra deserves to die for what she did to my son, Ida thought.

"Yes," Sausga agreed. "Azra must die."

Ida's eyes fell upon Nac.

Though he was still in custody, he had at least been allowed to attend Abidos' funeral. He sat there among the other mourners, still bound, surrounded by the Palace Guard. Hatred burned in his eyes whenever they fell upon Mursili.

"Mursili must also pay," Sausga whispered to Ida. "He could have saved Abidos if he had truly wanted to. The gods showed him what was to come. Yet, he let it happen anyway."

Ida could take no more, her rage and grief consuming her from the inside as fiercely as the flames licked at her son's charred remains.

She stood abruptly, stalked determinedly into the citadel. Few guards were about – most being friends of Nac and Kadar and thus, at the ceremony.

Ida easily found Azra's room. It was the only one that had guards posted outside of it. But a few shiny trinkets bought her easy entry.

As she moved though the suite, she pulled her long veil from her head and let it fall to the ground. She needed nothing to get in her way.

It was not long before Ida found the girl asleep in the bed chamber, Azra's eyes swollen as though she had cried herself to sleep.

Ida stared down at the brown-skinned girl, at her tightly curled tendrils of reddish brown hair. How beautiful and innocent she looked in her slumber.

"The better to entrap Abidos," Sausga whispered from behind her.

Sausga, now the red-headed Hawara, was dressed elegantly - as Saphik's wife.

"Just look at her," Sausga taunted as she came around Ida and stared down at Azra. "How sweet and sensual she looks – a cherry ripe for the plucking.

"She could have had a good life. She could have had any man she wanted, yet she chose to use her beauty to murder Abidos. She chose to use every last ounce of that beauty to lead your son to his doom."

Ida took out the small dagger she carried for protection, slowly pulled the knife from its sheath.

"And cruelest still," Sausga pressed, "she dragged it out for as long as she dared. How long your son believed she loved him. How long he imagined he had a future with her."

Ida swallowed hard, her vision starting to blur from her tears.

"Thanks to her," Sausga pressed, "the Amarna line is dead, the one person who bound you to your beloved Pharaoh Tutankhamun is dead, the one hope you had of reclaiming your family's lost glory is dead, Mursili's one hope of saving Egypt and Hatti is dead."

Slowly Ida raised the dagger, the point held downward, over Azra's heart. Though she closed both hands on the hilt to still her trembling, the blade continued to shake.

"Come on," Sausga taunted. "Do it. No one deserves to die more than she. No one.

"I have seen the future. If you let her live, she will only go on to do the same to someone else. She will only go on to make another mother feel just as you do right now."

"Your son's soul cries out for vengeance!" Sausga exclaimed.

Ida looked up at her, instead saw her dead son. His skin was charred, accusation burning in his eyes.

Ida cried out, dropped the knife as she stumbled backwards.

Azra shot up in bed, her chest heaving. Her eyes widened as she realized who was in the room with her and what the other woman was about.

Seeing Azra awake, Ida regained her focus. She scrambled to retrieved the knife. As Ida scrambled for the knife, Azra scrambled across the bed and away from her.

"Help!" Azra cried. "Someone help me!"

Ida stood facing her, madness and grief burning in her eyes.

"Help!" Azra cried once more as Ida slowly closed in on her.

Just as Ida was within striking distance of her prey, one of the guards burst through the door.

As Ida lunged for Azra, the guard lunged for Ida. He managed to grab the wrist that welded the knife and pull Ida away from the trembling girl. Though Ida struggled to break free, the man held her fast.

Ida was screaming at the girl, Azra cowering in the corner of the room – afraid that at any moment Ida might break free.

The commotion brought even more of the guard. One of them went to Azra's side and escorted her from the room while others formed a protective barrier between the two women.

"Take Raia to her quarters," their commander ordered, "and inform the king."

XVIII

King Mursili hurried to Ida's quarters as soon as he could get away. He barely even heard his commander as the man tried to brief him on what he had witnessed - so lost in his thoughts was he.

All he understood was that Ida had just tried to kill Azra.

Yes, Ida was in shock. Yes, Ida was in grief, but what had possessed her to do such a thing? Had not Ida finally learned her lesson? Had not Ida already done enough to ruin everything?

He shook his head.

Would Ida not stop until she saw them all dead, until she saw both Egypt and Hatti crumble to the ground?

He burst into Ida's quarters, immediately dismissing all of his men.

She sat in a chair, her eyes resolutely ahead, her hands clutching the chair arms so tightly that her knuckles whitened. Her posture was rigid. When finally she turned her eyes to meet Mursili's there was not an ounce of remorse in them.

He opened his mouth to speak, could not even calm himself enough to utter one coherent word. He exhaled loudly, paced the room a few times before he finally turned to face her.

"Look, Ida," he said struggling to keep his tone even. "I know you're hurting right now. I know you're angry and you want someone to blame for what has happened to Kadar –"

"Abidos," Ida corrected. "He's dead now. Can we not finally use his true name?"

Mursili closed his eyes, struggling to control his frustration. "To Abidos," he amended, "but Azra is blameless."

"Blameless?" Ida asked incredulously.

She rose from her chair, trembled with the force of her anger. "Was Azra not the spy Faium planted to ensnare my son? Did not Azra pretend to love him all the while feeding information back to his enemies? Was it not because of Azra that he was there in that shitty little hovel – alone and defenseless?"

"Yes," Mursili replied quietly.

"Then why then do you coddle her?!" Ida demanded, tears pooling in her eyes. "Why then does she lie about in quarters no less luxurious than my own while my son burns?"

"Azra had a part to play in Abidos's, in Amarna's, destiny," he replied. "Nothing more. Nothing less. How can I hold her to blame when she was only doing that which she was born to do?"

Ida laughed humorlessly. "Of course you wouldn't be on my side," she mocked. "What else could I possibly expect of you, Mursili? You who use the gods and prophecies to excuse all manner of cowardice, all manner of cruelty."

"Careful," Mursili warned.

"Careful or what?" Ida demanded.

Mursili did not answer though he clenched his teeth tightly, though the muscle in his jaw spasmed.

Ida nodded to herself. "Maybe you're right. Maybe I'm being unreasonable. Maybe I'm taking out my anger on the wrong person.

"After all, was it not you and your gods who said Abidos would be fine? Was it not you and your gods that promised that this would be the end, that all would work out for the best?" she choked.

Unable to hold her grief and anger at bay any longer, she turned away from him.

Mursili immediately felt regret for his earlier callousness - his sorrow burning in his eyes as he watched the woman he loved crumble.

"I'm sorry," he said quietly. "I'm so very sorry."

Instead of soothing Ida, the pain in his voice pricked her. It made her even angrier. What right did Mursili have to feel sorrow?

She whirled around to face him, allowed her grief and pain to turn into rage. Anything was better than feeling so much pain.

"You promised me!" she cried. "You promised, yet here my son is... dead!"

"I know," he repeated in that same quiet tone, "and I'm sorry."

"You know?" she mocked. "You're sorry?

"Well, guess what Mursili? I neither want nor need your sorrow! What I need now is for you to tell me the truth! Why has this happened to my son?! Why didn't you save him?!"

"Ida, I..."

"You what?" she spat.

He looked away from her.

"Come now, Mursili," she pressed. "There's nothing more you can say or do to me that would hurt me any more than I hurt right now."

Mursili sighed heavily, suddenly more tired than he had ever been in his entire life. He didn't have it in him to lie to her any longer.

"Ida, I warned you," he said. "I warned you that there would be consequences for disobeying the gods. I warned you to stay out of it, to not interfere."

Ida laughed humorlessly. "So what are you saying? That this is my fault?"

Mursili turned away from her – his pain so intense he couldn't stand it.

Ida grabbed his arm, forcing him around to face her.

"Answer me damn you!" she demanded.

Though tears stung at his eyes, he did as she wished. "The gods came into me," he said.

"And?" she prodded.

"And they showed me the truth - that it was not Azra who led Faium's men to Abidos but you."

"What?" she breathed, the air in the room suddenly too thin.

Mursili's face contorted in pain. "Azra had Faium's men convinced they were in Carchemish. It was only when one of his scouts recognized Galeno, spied you and Galeno's men conspiring to head to Mittani that they put two and two together, that they followed."

Ida shook her head. "No," she said, even as the truth of his words seeped into her soul.

She could still see herself now, waking up in her room in Carchemish - Sausga standing at the foot of her bed.

"You're wasting precious time," Sausga had said. "Abidos is not here but in Washshuganni Mittani. You must leave now, before it's too late."

At the time Ida had assumed Sausga had been implying it would be too late for Kadar to escape…but what if she had been wrong? What if it had been Sausga's intention all along for Ida to lead Faium's men to Abidos? What if it was Sausga's intention to soak Ida's hands with her own son's blood?

Ida suddenly felt sick to her stomach.

"No," Ida repeated sinking to the ground.

Mursili sank down next to her, tried to pull her into his arms.

This too made Ida angry. She deserved no love. She deserved no comfort. She who had just betrayed her own son.

With no one else to take her anguish out on, she began to strike Mursili.

"Leave me alone, you liar!" she cried, her words sounding hollow to even her own ears. "This is all your fault, all your doing!

"It wasn't me! I didn't kill my son! I didn't!"

Though Mursili did not say, he knew well it had been Sausga who had tricked Ida into betraying Abidos.

In his infinite arrogance, in his foolish complacency, Mursili had believed it was finally over, the prophecy finally fulfilled.

He had believed that allowing Sausga to have Ida would ensure Abidos remained safe – at least until Mursili and Muwa found a way to neutralize the goddess for good. He had believed Ida's suffering would finally set the Amarna free.

Mursili had been wrong.

He had underestimated Ida's determination, the reckless power of a mother's love. He had failed to recognize the immensity of the threat that Sausga and her influence posed to them all.

And now, as a result, the destiny that was to be the Amarnas' would not come to pass.

Kadar would not make it to the safety of Sarri's compound in Assyria where he and Sarri's guard would destroy the Egyptian threat once and for all. Kadar would not eventually reconcile with his true love, Hazrene, nor would the two marry, have many sons and daughters or live until ripe old age.

Now Faium would never realize the opportunity he had in Azra, falsely report Mal-Nikal a liar and Kadar dead to Pharaoh Horemheb. Mal-Nikal would no longer be punished for her sins. Horem would not finally end his obsession with Ida and her line.

No longer would Faium conspire with Vizier Paramesse to place the vizier's son and Kadar's daughter upon the Egyptian throne, unknowingly restoring the Amarna line to power.

Now, knowing well the wrath of the gods, none of this would come to pass. All of their fates – his, Ida's, Nac's, Abidos's, Hazrene's, Azra's and that of Kadar's unborn had been changed, forever. Now, there was only more torment, more pain to come for them all.

Feeling more than his fair share of blame for the calamitous turn of events, Mursili did not hesitate to let Ida rail at him and hit him until she was too exhausted to rail and strike at him any more, until she collapsed into his arms and sobbed, until she was too exhausted to weep any longer.

Then carrying her to his bed, he watched over her while she slipped into a fitful slumber.

XIX

The scribe Mittanna-muwa came bursting through the door of King Mursili's rooms, startling the king awake.

"My King," Muwa called. "I have news."

Irritated, Mursili motioned for Muwa to stop, to hold his tongue. He carefully leaned over Ida, making sure she still slumbered before he slipped from his bed.

Pulling on his clothes, he grabbed Muwa's arm and hurried him from his rooms and into hers. Only once the door was closed did Mursili speak.

"What news have you?" Mursili asked.

"I think I might have found it," Muwa said excitedly. Setting down the satchel he carried, he pulled a document from its recesses and handed it to the king.

Mursili took the sheets and read through them, a slow smile spreading across his lips.

"And you're sure this will work?" the king asked his chief scribe.

"No," the scribe replied, "but what other option do we have?

"Every other binding spell we've tried has failed. This one, at least, is the most promising we've have found so far."

Mursili nodded, continued to read.

"And the amulet?" the king asked.

"Right here," Muwa said riffling through the satchel until his fingers closed on the charm. He handed it to the king.

Mursili held it up to the light, examining it.

"It's kind of ugly," the king said at length. "It will be difficult to get Raia to wear it and never take it off, especially without tipping our hand to Sausga."

"Already taken care of," Muwa said reaching into his satchel again. This time he pulled out a beautiful pendant large enough and discrete enough to house the charm.

Mursili smiled as he took the housing from the scribe and placed the charm inside of it. It fit perfectly.

"I think this just might work for now," the king said clapping Muwa on the shoulder. "At least until we can get something of Kadar's to replace it."

Muwa nodded his understanding. Even this beautiful pendant Raia might take off if it did not please her that day or compliment her dress. Something from her dead son, she would never remove.

"Go and fetch the priests," Mursili commanded, "while I prepare the sacrifice."

XX

The goddess Sausga watched Ida sleep from the corridor between her and Mursili's apartments. It had been weeks since she had visited Ida last – the many wars between the lesser kingdoms distracting her from her games.

Sausga sighed. Though it had been fun toying with Mursili's little pet, fun bringing Mursili to his knees, Sausga was already growing bored. She had more important, more interesting matters to attend to and no more time to waste on such trivial things as these mortals.

Still, in Sausga's eyes, it had been time well spent. Seeing that arrogant bastard Mursili suffer had been worth it.

No, it had been more than worth it.

A slow smile spread across Sausga's lips as she visualized Ida throughout the years, as she settled on just the right Ida for the occasion.

There. Tonight she would be Ida's current Greek incarnation - Raia.

Closing her eyes, Sausga willed her form to change.

Her transformation complete, Sausga reopened her eyes and moved towards Ida's rooms.

Sausga couldn't wait. Tonight would be her best work yet. Tonight, she would push Ida and Mursili over the edge.

Sausga's smile widened.

However, as soon as Sausga penetrated the threshold of Ida's rooms, a sharp, painful jolt – like a thousand bolts of lightening - shot through her.

Sausga cried out in agony as she stumbled backwards and out of Ida's rooms. Even still, the pain from the jolt continued to radiate throughout her entire being.

Sausga was in shock. She had never felt such pain before, had never even known it was possible for mere mortals to hurt her.

As the pain finally began to subside, the deeply shaken goddess regained her confidence. This had to be some kind of fluke. Whatever barrier they had erected against her, whatever charm they had used, surely it would not work a second time – especially not now that she was prepared for it.

Re-gathering her courage, Sausga tried once more to enter Ida's rooms.

Yet again she was repelled, the pain she felt this time redoubled.

Sausga cried out in agony and anguish, her will to destroy Mursili once and for all multiplied a thousand-fold.

XXI

Nacamakun was plagued by violent dreams.

Though he had not witnessed it, he saw Horemheb torture, kill and desecrate the body of his son Kadar. Though he had not been there, he saw Faium's solider deliver the mortal wound that had killed Abidos.

"Mursili could have saved them...if he had truly wanted to," a familiar voice whispered in his ear.

Nac jerked awake. He sat up in his bunk - his chest heaving and tears falling from his eyes as they searched the darkness.

Though it was cold in the dungeons, sweat covered his body. Though men were crowded by the dozens in the small cell, no one else stirred.

"Nacamakun," the female voice whispered in the opposite ear.

Nac's head turned towards it, the hairs on the back of his neck standing to attention as he saw the cell door unlock and slowly creak open.

He hesitated for a long moment before he rose from his bunk. Then, carefully crossing over the men strewn about the floor, he moved towards the open door and through it.

Though he peered down the corridor in both directions, he saw no one about.

"Nacamakun!"

It was coming now from further down the darkened hallway.

Nac hesitated once more. This was obviously the work of something unnatural. What if It meant to lead him to his doom?

Nac shook his head, forcing his doubts aside. Unnatural or not, this might be the only chance he would ever have to avenge his sons.

His mind made up, Nacamakun crept down the hallway - towards the sound of his name.

XXII

Nacamakun continued to slither down the dank corridors of the dungeons, his body pressed flat against the damp walls.

Each time he came to a security door, the lock was turned and the door opened by unseen hands. Each time he came within sight of a guard, a gust of wind would blow down the corridor – simultaneously snuffing out the torch light and the guard's consciousness.

As he came to the final door of the dungeons, Nac could taste his freedom on his tongue. Only one more door separated him from the rest of the citadel. Only one more door separated him and his vengeance.

Yet, as he moved towards it, the lock did not turn and the door did not open. The wind did not blow and neither the light nor the guards' consciousnesses stolen away.

Still, ever so patiently, Nac watched and waited.

Watched and waited.

Watched and waited.

Still, no matter how long he stood there – his eyes intent upon his captors, his sweat drenched body pressed against the dark stone walls, the door stood immobile, impassable.

No matter how his muscles strained with the effort to hold his patience, the torches continued to blaze – a golden halo in the otherwise blackened room. No matter how his chest began to heave in his despair, the guards continued to gamble and carouse loudly just beyond him.

Just what kind of game was this Thing playing with him now? he wondered, the bitterness of this new reality finally beginning to settle in.

Still, he waited.

As the minutes stretched endlessly onward with no further aide from his unseen ally, Nac finally withdrew.

Careful not to make a sound, he slowly crept backwards - away from that damnable door, away from the blazing torches and away from the all too conscious soldiers.

Now, halfway back to his cell, he could barely contain a cry of anguish.

One measly door and six measly guards!

He smashed his fist into the wall, pain shooting up his wrist. He closed his eyes as he struggled to regain his composure - the physical pain a welcomed, though temporary distraction from his deeper mental anguish.

"Frustrating isn't it?" a familiar voice asked. "To be so close to vengeance yet still so very far away?"

Slowly, Nac's eyes drifted open.

He turned towards the voice. Before him he saw not Sausga's true form but that of his former lover – Mal-Nikal.

"I know exactly how that feels," she continued.

"What are you playing at?" Nac demanded through clenched teeth.

"Playing?" she repeated with a slow, sensuous smirk. "I'm not playing at anything. I'm....negotiating."

"Negotiating?" Nac repeated.

"Mmmm," Sausga replied. "I want to see Mursili brought down to his knees just as much as you do – maybe even more. But neither you nor I will be able to do it on our own. His patron gods still protect him.

"Still, there is a way, a way for both you and I to reap the vengeance we seek"

"I'm listening," Nac replied.

Sausga's smirk widened into a devious grin.

XXIII

King Mursili II stood at his altar - his eyes closed, his lips moving as he silently recited a prayer to his gods.

The door to his chamber slowly creaked open.

Though he heard it, he did not open his eyes. Instead, he waited for his guest to slowly creep his way into the room.

"I've been waiting for you," Mursili said, his eyes slowly drifting open. Yet, Mursili's gaze did not fall directly upon Nacamakun but just beyond him.

"Have you now?" Nacamakun replied.

Mursili's eyes drifted to Nac's face. "Of course."

"So you know what I mean to do?" Nac asked as he slowly drew the dagger he had taken from one of the unconscious guards, as he continued his slow creep towards Mursili.

"Yes," Mursili replied though he did not move.

XXIV

Ida rolled over in her bed, her eyes slowly drifting open.

Something had disturbed her slumber. She listened.

Voices. Mursili's and.... Nacamakun's?

Ida sprang from her bed, the amulet that had loosened in her slumber falling to the floor unnoticed as she hurried from her rooms, as she raced through the corridor that connected them to Mursili's.

Nac was but a few feet away from Mursili now, his dagger raised, a vicious snarl upon his face as he spat his accusations at the king.

"Nac don't!" Ida cried as she came to stand between the two men.

Nac froze - the sight of his friend, the only other person who truly understood the pain he felt, temporarily unnerving him.

Dare he hurt Ida – especially now that she was great with child? Dare he murder Mursili, the father of her child and her protector, right in front of her?

Mursili grabbed Ida by the arm, forced her behind him.

"Are you mad?!" Mursili demanded, his eyes drifting between Sausga and Nac.

"Go back to your rooms and stay there," Mursili commanded, his eyes continuing to drift between the two intruders as he slowly began to back he and Ida towards the corridor. "No matter what happens, stay there."

"And leave you to pay for my sins?" Ida cried incredulously, anguish in her voice.

"And protect our sons," Mursili replied through clenched teeth.

Sausga's eyes burned holes through Nacamakun's back. Why was he just standing there?

"Do something!" Sausga demanded.

Nac did not seem to hear her, his troubled gaze still upon the retreating pair.

Sausga grew even more agitated.

What good was this hulking beast of a man if all he could do was stand frozen as Mursili and Ida continued to put more and more distance between themselves and he? As he stood there struggling with his conscience?

"They're getting away, you idiot!" the goddess snapped. "You've already failed both Kadar and Abidos once! Are you already willing to do so again?"

The sting of the goddess' provocation pulled Nac from his thoughts. He once more began to advance upon the pair.

"Abidos' death wasn't his fault," Ida cried desperately from behind Mursili. "It was mine."

Nac froze once more, the weight of Ida's words striking him like a typhoon.

"Don't say another word," Mursili warned through tight lips as he continued to force Ida towards the corridor.

"*I* led Faium right to our son," Ida sobbed, her pain so intense it reached across the room and seeped into Nac. "*I* killed him."

Tears came to Nac's eyes, his whole body shaking in his grief.

Sausga had had enough. This human was too weak to do what needed to be done. She would have to take care of Mursili and Ida herself.

Without further hesitation, Sausga entered Nac's body.

Nacamakun's entire being shook, his head flying backward and his eyes rolling back in his head as his weak mortal frame struggled to contain the awesome power of the goddess.

"Your room, now!" Mursili yelled shoving Ida down the corridor as he ran back towards his altar.

Nac's body stilled, his eyes rolling back into position. His head slowly turned to track Mursili before his attention settled once more upon Ida.

Ida was frozen in the middle of the hallway, her eyes wide and chest heaving in horror.

A slow, malicious smile spread across Nac's face before Sausga moved towards her.

"Ida, run!" Mursili cried.

Ida stumbled backwards before she turned and ran faster than she ever had in her life, Sausga right behind her. She triggered the panel that blocked her rooms from Mursili's as she went. Though it was nearly closed by the time Sausga reached it, the goddess effortlessly halted its progress, shoved the heavy granite slab back open with ease.

Ida could almost feel Sausga's breath on her back now. As Sausga reached for her, Ida pitched forward, fell across the threshold of her room.

As Ida tried to scramble all the way inside, Sausga grabbed one of her ankles, pulling her down flat. Ida cried out in agony, Sausga's hand literally burning through her flesh.

Try as Ida did to pull her leg inside, she could not. No matter how she kicked at the goddess, the goddess would not let go. No matter how hard she pulled at the doorframe, she could gain no ground. It was like a mouse trying to escape a lion who had it by the tail.

Raising the knife, Sausga stabbed Ida in the leg.

The opening prayer finished, Mursili picked up his sacrificial knife and sliced it across his hand. His only hope of saving her, of saving them both was the completion of the ritual.

Though his body trembled and his voice shook with adrenaline, he continued. Even as he heard Ida cry out in pain, he continued.

Sausga felt her host's body jar. It was trying to expel her.

No! the goddess' mind screamed as she struggled to regain control of Nac, her grip on Ida beginning to give way.

Sausga's momentary distraction was enough. One well placed kick to Nac's face finally earned Ida the upper hand. She pulled with all of her might, dragged not only her leg but Nac's arm across the threshold.

As Nac's arm crossed the barrier, his body jolted - as though he had been struck by ten thousand bolts of lightening. Sausga's spirit was hurled backwards, forcefully expelled from the aging soldier's body.

No longer hampered by the effort of maintaining control over Nac, Sausga could hear Mursili's incantation – the incantation that would forever bar her from the mortal world. She had to stop him. She had to stop him now.

Pushing through the pain, Sausga forced herself to her feet. Still, with each step she took, she felt herself growing weaker, felt her power draining away from her.

Sausga was nearly to the altar now - Mursili's voice growing in volume and power as he repeated the incantation, as a bright white light pulsated around him and his long hair blew about.

Sausga's eyes widened. Arinna and Telipinu were with Mursili now.

Knowing better than to directly challenge the storm god and sun goddess, Sausga tried to flee instead.

Still, try as Sausga did to dematerialize, she could not. Too much of her power had been drained.

Desperate, she ran for Mursili's main chamber door. However, as she tried to go through it, she found herself jolted by yet another protective seal - this jolt bearing the agony of a thousand hells.

Sausga fell to the floor, her body racked with so much pain that even she, the great goddess of war, could not stand it.

Mursili's voice grew louder and more powerful still. It seemed all at once to surround her, to seep inside of her.

Sausga cried out in agony - a cry so powerful it shook the very foundations of citadel. Still, Arinna and Telipinu would not be moved.

Though bloody tears poured from her eyes, Sausga would not relent. And so, the incantation continued.

Sausga was half laughing, half crying in her despair, as Mursili's voice devoured her from the inside out. Using the last of her strength, she levitated a knife and flung it towards Mursili. The knife, however, disintegrated as it reached the field of light surrounding him.

Sausga cried out once more, this time in anguish. It was not going to end like this. It *could not* end like this.

Yet.... it was.

The goddess knew it was so as Mursili's incantation neared its crescendo, as the light that surrounded him pulsated, expanded, slowly filled the room. As its rays licked at Sausga's being, she felt the last of her earthly form begin to melt away.

Then, with one last, great pulse, the blinding light flared. In an instant, Sausga was gone, Mursili collapsing at his altar as the light fled back inside his chest.

As Mursili's consciousness fled, Sausga's spell was broken.

He could hear the sound of the citadel reawakening. He could hear Ida cry out as she ran to his side, as she tried her best to keep him in the land of the living.

His head lolling to the side, Mursili watched a dazed Nacamakun stumble into the room.

Nac held his side, his body racked with cough. Though he covered his mouth with his hand, Nac could not contain the blood his lungs had expelled.

As Nac struggled to regain his breath, his arm fell heavily to his side, the blood dripping from his fingers to the floor.

It was then that Mursili knew. The goddess' possession had been too much for the already weakened, grief-stricken man. Nac would not be much longer for this world.

Mursili's attention drifted in the direction of the main door of his suite. He could hear the guard outside of it now, trying to force it open.

His breaths growing slower and deeper, Mursili's eyes at last drifted closed.

XXV

Nac's head lolled wearily towards the main door for a long moment before he turned and slowly trudged towards Mursili and Ida.

He would be dead soon. He knew.

It was now or never.

Ida was still focused upon Mursili as Nac sank heavily to his knees just behind her. He watched for what seemed to his hazy mind an eternity - as she shook Mursili, as she called out to him, as she begged him not to leave her.

She was completely oblivious to Nac's presence and of that of the knife he had picked up off the floor – the knife which now lay glistening in his grip.

It was only when Nac forcefully yanked her away from Mursili and she saw the knife propelling downwards towards Mursili's chest that the spell was broken, that she realized what was happening. It was only then that she did the one thing she could think to do to save the man she loved.

She flung her body across Mursili's.

Still, Ida was too late.

Carried by momentum, Nacamakun could not stop the knife before it made contact - his face contorting in horror as the knife pierced Ida's flesh, as she cried out in pain then fell limply across Mursili's body.

Time stopped.

In that moment, nothing seemed real to Nacamakun - everything seeming from that point forward to move in slow motion.

Nac was still holding the knife, still staring down at Ida as the door to the king's chamber gave way, as the king's soldiers flooded the room.

It was only when he felt the first blade in his back that he jolted back to the present, that he realized the three of them were no longer alone. As he felt another stab, then another and another, he welcomed the pain.

As Nac finally collapsed, his body jerking with each new stab, a slow smile spread across his lips. Soon he would be away from this mortal world – a world full of pain and betrayal. Soon he would be free of Mursili and his gods and prophecies. Soon he would be reunited with his sons.

As the last vestiges of life slipped from Nacamakun, he was at last at peace.

XXVI

Ida awoke in near darkness, in both great physical and emotional pain. A solitary figure sat next to her bed, barely illuminated in the spare lamp light.

"Mursili," she whispered hoarsely.

"No," the man replied, drawing closer so she could see his face.

"Galeno?"

He nodded, reaching over to gently stroke her hair.

Ida's eyes drifted around the room. Mursili. Where was Mursili?

Of its own accord, her mind flew back to the events of the previous night – to the crazed look upon Nac's face as he had pulled her away from Mursili and brought the knife down towards the king's chest.

She tried to rise from her bed, was restrained by Galeno.

"Galeno, please," she begged, her voice trembling and tears pooling in her eyes.

"It's too soon," he replied firmly. "You must rest....at least for the sake of your sons."

"My sons?" she repeated as her eyes lost focus, as both hands flew to her midsection. Though her body remained tense, she allowed Galeno to lay her down again.

"They are well," Galeno reassured her.

Still, Ida did not quite trust his words. So much had happened of late that she was still not quite ready to believe that something good had come of it – that she had at least been spared the lives of the children she carried inside of her. But then, Sausga was also the goddess of fertility, was she not?

Still, it was only the twins' gentle press against the pressure of her hand that gave her a small measure of comfort. If she had lost them too...

She squeezed her eyes shut and shook her head against the thought. She shoved it from her mind.

Of course this only made room for another thought – one just as dark and painful.

Ida slowly reopened her eyes, tears breaking free as she felt herself drowning in her own chest.

"And Mursili?" she asked quietly.

"He lives."

"What?" Ida breathed, still not willing to allow herself to accept Galeno's words - though he was one of the few people she still trusted.

He nodded.

Her mind raced with the implications. "Where is he?" she asked.

"He sleeps," Galeno replied.

AMARNA BOOK III: BOOK OF RAIA

Her mind fled once more to the events of that terrible night.

"What do you mean he sleeps?" she pressed, dread rising within her.

"As you have," Galeno explained gently, "he has slept for the past three days straight."

"Three days?" she repeated.

She had been sleeping for three days? *Mursili* had been sleeping for three days?

Ida sat up despite the intensity of the pain that radiated from her back to her chest with the motion.

"Is he hurt?" she asked in a broken voice.

Galeno shook his head. "Not that the doctors can tell."

"And Nacamakun?"

For the first time Galeno couldn't meet her gaze.

Alarm bells went off in her head. "Galeno, what happened to Nac?" she pressed.

"He -" Galeno shook his head as his tears finally broke free.

Ida's dread began to rise once more. "What are you saying?" she demanded.

"Nacamakun is dead," Galeno admitted at last. "When the guards broke down the door and found him hovering over you and the king with a blood-soaked dagger..."

Galeno shook his head. "Nac left them no choice."

Ida covered her mouth with her hand as her body shook with the force of her sobs.

Whatever else Nac had been, he had a been a good friend, a good father to Abidos and a good father figure to Mursili – both boys not even of his blood. He had stood by Mursili when Mursili's mother was exiled for sorcery and replaced by Mal-Nikal. He had stood by Mursili and kept his secret when Mursili was given the gift of prophecy. He had stood by Mursili when Mursili told him of the Amarna prophecy and plotted with him to rescue a poor, undeserving slave girl from the vengeance of the Hittite people and their King. He had stood by Mursili when Mursili concocted the ridiculous story that Nac was the father of the child that grew in Ida's womb.

Even after Mursili had sent Ida to Lord Bietek, Nac continued to care for Abidos as his own. Even after his true son Kadar was taken by the Egyptians, Nac continued to protect the boy – even sacrificing the memory of his own child and giving Abidos Kadar's name.

And though his heart ached to no end from Mursili's betrayal, when Mursili truly needed him, Nac had returned and stood by his side.

Now, all of that would be forgotten. Now, Nacamakun would be remembered as nothing more than a traitor - except by those close enough to have had the honor of truly knowing him.

Yes, now, Nac would be made an example of. All of the spotless years of service he had provided to not only Mursili but to his father would be forgotten. All that he had done in their honor would be dissolved, his military titles and honors stripped.

The bravery, the honor, the devotion that had been Nacamakun would be no more. There would only be Nacamakun the traitor and in less than a moon, everything that was of Nacamakun, everything that belonged to him, would be gone.

Ida sickened at the thought.

Everything that belonged to him...

Clizi!

"What of Clizi?" Ida asked.

Galeno sobbed pitifully. "Clizi, along with the slaves of all of Nacamakun's households, were taken from his homes and executed in the square last sun."

Ida was stunned.

Even Clizi dead? Clizi who had first informed Ida of Abidos' existence. Clizi who had tended to her throughout her pregnancy and birth. Clizi who had been nursemaid to Abidos and Kadar their entire lives. Clizi who had never harmed even a fly.

"But why?" Ida asked, her voice thick with sorrow. "Why would they do that?"

Galeno shook his head.

They were interrupted by a light knock at Ida's main door. Ida listened as the man spoke briefly with the guards.

As the man entered the room, he was surprised to find Raia awake. He quickly fell to his knees, the object in his hand swiftly retreating behind his back.

"Lady Raia," Mittanna-muwa said, his head bowed.

Though Muwa had originally known her as Hawara, though he was more than a tad bit curious as to why she now slunk about in the shadows under the name of Raia, he dare not ask. Muwa's unwavering loyalty to the king, his unfailing ability to keep the king's secrets, Muwa knew, had helped him rise quickly among the scribes. He also knew, that should he ever fail in those virtues, he too would share a fate as bleak as Nacamakun's – or worse.

"Please rise," she said hurriedly swiping at her eyes.

"It's good to see you awake," the scribe said as he slowly approached the bed.

"Is it?" she asked suspiciously.

"Of course, My Lady" he replied.

"Then what is it you hide?" she asked. "And what brings you to my quarters so late at night?"

Sheepishly, Muwa pulled the new amulet from behind his back. He had meant to replace the previous one with this one while she slumbered.

"I brought this," he said. "It belonged to Kadar."

AMARNA BOOK III: BOOK OF RAIA

Ida's eyes narrowed. Why would he be bringing her something that belonged to Kadar, and in the middle of the night?

Muwa was unsettled by the intensity of Raia's gaze.

"It's protection," he explained.

"Protection?" she repeated.

Muwa nodded. "From the goddess Sausga," he admitted. "Though we were pretty sure the incantation would...did work, until the king awakens, it would probably be best if you wore it at all times."

Ida nodded her understanding.

Nervously Muwa handed the amulet to Galeno, watched as Galeno helped her put it on.

Ida returned her attention to Muwa. "You knew of the incantation?" she asked.

Muwa nodded again. "It was I who found it," he admitted.

"And what of its effects on the one who invoked it?" she pressed.

Muwa shook his head. "The incantation is thousands of years old and it hasn't been used for centuries...that we know of."

"I see," she said.

"However," he began again, before he could stop himself.

"However what?"

He hesitated for a long moment before he continued. "The incantation involved the taking of a great deal of power into his body – more power than even the king has ever attempted.

"You yourself have seen what it costs him even to have...." his eyes shifted uncomfortably to Galeno before they returned to Raia. "Well, you've seen how it drains him.

"This..." He shook his head. "This is that times a thousand."

Ida considered Muwa's words for a long moment.

"So you're saying he might yet succumb," she surmised.

Muwa mulled over his next words carefully before he spoke.

"Yes...and no," he replied at length. "While it's certainly possible he may never awaken, that he still draws breath means he might yet survive. Only time can answer that question. Time and the gods."

Ida nodded her understanding.

"Thank you, Muwa," she said. "For everything."

He bowed to her.

"I am only honored that the king trusted one so lowly as I enough to seek my assistance," Muwa replied.

"You did well," she replied.

Muwa struggled to hide his proud smile. "Now if you'll excuse me, My Lady," he said.

"Of course," she said.

He turned to leave, made it but a few steps towards the door before he turned back to face her.

"Yes?" Ida asked.

"Its Queen Tanuhepa and Prince Hattusili," he said. "They've been, as have most in the inner circle, eagerly awaiting news of your recovery. What might I tell them?"

Ida sighed heavily. She was hardly ready to deal with the onslaught of visitors and the questions they would surely bring with them.

"Tell them that while I have awakened, I will need a few days of complete seclusion, that I am not to be disturbed."

"Yes, My Lady," Muwa replied.

He turned to go once more. He was at the door when Ida called to him again.

"Muwa wait," she called.

He turned back towards her.

"They don't know anything about what truly happened here...do they?" she asked.

Muwa shook his head. He knew as well as she that Mursili was very selective about whom he let know of his abilities. With the king's mother and Nac gone, the only ones left who knew of Mursili's true nature was she and Muwa himself, possibly this man Galeno.

"They only know what the guard told them," he replied. "That Nacamakun somehow broke into the king's chamber and made an attempt on the king's life - only to be thwarted by your interference. The king's slumber they attribute to a blow to the head attained during the struggle. As for the missing time..." Muwa shrugged. "They simply pretend it didn't happen."

Ida nodded her understanding as her hand rose to her throbbing head.

Everything was bearing down upon her at once – sadness, despair, anguish, pain. In that moment, she wanted nothing more than to sink into the oblivion of sleep.

Galeno was quick to notice. "Thank you...once more, but as you can see Our Lady grows weary."

Muwa nodded his understanding. He stood watching for a long moment as Galeno helped Ida resettle on the bed, before he turned and left the room.

AMARNA BOOK III: BOOK OF RAIA

XXVII

The city of Nineven, Assyria.

Kadar's former intended, Hazrene, hid – listening, watching, as Lord Bietek barged into her Uncle Azil's home.

"Where's the girl?" Lord Bietek demanded.

"What girl?" her uncle asked. "I have only sons."

"What girl?" Lord Bietek snarled. "Hazrene! I know she's here!"

"I'm afraid My Lord that you are mistaken," her uncle lied. "Hazrene left with the caravan two morrows ago."

Lord Bietek ran a hand agitatedly down his face.

"You wouldn't be lying to me... would you Azil?" Bietek demanded.

"Of course not, Lord Bietek. I would never lie to you."

Bietek's eyes narrowed. "Because if you did, I would not take it lightly. It was, after all, you who came to me. You who begged me to save your family from financial ruin. You who begged me to help get your ailing Great Aunt out of Thebes.

"And it was she, Hazrene herself, who offered herself up to me as payment. She who vowed that she would do anything I asked of her."

"I remember, My Lord," her uncle replied.

"And do you remember as well that I could have done any number of things with a young beauty such as Hazrene, but instead I was merciful? That I gave her family the property and riches to resettle in Hattusa? That I trained her to be everything a young man could want, that I made her a warrior? That I chose her to marry the rightful heir to the Egyptian throne and to bear the seed of Amarna? That I did everything in my power to make it so?"

"Of course I remember, My Lord," her uncle replied. "We are forever in your debt."

"Then where now is Hazrene?" Lord Bietek demanded once more. "Saphik is dead. Kadar is dead. The girl who stole him away from Hazrene is missing. Everything is falling to ruin, yet Hazrene is no where to be found."

"Though I do not see what further assistance Hazi can be to you," her uncle replied, "it is as I have said, Hazrene left Nineven two suns ago."

Lord Bietek slammed her uncle against the wall and held his blade to the man's throat

"You do not see what further assistance Hazrene can be to me?" Lord Bietek mocked. "It is not for those so lowly as you to understand my motives. I've trained Hazrene. I've made her and her family into what they are today. I *own* her and I own you – all of you."

"Of course, My Lord," Azil replied. "Still, Hazrene is but a woman. Surely, with all of your forces -"

"I do not seek Hazrene to put her in danger's way! I seek Hazrene because the Oracle speaks of Kadar's seed. Either it resides in Hazrene or it resides in the other one. I need only to be sure of which."

"Hazrene is pure," Azil replied. "I'm sure of it."

Bietek smirked. "That's what they all claim," he said. "I'd just as soon let my physician be the judge of that."

Bietek snarled at Azil. "Just you remember your place, Azil. I need not your opinions, only the location of the girl."

"She is not here," Azil repeated defiantly.

Bietek's eyes narrowed. "I hope for your sake that you speak the truth," he said. "Because if I find out you've lied to me, that you took my money, that I wasted my time calling in favors to save some old slave, and you are lying to me, your entire family will suffer the consequences. Have I made myself clear?"

"Yes, My Lord," her uncle replied.

Lord Bietek released him.

"Now start from the beginning," Bietek commanded, "and tell my men everything you know of this caravan."

Azil did as he was bade, watched anxiously as the bulk of Lord Bietek's guard filed out of the house in pursuit.

When Lord Bietek and a handful of his men stayed behind, Azil turned to face them.

"Is there anything else you require of me, My Lord," he asked.

"Only your hospitality," Lord Bietek replied with a slow smirk.

Azil swallowed past the lump in his throat, his glance going to Hazrene's hiding place but an instant before he replied. "Of course, My Lord."

XXVIII

Thebes. Egypt.

Pharaoh Horemheb stared unseeingly out of the window as Mal-Nikal awaited her fate, as he mulled over all he had learned from Faium to date.

While it could not be determined with true certainty whether or not Idamun lived, there was a boy. A boy who had her face. A boy raised by the very same man who had fostered Ida's son before Horem's men had attacked his home and taken him. A boy who quite likely was Tutankhamun's son.

Then, before verification could be made, Ay and Esnai's daughter, Azra, one of Horem's favorite toys and one of his best double agents, ensnared the boy, ran away with him.

Just as everything seemed to be going to plan, somewhere along the line, Azra's loyalties shifted. Instead of doing her job, she began feeding her contact false information.

Yes, dear little minxy Azra made fools of them all for months before the two young lovers and a small band of defenders were cornered in Washshuganni of all places.

Defeated during the subsequent scuffle, few of his men made it out alive – Faium included of course. Though Faium swore that there was a woman warrior present and that she could well be Ida, her face had been covered. He could not say for certain.

Now, as it stood, Kadar was dead, Faium was wounded, Azra was on the run and he was no closer to finding her than he was to finding the *allegedly* twice resurrected Idamun.

Mal-Nikal shifted uncomfortably behind Horem. He turned to face her, his glare unsettling.

Nikal reminded Horem of Ankhesenamun in so many ways – negative ways. Just as Ankhe had been so willing to sell out the only living heir of her dead husband and its mother, Nikal was willing to sell out her own step-son, the king of Hatti.

A slow smirk spread across Horem's face. He had taken care of Ankhe and he knew well it was only a matter of time before he would have to take care of Nikal too.

"Your highness?" Nikal asked, her bravado for the first time faltering. She did not like the look in his eyes.

He turned his attention to his men. "Have her prepared and brought to my rooms," he said.

The men seized Nikal.

"But, Your Highness!" Nikal cried indignantly as she struggled against her captors, "You promised!"

"Yes, I did," Pharaoh replied. "I promised that I would provide permanent asylum and a comfortable living allowance if I found proof that Idamun lived....just as you promised to give yourself as collateral. Ida's existence, or lack thereof, has yet to be proven either way and you my dear have run out of time."

Nikal's eyes blazed. "How dare you?!"

Horem's attention returned to his men. "Oh, and see that she is tied down."

"No!" Nikal screamed in anguish as his men continued dragging the struggling woman away, as she cursed Horem and Egypt, as she promised her revenge.

Yes, Horem thought as he watched the spectacle, women like Mal-Nikal could never be trusted.

Still, that didn't mean he could not enjoy her in the present or that he might not have use for her in the future.

XXIX

Nineven.

The house had been still and dark for hours by the time Azil released Hazrene from her hiding place.

He motioned for her to be silent as they stealthily made their way through the house and to the rear door. Once outside, Azil led her through the back gate to a well-packed horse.

Hazrene mounted.

"Thank you, Uncle," she said. "I will not forget what you have done for me today."

Her uncle nodded. "Just keep to the back trails," he whispered, "and ride hard for the caravan. It will pass through Mari not Washshuganni. By the time Lord Bietek's men figure out they're on the wrong trail, you should well have reached the caravan and settled in."

"It matters not," Hazrene replied. "I ride not for the caravan but for Azra."

"For Azra?" her uncle repeated in surprise.

Hazrene nodded. "Don't you see Uncle? We have an unprecedented opportunity here. Lord Bietek, a distant relative of the Amarna line and the one person who could lead a successful uprising against Pharaoh Horemheb, believes that either Azra or I carry the seed of Kadar - a seed he would see sit upon the Egyptian throne.

"Both you and I know it is not I who carries Kadar's child, but she. If I can get rid of Azra and pass her child off as my own, it will be *us* and not Lord Bietek who rule Egypt.

"Surely, that is worth the risk?"

Azil thought her words over carefully.

Yes, a relative close to the Egyptian throne, above Lord Bietek, would not be a bad thing for the family. Still, what chance did Hazrene, a mere woman, have of pulling this off alone?

"Perhaps," he replied at last, "but everyone who knows of Kadar has been searching for Azra, in force, for months, without success. What would make your efforts any different? How would you even know where to begin?"

Hazrene considered his question for a long moment.

At last, it came to her.

"Grandma Batau," she said.

"Batau?" Azil repeated.

Hazrene nodded. "She was head slave under Pharaohs Akhenaten, Tutankhamun & Ay was she not? Surely she would know of Azra and her people. Surely, she would have better idea than most of where to start."

Azil scoffed. "That might have been possible….once," he agreed. "But in her current condition?" He shook his head.

Hazrene visibly deflated.

Her uncle was right. What chance did she have when so many others of greater means had failed? If the combined forces of Pharaoh Horemheb, Lord Bietek and the gods knew who else could not find Azra, what chance did she stand alone, guided only by her invalid Grandmother?

Hazrene sighed heavily.

She had visited her grandmother many times since Lord Bietek had settled the old woman in Assur. From one moment to the next Grandma Batau was a different person.

One moment her grandmother knew them all and remembered everything with startling clarity – even things from her early childhood. The next moment she barely remembered her own name, her own face.

"Still," Azil said breaking into Hazrene's thoughts, "it's worth a try. The road to Assur is but a short detour from the trail to Mari."

He nodded, his confidence growing by the moment. "Yes, try the old woman. If you can get nothing from her, it will take you but one lost night of sleep to join the caravan before Lord Bietek's men find it."

Hazrene's spirits rose once more, a bright smile breaking across her face. An answering smile formed upon Azil's lips.

Azil had always adored Hazrene. Although he knew he was blessed to have so many sons, Hazrene made him sometimes wish for just one little girl of his own.

"Now go," Azil instructed. "You've already lingered too long as it is."

Hazrene nodded.

Then, without further delay, she spurred her horse into motion.

XXX

Nubia.

Azra anxiously paced her rooms. She didn't like this. She didn't like this at all.

Before King Mursili had sent her away from the citadel, he had told her of the Amarna Prophecy, had told her that she carried twins – the last remaining direct descendants of the Amarna line, and that for their safety no one could know their true lineage. At least until the time was right for them to reclaim the throne.

Though she had not entirely believed what the king said about the prophecy or her children ruling Egypt, she knew well that Kadar was Tutankhamun's son and that there were many – Pharaoh Horemheb among them – who would do whatever it took to ensure the Amarna line did not survive. Whatever else this child or children were, they were a part of her. She would do whatever she must to protect them.

So, as the king had advised, Azra had taken one of his soldiers to husband - the date of their marriage conveniently pushed backward to ensure all would believe the child his, and returned with her new husband to her remaining relatives in Nubia.

Still, Azra was unsettled. Anytime anyone would touch her ever-swelling womb, anytime they would ask after her health or of that of the child she carried, she would become afraid. She would become convinced that on some level they knew.

Every time she would feel someone's eyes upon her, no matter how innocent they appeared, she felt like they knew the truth. Every hour of every day, she felt like she was living on borrowed time, as if any moment one of her enemies or one of Pharaoh's spies or one of the Amarna fanatics would drag her and her child away to some hell.

Azra's hands flew to her womb.

Soon. In less than 2 moons, the child would be born.

And then what? What if the child resembled Kadar or Ida? What if worst still it resembled Tutankhamun?

The thought chilled her.

All of this weight on her shoulders, and here she was alone now, near term, with these strange people.

Galeno had gone as soon as word had come down from Hatti of an attempt on King Mursili's life, an attempt hindered only by the near sacrifice of one of his concubines – Lady Raia. The same crazed lady who had been Kadar's mother, who had come for her life.

Not long after Galeno's departure, even her new husband had gone – called back to the Citadel by the head palace guard, a man who was still too paranoid to have anyone other than the most trusted around the royal family.

Now here she was alone in this house, amongst a bunch of people she barely knew though they shared her blood. People who blamed her behind her back for her mother's imprisonment – a mother she had had no choice but to leave behind at Pharaoh Horemheb's mercy.

Even this morning, as she returned from her walk, she found two of the elders huddled in the kitchen, speaking in hushed voices that fell to silence as soon as she entered.

They would betray her. She could feel it in her bones.

Azra only prayed that her husband and Galeno returned in time to save her.

XXXI

Hattusa. The citadel.

A week had passed since Ida had awakened. Then two.

Still, Mursili slept.

The shape of her womb had changed – the twins preparing themselves to enter the world.

And still Mursili slept.

The royal army continued to hunt down, torture, persecute and kill all who were close to Nacamakun.

And still Mursili slept.

Ida sighed heavily.

She stood now over Mursili's bed, staring down at him.

Though his eyes remained closed, though his chest moved almost imperceptibly, he was still in the land of the living. That meant there was still hope. Wasn't there?

She blinked back the tears that threatened to fall, one hand rising to lovingly stroke his head.

Of course there was still hope.

There had to be.

Ida swiped hastily at her eyes as she heard the main door to his chambers open. She hurriedly repositioned her veil over her face as the footsteps drew nearer.

She turned to face the intruder. Queen Tanuhepa.

"Tawannanna," Ida greeted with a bow.

"Lady Raia," the queen acknowledged.

Tanu moved closer to Mursili, stared down at him for a long moment before she spoke again. "Still no change?" she asked.

Ida shook her head. "I'm afraid not, Your Highness."

Tanu bent, gently stroked his hair. Though they were not intimates, Mursili was a good king, a good husband. Though she herself could no longer conceive, through his concubine Raia, he had even made her a mother again.

Ida watched the other woman, the large cushion under her dress bending unnaturally with her movement.

"Your cushion is too soft," Raia said. "It looks unnatural when you bend."

Tanu stood, her hands self-consciously repositioning the stuffing.

"And now?" she asked bending once more.

Ida nodded. "Better.

Tanu stood, smiled sheepishly. "It's times like this that I miss Clizi. She was always so good at this.

"This new girl I have is simply useless."

Clizi. Ida blinked back her tears.

"Oh, did I say something wrong?" Tanu asked innocently.

Ida shook her head though she turned her back to the queen. Though she managed to silence her sob, her shoulders shook.

"Oh no," Tanu said coming around Mursili to stroke Ida's back. "Don't cry. It's not good for our boys."

Ida's shoulders tensed.

Our boys.

Though she knew Tanu meant no wrong by calling her twins "our boys", it still pricked her – the thought that she would have yet more children who would not know her as mother.

"I did it again, didn't I?" Tanu said as her hand slowly fell to her side. Why was she always putting her foot in her mouth?

"I didn't mean it like that," Tanu tried to explain. "I only meant that Mursili and I will do everything in our power for the twins to have you in their lives, that they belong to all of us. That's all."

"I know," Ida replied quietly.

Tanu smiled, once more smoothing her hands over her fake womb.

She exhaled loudly.

"Well then," the queen said cheerily, "with Mursili out of commission, I have much to do. If you'll excuse me."

"Of course," Ida replied. She turned and watched as the queen crossed to the door.

Just as the Tawannanna was about to go through it, a sudden, deep contraction ripped a groan from Ida's throat.

The queen turned to face Ida, found her doubled over, one hand on her womb.

"Quick!" the queen called as she rushed to Ida's side and helped her to the nearest seat. "Someone fetch the midwife!"

XXXII

Nubia.

It happened sooner than Azra thought. She had been deep in slumber when her husband had come into their rooms and roused her.

"Get dressed," he said as her eyes slowly drifted open. "Now."

"What's going on?" she asked as she carefully sat up then stood, as she watched him furiously pulling her things from her trunks and stuff them into one small bag.

"We've been found," he said as he tossed some clothes on the bed for her to wear.

"Found?" she breathed as she hurriedly began pulling on clothing, though her hands trembled. "By whom?"

"Hazrene," he said.

"Hazrene?" she repeated.

Kadar's intended, Hazrene? Azra wondered.

"But how?" she asked.

"I don't know," her husband replied as he placed a cloak over her shoulders.

He grabbed her wrist and hurried with her towards the door. Motioning for her to be silent, he slowly pulled it open – one eye surveying the hallway before he felt confident enough to open the door and lead her down it, towards the front door.

Once more he was careful before he opened the front door wide enough for them to pass through. They were down the dusty streets and at the stables before Azra's mind could even make sense of what he had told her.

Even as he tied their bags upon their mount and set her atop a camel, it did not seem real. Even as the camel stood, as her husband carefully led them from the stables, through the town and out into the desert, it did not seem real.

XXXIII

Azra had fallen asleep, lulled by the gentle sway of the camel padding across the sand dunes. It was only when the animal jerked to a halt, that she heard the sounds of skirmish that she snapped awake.

There. Hazrene and her husband were fighting - knives drawn, fists and flesh colliding with vigor.

Much to Azra's horror, before Azra could spur the camel into a run, one of Hazrene's daggers came flying towards the beast, piercing it in the chest and collapsing the hulking animal.

Azra was stranded, panicked. All she could do was watch helplessly, hoping against hope her husband would prevail.

However, though Azra's husband was able to hold his own for quite some time, Hazrene, faster and more agile, began to get the better of him.

Realizing her husband might well fall, Azra clumsily dismounted.

She turned and looked around her. Her husband's stead nowhere in sight, she desperately sought some indication of where to run.

It was useless.

Far as her eyes could see in all directions was sand. No matter what path she chose, it would not end well for her and her child.

She knew it. The gods knew it - even the first fingers of dawn seeming to mock her.

She turned back towards the fray. Her husband was on his knees now.

Not knowing what else to do, Azra ran. She had barely made it over the first mound when a sudden, deep contraction brought her to her knees.

"No," she whimpered.

This couldn't be happening. It was much too soon.

Forcing herself back to her feet, she ran on.

The Citadel. Hattusa.

Ida's contractions had increased in frequency and duration throughout the night. Near dawn, her water finally broke.

She lay now in her bed, a birthing stick in her mouth as tears fell from her eyes and perspiration covered her body.

Queen Tanu sat next to her.

Though Ida squeezed Tanu's hand tightly enough to make the queen cry out every time another powerful contraction shook her being, Tanu refused to let go of Ida's hand.

Ida cried out in pain once more, the weight bearing down upon her for release becoming too much to bear.

"Not yet," the midwife coaxed, though Ida sobbed in her exhaustion.

Ida cried out again, this time in anguish.

"Alright," the midwife coaxed. "Now."

Nubia. The desert.

Yet another powerful contraction brought Azra to her knees. It was the 4th time.

This time, however, as she struggled to regain her footing, a great flood of liquid burst forth from between her thighs.

"No!" Azra cried, no longer able to contain her hysterical tears.

She sank back on all fours, sobbing uncontrollably at the hopelessness of her situation.

It was only when she heard the heavy trudge of the battle wearied Hazrene growing louder behind her that she forced herself to stand once again.

Back on her feet, Azra stumbled away but a few steps before Hazrene grabbed her by her hair and yanked her back to the ground.

Azra pushed, hit and kicked at the other woman in her futile efforts to stay her.

It was useless. All it did was make Hazrene angrier.

Hazrene was straddling Azra now, her fist rising to deliver yet another blow to Azra's face. However, just as Hazrene's fist was about to make contact with Azra's jaw, another contraction wracked Azra's body.

Realizing that Azra was about to give birth, Hazrene got off of her. She watched, shock and revulsion on her face as Azra's face contorted, as Azra pushed with everything she had in her.

XXXIV

The Citadel. Hattusa.

The first of the twins emerged from Ida with great vigor, the sound of his cries echoing throughout the king's rooms.

The second twin, however, was much more docile. Only the slap the midwife administered to his backside elicited an angry cry from the boy.

Though tears streamed down her face, Ida laughed with joy as she heard her sons' voices for the first time.

The afterbirth finally passed, Ida watched anxiously as the midwife's assistants cleaned the babies. How her arms ached to hold her tiny sons.

Her joy, however, was short-lived. As the midwife's assistants brought the babies towards Ida, they were stopped by the queen.

"Not yet," Tanu said taking first the eldest son into her arms.

She held him in the air, inspecting him. He was perfect.

Handing the boy back to the assistant, she claimed the younger of the two. Though he too was flawless, he was considerably smaller than his brother.

He too she handled back to the assistant.

Claiming the eldest once more, Queen Tanu stared down at him lovingly, her face beaming with pride.

As the assistant tried to move past her to hand the other over to Ida, she was again stopped by the queen.

"I said not yet," Tanu admonished. "Raia needs her rest."

"Yes, Your Highness," the assistant replied.

"Come," the queen ordered as she turned to leave the room.

The assistant who held the youngest twin spared Ida one last sorrowful glance as she turned and followed the queen.

Even before the midwives and queen cleared the door, the queen was already making plans.

"What shall we call you?" Tanu asked the babe in her arms. "Ah, I know. Telisili for the god Telipinu."

"And you?" the Queen said turning to face the child the nursemaid's assistant carried behind her.

She wrinkled her nose as she considered the possibilities.

At last the Queen smiled. "I've got it! Arrinutu. Yes. Arrinutu in honor of Arinna."

Thoroughly pleased with herself, the queen passed out the door.

AMARNA BOOK III: BOOK OF RAIA

Ida sank back against her pillows, her already battered heart splintering into a million pieces.

The twins were barely out of the womb and already it had begun.

Already Tanu was claiming them as her own.

The desert. Nubia.

Hazrene wrapped Azra's daughter in her cloak, hastily wiping the baby's face clean as its shrill cries pierced the early morning sky.

She couldn't help but feel more than a stab of disappointment that the child was female.

Still, female or not, that she was of the Amarna line gave her value – even if that value was only in marrying into the throne.

Setting the unhappy bundle down upon the sand, Hazrene stood. She slowly drew her knife as she advanced upon its exhausted mother.

Feeling Hazrene's shadow fall across her, Azra wearily opened her eyes.

"So this is how it ends," Azra remarked.

She began to laugh at the ridiculousness of the situation – she sprawled half naked in the middle of the desert, covered in birth waste. She, the daughter of Pharaoh Ay and of the Royal Concubine, Esnai. She, the former lover of yet another Pharaoh and mother of the grandchild of Pharaoh Tutankhamun, about to be butchered like a Flood Feast hog.

Hazrene studied Azra for a long moment. For not the first time, she wondered what it was Kadar saw in this girl that he had not seen in her.

Dropping to her knees next to Azra, Hazrene took hold of Azra's hair, used it to tilt Azra's head backward - exposing her neck.

Azra's eyes sank closed. It was time – time for Azra to die.

Yet, the hand that brought the knife to Azra's throat trembled.

Hazrene had killed before, yes....when she had to. But this was different. This was....barbaric. This was....wrong.

Just as Hazrene released her hold on Azra's hair, as she began to pull the knife away, Azra jerked forward - a new round of contractions forcing her throat against the retreating blade.

Hazrene fell back in horror, her chest heaving as Azra's head fell awkwardly against the sand. She watched in disbelief as blood poured from Azra's throat, as Azra's blood-filled mouth worked spasmodically to claim but a few more gasps of air.

Hazrene's eyes fled to Azra's womb.

Could there be another? Perhaps a son this time?

Quickly regaining her senses, Hazrene scrabbled between Azra's legs. She could see the crown of a second head.

"There's another one!" Hazrene called to Azra. "Push! You must push!"

Nothing.

Hazrene scrambled towards Azra's head, stared down at her. Already Azra's eyes were glazing over, already she stared into the abyss.

Panicked, Hazrene hurried once more to the 2nd child, its head now firmly lodged in an impossible position in a dead woman's womb.

She tried pushing down on Azra's stomach, to massage the baby outwards.

It was no use. The birth was not progressing.

Hazrene stood. She began to pace erratically as she tried to figure out what to do.

This wasn't happening! This *couldn't* be happening!

She stopped. What if that was him? What if that was the boy who would steal away the throne?

Her chest heaving, Hazrene flung herself back to the ground. Picking up the discarded dagger, she began to cut.

Once she had enough room to stick her hands inside of Azra, she closed her hands around the second babe and pulled with all her might. She pulled until at last the child broke free of its mother.

Tears of relief springing to her eyes, Hazrene set the child down upon its mother's chest.

Cutting a piece of cloth from Azra's body, she hurriedly wiped the baby clean.

She held it in her arms now and stared down at it.

Yes, it was indeed a boy. Only...only it was not breathing.

Hazrene was in a panic.

Why wasn't it breathing?!

Think Hazrene! Think!

Flipping the baby over on its stomach she began slapping it along its back. However, when she turned him over again, he was just as still as his dead mother.

What was she doing wrong?!

At last out of ideas, Hazrene covered the child's nose and mouth with her own mouth. This child would live even if she had to breathe life into it herself.

Hazrene tried, several times, to will it alive. Though she saw his tiny chest rise and fall with each of her breaths, the babe simply refused to breathe on his own.

Finally accepting defeat, Hazrene began to cry.

King Mursili's eyes opened as Azra's second born drew its last breath.

It was done. The life of one of the Amarna born for his – the price of exiling the goddess Sausga from the world of mortals and saving both his twins & Ida. A price he would not have chosen to pay if he had known, if he had had any choice.

Still, what was done was done.

Mursili tried to rise, found his body still too leaden to move. He tried to call out; however, no sound came forth from his throat.

Mursili closed his eyes once more - the cry of his second born echoing down the corridor as fatigue began to reclaim him.

XXXV

It was nightfall by the time King Mursili II reawoke.

He could hear Ida shuffling heavily, moving slowly between her rooms and his. She was sobbing noisily, anguish in her voice as she came into the king's bed chamber, as she took her pain and frustration out on Galeno.

"Ida, please," Galeno begged. "It's too soon for you to be about."

"It's too soon for a lot of things!" Ida cried. "Like losing Abidos! Like losing Mursili right before I give birth to his sons! Like losing those sons to a dingbat like Tanihoohoo!" She sobbed pitifully.

Galeno's heart broke for his friend. "I know how you feel," he began sorrowfully.

"Do you now?" Ida interrupted as she whirled around to face him. "You've carried a life inside of you? You've brought a life into the world? You've had that life snatched away from you?"

"Of course not. What I mean is..."

He sighed heavily, every thought that came to his mind seeming somehow inadequate.

"What you mean is what?" Ida challenged.

His brow furrowed, his eyes fleeing downward as he struggled to find the right words to placate and comfort the angry, hysterical woman.

At last he answered. "All I'm trying to say is that even if you care nothing for your own life and well-being, think of the people you love. Think of the king and your beautiful sons. You will do neither any good if you run yourself into the ground."

Galeno was right. Ida's anger began to dissipate.

She suddenly felt tired – more tired than she had in her entire life. Her whole body shook as she sank heavily into the nearest chair.

Galeno sank at her feet, stroked her comfortingly.

Mursili could stand no more. He needed to go to her, to let her know he was back in the land of the living, that he would move heaven and earth to ensure she would not lose her sons.

Using what strength he could muster, Mursili tried to rise. Though he had not the strength to do more than move his right arm, it was enough - his right hand sending one of amulets that the priests had placed around him crashing to the floor.

Both Galeno and Ida startled, their attention turning towards Mursili. Seeing Mursili's hand jump once more, Galeno rose.

"By the gods," he whispered, his eyes wide as he rushed over to the king.

Ida followed as quickly as her sore body would allow, Galeno already in the process of helping the King resettle against his pillows.

"You're awake," Ida whispered, tears of relief falling from her eyes as she lovingly stroked her face. "Thank the gods, you're alive."

Mursili tried to speak, but once more, no words came – the left side of his mouth frozen in place.

"Galeno, water," Ida instructed.

Galeno did as he was bade, Ida helping Mursili to drink.

XXXVI

Nineven.

"Hazrene!" Azil called as the pale, traumatized girl collapsed in front of the gate to his house. It was the middle of the night, his entire household startled awake by her urgent pounding.

"Bring her inside," he ordered his slaves.

Leading the way to one of the guest rooms, Azil illuminated it as Hazrene was settled upon the bed.

"Fetch the doctor," he said. "Now!"

As the man hurried from the room, Azil turned his attention to his niece. She was trembling, pallid, her hair plastered to her sweat soaked scalp.

What in the hell had happened to her?

As Azil stared down at his niece, his eyes taking in every detail of her appearance, the bundle tied to her chest wiggled then cried out.

Carefully untying it, Azil pulled back the covering.

It was the child! Hazrene had done it!

He smiled widely for a brief moment, his excitement at the realization of their dream momentarily distracting him from the state of his niece.

Hazrene grumbled in pain, banishing the smile from Azil's lips. He set the baby down next to his niece, stroked her hair as he spoke softly.

"You did well, Hazi," he said. "Now stay strong. The doctor will be here soon."

Hazrene nodded, even as her heavy eyes began to drift closed.

"How is she?" Azil asked the physician, as he at last came out of Hazrene's room. "What's wrong with her?"

The doctor's gaze drifted just beyond Azil, to the many ears and eyes focused upon them.

"It is a delicate matter," he said at last. "Perhaps we should..." He nodded his head towards Hazrene's room.

Azil nodded his understanding, led the doctor into Hazrene's room and shut the door.

"Well?" Azil asked anxiously.

The doctor's face shriveled in discomfort.

"Out with it!" Azil demanded.

"It's her...It's her womb," the man said at last.

"Her womb?"

The doctor nodded.

"What about her womb?" her uncle pressed.

"It's..." he shook his head. Without another word, he pulled back the blanket.

Azil was horrified. "Who's done this to her?" he demanded.

"She says she did it to herself," the doctor replied.

"What?" Azil breathed. "But why would she..." His brow furrowed.

The doctor shook his head. "I don't know. But the tear has become infected and that infection has spread deep inside of her. The only way I can save her life is by removing her womb."

"Then do it," her uncle urged.

"Doing so means she will never bear children of her own," the doctor replied.

Azil looked to his niece. She was delirious now - taking to herself, cursing at and begging for forgiveness from some unseen figure.

He nodded at last.

"Do it," Azil said. "Do whatever you have to to save her."

XXXVII

Nineven.

Hazrene awoke to find her uncle asleep in a chair next to her bed.

She slowly pulled herself into a sitting position, the sharp pain that shot from between her legs a glaring reminder of all she had done – of what she had sacrificed in order to ensure Lord Bietek's physician would pronounce the child of Amarna to be of her womb.

The pain she felt now was but a small fraction of the pain she had felt as she had forced the infant-shaped effigy up her birth canal, as it had torn her in two.

Now, no one would know she was not the child's true mother. Now, no one would know she had been a virgin.

"Uncle Azil," she called to her uncle.

Her uncle's eyes shot open as he sat up in the chair.

"Hazi!" he cried in relief. "You're awake!"

She nodded, a small smile of pride coming to her face. "Did you see her? Did you see the child of Amarna?"

Azil nodded.

Her smile widened. "I told you I could do it," she said.

"That you did," he agreed.

Hazrene's neck craned as her gaze scoured the room, her smile faltering when she realized that the babe was not there.

"Where is she?" she asked at last.

"Sold," Azil replied.

"What?" Hazrene breathed, incredulous - tears coming to her eyes. "How could you? After all I've sacrificed, how could you?"

"I did it for you," he said taking her hands in his. "A girl child is of no use to us. At best, Lord Bietek would have married her, used her to solidify his own claim to the throne. And we....we would still end up in little better position than we are now."

"So all of this was for nothing?" she asked, on the verge of hysteria.

"Of course not," he reassured her, stroking her hair. "I too have been busy while you were away.

"I've found a babe – a boy child of our line. It is he you will present to Lord Bietek as the child of Kadar, as the heir to the Amarna line."

Hazrene pulled away from him.

She shook her head, her brow furrowing. No woman of their line had been pregnant when she left. Unless...

"A slave's child?" she asked.

"Your *cousin's* child."

Hazrene shook her head again in disbelief. "You'd put the offspring of a slave, one not even of royal blood upon the Egyptian throne?" she whispered.

"Your *cousin's* child," he repeated. "One of *our* blood. One loyal to us, that we could control."

Hazrene shook her head, tried to rise from the bed. "This is madness. I have to find Kadar's child."

The pain that accompanied the effort, more than her uncle's hand upon her shoulder, kept her there.

"This is your only chance," Azil said. "Either you take this child or you live without."

Hazrene's blood turned to ice as she looked up at him.

"You have no womb – not anymore," he supplied.

"What?" Hazrene breathed.

"It had to be removed to save your life," he said.

Hazrene sank back against her pillows, tears falling from her eyes.

"I'm sorry, Hazi," he said. "For everything."

XXXVIII

Fifteen years later. Approximately 1292 B.C.

The last decade and a half had been a struggle for King Mursili II. Though he had eventually regained the majority of movement in the left side of his body, though he had eventually regained muscle control over the left side of his face, he was still noticeably weaker on that side. Though he had prayed to the gods, though he had made sacrifice after sacrifice of sacred bulls in the name of a cure, he was still without the ability to speak.

The twins, who were already almost as tall as he, took after their father. They were the spitting image of Mursili.

Though Arrinutu and Telisili shared the same build, the same height, the same face, they could not be more different.

Arrinutu was soft-spoken, thoughtful, introverted. Though he was careful to hide it, Mursili knew the boy had been touched by the gods, that he shared the curse of prophecy.

Telisili, on the other hand, was boisterous, impulsive and outspoken. Though he was spared the curse of prophecy, he excelled in his ability to interpret visions.

This made him a favorite among the priests and oracles.

And then there was Ida. After all that had transpired, she wanted no part of the gods.

She kept their sons from the priests and temples as much as she could. No longer did she ask about his visions. No longer did she ask about the prophecy.

Even on the rare occasion when Arrinutu would slip and allude to his curse, Ida turned a blind eye.

Mursili sighed heavily. He rotated his weary shoulder before he continued to scribble in his great book.

In pain or not, he had to finish.

"Lady Bietek?" Hazrene's personal slave called to her.

Hazrene sighed heavily, her attention shifting from the boy who horse-played with his friends in the courtyard below them to the maid behind her. "Yes?" she asked.

"Lord Bietek requests your presence in the receiving room," the slave replied.

Hazrene nodded absently, her attention returning to the boy.

How he had grown – the puppet prince. Even knowing that he would be the only child she would ever have, even knowing that the only reason Lord Bietek had taken her to wife after his first wife's passing was because of the boy, she still could not bring herself to feel anything even remotely resembling motherly love or even passing affection for the imposter.

Even though her family was well cared for and she lived a life of opulence worthy of great envy, she found she could not truly enjoy it. Instead, she was always uncomfortable in her own skin, always ill at ease.

It served her right. She deserved no peace after what she had done.

She had hunted Azra, the mother of Kadar's children, down like a dog. Then, accidentally or not, she had slit Azra's throat and in doing so, killed his only son.

Because of this sin, the gods had taken away her womb. Because of this sin, not a night went by that she didn't see them there – lying like broken dolls in the desert.

And Kadar's daughter....his poor, beautiful daughter – stripped of her family and sold into slavery.

Hazrene inhaled sharply, blinked back her tears of sorrow.

Kadar had loved Hazrene. He had truly loved her though he had been led astray by Azra. In time, had he lived, he might yet have realized his folly and returned to her.

And Hazrene, Hazrene had loved him – too much. That love, even without her wanting it to, had transferred to those babes. They were all that was left of him in this world, and therefore, precious to her. Whether she wanted them to be or not.

With each passing year, her drive to protect the last remaining child of Kadar, to right the wrong she had done to the children of Amarna grew stronger.

So, though it had taken Hazrene many years to find out just what had become of Kadar's daughter, she had finally done it.

The girl, named Bahara by the slavers, was at first considered more of a burden than an asset. She went for less than half of the sale price of a babe whose lineage was known.

She passed from buyer to buyer until she was old enough to be of real service – at the age of 5.

As Bahara had grown more capable, older, more beautiful, her value had also increased. At the age of 12, the pristine virgin was presented to Pharaoh's slavers and accepted into service despite her questionable heritage.

Now, at 15, Bahara was among the aging Horemheb's favorites.

Hazrene scowled. The irony disgusted her – that the true heir to the Egyptian throne was in the service of the throne's usurper, that Horemheb might yet create a true Amarna heir, without even realizing it.

And it, all of it, was Hazrene's fault.

Hazrene snarled as the boy threw back his head in laughter.

Her and her family's only hope was this imposter, her cousin's bastard. Still, a part of her hated him – almost as much as she detested Lord Bietek...almost.

Though a part of her fought desperately to keep up the ruse, another part of her would see them all destroyed, would see them all suffer for what they had done to Bahara.

So, in the dead of night, she had sent one of her guard, her lover, to seek out Lady Raia.

"My Lady?" the slave called uncertainly.

"I'm coming," Hazrene replied, neutralizing her expression before she turned to face her slave.

XXXIX

Thebes. Egypt.

Pharaoh Horemheb had never been superstitious. Superstitions and gods were for other men – lesser men.

Horem knew better than most. Having clawed his way from common origins to soldier, then military commander to Pharaoh, he knew well that the only belief a man needed was belief in himself – and enough ruthlessness to do whatever it took to reach his goals.

So, when Idamun had spat her curse upon him decades before – that he would be without heir, he had laughed. He had by that time already fathered four strapping sons, sons who were as driven and ruthless as Horem had been.

Then, one by one, over the years, his sons had fallen to the wayside. One was killed in battle. Another in an unfortunate accident. One had sided with Lord Bietek against him and been cut down by Horem himself. The last was taken by illness not 2 months ago.

In all of the years since Ida had cursed him, not one of his concubines, not one of his wives had taken his seed.

Now, as he raced towards old age, towards infirmity, he found himself without heir.

Now, the sharks were circling…again.

There was Lord Bietek. Using some false heir he had plucked from Nineven, he had given Horem's enemies in Lower Egypt new courage to challenge his rule.

There was Prince Muwatalli II – young and eager to take over from his ailing father, King Mursili II, and prove himself just as great a warrior as his father had been.

Even the kings of Assyria and Nubia were emboldened - watching, waiting for the chance to pick his carcass clean.

Worst still were the enemies that surrounded him, the enemies who lived in Upper Egypt, who lived in Thebes, who lived inside the palace walls. They were advisors, priests, commanders – all with their own plots against him. All with their own plans for the future of Egypt.

With each passing year, the number of people Horem could trust decreased and the number he couldn't grew. With each of his sons' deaths, the bolder his enemies had become.

Now, with the death of his final son, Horem had a target on his back. He knew it. His only chance now was in securing an heir, an heir of his own loins.

So, Horem, for the first time in his life, began to pray. For the first time in his life, he went to the temples and made sacrifices to the gods in earnest.

For the first time in Horem's life, he listed to his physicians. He took every poultice, tried every fertility remedy his physicians could find.

Still, none of his seed took root.

Yet, when first he saw Bahara, her grey eyes magnificent against the brown of her skin, he saw his salvation. They were the eyes of his mother – the one person who had always believed in him, who saw before him a destiny of greatness, even before Horem saw it himself.

Still, no matter how many times he spilled seed inside of the girl, her womb remained empty.

Horem sighed wearily.

Was this it? Was this to be the end of his bloodline's turn upon the throne?

Horemheb scowled.

No, he would never again let the throne revert to the lazy, useless hands of so-called god-kings. Even if he could father no heir himself, he would see an heir upon his throne – one of common origins like himself.

Yes, someone who had grown strong clawing and scratching himself to the top – just as he had done.

A slow smirk spread across his lips as he called to his guard.

"Guard! Fetch me, Vizer Paramesse."

XL

Thebes. Egypt.

Bahara sat awkwardly upon the edge of the bed, her arms covering her nakedness as best they could. Though she was hardly a virgin, she trembled in fear and anticipation.

Tonight, this night, would be the first she would be with a man other than Pharaoh. Tonight she would be with one of his officers – no doubt in a last-ditch effort to sire an heir to the Egyptian throne.

It seemed forever before the door to the bedchamber opened.

Slowly, Bahara hazarded a peek at the man-child. She blushed, her eyes hurriedly turning away again.

He was tall and young – close to her age or maybe even younger than she. He was well-built and handsome. Most of all, he seemed as uncomfortable with the situation as she did.

Bahara's chest heaved, her breath leaving her mouth in loud gasps.

She concentrated so hard on avoiding his curious gaze that she startled when she felt his rough hand gently slide up her back. Her heart beat out of her chest as she felt his breath upon her neck, as she felt his lips softly graze its tender flesh.

Her eyes fluttered closed despite the tension in her shoulders, as his lips made a gentle trail up her neck and to her ear.

When she no longer felt his lips upon her skin, she slowly opened her eyes, turned her head towards him.

Their eyes held for a long moment before he spoke.

"Lie down," he whispered.

Slowly Bahara complied.

As he slowly moved to cover her body with his, as his lips slowly moved towards hers, Bahara finally understood the meaning of the word desire.

XLI

King Mursili II had just scrawled the final words in his great book when he was seized by a fit of tremor.

It was done.

As Mursili collapsed, Ida called for the guard to fetch the king's physician. She ran to his side, fell to her knees beside him. Tears fell from her eyes as she held him, as blood drained from his ears, eyes, nose and mouth.

At last, the tremors stopped.

As he lay limply in her arms, Mursili whispered her name.

Ida was in shock. It was the first time he had spoken since his battle with Sausga.

She leaned her ear closer to his lips, her eyes growing wider with each word.

Ida pulled back to look him in the eye, her eyes filled with disbelief. Yet, even when faced with her skepticism, he had nodded affirmation - one hand rising heavily to point to the great book.

Ida's eyes followed his hand. By the time she looked down at him again, he was still.

"Mursili?" Ida called giving him a shake. "Mursili?!"

She pressed her head to his chest, listening, feeling for even the slightest of heartbeats. There was none.

Frantically she pressed her ear to his nose and mouth. Nothing.

"No!" Ida cried out in anguish, as she pulled his limp body to her and rocked it back and forth. "No!"

XLII

Days after King Mursili's funeral, Ida still sat on the floor of his chambers.

Though people came to comfort her, she would accept no condolence. Though people tried to get her to eat, she would take no food. Though they tried to get her to rise, she would take no rest.

She just sat there staring at the spot where he had died.

It would take months before Ida was at least going through the motions of life again.

Still, she could not bring herself to open the great book.

She stared unseeingly out of her window now, her hand absently sliding the key that hung around her neck up and down its chain, her mind replaying Mursili's last words over and over again.

"It is done," he had whispered. "It's time for you to act. Time for you to save Egypt and Hatti. Time for you to ensure the Amarna line returns to the throne of Egypt and to make all that we have suffered mean something."

What could he possibly have meant by that?

Kadar was the last direct descendent of Amarna and he had been killed.

Azra, the only lover Kadar had ever had, had been found in the desert fifteen years ago - a dead baby not far from her body.

His intended, Hazrene, had claimed a descendant of the Amarna line. Yet, the moment Ida saw him, she knew the boy was a fraud.

Could there have been someone else?

Ida shook her head.

No. There couldn't have been. Kadar had been so young when he had died.

Still, Mursili had been sure. Even as his life ebbed away, his faith in his words had been unwavering.

Then there had been the missive sent from the current Lady Bietek.

Ida had found it only the night before - hidden amongst the letters of condolence. It was much thicker than the rest, the hand on the outside hurried.

Was it a coincidence – the timing of the letter from the mother of the imposter and Mursili's last request that she read the final entries in his great book? Or was it something more?

Had the gods finally made peace with Ida or was this simply another of their games?

Ida's hand stilled.

There was only one way for her to find out.

XLIII

It was done.

Bahara was with child – Commander Merenptah's child.

Still, she hid her pregnancy from Pharaoh Horemheb.

Bahara's pregnancy meant more than that Horem finally had an heir, one he could pass off as his own. It also meant there would be no more need for Meren's visits to her bed, and that was a thought Bahara could not bear.

Still, the girl had her duty to Pharaoh.

That she shared the young officer's bed changed nothing between them. Horem still expected her to lie with him, to satisfy his sexual urges - though less and less often was he able to achieve erection.

Still, it would not be long before no amount of lies would be able to disguise her swollen belly.

She sighed heavily.

Running away with Meren and marrying him was no option either – though he had begged her to do so. Pharaoh would only find them and punish them as only he had the stomach and imagination to.

No, running away would never work. What she needed was to get rid of Pharaoh Horemheb....and soon.

A slow smile spread across Bahara's lips as she imagined all of the ways she could dispatch the old man.

They were brave thoughts indeed for one so young and powerless. Yet, when the knock sounded at her chamber door, she startled guiltily.

Swallowing past the lump in her throat, she went to the door and opened it.

Vizier Paramesse! Hurriedly, Bahara fell to the floor in subjugation.

The Vizier smiled.

"You may rise," he said, his smile well under control by the time she reclaimed her feet and looked up at him.

"My Lord," she began. "What brings you here?"

He looked around the room. Sure they were indeed alone, he closed the door behind himself.

"Might I speak with you candidly?" he asked, his eyes narrowing as he studied her face.

"My Lord?" she asked.

"I mean, can you be trusted to hold a confidence?"

"Of course, My Lord."

"Even from Pharaoh?" he questioned.

Bahara looked away guiltily, color flooding her cheeks. It was all the confirmation Param needed.

"Well, young Bahara," he said. "I have a proposition for you."

"For me?" she asked.

He nodded. "For you."

She looked confused.

"You see, Bahara," the Vizier explained, "you find yourself in quite a unique position - as the woman Pharaoh has placed all of his confidence in to produce an heir. Unique in that if you should for some reason...fail, Pharaoh will have no choice but to appoint an heir. Someone who would be very grateful to you. Someone like me for instance."

"And if it is too late for me to earn your grace?" she asked.

Param's eyes widened. Could she already carry Meren's child?

Bahara looked away from him.

After a long silence, Param spoke again. "Does anyone yet know?" he asked at length.

Bahara shook her head. "No. Not even the child's father."

"Not even Pharaoh?" he pressed.

"No. Especially not Pharaoh."

Param studied her for a long moment. Could it be? Could Bahara have already fallen in love with his son?

"Do you love him?" the Vizier asked. Do you love Meren?"

Bahara hesitated a long moment before she finally nodded, tears pooling in her eyes.

"I see," he said at length. "Or at least I think I do."

He paused before he continued. "Does Merenptah feel the same away about you?"

"He wants me to run away with him, to become his wife."

Though she hadn't meant to tell him, or anyone else for that matter, there was just something so understanding in his manner, in his tone, that she really couldn't help herself.

However, she quickly realized her mistake.

The man smiled wirily. "And would you?" he asked. "If you were free to?"

She looked away from him again for a long moment before she replied.

"In a heartbeat," she breathed.

"Good," Param replied.

Bahara looked up at him again. "How is this good? Pharaoh will never let me go. Whether I tell him or not, it won't be long before he figures out I'm with child."

"Perhaps," he replied. "But what if there's a way he would *never* find out?"

"The only way that could ever happen is if he – " She dared not utter the word.

"Died?" Param pressed.

Bahara shook her head furiously, tears coming to her eyes. "We must not ever speak of such things."

"And why not?" he pressed. "Pharaoh is an old man, as am I. Both of us are on borrowed time, both of us desperately fighting to fortify our legacies before we pass on to the next world."

He walked around her, his eyes drinking her in as he did so. Now that he looked at her closely, he did indeed see it. This girl, this slave, was of the Amarna.

And to think she had been for the last four years right under his nose.

Bahara began to grow increasingly uncomfortable under his scrutiny, was grateful when at last he spoke again.

"Lord Bietek and his forces were defeated once again. Did you know that?"

Bahara nodded.

Param continued. "Did you also know that they weren't defeated by Pharaoh but from within?"

Bahara was in shock.

"Mmmm," Param said. "It seems Lord Bietek was trying to pass off some Assyrian bastard as the long-lost heir of Pharaoh Tutankhamun.

"Unfortunately for him, the boy's true mother, not the current Lady Bietek by the way, was still alive.

"One word from the mother backed up, surprising enough, by Lady Bietek, and the whole ruse unraveled. His own men turned against him.

"And poor Lady Bietek - desperate to save her own life, claimed that there exists a true heir of the Amarna line. Only that this heir was sold into slavery at birth – a victim of its sex.

"I, of course, like everyone else, didn't believe her. Pharaoh, however, was another matter entirely.

"Paranoid bastard!

"As he commanded, I did some checking into Hazrene's story. Checking that led me to you."

"What?" Bahara breathed.

"The true Amarna heir is you, Bahara."

Bahara shook her head.

"No," she said. "You're mistaken. You have to be."

"I'm afraid not my beauty. I can see it in your face. You are the spitting image of your great-grandmother Nefertiti."

Bahara sank to the floor, the tears finally falling from her eyes.

How many times had she heard Pharaoh talk of what he planned to do to this Amarna heir should he ever get his hands upon him?

The things he had said had given her nightmares.

And the rumors she had overheard – about him murdering Pharaoh Tutankhamun, about Pharaoh burying some poor girl alive with a desiccated child to hold on to the throne, about him having a hand in the death of Ay and Queen's Ankhesenamun's disappearance.

If he had been so ruthless to such as they, what might he do to someone insignificant like her.

She shook her head again.

No, she could not be the true heir. She would not be.

"Despite what he says," Parma pressed, "even now, even the thought, the hint that there might be an heir out there has him squirming on his gilded throne.

"And I am not the only person he has set to the task of finding out if this true heir does indeed exist.

"He has agents everywhere. It's only a matter of time before he too figures out that the loose end he seeks is here under his very own roof, is warming his very own bed."

Bahara looked up at him, her fear and desperation burning in her eyes.

"Why are you telling me this?" she asked.

Param sank down to his haunches before her. "Because I believe that you and I can help each other."

"But how?" she asked.

He reached into his purse and withdrew a small vial, handed it to her.

"What's this?" she asked.

"It's poison," he said.

Bahara dropped it, the Vizier catching it before it hit the floor and shattered into pieces.

"Careful now," he warned. "Poison of this caliber is very difficult to come by."

Bahara rose, walked away from him.

He stood, watched as she wiped her suddenly sweaty palms on her dress.

At last she turned back to face him. "I can't," she said.

"You must," he replied. "You must kill him before he kills you."

"And if I fail?" she asked. "If I'm caught?"

"Then you'll be in no worse position than you'll be in when he learns the truth.

"However, if you succeed, you will be free to marry your young officer, free to raise your child in peace.

"As Pharaoh, I will make sure of it."

Bahara considered his words a long moment.

He was right. She was trapped and there was only one hope.

"Alright," she said at last. "Just tell me what I have to do."

XLIV

Bahara had never been so terrified in her entire life. Though she tried not to think of what was to come, she couldn't stop trembling.

As her dressers entered her chambers that evening to prepare her for Pharaoh, she was on the verge of tears.

She had closed her eyes, willing the tears away as the warmth of her bath water seeped into her bones.

Now, as she sat alone on the bed in Pharaoh's bed chamber, the tiny vial felt heavier than a pyramid cornerstone in her hand.

Fearfully, she rose.

She crept towards his wine jar, her hand shaking so violently by the time she reached it that she could barely even open it.

Setting the wine jar back down, she clumsily fumbled with the cap of the vial – her adrenaline pumping so fast that she had not the coordination to open it. Instead, the vial fell to the table.

"Shit!" she swore in a loud whisper, as she gave in to her despair.

She couldn't do this. She wasn't a killer.

No matter what Pharaoh had done or might do to her, she couldn't do this.

She began to sob.

"Quiet!" an unfamiliar voice breathed in her ear.

Bahara's heart stopped.

She had heard no one enter the room, had not even heard as whomever it was crept up behind her.

Her breath frozen in her chest, she slowly turned around. Before her was a specter - a specter in a long, semi-transparent veil.

"Go," the specter ordered.

Bahara needed no further encouragement.

Ida watched, amused, as the girl fled back through the hidden passageway and into her rooms.

Pulling back her veil, Ida picked up the vial and inspected his contents.

Just as Mursili had written, the Vizier had spared no expense. Just a few drops and Horemheb would be dead before dawn – seemingly of natural causes.

Picking up the wine jar she went to his bathing room and poured out most of its contents – leaving just enough for a single glass.

Done, she returned the wine jar to the table. Then, removing the cap of the vial, Ida poured the vial's entire contents into it.

Bahara sobbed in relief as she flung herself into her lover's arms.

She was so shaken up, so glad to see him that it didn't even occur to her to ask him how or why he came to be in her rooms. She just needed to feel his warmth, to feel, even if only for a few moments, like everything was alright.

"What's wrong?" he asked pulling back to look at her face, as he stroked her cheeks.

She shook her head, pulled him back to her.

XLV

Ida watched as Pharaoh Horemheb arrived in his chamber, watched as his dressers prepared him for bed, as he took his nightly wine.

It was only when they were alone again, that she spoke.

"Enjoying the wine?" she asked.

Horemheb slowly lowered his nearly empty cup, the hairs on the back of his neck standing at attention.

He turned towards her, a slow smirk sliding across his face.

"Well, well, well," he said. "If it isn't Idamun – back from the grave yet again."

Ida smiled sardonically.

"I see you've returned to your natural color," he remarked. "Black hair always was the most flattering."

"So happy you approve," she replied. "Bringing a smile to your lips is the least I could do – what with these being your final hours and all."

Horemheb's smile faltered, almost imperceptibly. Still, he took the last sip of wine.

"You have your Vizier to thank for this by the way," Ida taunted. "If it was up to me, you would have died as slowly and painfully as possible."

"Then I thank the fates it was not up to you," he remarked.

Yet, even as Horemheb tried to maintain his bravado, he felt numbness begin to spread through his limbs.

He plopped down heavily in the chair nearest him.

Ida went to him, leaned over him. "And you want to hear something else funny?" she asked.

"Sure. Why not?" he smirked.

"Bahara is my granddaughter," Ida whispered.

Horemheb laughed at the absurdity of her words.

Ida stood. "Don't believe me?" she asked.

"Not for a moment," he spat.

"Then try this on for size, Horemheb.....I *can* call you Horemheb now, can't I?"

"Sure," he replied. "Why not?"

Ida smiled with false sweetness.

"You see, Horemheb, Faium was right all along," she said. "Kadar was indeed my son."

He laughed humorlessly, his reason fast abandoning him as he finally began to realize the futility of his situation.

Ida continued. "Kadar is also Bahara's father. So you see, all of this time, you've had Tutankhamun's rightful heir right here, right under your nose, without even realizing it."

She laughed haughtily. "It's poetic justice when you think about it. Especially now that you know the truth and it's much too late for you to do anything about it.

"You're going die. The man who masterminded your death is going to take over your throne – with your blessings I might add.

"My granddaughter's going to marry the man the Vizier used as your stud, his own son and future Pharaoh, Seti.

"Best of all, my great grandson, Ramesses II, a true Amarna, will sit upon the throne once more."

Horemheb opened his mouth to speak, instead clutched painfully at his chest. He lunged towards Ida, she easily stepping out of his reach and sending him crashing to the floor.

As he struggled against the pain, as he fought with all his might to survive, Ida watched.

As he drew his last, the veins in his neck bulging, his face beet red and his eyes popping out of his head, a slow smile spread across Ida's lips.

XLVI

1274 B.C. Reign of Pharaoh Ramesses II.

Queen Tuya needed to read no further. She knew the rest.

The next morning, Horemheb was found dead – the apparent victim of a heart stoppage.

Horemheb would be barely cold in his sarcophagus before Vizier Parma was coronated Pharaoh Ramesses I.

As for Bahara, she would learn that the man she loved was not just any commander but the Vizier's very own son. It was no doubt just another contingency plan in the Vizier's bid to control the throne - whether or not Horemheb was disposed of.

She would marry Merenptah with Ramesses' full approval – the Vizier desperate for the dynastic blessing that only one of royal blood could guarantee. Sety Merenptah would be coronated Crown Prince Seti and she Princess Tuya - the change in name designed to distance her from her past as Horemheb's concubine.

To further solidify her new identity, Tuya would be officially adopted by one of the Vizier's closest friends – Commander Inar. Inar, in turn, would prove to be a father to her in more than just name only. He would become a man she would grow to love and trust.

Her and Seti's son, Ramesses II, would go on to take over the throne after Seti's death.

Now here they all were, but a generation later – the Amarnas and Hittites at war once more. The very same Hittites that had once been their only true allies. The very same Hittites to whom they were tied not only by fate but by blood. The very same Hittites her son faced now at Kadesh.

She rose, hurriedly stuffing the scroll pages back into the chest and shutting it.

She had to stop this. She had to stop it before Egypt and Hatti destroyed each other.

XLVII

Pharaoh Ramesses II's encampment. Just outside the city of Kadesh.

Ramesses paced his tent like a caged tiger.

Fools! They had all been made to look like fools – especially he!

He swiped the figurines, maps and battle plans to the floor.

The Shasu nomads had been plants – no doubt designed to lull him into a sense of false security. And he, haughty king that he was, fell for it - the advice of his commanders unheeded.

It was only when his generals provided proof - in the form of two captured Hittite spies - that Pharaoh realized his folly. By then; however, it had been too late.

The Hittite forces he had arrogantly believed to be more than a week's march away had already sprung upon the Ra division of his foolishly divided force.

The Ra division had fallen quickly – alone and easy pray for the Hittite army. Quickly overrun and scattered, the shattered remnants of Ra had retreated back to the main encampment.

Now, as Ra Unit survivors trickled into Pharaoh's camp, his men were thrown into a panic - the precious, fragile respect he had only just earned as their new Pharaoh, that he had earned during their successful campaigns in Southern Assyria, already threatening to fray.

Could his detractors be right? Could Ramesses be better suited for the role of division commander than leader of the entire Egyptian army, than the leader of the Egyptian empire? Had the military prowess he had demonstrated as Prince Regent only been possible because he had not the burden of the crown?

Or was it something else?

Had Ramesses grown too complacent in his new role? Had he let himself become too fat and contented while building his cities and monuments, and thus lost the edge that had earned him victory after victory against the Nubians, Hittites, Libyans & Sherden pirates in the past?

Ramesses shook his head.

No, he could not doubt now. He had to act.

The longer he stayed sequestered in his tent, the larger the specter of defeat grew, the less his men trusted him to lead them to victory. Either he act now and prove his enemies to be the fools they were or he do nothing and prove them right.

Grabbing his helmet, Ramesses' turned to storm from his tent, was frozen in place by the all too familiar sound of his mother's tattoo.

No. It couldn't be. He had to be imagining it.

Yet, as he tried to advance towards the flap of his tent, she entered.

"Mother," Ramesses cried, sinking to his knees before her, his head bowed in shame.

He had no idea why he had done that. He was no longer a child, no longer just a prince. He was Pharaoh now and Pharaoh bowed to no man.

Yet, he had.

Perhaps the bitter taste of his first major military defeat was already ripping cracks in his ego. Perhaps it was his mother's presence that solidified the doubts about his skill as a leader - doubts that had begun to overrun even his own mind.

Embarrassed, he stood - his usual bravado overtaking his despair as he led her deeper into his tent.

Still, he could not quite face her. She could read him too well. She, of all, people would know something was wrong – terribly wrong.

"Why have you come?" he asked, a haughty edge to his voice.

"I came to warn you," Queen Tuya began.

"Warn me of what?" he spat bitterly, as he finally faced her. "Of some Oracle's prediction? Of some prophet's prognostication?"

Tuya shook her head. "I came to warn you of the dangerous path upon which you currently tread – the same one as your father, only worse."

"Father lies cold in a tomb," Ramesses replied. "How can my fate be worse than his?"

"These people, these Hittites you fight...." She sighed heavily. "They aren't your enemies. They're blood – more than blood."

Pharaoh stared at his mother as though she were mad.

"Please believe me," Tuya pressed. "There are things you don't know - things you don't understand about my past, about our family's history and our deep connection to the Hittites."

Ramesses laughed, shaking his head.

"Ramesses please," she begged. She pulled the last remaining scroll from its hiding place on her person and proffered it to him.

Pharaoh went to her, looked down at it for a long moment before a cruel smirk curled the corner of his lips.

"I've no time for fairy tales, Mother," he said.

"Now if you'll excuse me, I have a war to fight."

Without another word, he brushed passed her and out the tent.

XLVIII

Pharaoh Ramesses strode purposefully though his encampment, back towards his tent. His regal head was held high, his shoulders proud and broad.

He seemed a man full of confidence. A man who knew exactly what he was doing.

It was only when Ramesses returned to the privacy of his tent, that his facade crumbled. He sank heavily into his gilded chair, tears pooling in his eyes.

Useless! It had all been useless.

Like Horus, the sun god himself, Ramesses had charged unflinchingly forth from his encampment – a small chariot division in support. They had assaulted the much heavier, slower Hittite chariots with the vigor of young gods.

Though the daring assault helped Ramesses prove to both himself and the Hittite King that he was as much of a threat as he had ever been – perhaps even more so, though the initial success of their bold charges had restored his men's confidence, though he could almost taste victory on his tongue, his efforts had proven for naught.

The Hittites and the Egyptians each stood victorious in their own right, a third clash having resulted in a stalemate. Though men fell, both Hittite and Egyptian, neither army had managed to move any closer to crushing the enemy force.

For several hours it lasted – this third clash between the Hittites and Egyptians.

First Ramesses would gain a slight advantage, then Muwatalli, then he again. Back and forth, forth and back it went with neither gaining enough advantage to push through to victory.

And there she had stood – the City of Kadesh. Kadesh which was so close yet still so far away. Kadesh which seemed to glitter mockingly - like a jewel just beyond an abyss.

As day began to give way to night and the men grew wearier, it had become clear. No easy victory would be won here – for either side.

So, not by victory but by mutual agreement, the two sides had adjourned to their separate camps – at least until the next sun.

And then what? Ramesses wondered with a sigh.

More useless clashes? More lives needlessly lost? Both armies so broken and bloodied that they became easy pickings for some new power that waited unseen in the wings?

Ramesses sighed again.

XLIX

Queen Tuya stole away from Pharaoh's encampment, unseen, in the dead of night.

It was only the heavy clouds that blocked the stars and the moon, the will of the gods that protected her.

As she neared the Hittite encampment, someone called out to her.

"Halt!" the man said, his bow stretched taught in one hand as the other directed the arrow towards her.

The Queen froze in her tracks.

"State your name and purpose," he demanded.

"I am Tuya, Queen Dowager and mother of Pharaoh Ramesses II, adopted daughter of Inar and...granddaughter of King Mursili's concubine, Raia. I come now to talk terms."

"Stay where you are," the man ordered.

It seemed an eternity that Tuya stood there, the arrow trained upon her heart.

When at last a solitary figure approached, Tuya's heart sped up in her chest. It was a woman – an old woman with Ramesses's eyes.

Seeing Tuya, a slow smile spread across the old woman's face.

"Tell me, *Tuya*, daughter of Inar and granddaughter of Raia. Do you speak the truth or is this just another of Pharaoh's temper tantrums?"

"Grandmother," Tuya said sinking to her knees before Ida, tears welling in her eyes.

"Rise, granddaughter," Ida instructed. "We have much to discuss."

L

"You did what?!" Pharaoh Ramesses demanded of the Queen.

He had been furious when he had found she was not in her tent – more furious still when she was nowhere to be found in the camp. By the time she dared return, only a couple of hours before dawn, he was enraged.

"I went to the Hittite camp," Tuya confessed.

"To what end?" he demanded. "And upon whose authority?"

"I went to stop this madness," she replied, "and did so under the only authority I need – that of the gods."

"I may be your son, woman," Ramesses snarled, "but I am no longer a child. I am Pharaoh."

"Then act like it," she snapped.

Ramesses was momentarily taken aback by her tone. She had not dared speak to him so in years – not since he began to show signs of manhood.

Tuya blinked back her tears of frustration, struggled to regain her composure.

When next she spoke, her voice was even. "You left me no choice. You would not hear me."

"And you think this? This reckless act of defiance speaks in your favor?"

Tuya stared at her son, her eyes pleading, her brain frantic as it searched for a way to get through to him.

However, before she could reply, there was a rustling near the entrance of her tent. Someone was coming.

Hurriedly wiping at her eyes, Tuya turned to face the tent's entrance. Pharaoh's eyes too fled to the intruder, an intruder whose eyes looked so much like his own that it unnerved him.

"I thought you might need some help," the old woman offered Tuya by way of explanation, though her eyes were trained upon Pharaoh.

"Who is this woman?" Ramesses demanded of his mother. "Why is she here?"

Before Tuya could answer, Ida raised a hand, silencing her.

"Who am I?" Ida repeated. "I am Idaten, disgraced descendant of a once great and noble family and former slave of Pharaoh Akhenaten. I am Idamun, lowest and final wife of the former Pharaoh Tutankhamun and mother of his only son. I am Hawara, former wife of the warrior Saphik and mother of Kadar, the last descendent of the Amarna line. I am also Raia, former concubine of King Mursili II of Hatti, mother of the Hittite Princes Telisili and Arrinutu, paternal grandmother of Queen Tuya of Egypt and great grandmother of Pharaoh

Ramesses II."

Ramesses was speechless, his eyes darting between his mother and the woman.

As the woman continued her careful advance, as she slowly moved passed his mother, his sharp eyes picked up on but a sliver of resemblance between the two.

Yet, as the strange woman crept closer still, he found himself still unable to move, unable to speak.

Ida stood before him now, seemingly hypnotized as her eyes drank in every detail of his face.

"By the gods," Ida breathed, tears pooling in her eyes. "You look so much like him, like your great grandfather."

Slowly, she raised one hand to touch his face.

Ramesses backed away before her fingers brushed his flesh, turned his back to her. His shoulders rigid, his chest heaved.

"You're just as mad as my mother," Ramesses spat.

"Am I?" Ida asked.

"Tutankhamun had no heir," Ramesses replied. "Everyone knows that. That is why Ay and then Horemheb were able to ascend the throne.

"As for his wife, Idamun..." He shook his head. "No record exists of such a person."

"Except for this one," she said reaching into her garment and pulling out the marriage pendant Tutankhamun had given her.

Ramesses was shaken as his eyes drank in the characters that ran down it, characters naming this Idamun, whomever she was, as Tutankhamun's one true wife.

He turned away from her, his brain struggling to comprehend what he had seen.

The pendant looked genuine enough.

Still...

"It's a fake," he said turning back to face her. "You somehow got your hands on one of the real marriage pendants and you paid someone to make it look like you and Tutankhamun were bound."

"To what end?" Ida asked, blinking back her tears. "You have no idea how I have suffered, how our family has suffered, how Mursili and those he loved suffered because of this stupid little piece of gold, because of what it meant.

"Your grandfather, my son, was hunted down by Horemheb not once but twice – and left for dead because of it. Your grandmother had her throat slit and was left bleeding to death, along with your mother's dead twin brother, in the middle of the desert because of it. Your own mother was enslaved, used and abused by many including Horemheb and your Grandfather Ramesses because of it."

"If it was such a mighty burden, why not destroy it?" Ramesses demanded, anguish burning in his eyes.

"Because I couldn't! Because it wasn't just about me and my son or even Tutankhamun. Because it wasn't just about the Amarna."

"Of course it wasn't. It was about you wanting power in Egypt. You had already gained power in Hatti by spreading your legs for its king and now you wanted power in Egypt too – power only that pendant could give you."

Before she could stop herself, Ida slapped him.

The eyes that fell upon Ida afterwards were murderous. Only the fact that Tuya had put herself between Ida and Ramesses kept Ramesses's hands from closing around Ida's throat.

"Get her out of here," Ramesses hissed through clenched teeth.

"Not until you listen," Tuya replied.

Her son's eyes fell upon her – anger burning in them. "To what? More lies? More fantasies?"

Ida's lip curled in distaste. "Maybe he's right," she said. "Maybe we should just stay out of it. Maybe we should just leave him to his fate."

Tuya turned around to face her. "Grandmother please," she begged. "You don't mean that. You can't mean that."

Ida looked away from her.

"By the gods!" Tuya exclaimed exasperated with them both. "This is not just about you or I or Ramesses. This is about the future of Egypt. The future of Hatti."

When Ida still refused to meet her gaze, she turned to face Ramesses. He too continued to sulk.

The queen laughed humorlessly, throwing up her hands. "So this is it? This is how both Tutankhamun's and Mursili's dynasties end?"

She laughed again, nodding her head.

"Maybe you're right," Tuya said returning her attention to Ida. "Maybe we don't deserve to survive."

As Tuya pushed passed Ida and out of the tent, Ida slowly raised her eyes to stare across the room at a brooding Ramesses – found that he had done the same.

Epilogue

1273 BC. Thebes. Egypt.

Pharaoh Ramesses sat upon his gilded throne, his mother, Queen Tuya, just behind him.

It was all he could do to sit still as he listened to the latest public accounting of his great victory over the Hittites in Kadesh. The same great victory, he did not doubt, King Muwatalli's scribes were writing into their own annals as their victory.

His eyes slowly swept the crowd.

All were raptly attentive - eagerly accepting every word as the gods' own truth. All except for one. *Her.*

Her eyes were fixed upon him – something in her expression causing unease in the pit of his stomach. It was like staring into the eyes of a cobra.

Was she not satisfied?

This was after all her doing, after all: a hollow, empty "victory" for both Egypt and Hatti which had in reality been a victory for neither. A secret, uneasy truce between the two families which was to be replaced by a formal treaty between the two empires - once enough time had passed to avoid suspicion - and solidified by his union to one of the Hittite Princess.

Ramesses pulled his eyes away from his great grandmother, suppressed a sigh.

What did any of it matter anyway?

He was still Pharaoh. He would still go down in the annals of Egyptian history as the great victor in the Battle of Kadesh.

And one day.....one day he would be something more.

One day, he would be great.

Ida could almost read her great grandson's thoughts in the haughtiness of his expression, in the pride of his bearing – even in the face of such a farce.

This young god, with no sense of humility, who had not been humbled even by his glaring failure to capture Kadesh, was strong – not just physically but mentally and emotionally. This young, bold god knew exactly how to play the game, would not be manipulated, bullied and dispatched as easily as his great grandfather had been.

Though she and Ramesses were both much too proud to speak the words aloud, they had come to an understanding. Egypt and Hatti would be safe with him.

As Ramesses' eyes fell upon her once more, she offered him the slightest of nods.

Though Pharaoh hesitated for a long moment, in the end, he returned the gesture.

Satisfied, Ida turned and walked away. She had no real destination in mind, allowing herself to be carried along by the ebb and flow of the crowd.

With every step she took, she became more and more aware of her many, many years. With each step, she became more and more aware of just how tired she had become.

As the sun bounced off the sandstone buildings in blurred waves, the specters of her long life arose once more. Specters of her past. Specters of the people she had once known.

Everywhere her eyes fell, she saw them.

She saw she, Ankhe and Tutankh playing as children in el-Amarna, the kindly Pharaoh Akhenaten & his beautiful wife Nefertiti looking on with amusement. She saw she, Batau and Esnai at the market, bickering like sisters over which fabric to buy for the Queen. She saw Galeno and his fiancée, before the scandal that had destroyed them, stealing kisses in the alleyway.

She saw Ankhe beaming at Heketya as the very animated child relayed news of her day. She saw she and Tutankh – so young, so in love, so oblivious to what was to come.

She saw the young, determined man-child Mursili convincing the scared little girl she had been to fight for her life and that of her son. She saw Nacamakun playing with Abidos and Kadar at their courtyard in Assyria. She saw Clizi brushing her hair and playfully chiding her in that motherly way she had about her. She saw Mursili, bathed in the moonlight the first time they had made love.

She saw the Bietek baby cooing as it lay in her arms, as it brought the few smiles she was capable of those days to her lips. She saw Saphik and Lord Bietek in the midst of one of their passionate and animated discussions on the latest weaponry. She saw she and Saphik on their wedding day – so optimistic and full of joy. She saw Hazrene and Kadar holding each other near the fountain, as they spoke of the future.

She saw Tanu doting upon her twins – as good a mother to them as she was to her own children. She saw her twins playing hide and seek in the Citadel with their half-brothers and sisters. She saw Galeno, Muwa and Mursili - their heads pressed together as they considered a matter of great importance – a surprise for her 40th birthday.

It was only when Ida felt the tears upon her face - tears that were not her own, that she returned to her senses.

The specters fading, she found herself lying in a great bed in the palace, her granddaughter hovering over her.

"Bahara," Ida breathed, gently stroking the crying woman's hair.

Tuya looked up at her, but instead of the woman she was now, Ida saw the terrified woman-child she had been that fateful night in Horem's bedchamber.

Though Tuya spoke to her, it grew harder and harder for Ida to hear her.

They were calling for her – those that she had lost.

She lifted her gaze, looked just beyond Tuya's shoulder.

Yes, they were there. All of them. The ones who had passed on. They were calling for her, beckoning her to join them on the other side of the abyss.

With each passing second, Tuya and the opulent room grew dimmer. With each passing second, the sounds of the world grew farther and farther away.

Then, with one, last shaky breath, Ida closed her eyes and was no more.

Coming Eventually….Maybe
Hatti

How True is Amarna Book III: Book of Raia?

Okay, this is all being done by memory of research done decades ago. It's as accurate as I can make it without trying to dig up said research.

- The only people who did not specifically exist in reality (though they can be said to be composites of real people) are all of the non-royals and one royal. Even the non-royals who would become royals are real people (from the Vizier's line).
- Mal-Nikal really did escape Mursili's wrath after the oracle granted Mursili II permission to punish her for the murder of his wife, Gassula.
- Mal-Nikal's flight to Egypt, however, is fictional. I've no idea of where she really went or what happened to her afterwards.
- Sausga was a real goddess in the Hittite pantheon of gods. She was also known as Ishtar and responsible for fertility (both human and earthly), protection and healing.
- Sausga was also responsible for military success/war.
- Some goddesses with whom Sausga is compared/considered to be the same as were also notorious for interfering in human affairs. However, I have no idea if Sausga was one of Mal-Nikal's go to gods or not.
- Mursili's youngest son at the time, Hattusili III, really was dedicated to Sausga instead of one of Mursili's two patron gods, Arinna and Telipinu.
- Hattusili had fallen into a terrible illness. It was believed that this would/did save the boy's life.
- Hattusili would remain faithful to Sausga/Ishtar his entire life.
- Mursili really did remarry and was believed to have sired additional children. I made two of these children the adopted sons of his fictional relationship with Ida.
- Mursili really did have what modern analysts describe as a stoke and he really did suffer from the symptoms as described in the book.
- Mursili really did write the prayer attributed to him in the book.
- Mursili really did sacrifice a bull in order to appease the gods after his stroke.
- Mursili died around the age of 40.
- Muwa really was one of Mursili's scribes.
- Horemheb really had no heirs. He appointed the real-life Vizier Paramesse as his successor.
- The Vizier already had a son (future Seti I and Tuya's husband) and grandson (future Ramesses II) at the time of his appointment.
- Vizier Paramesse's would go on to be Ramesses I.
- Seti I's birth name was Sety Merenptah. Yes, like the Merenptah that conspires to run away with Ida's granddaughter. (wink)

- Raia was the name of the man who fathered the real-life Queen Tuya. He was a military officer.
- During this installment, Ida's alias is also Raia. For my purposes, I made Tuya into Ida's descendent (considering how much these Egyptians enjoyed rewriting/erasing history that didn't suit their needs I felt right at home (wink)).
- Though Tuya and events after her marriage to Seti I are real (excluding the Ida scrolls), her connection to Ida and life as a slave is fiction.
- Ramesses II really did go to war with the Hittites. Though stylized, the events of the Battle of Kadesh are largely accurate - including the two spies.
- Both the Hittites and Egyptians claimed victory at Kadesh – though historians largely agree that it was likely a tie.
- Ramesses II would later go on to marry one of Mursili II's descendants (a granddaughter I want to say).

Other Titles Currently Available from Seamonkey Ink, LLC & Grea Alexander

Rebellion Book I: Book of Quay
Genres: Historical, Drama, Romance, Fiction

Intrigue, deception, betrayal. What are a few knives in the back between two lovers?

Qing Dynasty, China.

Some wounds cut too deeply to ever truly heal, to ever be forgotten. For the rebel Phong Quay, The Princess Ni Soung is one of those wounds - a remnant of the most painful chapters in his life, a pawn in his never ending war with his greatest enemy, the Emperor Ni Fehn.

As the Han rebellion against the Emperor intensifies, The Princess Soung becomes caught in the middle. As bait in the Emperor's most brazen bid to date to bring Phong Quay down, the princess may just find herself a casualty in the battle between the two men - a battle between the past and the present, between the truth and lies, between love and revenge.

Rebellion Book II: Book of Soung
Genres: Historical, Drama, Romance, Fiction

What if the person you could trust the least was yourself?

Although Lord and Lady Choi had promised each other that there would be no more secrets between them, no more lies, neither of them was capable of holding to the bargain. He still had his secrets and she still had hers.

While Lady Choi loved her husband with everything she had in her, she would never be foolish enough to trust him again, would put nothing past him.

When new enemies and old ones ally to seek revenge, the very foundations of their faith in one another is shaken to the core. As old lies unravel, new deceptions are revealed and old insecurities resurface, can a love without trust survive?

Rebellion Book III: Book of Choi
Genres: Historical, Drama, Romance, Fiction

What if everything you thought you knew about yourself and everyone around you was a lie?

For the past two decades, Ni Soung has been living a lie – a lie of her own creation. A lie perpetuated by everyone around her, even her own husband and father. A lie her enemies have used to twist and destroy everything she once believed.

Now, held captive and separated from her husband and children, her only hope to save them all is the truth.

As the lies are stripped away and her memory returns, will Ni Soung uncover the truth in time to change the future or will she be destroyed by it instead?

Cabello
Genres: Horror, Supernatural

Nightmares are the stuff that answered prayers are made of.

In Saintsville, TX, fewer than five people under the age of 70 have died in the past ten years. Now, in the course of a few weeks, the residents of Saintsville are dropping like flies.

When everyone involved in the cover up of Mineau December's abuse and brutal assault begin to die under mysterious circumstances, Mineau believes her prayers are finally being answered. Answered prayers, however, quickly turn into a nightmare when Mineau finds that her savior is more dangerous than anyone she has ever known, than anything she could possibly dare imagine.

Cabello.

The Pack: Addison
Genres: Horror, Supernatural

Addison Savaughn's only sin was being born at the wrong time, to the wrong bloodline.

Celestine Savaughn kept her daughter isolated, locked away from the world.

As the last descendant of the Devinforge blood line, Addison had a destiny greater than she had it in her to imagine, a destiny that required sacrifice - great sacrifice.

So instead of dolls and pretty dresses, Addison had her knives and pistols. Instead of school, Addison had drills and patrols. Instead of friends, Addison had Mama and the Hunters' Guild.

Still, there was just one problem. Addison didn't believe a word of it.

She didn't believe in Mama. She didn't believe in the Guild. And she certainly didn't believe in wolves with hair on the inside.

Also look for these upcoming titles from Grea Alexander & SeaMonkey Ink, LLC:

Miael (formerly M)

The Pack Book II: Bristol

Cabello Book II: Descendant

Sedition Book I: Book of Xian

Printed in Great Britain
by Amazon